EMBERS AND ASH

MELANIE MURPHY

Embers and Ash

Copyright © 2025 by Melanie Murphy

All rights reserved

Published by Emperor Books

Bellerose Village, New York

Library of Congress Control Number: 2025917311

ISBN

Print 978-1-63777-761-9 | 978-1-63777-762-6

Digital 978-1-63777-760-2

No part of this book may be reproduced in any form or by any electronic or mechanical means, including information storage and retrieval systems, without written permission from the author, except for the use of brief quotations in a book review.

This is a work of fiction and any resemblance to any person, institution or organization alive or dead is purely coincidental.

This one is for my readers. Your support continues to stoke the flames within me. Thank you.

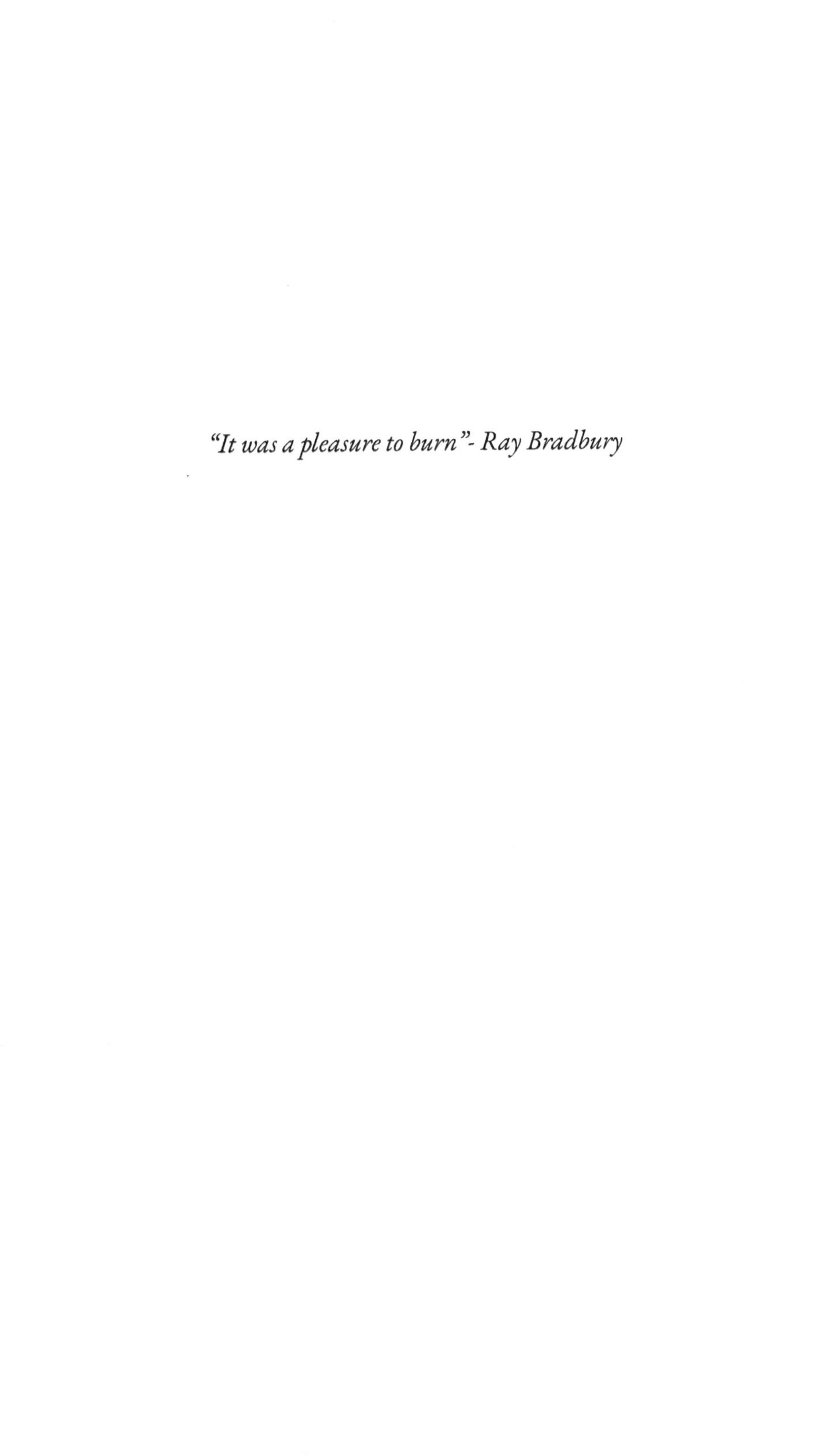

"It was a pleasure to burn"- Ray Bradbury

F ire. Whose eye is not drawn to the flame? The crimson, golden, and orange embers that dance hypnotically before us, sending out their warmth to inhabit every crevice of our being, filling us up to the brim with light. The brightness that remains etched into our closed eyelids long after it has been extinguished—as if our psyche mourns those fleeting images that were once so full of brilliance and life. The heat absorbs into our clothes and skin, beating against our fragile faces as we hover around it—turning our cheeks flushed with pulsing waves of flickering energy.

Gray smoky tendrils curl into the air like unraveling ribbons, sending their signals into the heavens above. Crackling wood speaks a language all its own—conjuring pictures of both fire's beauty and destruction. After all, warmth is a dangerous gift; it can give and it can take-away. It can nourish us in the deepest, darkest of winters, but can also consume the mightiest of forests, burn the most noble of structures to ash. Don't ever be fooled into thinking that humans can tame fire. When it so chooses, we are but naked and defenseless against its raw power.

A little bit of fire burns within all of us—perhaps that's part of its magnetism, its intense beauty; after all, Prometheus stole the fire from Zeus and gave it to man, imbibing us with a life force that burns from deep within. It lives in our anger and desire—unquenchable emotions which have the power to swallow us whole, that seethe uncontrollable, rattling around inside us with blazing tenacity.

Describe fire as you will: sultry, frightening, enthralling. The one thing to remember however, is that it leaves only ashes in its wake.

Part One

Chapter One

T hump.

Thump.

The sound came from within. A deafening screaming in Fiona's brain sent violent shock waves throughout her core. It felt like someone was drilling inside her skull–digging around with metal spades and shovels in the gray matter between her ears. Fiona experienced headaches before, but never one like that.

Thump.

Thump.

Then there was another sensation. Heat. Blazing, searing heat. Fiona could feel the waves pulsing against her skin.

Fiona. Open your eyes. That was her thought, what she tried to tell herself. *Open. Your. Eyes.* But she couldn't open them; they were so heavy. So very heavy. And she was so tired.

"Fiona. Open your eyes."

That time, the words came from outside of her. They weren't in her brain anymore. Someone was speaking to her. Everything was so jumbled. So confused.

Louder then, "Fiona. Open. Your. Eyes."

She did...but she wished she hadn't. At that moment, Fiona wished that she just allowed herself to be consumed. Eaten. Devoured. It would have been easier.

Fiona couldn't see. She opened her eyes, but she couldn't see. She moved her hands in front of her face. She saw them. Why couldn't she see past them?

Despite the incessant thumping in her brain, Fiona sat up. Who spoke to her? She couldn't see anything past her trembling hands. And then she understood why. Smoke. She was consumed in thick, dense smoke. It blanketed her surroundings.

Panic. Fiona's eyes adjusted to the hazy atmosphere. She was twisted up in the white sheets on a bed. Her fancy bed in that fancy suite at the Garden City Hotel. Slowly the events of the night came back to her. The party. Gio. The tequila. Don Julio. Frantically, she unwound herself from the bedding and stood. She was completely naked. What the hell happened to her? Every single pore of her body hurt.

She tried to think. What happened after that tequila shot? How did she get back to her hotel room? But before she could process anything, out of the corner of her eye she noticed the flames. Orange, Red, Blue. *Fire turns blue when it's really hot...*she remembered learning that somewhere, maybe in science class. The towels in the bathroom were blazing with fire. Fiona's pulse flared in her throat, her temples. Her mind was hazy, confused. Then, she perceived the wailing.

Sirens.

Alarms.

Screaming.

The thought hit her like a slap to the face, like someone dumped a bucket of ice water on her: *I did this. Holy shit. I did this!* She knew it with a certainty she could never explain. *I. Did. This.* The fire felt like part of her. She could sense the crackling, could sense the damage it would inflict. *Oh God.* She couldn't pull it back. She kept it bottled up for so long. She thought she had it controlled. Oh how wrong she was. How careless. How reckless.

Fiona careened around the room, looking for clothes. She had to get out, and had to see if everyone was ok. Everything she touched went up in flames. The heat was within and without. Burning her from the inside, but of course, it left no marks on her pale, freckled skin. It never did. She was immune to the flame.

Chapter Two

"Fiona."

That voice again.

"Fiona. Look what you did! It's time to get out of here. Hurry!" The voice said.

"Who are you?" Fiona screamed. "Help me."

"I can help you. But we have to leave. Now. Trust me."

Fiona didn't trust him, but what choice did she have?

"I trust you. Please," Fiona sputtered. "Just help me. Help everyone."

Why weren't her legs working? Why couldn't she see straight? The figure before her was blurry. He turned around to grab something–his movements jerky, betraying his fear. What did he grab? Fiona couldn't process what was happening. She was disoriented. Desperation settled in the pit of her stomach. The fear mixed with the fire vibrating through her as she collapsed to the floor. The dizziness in her head made the room spin. *What's going on with me?* she thought angrily. Her eyes felt heavy and the smoke consumed her senses. She couldn't get up. It felt as though her head weighed a thousand pounds. Nausea consumed her.

Dimly, she perceived a male figure placing something around her shoulders and lifting her. Horrible glimpses infiltrated her vision as she sailed down the hallway, carried by an unknown force.

Burning.

Screaming.

More sirens.

More alarms.

The rug went up in flames behind her.

Fiona tried to get down, but someone was holding her. Gripping her.

"No!" she screamed. "We have to help them!"

"We can't help them if we burn with them," he responded.

"I don't burn," Fiona said. "I can't."

But the person carrying her didn't slow his gait. She could feel his heartbeat against her ribcage.

Chaos ensued. People flew out of the rooms in blinding panic running this way and that, disoriented...scared. Some followed Fiona and this stranger who had her in his grasp. Others fluttered around not knowing what to do. Fire was every-where. The canvas paper peeled off the wall like dead skin exposing bare wooden beams and insulation. The lights flickered out, leaving everything in hazy darkness. Fiona saw an old man open the door to his hotel room wrapped in a wet towel, but when he saw the pandemonium in the hallway he just closed himself back in. Fiona imagined his fancy suite turning into his tomb.

But then her eyes closed again and her head lolled backward. But the screaming, the scent of burning flesh, burning hair invaded her senses.

After what felt like eternity Fiona felt grass beneath her and smelled clear air.

"Fiona. Open your eyes."

Again, that directive. Fiona did open her eyes. Cautiously. Fearful of what she would see. It was slightly easier this time, but the thumping was still there, in her head. The alarms, the sirens, the noise still pierced her consciousness. But she was no longer straining to see through the smoke. Instead, Fiona was gazing directly into dark, somber eyes.

"Who are you?" Fiona screamed, scuttling backwards across the grass on all fours.

The fear was tangible, leaving an acidic taste in her mouth.

"What happened? Where am I?" She couldn't stop rapid-firing questions.

The dark eyes assessed Fiona silently, calmly.

Again, Fiona screamed with a voice that was hoarse and raspy, "What the hell just happened? Who are you? Is everyone ok?"

The stranger just pointed into the distance to the smoke rising up into the air. Fiona could hear the sounds of the sirens, the sound of the screams...or were those in her mind. Burned into her subconscious?

"What is that?" Fiona asked, even though she knew the answer. "Where am I?"

The fight was beginning to drain out of her body and she again felt tired and dizzy. She felt sluggish as though she was trying to run under water, only to wade through mud.

Finally the stranger spoke, "You don't remember?"

Fiona tried to rewind her thoughts like the old video cassettes of her youth. And she did remember...some things. She remembered the screams, remembered brief glimpses of hotel rooms ablaze with orange flame as she passed by somehow–almost like she was floating. She remembered the inferno blazing in the bathroom at the Garden City Hotel. But what she remembered above all else, was the blinding, crushing knowledge that she had done it all. That she was the one responsible. *I. Did. This.* Suddenly she was transported back in time to her Senior Prom where the exact same phrase reverberated through her mind like an incantation. How long had she been telling herself she had it all under control–that she had her emotions under control: the catalysts for her fire. That her condition was simply one part of her personality, not a defining trait? And how selfish she had been. The thoughts tumbled forth unchecked.

Again the stranger said, "Tell me what you remember."

Fiona didn't answer him; she just asked another question, "Where am I?"

This time, he did answer, "You're in a field about a block from the Garden City Hotel. I carried you here."

She looked down at the white bathrobe she was wearing. Even though dawn had not yet broken and it was still dark outside, she could perceive the gold embroidered monogram on the breast pocket: GCH. Garden City Hotel.

"Who are you?" Fiona asked again.

"My name's Micah," he responded.

"Ok," she replied. "Micah. But...*who* are you? Why are you here? How did we get here?"

Without missing a beat, he replied, "I'm your savior."

Chapter Three

"My savior?" she asked, trying to choke back the tears that threatened to explode. She felt cold, numb, used in a way she couldn't explain or understand.

"I just saved your life," he explained.

His calmness was infuriating. It stood in stark juxtaposition to the terror, to the sheer panic she felt within.

Her anger burbled, "Can you stop being cryptic. Tell me what the hell just happened. The last thing I remember is–"

"Yes Fiona. Tell me. What is the last thing you remember?" he asked.

"I remember a shot of tequila. I remember Gio–"

"Well," Micah replied. "Let me fill in the blanks. Gio roofied your drink...his intentions were far more sinister than his appearance."

That explained why she blacked out after taking that shot of tequila. But there was a more pressing question rumbling in her head.

"Did he..." she struggled with how to word it, and decided on simplicity, "Did he rape me?"

The thought brought with it fear, anger, shame, and bitter, bitter disappointment. She gripped the bathrobe more tightly around her feeling suddenly too exposed. She tried to take stock of herself and her panicked hands fluttered around her body, searching for bruises, for sore spots. She couldn't even wait for an answer.

"Holy shit," she said in a ragged gasp. "I need a doctor. I need–"

Micah took hold of her hands to still them and Fiona tried to shake him off.

"Don't touch me!" she screamed, unable to deal with even the softest of human contact.

"Fiona, calm down," he spoke softly. "He didn't rape you."

Fiona paused in her desperate inspection, "He didn't?"

"No. He didn't. He certainly tried to. I arrived before he was fully...successful," he said, again assessing her with those dark eyes.

"But why were you even there? How do you know all this?" Fiona pressed on, the fear turning to confusion.

"Those are questions for another time," he answered cryptically.

Fiona wanted to ask more, needed to, but her mind was reeling–the fire, smoke, death. Gio. Despite the mystery of this man's appearance, she couldn't say that it didn't come with a sense of comfort and safety. He seemed so sure of himself, so logical–her mind clung to that like a life raft.

When she didn't say anything, Micah continued, "After the incident with Gio, that's when you made the fire come."

He spoke with a sense of awe, of admiration. His tone disgusted Fiona and her eyes snapped to attention.

"How do you–" she began.

Micah interrupted with a wave of his hand, "I've known about you for a long time, Fiona. I've done my homework on you. You've been sort of a...hobby of mine. This was the perfect time to swoop in. But, as I said, all of that's a story for another time. There are more pressing concerns to consider now."

"What could be more pressing than that?" Fiona sputtered

back. "You just happen to be there when I wake up? You just happen to know about me? I'm your...*hobby*? What the fuck?"

That sense of comfort and security was fading as she gazed up at this human before her.

"What's more important than those questions?" she went on.

"Getting you out of here safely–with your freedom still intact," he responded, enunciating each word with care.

Fiona didn't know what to think. Her mind was still hazy from the drugs coursing through her system. As she tried to process his words, all she could think about were those screams she heard. Of the fire pummeling through the narrow hallways turning what was once beautiful into a burning hellscape. The painful admission, *I. Did. This.*

So instead of asking for more clarification she blurted out in a hysterical pitch, "Did I hurt anyone? Did everyone get out?"

The thought was too much to take. So many of her friends were in that hotel. So many families. Fiona remembered seeing that adorable blonde-haired boy when she checked in. Had he escaped?

"Some people got out," Micah replied simply. "Others did not."

His words brought in a wave of sorrow so deep, so dark that Fiona simply hung her throbbing head upon her knees while her shoulders heaved with bone-shattering sobs. She vomited the contents of her gurgling stomach onto the ground beside her. Once she started, she couldn't stop. She heaved until she couldn't breathe anymore, until her stomach and chest ached from exertion. The hair that hung in front of her burning face smelled rotten and acrid; it smelled like death. Death she caused.

Micah let Fiona cry. He let her puke her guts up. He didn't try to console her. Fiona craved more detail, needed more answers. But she couldn't muster up the courage to ask for them. If she was being honest, she was too afraid to know. Too terrified to understand the depth of the destruction, the wrath of the gruesome condition she attempted to hide for so long.

After a few minutes Micah said with a warning, "Careful Fiona."

Looking up at him with a question in her eyes, Fiona saw him gesture downwards. Following his gaze, Fiona saw that the sleeves of the bathrobe she was wearing, along with the grass surrounding her bare feet were glowing with smoldering embers that threatened to turn into a full-blown fire...again.

Standing up abruptly, she tried to stamp out the sizzling grass. What was happening? Her condition was under control. Wasn't it? It had been years since she caused any real problem. And never, ever, had she caused anything like this. This was just beyond anything she thought possible. Now, everything Fiona knew or thought she knew about herself was going up in smoke... literally.

Micah held out a bottle of water and said simply, "Drink."

Fiona did as he ordered and wiped her mouth with the back of her forearm. Then he poured the remaining contents onto her hands. Tendrils of steam wove into the brightening sky. How could the sun dare to rise on a day filled with such sadness, such terror? After a few breaths, Fiona was able to push that heat back down.

"What am I going to do?" she sighed out with shaking hands, overwhelmed by the devastation she created. "What the hell am I going to do?"

"That's where I come in Fiona," Micah said with a small smile playing against the edges of his mouth.

Fiona looked at him with tear-blurred vision without responding.

"You, like the others, have died in the fire," he continued slowly, letting each word sink in.

"But I didn't die. I'm alive. I'm a murderer. I deserve–"

"You deserve to live your life. You are the victim here. You didn't ask to be drugged. You didn't ask to be nearly raped. You are not the one responsible for what happened. Gio is," Micah reasoned.

"What happened to G-G-Gio," Fiona almost couldn't even utter his name.

He truly fooled her; Gio seemed so kind, so wholesome. Fiona's lapse in judgment scared her. *How stupid could I be? Why would I go to the bathroom and leave an unattended drink on the bar? Hadn't my mom drilled that into my head before I went off to FIT?* The thoughts ricocheted off the cages of her mind.

"He burned with the rest of them," Micah answered.

Fiona was shocked to feel no remorse at the thought.

"So..." Fiona began. "What you're saying is that... Is that..."

"Say it Fiona," Micah goaded.

"So what you're saying is I should fake my own death?"

The thought was so extreme. Faking death was something reserved for the movies, wasn't it? This was real life. Was that something real people did?

"Why would I do that? How could I do that?" Fiona asked.

"Well the 'how' is the easy part. I have the 'how' covered. As far as the 'why'...well. The entire fourth floor was completely consumed in flame...and that was where your suite was. If you emerge as the lone survivor, the authorities will be forced to investigate further. It wouldn't bode well for you."

Fiona tried to follow Micah's logic, but her head swam with confusion. There was simply too much to process at once.

"Are you saying the authorities could learn I was the one who started the fire?" Fiona asked.

"I am very much saying that," Micah replied. "And if they identify you as the cause, your life as you know it, will be over. You will be sent to prison...especially once the death toll is–"

Fiona cut him off, "Maybe I deserve prison. Actually, prison is too good for me. I deserve worse...the death penalty. That's the only way to make sure I never hurt anyone again," Fiona was hysterical. She kept going, unable to stop the words from pouring out of her mouth, "What kind of a monster am I anyway? I'm a liability. I deserve to pay for what I've done. I could do this again and again and again–"

"I can help you learn to control it," Micah interrupted.

"How?" Fiona spat back. "There is no controlling this. I've tried to control my condition for years... I thought I had it under control. Thought I had my emotions under control. But I was wrong."

"Just trust me," he said.

"I don't even know you," Fiona replied.

"You will get to know me. I'll take care of you. It's the right move Fiona. It's the only move you've got," Micah reassured.

"Faking my death? Is that even possible?" Fiona asked, still gazing up at him from the ground.

"It is possible. But you have to decide quickly. You do not have the luxury of time," he explained.

"What about my mom...oh God.. What about Noah?" Fiona nearly gagged as she spoke the names of her mother and little brother. The shame rising inside was nearly palpable.

"What do you think is better for them Fiona," Micah began. "To mourn your death, or to know the truth about you?"

He was right. Her mom and Noah could never lead a normal life if Fiona was arrested as a murderous arsonist. Better for them to mourn her and move on. They would heal. In time. And they would still be able to view Fiona, a daughter...a sister, with pride and positivity. The thought nearly broke Fiona's heart.

"What about–" Fiona tried to wrap her head around the enormity of the decision and her brain was desperate for logic and concrete facts. "Won't they know I escaped? They won't find my body–"

Micah responded, tucking his hands into the front pockets of his dark jeans, "Do you know what happens to the human body in a fire of this caliber? First the skin chars and splits. Then the muscles and fat carbonize. Then–"

"Stop. Please," Fiona interrupted. "I can't hear anymore."

"What I'm saying is that any human remains will be exceedingly hard to identify. You don't have to worry about the authorities recovering your body. All the corpses in that fire will be unrecognizable. Embers and ash—the only things left."

"Stop," she said again.

"It's the truth," he said simply, looking off into the distance at the smoke still rising into the sky.

"Embers and ash," Fiona repeated, as though the words helped her come to a final decision.

Without any further objections, Fiona felt something inside crumble that day. Something she didn't think could ever be fixed. Maybe it was her heart. Maybe her soul. But Fiona actually felt the life draining out of her as she struggled to come to a decision.

Fiona sat still for what felt like an eternity before answering. Over the next few years, she often found herself wondering if she would have made the same choice had her mind and emotions been clearer.

"How would this even work? Tell me," she demanded.

He didn't hesitate, "It's easier than you think...for me. I have contacts, connections—ways to ensure your anonymity. You come with me. Lay low. Change your appearance, your last name. We work on controlling your ability. I get you all the documents you need: passport, credit cards, identification documents. This comes with financial stability too."

She considered this. His answers were forthcoming; he made it sound easy, logical. But the emotional part was harder. This also meant leaving her mom, her brother, her life. But what else could she do? He was right; this was the only path left. Everything else, every other possibility had burned up inside the hotel.

Ultimately, she turned to Micah and said softly, "Ok."

He raised his eyebrow in question.

"I'll do it. I'll fake my own death. I'll come with you. Only if you promise to teach me how to control this demon inside of me. I'll never hurt another living soul again."

"I promise," he said.

Fiona's shoulders sagged in defeat. All those lives lost. She thought to herself, *What have I done? How can I ever come back from this hideous act?*

He continued, "My offer comes with conditions."

Fiona didn't have the heart to talk anymore–nor the stomach for it.

"I agree to whatever you ask," she replied. "What do I have to live for anymore anyway?"

"You'll find your purpose again, with me," Micah replied.

Fiona looked at him. He would be her life from here on out. She loved and hated him at that moment. A very large part of her wished she could have just burned along with all those victims. But she wasn't that lucky. Her penance would come in a different form.

Fiona broke that day. That was the only way to explain the change that overcame her when she agreed to Micah's plan. When she agreed to leave what she had known, what she had worked so hard to achieve. But as Micah explained, there really wasn't another option. It was the only play. Checkmate.

As she stood back up and followed Micah across the field–with the hazy images of her mom and brother flashing like lightning in her jumbled mind–she knew she would never be the same. The trajectory of her life had changed for good...and in that moment, Fiona was powerless to stop it.

Chapter Four

Still dressed in that white, terry-cloth bathrobe, Fiona opened the door to Micah's car–she couldn't even notice the make or model–and climbed in almost as though she was climbing into bed. It felt like someone else was controlling her movements. All connection to her body, to thought, logic, or rationality had been severed. It was almost like her whole being was on auto-pilot and her emotions were in a locked box–compartmentalized somewhere deep within for survival.

Her hysterics transformed into soft whimpers and tears leaked down her hot cheeks from eyes swollen into slits. She dimly perceived Micah start the car–felt movement as he pulled away from the curb.

"Where are we even going?" Fiona asked robotically.

Not that she really cared. What did it matter *where* they were going? It didn't. Not at that moment, but she didn't know what else to say. The black cloud of depression descended with such a heavy hand that she felt weighed down, suffocated. God, she had been at the top of the world just a few hours ago–celebrating her success with her co-workers cheering her on. Her mom and brother, safe at home–proud of her. And now... The juxtaposition was startling. It gave her a sort of mental whiplash. The screams still reverberated through her mind. The acrid scent of burning still so strong in her hair.

"Close your eyes, Fiona," Micah instructed. "You're exhausted."

He was right; she was exhausted. Mentally, spiritually, bodily–the drugs still coursed through her blood stream.

"What's my new last name going to be?" Fiona mumbled through lips that felt alien.

"Smith. Easy. Simple. Common," Micah said.

"Fiona Smith," she said, the words feeling foreign and uncomfortable against the roof of her mouth.

"Go to sleep Fiona," Micah said again. "Your body needs rest."

Fiona had never been one to go to sleep in front of others; it even took time for her to adjust to sharing a bedroom with her college roommate–something about feeling vulnerable like that made it difficult for her to truly relax enough to fall into deep slumber. But in that car, with Micah, exhaustion permeated through her body.

She then did something unexpected. She looked over to find Micah's hand resting on the gear shift of the car. It looked warm and solid. And Fiona desperately needed something warm and solid to grab onto. He let her envelop his hand in between her two palms. Fiona wasn't sure if the intimacy of the gesture was uncomfortable for him, but at that moment she didn't care. She needed someone. She craved human connection. And as much as she wanted her old life and her mom and brother, that was no longer a reality for her. She needed to find a new place–was this new place with him? She thought it could be. Once she had Micah's hand in her grasp, she floated to sleep as the road unwound beneath them.

What felt like minutes later, Fiona opened her eyes when the car finally stopped driving, and rested in front of a nondescript home.

For a blessed minute, Fiona thought everything that happened at the Garden City Hotel was a dream and she felt a moment's peace. But gazing down, she was still dressed in that bathrobe, which had slipped open a bit, revealing a sliver of thigh and though it was upside down, she could read the gold embroidered monogram: GCH. It wasn't a dream. It wasn't a nightmare either. The events crashed down on her like the relentless beating tide abuses the sandy shore.

She felt the tears come again; it was amazing that she had any left. All she could think about was her mom and brother–about their reactions when they learned of her "death." The image played like a loop in her mind–crushing and paralyzing.

Micah looked over and said, "Time to wipe those tears, Fiona and put on your big girl pants."

The bluntness of his comment startled Fiona, but she didn't have the energy for rancor.

"Where are we?" she asked, through lips that felt like steel; it was painful to even open them. She felt like the Tin Man in *The Wizard of Oz,* when Dorothy finally put enough oil in the crevices of his mouth to allow him to speak.

"We're in Plattsburg," Micah responded. "And it's time to go inside. They're waiting for you."

Chapter Five

PAST

"They're waiting for you, Fiona," Angela Blake called up the stairs as the minutes ticked slowly away. "Fiona," louder this time. "It's 7:15. Your ride's here. It's Alexa's turn to drive, don't you remember? It's a Day 1."

Fiona and her neighbor, Alexa, had worked out carpool arrangements based upon Day 1 and Day 2 schedules. They were both seniors and therefore eligible to drive to school. A few other girls also benefited from the arrangement and whether Alexa or Fiona drove, the car inevitably reeked of designer perfume and the unmistakable scent of Strawberry Pop-Tarts. Fiona's mom tramped up the steps with the express purpose of getting her daughter moving already.

"Fiona, I don't have time to play around this morning. I need to get Noah ready and be out the door asap."

Fiona met her mother at the door of her bedroom, still in her pajamas and wearing that puppy dog expression that worked so well. Her mother's gaze softened as she took in her daughter's worn appearance. She brought a hand up to Fiona's face to caress her cheek as the frustration in her tone melted away.

"Jeez. Fiona, you're burning up," Angela, spoke softly, pressing her cool lips to her daughter's temples.

That was how Fiona's mom assessed whether or not she or her brother had a fever. She insisted her own lips were more accurate than any thermometer on the market. Fiona squirmed away from her probing eyes...and her lips. Fiona always ran warm, and it's no wonder why. But that's something even her doting mom didn't know about–or at least Fiona hoped her mom didn't know about it. Sometimes, the tilted gaze Fiona's mother gave her, or the way she stared at Fiona, wearing a puzzled expression, made Fiona wonder if she knew more than she led on–made her wonder what questions hid behind those kind eyes.

"Warm enough to stay home from school today?" Fiona asked her hopefully.

She had a test in Calculus and a major essay due for Mrs. Douglas by the end of the week that she hadn't even started yet. Fiona really needed the day to both study and finish that English assignment if she was going to continue to stay on the Honor Roll. She didn't know why she cared so much about that anymore, having already been accepted into FIT; they wouldn't rescind their offer–or probably even know about it–if she didn't get her usual grades. Yet despite that logic, she wanted to be in the running for the top ten highest achievers in her graduating class. Call it ambition, call it stubborn pride. Maybe it was a bit of both.

"I think so," responded her mom with a worried expression on her face. "We may even end up at the Walk-In clinic later this afternoon if your fever doesn't break."

That won't happen, Fiona thought to herself. As always, she would make sure to take a cold shower before her mom got home from work and came at her again with those lips. She had learned a thing or two about her condition...and parental deception. It was the only thing that worked to fool her mom into thinking Fiona was well, the only thing that lowered the dial on the fire burning inside. And despite what her mother thought, Fiona *was* well. She never *really* got sick, so she usually managed to avoid her mom's inaccurate assessment of her body temperature. Well, her mom *was* accurate about the temperature...just not the wellness part. But Fiona was still a teenager after all–even though she would be going off to college soon–and she really needed a day off. So, Fiona used her condition to her benefit. Wouldn't any other teenager do the same?

That's what Fiona started calling it...her *condition*. What else was it? What other labels would apply? It had always been there, inside of her. It flickered weakly in elementary school, but once middle school started, it got stronger. And at this point, at 17, almost 18 years old, it scared Fiona sometimes. It seemed unquenchable. Fierce. Bubbling beneath her skin. Scorching her from the inside out. And it was heavily tied to her emotions.

What about next year, in college? Fiona would have a roommate. And doesn't a roommate see everything? It would be hard to hide those secrets when sharing such intimate space with someone else. A stranger. Yes, Fiona would get to select a roommate, but how much can you really know about a person from a few phone conversations, some texts and some social media pictures?

Maybe I should have chosen a college more local, a university allowing me to keep my privacy and remain at home, Fiona often thought to herself. Yet, part of her needed to go, needed room to breathe, room to become someone more than who she was at that stage in her life. Fiona was smart; she knew that. And talented. Her curated and carefully crafted portfolio was a testament to that. As most high school seniors do, she had such dreams. Life hadn't gotten real enough yet to quench those sky-rocketing ambitions. 17 years old is the perfect blend of both fantasy and reality; as the line between adulthood and childhood blurs and the real world begins to lose that misty haze–almost like turning the focus wheel on a camera–some of the glamor begins to fade too. But that hadn't happened yet for Fiona. She remained safely behind those rosy-hued glasses the older generation wishes they could wear once again.

But, in contrast to the excitement that often raced within her veins about the changes that would come upon graduation, Fiona was also worried–worried her condition would continue to grow. Continue to consume. Continue to eat away at her until there was nothing left at all. Just ashes.

Chapter Six

Angela Blake dropped her 7-year old son Noah off at the bus stop and drove into the office promising her daughter she would check in a little bit later and insisting Fiona call her if she started to feel worse. All morning, Fiona luxuriated in her bed and in the empty home. She loved having the house to herself. Her rumbling stomach brought her to the kitchen.

Standing in front of the open freezer Fiona decided on Totino's Pizza Rolls. Not exactly a breakfast of champions, but those little pockets of volcanic cheese and sauce were her favorite. She typically tried to stay away from overly processed foods—especially after learning about some of the chemicals on the ingredient list in Health Class last year—but these were Fiona's one exception. Shaking out a handful of the frozen pieces, she spread them out on the wire metal basket of the toaster oven and watched as they turned brown; she knew they were ready when the insides bubbled out from between the seams.

Even though her mom would have scolded her for eating anywhere other than at the kitchen table, Fiona carried the plate back up to her bedroom. As much as she wanted to veg out in front of the television, the whole purpose of faking an illness today was to plow through all that accumulated work. Just as she got herself into a groove typing that literary analysis on *King Lear* for Mrs. Douglas, Fiona heard a text notification. It was Jenna, her best friend:

You sick? Why aren't you in 2nd period?

Jenna sat right in front of Fiona in second period AP U.S. History, and frequently relied on her when it came to home-work and assignments. Jenna was innately intelligent, but didn't put much effort into her academics, and as a result didn't achieve the grades she was capable of. Fiona had basically been carrying her through the last two years of high school. Sometimes Fiona wondered what Jenna was going to do without her next year in college, but she supposed she would just ingra-tiate herself to someone else. Jenna had a magnetic personality; her beauty helped too. She was definitely likable; Fiona had to give her that.

Not sick. Needed a day off. Too much work to do

LAME!

Gotta finish that paper for Douglas.

It's due on Friday. You have 3 whole days.

Jenna herself lived her life through procrastination and was never able to understand Fiona's need to get all of her work done ahead of time. If Fiona waited until the night before to complete an assignment, anxiety would consume her—and anxiety fueled that fire within her that lately was difficult to suppress.

I need to ace it

You will ace it

You always ace everything.

Not true

I feel like ditching. Pick me up. Let's go to the beach.

Fiona wasn't a goodie-two-shoes by any means, but Jenna always made her feel like the Virgin Mary. Yes, technically Fiona was a virgin, but she did like to let loose every now and then. However, skipping school was not Fiona's idea of a good time, even though she reluctantly went along with Jenna's wild plans quite a bit throughout the course of their friendship. She pushed one way, and Fiona tried to push back...but she usually gave in. It was hard to say no to Jenna Hendersen and her pleading blue eyes. Fiona could almost see her standing at her locker with her hair styled in those perfect loose waves, rolling those blue eyes at the incoming messages. Fiona wouldn't have admitted this aloud, but sometimes she was glad they weren't attending the same college next year.

I'm not picking you up

The whole point of me taking the day was to get my work done. And my mom thinks I'm sick. I'll get caught.

Your mom doesn't get home until 6. We'll be home way before that. It's only 9 in the morning.

Fiona could feel her resolve wavering.

Almost as though Jenna could sense the shifting mood, she texted again,

> Do your work tonight. C'mon Fiona. Live a little. High school is going to be over in like 2 weeks.

> Fine

> I'll pick you up at 7-11 in 15.

Fiona couldn't very well drive up to the front of the building like Ferris does in *Ferris Buehler's Day Off*. This was real life. 7-11 was their designated meeting place. And a Slurpie was always a good idea.

> YES! I'll be there waiting! See ya in a few!

Fiona wondered if anybody ever said *No* to Jenna. Probably not. Casting one more fleeting look at the open laptop, Fiona saw the half of her literary analysis she completed over the course of the past hour staring back at her. She sighed; she would have been lying if she said that she didn't feel a bit bitter and a bit angry with her friend. Fiona would have been lying even more if she said she didn't feel angry with herself also. After all, Fiona was the one without a backbone when it came to standing up to Jenna.

Fiona sensed the fire ignite within her. This was happening with more and more frequency lately. She accidentally set the bathroom garbage aflame the other day when, after she got out of the shower, she saw a notification on her phone alerting her to a decline in her Physics average. She got a zero on a homework assignment, which brought her overall grade down 2 whole points. She knew Dr. Z would probably change the grade once she handed it in and spoke to him about it the next day, but just seeing that zero almost set Fiona into a tailspin. She was so focused on finishing high school with the highest GPA possible.

Luckily the garbage can was made of metal and with the sink right there, it was easy enough to extinguish.

Fiona sat still on her bed waiting for the flames to grow, wondering what could possibly spring into fire. It could be anything: the lace valances lining the two bedroom windows, the pink plaid comforter, the tan, shag throw rug beneath her feet. Fiona really needed to get a handle on this condition if she was going to keep it under wraps.

Another text message from Jenna provided some distraction.

> Wear that cute black bikini you bought the other day at the mall. I'm wearing mine too.

The fact Jenna was already wearing her new suit meant she planned to ditch before she even walked into Levittown High School. Fiona guessed she lucked out when she realized that her best friend, who also happened to just get her first car, was home for the day. Jenna must have felt like she hit the jack-pot.

Even though Jenna's comment annoyed Fiona, it was enough of a distraction to make her forget about the heat simmering under the surface, which helped quell the rising flames. Fiona shimmied out of her soft pajamas and tore off the tags still attached to the swimsuit. The material felt cold on her thighs as she pulled it up into place. Over the bikini, she threw on a soft pink tank and a pair of track shorts. She ran her fingers through her tangled red hair and grabbed the car keys, a towel, and her bag. Despite her better judgments and the worry running through her mind, Fiona headed out of the house.

Chapter Seven

Fiona's 2006 Toyota Corolla was her prized possession. It wasn't a dream car by any means, but it was hers. Yes, it was a few years old, and yes, there were a few tiny dents along the rear bumper, but the cherry red exterior and the soft gray upholstered seat had become Fiona's sanctuary ever since she saved up enough money to purchase it a few months ago. After an entire 3 months of pleading with her mom last year, Angela Blake, despite her trepidation, finally made her persistent daughter a deal.

Angela said, "Whatever you save up, I'll double it...But I still make the rules. Just because you have a car, that doesn't mean it's a free for all. I'm still the one in charge. If I say 'Be home by ten,' that means be in this house before the clock reads ten o'clock. If I say 'Noah needs a ride,' that comes before anything else."

"Deal," Fiona replied back, even though there was a twinge of guilt at the idea of her mother spending money she really didn't have.

And like most challenges in her life, Fiona went full-steam ahead with saving her money. She couldn't even say how many hours she worked at Saf-T. Swim, teaching reluctant swimmers to feel confident enough to put their heads beneath the surface of the pool, or jump off the side. It must have been hundreds of hours–at least it felt that way when she was engulfed in a chlorinated cloud of pool air and her fingers shriveled up like raisins before her eyes. She could never quite rinse her hair clean of that chemical smell, nor clear her ears of the terrified screams of infants as she held their wet, slippery bodies in her grasp. *When I'm a parent*, she thought. *I will never subject my child to the torture of swimming lessons. It should be considered cruel and unusual punishment!* She once shared that exact thought with her boss, who said, *We live on an island, Fiona. It's a safety concern for kids if they can't swim well. We have an important role here.* Fiona supposed that was true, but those screaming babies would have definitely disagreed.

Fiona was frugal with her paychecks, barely spending anything, and by the time she passed her road test, she accumulated a nice chunk of money.

Standing outside her car for a minute, Fiona noticed the sound of the birds chirping in the tree above. So careless. So free. Fiona could still turn back around. Text Jenna again and tell her that she changed her mind. She could even lie and say that her mother was coming home early from work. That would have been a believable story. But Jenna never would have let Fiona hear the end of it if she declined. Jenna was persuasive and aggressive–two traits that Fiona didn't possess. It was just too damn hard to put up resistance to those calculating blue eyes.

Fiona could see her distorted reflection in the passenger window, the red hair blowing gently around her face in the light June breeze. *Maybe Jenna was right,* Fiona thought to herself, trying to work up the courage to get in her Corolla. Trying to talk herself into what she was about to do. *It's way too nice outside to spend the day studying and doing work.* And it really was a stunningly beautiful day out–one of those rare days. You got only a handful like that, if you were lucky.

So swallowing her hesitation, Fiona hopped in the car and turned the key in the ignition, relishing the gentle purr it made. 7-

11 wasn't far away, probably a mile or less, but she turned the air conditioner on 'cool' and fiddled with the radio, finally settling on 92.3, her favorite rock channel at the time. Fiona was sure that once Jenna claimed her seat in shotgun, she would change the station anyway; Jenna preferred pop or hip-hop, those Top 40 hits that Fiona couldn't stand. But, in Jenna's presence, she always sang along to the corny lyrics anyway.

Pulling into the 7-11 parking lot, Fiona saw that Jenna wasn't alone. She was standing in the middle of two guys: Josh Taylor, with whom she was unabashedly flirting and Jared McLaughlin, the boy she shamelessly insisted that Fiona date. Fiona already agreed to go to the prom with him, but she didn't think she was ready for a boyfriend, especially considering the fact she would be living in New York City in a few months. But that wasn't the main reason Fiona remained reluctant to date; paramount on her list of concerns was this condition raging inside of her, the condition she found harder and harder to control.

Jenna waved enthusiastically as Fiona approached and when she hopped into the front seat, smelling of her Calvin Klein perfume she said, "Josh and Jar are going to tag along. You don't mind, right?"

What was Fiona supposed to say? It was just like Jenna to do that. Act first and apologize later–if there was even an apology. It would have been rude to kick them out of the car, but she was worried this day was gradually spinning out of her grasp. Maybe she should have stayed home. Was it too late to change her mind? Fiona felt that flush creep into her cheeks again as the three sets of eyes stared at her. Yes. It was definitely too late to turn back now.

"It's fine," Fiona said with a shrug, trying to conceal the turbulent emotions she felt.

Jared gave Fiona's shoulder a little shake from the back seat and as she turned around he mouthed the word, "Hey."

Turning around, Fiona gave him a small smile. He was cute, she had to give him that. Tall and dimpled with smooth, tan skin. Dark hair covered by a backwards Mets hat, deep blue eyes and a smattering of freckles splashed across the bridge of his nose–not as many as she had, just a sprinkling really, but they gave his face an endearing quality. His lips though, those were what Fiona had trouble turning away from. They were full, and soft–at least she imagined they would feel soft. *How would they taste*? She wondered. Fiona cleared her throat to stop the barrage of thoughts.

"Jones Beach Field 4?" Fiona asked, already knowing the answer.

"Yes," Jenna answered, almost shrieking with excitement.

Chapter Eight

Fiona eased the car out of the parking lot, onto Hempstead Turnpike, and then onto the Wantagh Parkway headed South. Even though the feeling of neglecting her unfinished work and lying to her mom nagged at her, Fiona didn't want to waste the day. She caught a glimpse of Jared's smiling eyes in the rearview mirror studying her profile, and felt her pulse quicken a bit. *I wonder if he notices my red cheeks*, she thought to herself, trying to force herself to cool down, to breathe. She was always self-conscious that her internal flame would reveal itself to others, but no one ever seemed to comment on it.

After a 15-minute drive, Fiona parked the car in the lot. The group exited her Corolla and, grabbing their bags and backpacks, headed towards the wooden planked walkway leading to the ocean. When they finally reached the white powdery sand, Fiona kicked off her flip flops, relishing for a moment the way the tiny grains felt against the soles of her feet. She loved the beach, always had. And even though her emotions today were a messy jumble, she couldn't ignore the reassuring sound of the waves in the distance or the friendly feeling of the sun as it shone down on her upturned face.

The teenagers sat themselves down on their towels just a few feet away from where the cerulean sea tumbled onto the vast shoreline. Fiona studied the sparkling Atlantic Ocean in front of her and inhaled the salty air; she told herself to just relax and let go. To enjoy the day; she felt some of the tension drain away.

Josh and Jared immediately shed their shirts and ran towards the ocean, kicking up sand as they went. The girls watched them go, silently studying the way the muscles in their arms and shoulders rippled with the movement.

"I'm going to hook up with Josh today. He's so hot," Jenna groaned.

"How have you not hooked up with him already?" Fiona responded. "It's just a matter of time until he asks you out. You guys are already going to prom together."

"I know right. Ugh. He's so cute!" Jenna almost whimpered. "And what's the prom comment supposed to mean? You and Jar are going to prom together too. And you haven't hooked up yet," she retorted, emphasizing the word *yet*.

"Not going to happen Jenna. I'm going away to school in a few months," Fiona answered.

"So am I," Jenna said. " And so what? You don't have to marry him. But he'd be fun to make out with a little. I bet he's a good kisser," Jenna said, nudging her friend's arm.

Fiona had to laugh. Hooking up with guys was all Jenna ever thought about. Boy-crazy would be putting it mildly. It seemed as though every week Jenna had a new crush, and she always seemed to attract the very person she wanted. Not surprising considering how effortlessly gorgeous she was. She left quite a few guys trailing after her with puppy-dog eyes and broken hearts. This track record made Jenna significantly more experienced in this realm than Fiona–which was an understatement. Jenna lost her virginity in 9th grade; Fiona wasn't even close to that. Aside from a small make-out session with Bryan Ferraday in 8th grade during an impromptu game of spin-the-bottle, Fiona had no experience whatsoever with boys. And she preferred it that way. Yet now, the thought of Jared made her pulse quicken. Her body hadn't responded to Bryan Ferraday the way it seemed to respond to Jared. Not at all.

Josh and Jared came back panting and collapsed next to the girls.

Jared turned to Fiona, studying her with those impossibly blue eyes.

She gazed back at him.

"Want to go in with me?" he asked. "It's not that cold, I promise."

Fiona peeled her stare away from him and glanced back at the water, noticing the rough waves crashing on the shore. Fiona wondered if a storm was coming.

"Maybe in a bit," she answered.

Jenna broke their conversation when she announced, "Me and Josh are going to take a walk. We'll be back."

Fiona tried to tell Jenna with her eyes to stay. She gave her that please-don't-leave-me stare that was supposed to mean something amongst girlfriends. It wasn't that she minded spending time with Jared, Fiona actually enjoyed it. But she was worried about what would happen if she let herself give into those wild emotions. Would she set the world on fire?

Jenna ignored Fiona—probably intentionally because she wanted some alone time with Josh; she could definitely be selfish when it suited her. The two walked up the beach hand in hand towards the boardwalk, and away from them. The sound of Jenna's laughter trailed behind them.

Jared and Fiona spend a few moments silently studying the water in front of them. The two hadn't spent much time alone. Fiona's heart thudded so loudly in her chest she was sure he could hear it over the surf. Why did she feel so nervous? This was Jared, the boy she'd known since kindergarten. But somewhere over those years, Jared transformed from that awkward little toothless 6 year-old, into an incredibly attractive teenager.

"Excited about going to Albany next year?" Fiona asked.

"Hell yeah," he said. "A little nervous too. I just decided on a roommate. I hope he's cool. He'll be playing baseball with me."

"I'm sure you two will get along," Fiona answered. "You're so easy-going. You'll make tons of friends."

Fiona was momentarily embarrassed for having complimented him so openly, but he turned to her and said, "Thanks Fiona. That makes me feel a bit better. Feels weird knowing I'll be somewhere else next year."

Fiona admired and appreciated him for making that admission. It made her feel less alone. He didn't turn away after he spoke. Their faces were so close together Fiona could see small drops of saltwater running down from his still-wet hair. His broad, freckled shoulder rubbed against her own; it felt cold from his swim in the ocean. Without speaking, he lowered his face and pressed his lips against hers, coaxing her mouth open with his tongue. He tasted like saltwater, and summer. Fiona felt her whole body respond to him. She pulled him closer with her hand on the back of his neck. He adjusted himself on top of her, his wet shorts pressing against Fiona's open thighs. What was she doing? Her insides were blazing.

"You're so warm," he whispered into Fiona's ear as he pressed a trail of kisses against her throat.

He had no idea what that statement did to Fiona. It did the opposite of what he probably hoped it would do. It made her aware she had to put a stop to this, no matter how right it felt. Heat radiated off Fiona in waves and she thought about the bathroom fire she started the other day. With a firm hand on his chest, Fiona reluctantly broke their kiss. He looked down at her with raw desire and disappointment written all over his face.

"How about that swim?" Fiona asked breathlessly.

He rested his forehead against hers, composing himself and then propped himself up on his knees. He wasn't the kind of guy who was going to push.

"I'll race you there," he responded.

Fiona tried to hide her own feelings of shame and embarrassment—and even fear. Fear she would never be able to have a normal relationship. Fiona had to get this condition under control. Maybe if she could do that, she and Jared could have a chance.

Jared and Fiona spent the next hour bobbing over the rough waves. Even though the choppy tide made her nervous, the cool water splashing over her skin smothered that internal fire. Jared kept a respectful distance, but every once in a while he playfully grabbed Fiona's foot or tickled her ribs. He was a good guy, and after being snubbed earlier, his touch didn't linger, despite the fact that part of Fiona wanted it to, wanted him to try again. But on the other hand, she knew she couldn't chance another intimate moment with him. The thought of prom crept into her mind and she didn't know what she would do when he asked her to slow dance with him. Maybe make sure they were directly underneath the air conditioning vent. Fiona almost laughed at the ridiculousness of that thought...but she almost cried too. How many girls at prom had to worry about accidentally torching the place? None.

"My fingers look like raisins," Fiona said, raising her voice so Jared could hear her over the waves.

"Want to dry off?" he asked.

They gradually made their way into shallower water and trudged up the sand towards their towels. Fiona's arms and legs felt rubbery from all the time in the ocean and a tiredness—and a bit of depression— pulled at her from deep inside. There was still no sign of Jenna and Josh, and Fiona almost gasped when she looked at her phone and saw that it was after 4pm.

"Let's pack up," Fiona said to Jared. "Don't you have baseball practice?"

"Supposed to. Josh came up with some sort of excuse. And since we lost the playoff game last week, Coach hasn't been as intense," Jared replied with ease.

"Well, I have to get going anyway. My mom is going to kill me if I'm not home when she gets back from work."

She quickly picked up everyone's belongings and threw everything into Jenna's oversized beach tote. Fiona noticed the sky above had changed from that blameless blue to a steely gray; when had that happened?

"Looks like it's about to pour," Jared observed.

"Let's go find them and head home," Fiona said, trying to hide the panic from her voice.

"I'm sure they didn't go far," Jared offered as they walked towards the boardwalk.

The beach had cleared out for the day, and aside from one or two remaining bikers, Jared and Fiona found themselves alone on the wooden planked walkway spanning the length of Jones Beach. Both Jenna and Josh left their phones behind, so they couldn't simply send them a text message to let them know it was time to go. And when Fiona glanced down at her own phone, she saw it was dead. She charged the laptop last night to make sure that it would be on full battery for all the work she had to get done and unfortunately neglected the phone.

Intermittent heavy droplets of rain began to fall from the sky as Jared and Fiona walked.

"Let's try the gazebo," Jared suggested, just as Fiona was thinking that Jenna and Josh might never be found.

The gazebo was an enormous wooden structure housing the bathrooms, snack stands, and souvenir shop. Last year Fiona's mom almost lost her mind when she gave Noah a 20 dollar bill to buy ice cream and came back proudly holding a boogie board still wrapped in its clear plastic coating. Fiona guessed he thought the boogie board was a more worthy purchase than a Chipwich. Fiona couldn't disagree.

As they neared the structure, Fiona saw Josh's fluorescent orange shorts and she knew Jared had guessed right. The two were vigorously kissing in an alcove near the now-closed snack stand and Fiona could perceive that Josh's hands were unabashedly exploring Jenna's chest underneath her bikini top.

Jared laughed and whistled to alert them of their presence.

When she saw them standing there, Jenna adjusted her bathing suit and without a blush said, "Hey guys!"

"Time to go," Fiona said, trying to keep the annoyance out of her tone.

"Bummer," Josh said. "Raincheck babe?" he asked, turning to Jenna.

"Babe?" Fiona repeated.

"Josh and I are dating now," Jenna responded walking towards them.

Fiona didn't have time to ask about the specifics of that revelation–she was sure she would get the full story later...if her mom didn't murder her first.

"Sorry guys," Fiona said. "We have to go. It's raining and I should have been home hours ago."

"Don't be such a prude," Jenna responded with laughter, not knowing how close she got to hitting the mark. Fiona's cheeks burned as Jared gazed sheepishly on.

The group ran back to Fiona's car in the downpour. The skies opened up and the rain fell in silent sheets. With goosebumps on wet flesh, Fiona started the car. When did it get so cold out? The windshield wipers couldn't even keep up with the onslaught of water as Fiona drove slowly home.

"I hate driving in the rain," Fiona uttered through stiff lips.

"Just take it slow," Jared instructed from the backseat.

The light-hearted vibe of the day was replaced with tension. They were cold and wet, and Fiona was sure Jenna sensed her annoyance. After all, she knew that Fiona needed to be home early. And she knew that this had all been her idea.

Jenna tried to reassure her friend by saying, "Relax. We'll get home before your mom does."

Chapter Nine

Jenna was wrong. As usual. After Fiona dropped off first Josh and Jared and then Jenna, Angela Blake–who had left work early–waited for her wayward daughter in the driveway with her hands on her hips and her mouth pressed into a hard line. The deluge quieted to a steady downpour and Fiona's mom's wet hair was plastered to her face like a helmet. She must have seen Fiona's headlights coming from the kitchen window and thought that she would "greet" her out front.

"Where have you been?" she demanded before Fiona even got out of the car. "I've been calling and texting you for the past hour and you didn't reply. I was worried sick."

"I'm sorry mom, my phone died and–"

She cut her daughter off immediately with a raised hand, "I left you home to go to work...my poor, sick daughter...and I come home to find your car gone and your bedroom empty! Fiona, please tell me you have an excuse because I don't think I have ever been this mad at you. I'm literally shaking. Noah couldn't get off the bus without a parent or guardian. The school called me at work to come get him! He was sobbing when I pulled up."

Shit! Noah! How could I have forgotten? Fiona thought to herself.

Her mom was completely correct in her anger. Fiona was furious at herself for such a terrible oversight. Her mother was also right about Fiona's track record; Fiona never got in much trouble–actually she never got into ANY trouble. She was dependable, reliable, responsible–the perfect daughter. Perfect except for her condition of course.

Fiona could have lied. She could have made up some excuse that she had to go to school because she forgot something in her locker, but she wasn't going to lie to her mom. She already lied to her every day about the reality of what burned inside of her–well, she lied by omission at least. And that was bad enough. Fiona wasn't going to start lying to her about other things too.

So Fiona just said, "I don't have an excuse, mom. I went to the beach with Jenna."

The admission shocked her silent, which was extremely difficult to do. Angela was anything but silent.

"You went to the beach? While you're sick?" She sputtered.

"I wasn't sick mom. I faked it. I wanted to stay home because I was behind on a bunch of work. My plan was to–"

"Fiona, you *were* sick. You were burning up this morning."

"Mom, you know I run warm. And you felt my head after I was underneath the covers all night," Fiona tried to justify the warmth she had felt coming off her head in waves earlier.

"And let me guess–Jenna talked you into going to the beach," she questioned.

Fiona's mom wasn't a fan of Jenna. As much as she pretended to like her for her daughter's sake, she wasn't fooled by the sugary sweet way Jenna spoke to her, and she definitely didn't approve of the revealing clothing she wore. But Fiona wasn't going to blame this on Jenna; she could have said no. And clearly, she *should* have said no.

"I'm sorry mom. It wasn't Jenna's fault. I guess I just wanted to have a little fun," Fiona responded.

Angela's eyes softened a bit, "I know you've been working so hard Fiona. And I know you must be feeling lots of emotions now that high school is almost over. If you would've just told me the truth, I might've even condoned a day off."

"It won't happen again mom. I really am sorry."

Fiona could tell that her mom's anger had dissipated by the way she looked at her. Angela had seen the stress and anxiety that Fiona carried around with her every day first hand. Many times Angela was the one telling her daughter to ease up, to be kinder to herself, more forgiving–reminding her that she didn't have to be perfect all the time. If Angela only knew how imperfect her daughter really was. Sometimes Fiona thought about telling her about the secret. She would know what to do...how to handle it. But then again, Fiona's mother had been through a lot in her own right–would it be fair to burden her with the weight of another nasty truth? After she had already said goodbye to her husband and embarked on the treacherous journey of being a single mother?

"It's ok, Fiona. But please. Don't let this happen again. If you need a break, let me know. I'm your biggest supporter. Don't you know that?" she asked.

"I do know that mom. Now I guess I really better go finish up all that work."

With a sigh of relief, Fiona trudged back up those stairs. Yes, she did have to complete that essay...and study for that test, but her mind reeled with images of Jared. His face, so close to hers. His smiling, blue eyes. The feel of his body against her. Fiona's heart fluttered in her chest just thinking about it. Again, she felt heat rush against her face. Her fingers tingled with energy and raw power.

Could Fiona actually have a relationship with him? She wondered. It was clear not only from today, but from what Jenna told Fiona in the past, he wanted to be more than friends. Maybe if she just told him the truth about herself, he would listen. Fiona mused that maybe he could help. Or...maybe he would tell someone. Maybe he would look at Fiona as a freak, a science experiment. Maybe Fiona would end up locked up in the basement of some lab with people sticking her with needles and drawing her blood. That was her biggest fear...that and accidentally hurting someone. *No,* she corrected herself. *It is definitely better that I stay on my own. That I keep to myself.*

But the cool water did help. Recently she had learned that much at least. As Fiona turned her attention back to her school work, she took some comfort in that knowledge. She could do this, she reassured herself. As long as she managed those pesky emotions, Fiona could keep this all under wraps. *And if I get too heated, I can just find a way to cool myself off,* her last thought before she turned her attention back to her neglected schoolwork.

After finishing up the literary analysis, Fiona opened up the study materials to prepare for her upcoming Math test. She was mostly able to keep Jared and his strong arms and soft hands in the periphery of her consciousness...and that was good.

Chapter Ten

PRESENT DAY

Fiona spent the first week in that house in Plattsburgh in a stupor. Sleeping mostly, barely eating. She lost weight and developed pale purple circles under her eyes. Upon walking in a week ago, she had been greeted with smiles and enthusiasm, none of which mirrored her oppressive feelings of sorrow and remorse.

She missed her mom and brother with a fierceness bordering on pain, as though her limbs had been torn off. It was the most profound feeling of loss she ever experienced. She didn't even know it was possible to hurt so much and not actually die. She thought about them constantly: How were they? Did friends rally around them? Did they cling to one another for support? Did they seek out a therapist? The lack of answers drove her insane; it impacted her sleep, her ability to think clearly, everything. Every miniscule act reminded her of them. When she showered, she half expected to see Noah's Suave Kids 3-in-1, the green bottle that made his hair smell of watermelons. When she managed to eat something, she thought of the love and care her mother put into food preparation, even when she was racing around like a lunatic living the single-parent life. The traces of her family lingered in her periphery and she wished that she could check in on them—

make sure they were ok. But she couldn't do that. She was helpless here. The knowledge of their grief, even though she couldn't observe it in person, was oppressive.

When she finally did fall asleep–because her body had simply shut down–cocooned in the darkness of that basement bedroom, she found momentary reprieve. But as soon as she opened her eyes again, it all came back as though a dam had been opened. The onslaught of melancholy was consuming and total.

Micah left her alone mostly, aside from insisting that she at least attempt to eat. There were others there too. But they felt like shadows and danced around the periphery like hovering ghosts. None of them seemed real to Fiona.

There was Spence, Maya, and Rhea. She was surprised she even cared enough to remember their names. Spence tried more than the others to draw her out, but Fiona wouldn't allow herself out of the web of numbness. A very large part of her believed that she deserved this anguish, this pain. Look at what she had done. She scoured the newspapers and found facts that haunted her–both in the daytime and throughout the night. All those victims. And the thought of what her mom and Noah must be going through–enduring the loss of a daughter and sister. When she was feeling really low, she imagined what her funeral would have been like–without a body. Her family huddled around an empty coffin. That thought pierced her soul afresh every single moment of the day.

At the one week mark, she heard a sharp rap at her bedroom door. Usually if she ignored the knocks, and the attempts at socialization, the person on the other side would eventually go away. But this time, the sound persisted.

"I'm sleeping," Fiona called.

"You're not," the voice said. "If you were, you wouldn't have answered."

Maya pushed open the bedroom door and stood there, leaning against the molding. She stared at Fiona with calculating eyes, not without a bit of disgust and said, "Get up. We're going outside."

"I'm not really–"

Maya cut her off, "Honestly, I don't care if you don't want to. You're going to. Now get up."

"Did Micah tell you to do this?" Fiona asked.

"Yes," Maya replied honestly. "But he's right. Are you just going to lay there forever and wallow in self pity?"

"That was my plan," Fiona said, surprised that a tinge of humor escaped her lips.

"Well, it's not mine. No offense, you're not here to just sleep your troubles away. Now get up. It's a beautiful day outside. Time to start earning your keep."

And Fiona listened. She wasn't sure what made her get out of bed. Maybe on some level Maya's logic sunk in. Maybe she was just sick of being tired. Tired of being sad. Pulling on a pair of leggings and a loose tank–Rhea had basically given her a whole new wardrobe–Fiona pushed the nausea and the dizziness down and got up. She followed Maya up the stairs.

Chapter Eleven

"Breathe in, Fiona" Maya instructed. "Now, breathe out for 1, 2, 3. Posture upright, face relaxed. And again. Breathe in. And out for 1, 2, 3."

Despite Fiona's reluctance to get out of bed, the warm sun felt good on her face and for the first time since she arrived in Plattsburgh, she was able to think with some clarity and find a bit, just a bit, of solace.

The two women had been sitting there for an hour already. It started with silence; neither found the need to fill the space with mindless chatter. Fiona appreciated the fact that Maya didn't try to make small talk. There was something about her manner and all her abruptness that was appealing. After a while, Maya offered to take Fiona through some meditation and breathing exercises.

"Humor me," Maya had said.

"Why not?" Fiona replied.

So now, Maya and Fiona sat Indian-Style–or was that phrase frowned upon now? Fiona couldn't keep up with what was and wasn't allowed in today's society. In the lush grass of the backyard, the sun shone, warm and friendly, on Maya and Fiona's faces in the late June morning.

"Ok. Now open your eyes," Maya continued.

Fiona did as instructed and blinked away the brightness of the day. Maya placed her two fingers on Fiona's inner wrist, testing the pulse. Surprisingly, Fiona didn't flinch at her touch. The act was clinical. Fiona didn't need Maya to tell her that it was slow and even. The rhythmic cadence of her heart-beat danced calmly in her ribcage. Thump-thump. Thump-thump.

"How do you feel?" Maya asked.

Fiona took stock of herself and spoke, "I feel better than I have felt all week. Calm. Light. Steady."

And Fiona wasn't just saying that. She meant it. The pressure had momentarily lifted. It was a beautiful and much needed break from the relentless crushing sadness of the past week.

"That's the goal. The better you can self-regulate, especially under duress, the better you can control your ability."

"How do you know so much about this?" Fiona asked.

"Lots of research," Maya said simply.

Fiona let out a small chuckle at that, and was surprised that she was even still capable of making such a sound.

"What?" Maya asked.

"How could you possibly research? Are there sources? Articles? Studies? Scholarly journals about women with the ability to make sparks with their minds?" Fiona replied. The thought was so ridiculous it elicited another two muted chuckles.

Maya didn't join in and simply said, "Actually, Fiona, yes. There are. Did you think you were the only one? Many scientists have studied certain mental phenomena that appear unexplainable or clinically perplexing. There hasn't been much written about thermal manipulation, which is what your *condition*, as you refer to it, is called. But there has been quite a bit written about Earth manipulation."

That shut Fiona up. For her entire life she had looked for validation for what she could do, some scientific explanation for this *condition*—there was that word again—that changed the course of her life and landed her here. Knowing she wasn't completely alone in her abilities, that others, throughout time had been burdened with the same heavy weight provided her with a feather of hope to tuck into her hat. Had anyone else who possessed these "conditions" killed all the people Fiona had? Had they faked their death? The lightness started to fade from Fiona's eyes.

Maya saw the change in Fiona's gaze and spoke again, "You just have to know where to look."

Fiona tried to subdue the bite in her tone, "Well, I would really appreciate it if you could share this information with me. I feel like you all know more about me than I know about myself. Maybe if I had known—"

"Stop with the shoulda couldas already. There's only now and the future," Maya interrupted.

Fiona tried to form a response in her mind, but couldn't bring herself to feel much–that numb, fuzzy feeling had returned.

"How about this," Maya replied, when Fiona didn't speak. "I can help you explore a bit. Spence was the one that helped me tap into the research I needed to help you. Sorting between the real stuff and the junk science presented certain challenges. It's kind of a rabbit hole once you get started."

"I guess you also knew about me? Just like Micah did?" Fiona asked.

"I did," Maya replied simply. "We all do. And you're one of us now. We need you."

"To do what exactly?" Fiona responded. "I don't really understand any of this."

Maya replied, "You will. Maybe once you come back to the world of the living, Micah will tell you all about it."

Fiona wanted to ask more, but there was something in Maya's tone that told her that pressing wouldn't work. And to be honest, Fiona wasn't sure she even cared. What kind of a life could she even live without her family? How could she possibly get past the awful things she had done?

Despite her searing exhaustion and sadness, Fiona asked, "How did you end up here?

She wasn't sure Maya would answer such a personal question.

Fiona knew first-hand how painful it could be to dredge up memories.

"In a similar way as you. Micah discovered me–"

She must have guessed at Fiona's misconception because she continued, "No. Not like that. I can't *do* anything like you can do, Fiona. But let's just say that I too have a propensity towards the flame. And I have been burned by it before. Just like you."

Her cryptic response didn't explain much, but Fiona didn't push. She was sure Maya had her own reasons for holding back. She certainly hadn't struck Fiona as a sharer, so even that much was better than nothing.

"Thanks for helping me today," Fiona said. "Those breathing exercises helped...more than you know."

Fiona wasn't lying either. Sitting there with Maya on the grass was the closest she felt to alive all week.

"Well. What's good for you is good for the group," Maya replied. "Plus, when else will I get to put all my Yoga instruction to use?"

That last reveal surprised Fiona. She never would have expected Maya to practice Yoga. Not with the thick black makeup outlining her inky eyes and her aversion to any clothing of color.

Maya must have read the amazement in Fiona's eyes and she said, "We all have a past, Fiona. And what? I don't look like the typical yogi to you?"

"No. You don't," Fiona answered honestly.

Even though Maya stifled it, a slight smile broke through on her lips. The gesture changed her whole face, lit it up. It was at that moment that Fiona started to like Maya. Started to think perhaps they could be friends. *Friends.* Could Fiona even make new friends after what happened to her co-worker friends at the Garden City Hotel? After what *she* made happen to them? Maybe she didn't deserve friends. But despite the darkness of that thought, she desperately wanted one. More than she ever had before.

But these thoughts came with bitter feelings of shame, of

anger–for how her life had gone so wrong, of crushing guilt. How dare she have wants? She didn't deserve friends. She didn't deserve anything. At that moment Fiona truly believed that all she *deserved* was to be burned along with her victims in that fire.

Suddenly her skin began to heat and she could feel the warmth radiate out from her core, pulsing off her skin in waves. She tried to breathe, tried to calm herself. But her emotions were raging out of control and those emotions stoked her fire afresh. What the hell? She was all out of whack. Everything she thought she knew about herself had gone out the window. She thought she could control all this...control her emotions. But now, she couldn't even recognize herself anymore. It was like she was back at square one.

Maya must have sensed the shift because she said, "Fiona? You ok?"

"Get away from me. Now!" Fiona screamed back.

But it was too late. The tiny patch of grass between her and Maya burst into flaming orange wisps and engulfed Maya's pale knee.

"Oh My God! Maya," Fiona screamed as she frantically stood up and pulled Maya up with her, swatting her skin and her fraying jean shorts that had sizzling embers studding the edges.

"It's ok," Maya said, even though her lips trembled.

Maya stomped out the small blaze and repeated, "Fiona, I'm ok. Look. It's fine–"

But Fiona didn't hear the rest because she was running towards the house. She had to get away from Maya. She needed that tiny dark bedroom to control her emotions. The only phrase repeating in her mind was *Oh my God. Oh my God. Oh my God.*

"Oh my God! Noah," Fiona screamed the following afternoon, turning around to take her brother's raw hand in her own, careful to avoid the worst of the blistering.

When had he come into the room? Fiona was so preoccupied with trying to put out the fire that she didn't see her younger brother enter and try to pat out the blaze himself with his soft, smooth adorable hand. The fire was out now and Fiona was trying to assess the damage and come up with a story to explain the burnt remnants of rug and clothing to her mother. That's when she heard Noah's cry of pain.

His face was red and his eyes were watery with suppressed tears. Noah was obsessed with superheroes and was fond of saying, "Superheroes never cry." No matter how often Fiona tried to tell him that crying is ok...good even, Noah wouldn't budge and she knew that those threatening tears were bothering him as he stood there shaking, trying to be brave.

"Why did you touch the fire, Noah? Don't you know that you'll get burned?" Fiona asked, enveloping him in a hug.

"But the fire was on your back," he responded. Your shirt was on fire. I thought I could use my hand and pat it out. Fire Safety

Prevention was last month and in school, the fireman told us that–"

He stopped talking as Fiona pulled him deeper to her chest. With her free hand, she felt the back of her shirt and was shocked to find that there was barely anything left of the fabric at all.

"What happened Fiona?" Noah asked. "Was it your candle again? Like last time?"

The comment broke her heart because it bespoke years of deception. After all, a candle was an easy alibi, but Fiona wasn't sure just how many more times she could use that excuse. It was starting to wear thin.

Before Fiona could answer, the two heard the unmistakable voice of their mom.

"Shit," Fiona said aloud, even though she didn't mean to. She quickly stood up and pulled the charred t-shirt off over her head. Good thing she was wearing a tank underneath.

"I won't tell," Noah said.

As Fiona ran to the bathroom to run cold water over the remains of the shirt and put out the last few smoldering embers, Angela Blake's voice rose upstairs, clear and insistent "Something's burning in here?" Her footsteps on the stairs. Fiona could even perceive the creak made by that pesky seventh step. "I'm not crazy this time. What's on fire?" Fiona's mom asked, panic lacing her voice.

At least once a week, Angela Blake would walk in the front door after a long day of work and ask her daughter that very same question. Fiona actively tried to convince her mother that this developing phobia of fire was simply her paranoid imagination, but it was becoming harder and harder to do. Mostly because when Angela asked that question, it usually did smell like smoke in the house.

Angela met her daughter at the doorway to the bathroom and must have known immediately, by the guilty expression on Fiona's face, that something was up. Like she always did, Fiona tried to downplay the scenario by saying, "Well I lit a candle earlier. Maybe that's what you're smelling."

"It's not a candle Fiona," her mom said. "It smells like burnt hair or something."

Angela walked frantically into Noah's room to inspect. Fiona followed her trying to hide her panic and attempting to hide the burnt, blackened–and still dripping–evidence behind her back.

Noah's door swung open, and Angela found her son in the picture of innocence: on the floor, playing with his super hero action figures. Only Fiona was able to perceive that his body was angled intentionally away from their mom, so she wouldn't see the angry red blisters on the back of his hand. He certainly was a good little actor.

"Is something burning in here?" Angela asked her son, making exaggerated sniffing gestures. "Don't you smell that?"

"Nope," Noah responded. "Nothing's burning in here, mom. I think you're just being paranoid."

The fact that he used the word "paranoid" would have been funny in a different scenario. He was trying to protect Fiona, using the exact terminology she always used to convince their mom that everything was ok. At that point, Fiona wondered if Noah was onto her. Onto what she could do. He was a perceptive little boy and loved his big sister with a tender fierceness that stole Fiona's breath sometimes.

Angela's appraising eyes snapped to her daughter, "What's behind your back?"

"Nothing mom–"

But before Fiona could spit back an excuse, her mother pulled the wet, charred fabric from her daughter's clenched fingers.

"What's this?" Angela said, examining what remained of Fiona's brand new Nirvana t-shirt with wide eyes.

Fiona didn't know what to say so she settled on, "It's my t-shirt."

"I see that Fiona. But what happened to it? It's nearly burned to ashes. And why is it soaking wet?"

It wasn't "burned to ashes" as her mother suggested. Noah extinguished the flames before that happened, but she didn't think she should argue with her mother over the proper terminology to describe the state of the garment.

"Well–"

"Spit it out Fiona," her mother said while her daughter stammered over her words.

"I was lighting my new candle and I was wearing that shirt...I guess I leaned over it and the bottom caught the flame," Fiona lied.

What really happened–and what Fiona could never reveal to her mother–was that the pile of laundry she was folding in front of her seemed to spontaneously combust while she was on the phone with Jenna. And thanks to Noah she learned that the shirt she was wearing had also been ablaze. It wasn't their typical conversation; they argued. Jenna was trying to convince Fiona to finally take the plunge and date Jared, and Fiona just...snapped at her. She was sick of her friend pushing her on this. She wasn't going to be forced into a relationship, no matter how much Jenna pleaded. As Fiona's anger sizzled inside of her, the threads of the clothing smouldered with heat. Luckily, Fiona removed the smoke alarm from her bedroom a few months before, after a similar incident occurred. That time, the smoke alarm *had* sounded and she had to stand on her desk chair and fan the area with her pillow to get the siren to stop while Noah looked on with his hands pressed firmly over his ears. *That* time she had to bribe her brother with a Slurpie from 7-11 to keep the situation a secret from their mom. And there were other times too. Many, many other times, where the fire just got away from Fiona. Nothing too bad ever happened. A few burnt clothing items. A burnt bedspread. A couple of char marks on her wooden bureau. Nothing she couldn't handle–or explain away. But today she burnt her brother...indirectly, but still, the fact remained the same.

Angela Blake's angry tone brought Fiona back to the

moment, "You have got to be more careful Fiona! You need to get rid of those candles...today. If you don't. I will. You could burn down the house!"

If her mother only knew how accurate that statement truly was. But Fiona was careful. Well, usually. Yes, things sometimes escalated a bit–but Fiona was always able to fix things. Always. At least that's what she told herself. Maybe it was a survival mechanism. If Fiona thought she was a living breathing spark, she wouldn't be able to sleep at night out of fear and anxiety. But despite it all, Fiona was a teenager. A teenager who wanted, more than anything, to be "normal." And like most teenagers, Fiona could convince herself of just about anything to achieve that goal. Even if what she had to convince herself of, was that she had her condition under wraps.

"I won't burn down the house mom," Fiona tried to reassure her mother, who still looked worried and unsure. "I promise."

Fiona secretly hoped this was a promise she could keep. Because as much as Fiona tried to convince herself she had everything under control, sometimes she wasn't so sure. Sometimes those emotions just got away from her; that's when things had the potential to turn bad.

Fiona watched her mother's gaze soften and saw tears well up in the corners of her eyes.

"Fiona–" Angela began.

"Please don't cry, mom," Fiona said. "It's ok. No one got hurt."

"You know that you can–talk to me, right?" Angela asked.

"I know that mom," Fiona responded, feeling ashamed of her deceit.

"I know it hasn't been easy having only a mom...that sometimes–"

"Mom, you're all we need...we don't need two parents when we have you," Fiona tried to console.

"Let me finish Fiona," Angela said softly. "I know that I'm not around as much as I should be...that I work a lot. But–you can talk to me, if something is happening...if something is going on with you."

"Nothing is going on with me, mom," Fiona said. "This was just an accident."

Angela spoke without missing a beat, "There have been a lot of accidents. I've noticed char marks on your dresser. Burnt bed sheets. A burnt t-shirt–"

"I guess I need to learn to be more careful with my candles and incense," Fiona said, averting her eyes from her mother's steady gaze.

"I just want you to know that you can talk to me Fiona. I'm here. And I would leave work in a heartbeat if you or your brother needed me...even just to talk."

"I know that mom. I really do," Fiona said.

"I just...I feel like...something is..." Angela couldn't decide on the right word to use. "I feel like something is...off...with you."

"Nothing is off," Fiona said too quickly.

"Ok, Fiona. Ok. Just please know...I'm here. I'm always on your side."

"I know that mom."

Angela embraced her daughter in a fierce hug before stomping down the stairs with a final command, "Now, throw out those candles. Right now. I want to see them in the garbage can."

Thankfully, she didn't enter Fiona's bedroom to see the other evidence of what just occurred. The interaction with her mom left her worried. Worried that her mother knew way more than she said. Her mother had displayed suspicion before, but nothing even close to as overtly as she just had. Fiona thought herself smart enough to hide the truth; maybe she wasn't as smart as she thought. Was it true what they said, that a mother's intuition is never wrong? Fiona didn't know, but she felt dejected and tired– guilty too. Bone-numbingly guilty. Should she just tell her mom? What then? What would her mom say?

Fiona walked back into Noah's room and said, "Thanks for covering for me. Let me see your hand."

"I'm fine," Noah responded.

"Let me see," Fiona repeated with firmness, wishing that she was the one who got burned. But she never got burned–it seemed as though she was immune. Lucky for her.

The blisters were angry and scarlet, but they weren't as bad as she initially suspected. She led him by his wrist into the bathroom trying to keep her own emotions in check and sat him down on the lid of the toilet. She applied a thin coating of Bacitracin and a small bandage to the affected area. Then, bringing her lips gently to the bandage, pressed a light kiss to the hurt spot.

"There," she said. "All better." And again, she hoped that was true.

When Noah trotted happily back to his room, Fiona let the tears flow. How could she have allowed this to happen? She hurt her brother...the most dear person in her world. If she was the Earth, Noah was the sun. Or maybe *she* was the sun...capable of fire and destruction. Burning those closest to her. She always tried to be so careful, but maybe she was simply an accident waiting to happen. The thought of those blisters on her brother's small hand etched itself into Fiona's mind. *Never again*, she swore. *Never again will I hurt Noah or anyone else for that matter.* The promise allowed Fiona to wipe the tears from her eyes and put the event into the periphery somewhere, where it hovered like a storm cloud about to burst.

No one bothered Fiona the rest of that day or that night as she cried stormily in her basement bedroom. But the next morning Maya came back. She didn't even bother knocking this time. She was wearing new shorts, and Fiona immediately noticed the bandage on her knee.

"Alright," Maya said. "Time to get up. More breathing and meditation today. Gonna help you train up."

Fiona couldn't believe what she was hearing.

"No," she said simply.

"*No* isn't an option," Maya spat back. "Get up."

"Are you insane?" Fiona asked. "You clearly must be. Look what I did to you. Look at your knee. I hurt you, just like I do everyone. Just—stay away from me. Trust me...you're better off."

"Not going to happen," Maya said. "Stop sulking. Get up."

"I'm not getting up," Fiona said, frankly sick of being pushed. "I'm not going anywhere. And I'll tell Micah that too."

"God Fiona," Maya said. "Grow up, alright. Yes. The Garden City Hotel happened. Yes, your mom and brother had to mourn your death. Yes. People died. All those things happened. I'm not going to sugar-coat it or lie to you. But *you* are alive. And while you may not agree with me, you should be happy that you are.

Life goes on. And you have a new life here...Micah gave you a second chance. And you're just going to waste it? By lying here day after day crying and sulking?"

"I don't deserve a second chance," Fiona responded.

She had so much more to say, especially about that word *sulking*. For some reason it grated against her. Maybe because it was true.

"No one in this world *deserves* anything. It's not how life works. You're here. With us. And we need you. So. Get. Up," Maya was not going to take no for an answer.

When Fiona didn't respond nor move, Maya said again, "Get. Up. Rhea and Spence are up there waiting for us to join them for breakfast. They're also sick of your bullshit. It's getting old."

"My bullshit?" Fiona repeated with a sardonic laugh. "If you're all so *sick* of me, how about just leave me the fuck alone."

She had never spoken to anyone like that and she felt momentarily guilty for snapping at Maya that way. She didn't deserve it. Maya wasn't the one responsible for any of this.

"Because we need you. And you might not see it yet, but you need us too. So get up and come with me," Maya concluded.

Spence took that moment to appear in her room.

"Aw a family reunion," he said with a giggle. "Come on up Fiona. Breakfast is ready."

"I don't want breakfast. I don't want to be here. I want to go home. No offense...But I just don't want any of this," Fiona sputtered out.

Maya exhaled a frustrated sigh and turned to Spence, "You try. I'm over this."

Maya turned on her heels and Fiona could hear her stomping up the steps.

Spence walked over to Fiona and kneeled next to the bed so he was eye level with her. Fiona didn't recoil; his gaze was friendly. There was still a hint of humor in his eyes, as there always seemed to be, but there was kindness there too–a genuine concern.

"I know this wasn't the life you chose," he said. "Yeah, you might have *chosen* to go with Micah. But you didn't choose this."

His words seeped into every corner of Fiona's soul. She felt like he understood...like he was the first person to really see her here, and she couldn't stem the flow of tears.

"I don't want to be here. I don't want to train. I miss my mom, my brother. I don't want to work for Micah," she said softly. "I want my old life back."

"Look Fiona," Spence began. "None of us ever planned to be here. We all had other goals in life. But this is where we landed. Just like you. You don't have the luxury of getting your old life back. But you can make a new one. Here. With us. We can't replace your mom and brother. I know that. But we can be your friends. We can give you a place in this world."

Fiona let his words sink in. She didn't have any other options. She couldn't go home. She didn't have any money to go elsewhere. She was terrified of hurting more people with her condition. As she stared into Spence's earnest eyes, a realization dawned on her...and an understanding. This was a place where she was wanted, needed. A place that would allow her to hone whatever ugliness resided inside her. Maybe it wouldn't be so bad.

"I don't know," Fiona began. "What if I can't do it? What if I can't do what you all want me to do?"

"Don't think about the what-ifs," Spence said without missing a beat. "Think about the now. Just put one foot in front of the other."

"I don't know how to do that," Fiona responded.

"Well how about come upstairs with me and get some breakfast," Spence said, standing up and extending his hand.

"I don't know," Fiona said; she couldn't even believe that she was actually considering the offer.

"Look..." Spence began. "I'm not asking you to marry me. I'm just asking you to drag your ass out of bed and have breakfast with us. You have to eat. You don't even have to get dressed."

"I'm in my pajamas," Fiona said, glancing down at herself. "I don't even have a bra on."

"That's fine. No one cares, and Micah isn't even here. Pajamas and no bra is fine clothing for sitting around the kitchen table. It's not prom, Fiona," Spence said.

Fiona pulled herself out of bed and re-did her ponytail. As much as it pained her to admit it, she was hungry. And Spence was right about one thing, it definitely wasn't Prom.

Chapter Fourteen

PAST

Prom at Levittown High School was always on the last Friday of the school year, the night before graduation rehearsal...and graduation rehearsal was a mandatory event. Administrators arranged it that way to ensure that prom-goers didn't get too drunk, nor head out to the Jersey Shore for what would undoubtedly be illegal activities for underage minors. After all, if students didn't show up at the school the next morning at 9am sharp, they wouldn't be permitted to walk in graduation. This theory mostly worked–at least in the sense that plans to go away were deferred until after graduation, but most kids showed up to rehearsal still in their prom make-up, and clearly hung over...or worse, still drunk.

For years, decades even, adults have tried and failed to try to instill restraints upon rambunctious teens, but as much as things change, they still mostly remain the same. When there is a will, there's a way. And for a senior in high school–with graduation hovering on the imminent horizon–there is more than a will, there's an insistence. An animalistic demand for more, that outmatches even the best of intentions.

Fiona stared at her reflection in the large mirror hanging over the dining room table as she waited for Jared to arrive. She wasn't used to wearing this much makeup and her green eyes stood out even more than they usually did against the heavy lashes and eyeliner applied by the make-up artist at the salon. She wore her red hair down in loose curls and a sapphire blue fitted dress that hugged all the curves of her almost 18 year old body. She never flaunted her figure, but when she tried this dress on in front of her mom and Jenna at Aurora Boutique, they both squealed in delight. Fiona smiled to herself, thinking of what Jared would say when he saw her. They hadn't spent any time alone together since the ill-fated beach adventure, but she had been experimenting with controlling her condition, and she had been mostly success-ful...except for a tiny little kitchen fire in the toaster oven a few days ago. *Maybe he'll try to kiss me again tonight*, she thought hopefully. Maybe she would even let him.

Angela's face came up beside her daughter and she gazed at her in the mirror with misty eyes.

"Oh Fiona," she sighed. "You are so beautiful."

"Thanks mom," Fiona blushed.

"You're going to have the best night. I still remember my own prom. It was–magical," she said.

Just then, the women heard a car pull into the driveway. Jared.

"I'm kind of nervous," Fiona admitted, fiddling with her hair.

"Don't be," Angela consoled, taking hold of her daughter's warm hands in her own. "Just make good decisions," her famous line.

Fiona's mother always told her to *make good decisions*. And Fiona always did. Her conscious decisions were always good. It was the unconscious ones that got her into trouble sometimes.

They heard the doorbell ring, and just before her mom left to go answer it, she put her hands gently on her daughter's shoulders and turned her around so they were facing one another directly.

"I wish your father could be here to see you now. He missed out on so much by leaving," she said.

Angela Blake didn't often mention Fiona's father; she thought it was too hard for her children. Too much of a reminder of the aching absence that they undoubtedly felt. What Angela didn't know was that to Fiona, she had been more than enough. She had been everything.

Unlike most women whose husband ran out on them, Angela didn't harbor that biting resentment, just a lingering sadness. Fiona knew that she still loved him, despite it all–that much was clear from the very few times she allowed herself to bring him up in conversation. Fiona often wished her mother talked more about him; maybe then she would talk more about him...it might make him feel more present, more real. Was he even still alive? Did he move on to another family? Have more kids? Did he run away from them too? Fiona wished she had answers to those questions. Fiona still had memories of him. She was nine when he left. But Noah, he was just a baby. Fiona wasn't sure what was better? Having the memories and feeling the pain? Or having no memories at all? He was in her life for the first nine years of her existence and then he was just...gone–vanished like smoke.

For a moment, Fiona wished Jared hadn't chosen this moment to show up. She would have liked to have had more time to talk to her mom about her father, this elusive figure whose absence had left a hole in her identity. But Fiona didn't have that luxury. Maybe there would be another opportunity where she could ask about him.

Jared entered the house, unabashedly handsome in his polished shoes and black tux. His eyes widened when he saw his date, but he had to play it cool in front of Fiona's mom.

"You look great," he said, approaching Fiona shyly. As expected, he slid a corsage of pink roses onto her wrist. The soft petals sent shivers up Fiona's spine when they brushed against her bare skin.

Noah, watching the whole time spoke up, "Those are weird shoes Jared,"

"Noah!" her mom scolded.

"It's ok little dude," Jared replied. "They are weird, aren't they?"

Jared did a little dance to showcase his footwear and they all laughed.

"Ok," Fiona's mom said, pulling out her camera. "Smile."

They did, and for the moment Fiona forgot about her dad, her condition...she forgot about everything except the warmth of Jared's hand against her waist.

Angela plugged on, "So remind me of your plan again."

Jared answered for them, "We're going to Jenna's house to meet up with everyone and take pictures. Then the limo is coming to take us to prom. Then...I don't know, maybe the beach or something."

"Don't be home too late," Fiona's mother replied. "You have to be at graduation rehearsal at nine o'clock, and if you're not there–"

Jared and Fiona chimed in together and finished her sentence, "...we won't be allowed to walk in graduation. We know."

"Sounds like you know the deal," Angela chuckled agreeably.

Pulling her daughter in for one last hug, Angela was careful not to mess up Fiona's hair or makeup.

"Don't go smooching with Jared in the bathroom," Noah chimed in, giggling.

Fiona gave her brother a playful punch on the arm to hide the redness that suddenly burst forth on her cheeks.

Ignoring her son's comment, Angela said, "Have fun Fiona." Then she whispered in her daughter's ear, "I love you."

"Love you too mom," Fiona said, as Jared led her out the front door.

Chapter Fifteen

The crystal chandelier at The Piermont cast rainbow prisms across the dance floor and the view of the sun setting over the Atlantic Ocean just outside the window added a sparkle of enchantment to the evening. Fiona and Jared, standing on the wooden deck outside the catering hall, watched as the red sphere sank below the horizon and just as its last glimmer disappeared below the water, he kissed her. Even though the heat raged within, Fiona was able to keep the flames from spewing forth; however, she did retire quickly to the bathroom with the intention of running cool water on her wrists...just in case. Progress!

She closed herself into one of the restroom stalls and as she lifted her gown to sit on the toilet, she felt small blisters forming on the heels of her feet, where the straps were rubbing her skin raw. But despite the pain, she couldn't keep the smile from her lips. Her mom had been right. The night was magical. Perfect. Like something out of a dream.

Just as she was about to flush, she heard the rustle of chiffon outside the stall and perceived high-pitched female voices, giggling harshly in the echoing space.

"She's such a fucking tease," said one of the voices.

Fiona immediately recognized the nasal, brittle quality. It was Jenna. Instead of exiting the stall, Fiona remained there, listening.

Jenna continued, "Did you see the way she kissed him? He's in love with her, and she's just leading him on."

Then, another girl laughing conspiratorially said, "Who knows, Jenna—maybe she has plans to take him home tonight and make that perfect red hair all dirty."

A round of laughter told Fiona there were more than just two of them out there.

"Yeah right," Jenna said with a snort. "Not Fiona. She's such a damn prude. She thinks she's better than everyone else because she's never let anyone fuck her. Poor Jar...he probably thinks he's gonna get lucky tonight. But he's just gonna go home with another case of blue balls."

Fiona felt the tears grow hot and heavy in the corners of her eyes. She couldn't believe Jenna was speaking about her like this. Jenna, who was supposed to be her best friend. The betrayal was piercing and suddenly the twinkling veil that covered the evening turned sallow and ugly. How many times had Fiona confided in Jenna over the years? Hundreds of times? Thousands? And how many of those confidences had been the fodder for gossip? How many times had Jenna laughed at her behind her back? How many of Fiona's secrets had Jenna revealed to others, while Fiona kept Jenna's locked away inside herself?

Fiona wanted to burst out of the stall and confront her friend—or maybe "friend" was the wrong word. Stand face to face with her and scream at her until her voice was hoarse. Yet, she couldn't quite force her hand to turn the lever of the bathroom stall. So Fiona remained there, while the girls, her classmates...her friends...prattled on.

Finally, the girls left the bathroom, their voices trailing echoes along the marble tiles. Fiona emerged from the stall and glanced at herself in the full-length mirror before her. Her mascara left streakmarks down her cheeks and her nose was red and running.

Yes, there was sadness there...and betrayal, but the anger

burbling forth from Fiona was the most palpable emotion of all, and as Fiona grabbed a paper towel from the stack, the flimsy paper went up in flames in her pale, freckled hands. She threw it into the sink and went for another, but the same thing happened. *Fuck. Not now*, she thought to herself. Then there was the smell—the same one her mother perceived a million times. She looked down to see that the plush carpeting beneath her feet—with an intricate rose lattice design woven throughout—was smouldering. Smouldering and spreading. She stepped rapidly towards the bathroom entrance and the fire trailed behind her, catching and unfurling like a vine. The carpet, the lavish velvet sitting sofas in the anteroom, the stair runner—all up in flames. She watched, frozen in horror, as the curtains lining the lobby erupted in gushing waves of blazing heat.

Then, there was the shrill sound of the fire alarms as the once-beautiful and bright and golden prom venue was engulfed in gray plumes of billowing smoke and angry crimson flames.

Fiona stood there in the center of it all as the prom-goers became a stampede. Chris Ferguson collided into her and she went sprawling on her butt as bodies raced past her. Suddenly she didn't feel beautiful anymore. She felt like Carrie White must have felt as she destroyed her own prom in Stephen King's fateful tale. She felt like a monster.

From the floor, Fiona could only dimly perceive the noises, the yelling, the screaming, the panic around her. She remained in a hazy state of confusion. What blared loudest in her head were three words that echoed over and over again, like a chant. *I did this. I did this. I did this. I did this.*

Then, she felt a firm hand grip her elbow and she peered up into Jared's face. His hair was disheveled and his once pristine tux now hung open, revealing a throat glistening in sweat.

"Let's go Fiona," he said. "I've been looking everywhere for you."

Fiona let Jared pull her to her feet and guide her to the door leading outside—the same doors they traipsed up two hours before.

Once they were standing in the parking lot in a huddled mass with the rest of the prom goers, Fiona took stock of her surroundings. She was trembling and Jared removed his tuxedo jacket and gently placed it around her quivering shoulders. If only he knew her shaking was not due to the slight chill in the air.

With Jared's jacket wrapped tightly around her shoulders, she perceived four firetrucks and three ambulances—the red lights blaring into the darkness, leaving their ghostly imprints upon her retinas. There had been a few minor injuries: Gina Docken was treated for a broken ankle as a result of tumbling down the front steps in heels, Gabe Rivera was getting stitches in his forehead for smashing his face into the molding of the exit doors, Richy Janus, Jamie Pelfley, and Alexis D'Agostino were the last ones out and were being treated for smoke-inhalation. Aside from that, there were bumps and bruises on some of her classmates, torn dresses, missing bowties, and some little scrapes and cuts, but every single student was alive and accounted for—the staff chaperones made doubly and triply sure of that—standing in the parking lot awaiting parent pick-up. All in one piece.

The thought that everyone was safe brought only a tiny iota of solace to Fiona's reeling mind. She ruined the night for everyone. She caused severe damage to the catering hall, and had brought pain to some of her classmates. And only some of that pain was physical. As she looked around, most of her female classmates were crying silent tears while their dates—looking worn and shell-shocked—tried to soothe them. And Fiona was the one responsible.

It could have been worse. Yes, of course that was true. But like always, it turned out alright. In the grand scheme of life, what was prom? A distant memory of adolescence. It was one of those milestone events that meant a great deal in the moment, but faded in importance over the years. Was it that big of a deal it ended in fire? Fiona tried to rationalize it. Talk herself into thinking it was ok.

At least no one was really hurt, right? Yet the ugliness of it all lingered in her mind like a bitter aftertaste. Guilt, confusion, regret, those emotions tumbled over one another–and then relief that it was over, and that everyone was safe washed over those feelings, assuaging the pain like aloe soothed her sunburns.

At that moment Jenna ran up to Fiona and threw her arms around her.

"Oh my God. Thank God you're ok," Jenna said.

And even though the anger was still there, and the feelings of betrayal, Fiona allowed herself to be embraced. Was she really going to throw stones at Jenna for what she said...after everything Fiona had done? Why ruffle the feathers? After all, they would both be going away to school soon enough. So, Fiona hugged her friend back. It seemed silly not to, and swore a silent vow that nothing like this would ever happen again.

After the initial relief that visibly passed over Angela Blake's face upon seeing that her daughter was safe and sound, Fiona climbed into the front seat of the car. Fiona felt drained in a way she had never experienced before. When she started driving, Fiona's mom cast a suspicious gaze at her daughter. She didn't voice her fears–perhaps she felt like the experience had been so traumatic that it wasn't the right time, Fiona couldn't be sure– but Fiona knew what they were. *Another fire. Another close call.* She could see her mom's brain working furiously, trying to process what had occurred. Fiona didn't offer any insight. Would her mom confront her about her fears tomorrow? Possibly. But Fiona would be ready for the questions, just like she always was. Questions played on her mom's lips, but nothing came out. In response, Fiona remained quiet. What could she say? But then again...nothing *really* happened, right? No one got hurt. Maybe she caused some damage, but nothing that couldn't be repaired. So, Fiona–like always–chalked it all up to just another close call. Was that an irresponsible mistake? Maybe. Probably. But Fiona was young, and again...she was determined to lead a full and normal life in spite of her condition. She could get it all under control. She knew she could.

Chapter Sixteen

PRESENT DAY

As she often did, Fiona found herself alone in the house. Silence echoed through her basement bedroom; no footsteps, no echoes of conversation, no creaks of wooden floorboards. The small clock above the door read 8am and Fiona extended her arms above her head in a full body stretch. It felt good. *She* felt good.

That breakfast Fiona had with the others the other day was a sort of breakthrough for her. She didn't expect to feel so comfortable with Maya, Rhea, or Spence–nor did she expect to find such solace in just being around other people. It allowed her to push past some of the pain and heartache and join the life of the living again.

So, a new sort of routine began, and it allowed Fiona to suppress the ugliness–if only a little bit. Fiona was surprised to find that the next few weeks passed quickly. Fiona worked with Maya on breathing and meditation and began to get her emotions under control. They fell into a rhythm in Plattsburgh. And rhythm was exactly what Fiona needed. She still mourned her mom and brother, and couldn't stop thinking about those 11 victims that lost their lives in the Garden City Hotel fire, but somehow, she was able to compartmentalize that. Fiona dedicated herself to her training with vigor and zeal. If for no other reason than the distraction it provided.

Still in her flannel pajama pants, Fiona trotted up the basement stairs and into the kitchen to find something to eat, the chirping birds and her grumbling stomach the only sounds. Looking around, she took in her surroundings. Maya's New Balance running shoes by the back door. Rhea's pack of smokes on the coffee table in the living room. Spence's laptop neatly charging on the kitchen counter. All evidence of life–an indication of the people who resided here, people she was still getting to know. But what about Micah? None of the possessions scattered about were his. Who was he? *What* was he? Sometimes, like right now, Fiona was desperate to know more about him. And not only him, but Kaleb too. It wasn't like she hadn't tried to dig for details. She had. But she didn't have much to go on. She didn't even know Micah's last name.

Then, a thought came to her. She tried to ignore it. *It would be an invasion of privacy*, she rationalized. She placed two slices of Pepperidge Farm Cinnamon Raisin Swirl bread into the toaster to brown. Tapping her fingers lightly on the counter, the thought was still there. The curiosity was still there.

Fuck it, she said to herself, turning her back on breakfast and heading down those basement stairs she had walked up just minutes before.

Standing in front of Micah's bedroom, with her hand poised on the doorknob, Fiona hesitated. He would be furious if he knew she had gone in there to snoop.

He won't find out, she told herself. *Just a quick look*. And she opened the door.

Being in his private space felt wrong, but Fiona needed to at least try to satisfy some of her raging need to know more. Not only about Micah and Kaleb, but about this whole little organization of which she was now a part.

The room smelled like him. Clean and masculine. God, she loved his scent.

Focus, she told herself. *Don't get side-tracked by how bad you want this guy.*

Looking around, his room was neat and bare–tidy. Queen-sized bed made with military precision with a plain gray comforter, simple black dresser without a speck of dust. Aside from a lamp and a black wooden box there was nothing on the surface of the dresser. Nothing on the walls either. No photos, pictures, plaques. Fiona didn't know what she expected–maybe part of her imagined a wall consumed with thumb-tacked photographs connected by string, newspaper clippings–like those CSI shows on television.

She rifled through his drawers, careful not to ruffle the folded t-shirts, boxer briefs and socks. When she opened his closet the smell of him was stronger. Shirts and jackets in various dark hues hung in an orderly row, just like the shoes that lined the bottom. The shelf at the top of the closet held folded sweaters; there was even a sweatshirt there and a folded pair of sweatpants, shockingly. Fiona couldn't even imagine Micah wearing anything so casual.

Closing the closet door, she let out a sigh of frustration. Nothing. There was nothing here that gave any clues about anything. Just as she headed towards the door, that dark box on the dresser caught her eye again. She approached it tentatively; it was about the size of a small shoebox, ebony wood with a metal clasp. Upon closer inspection it had a loopy 'M' etched into the top.

When she opened the lid, she saw, much to her dismay that this was a watch box. 5 watches in assorted shades of glimmering metal were lined up like sentinels, their soft ticks audible in the quiet space. Tentatively, Fiona traced her finger across one of the glass faces. As she did, the display tray moved a bit, and she realized that there was a second tier–an underneath compartment.

She gently lifted out the tray, careful not to disturb the watches. Underneath, was a folded newspaper article and a photograph. The photograph was creased, definitely a few years old. Who even printed out pictures anymore? Where did this one come from? The photo was a candid shot of a younger Micah–not much younger, only slightly...maybe a few years–smiling, shaking the hand of another man. Neither were looking at the camera. In fact, it looked like they didn't even know the photo was being taken. The other man was positioned away from the camera, so that only the back of his head and his salt-and-pepper hair were visible. Could that be Kaleb? Who had taken this photo? Why? Fiona's questions spun out like taffy as she drank up the image before her.

Reluctantly she placed the picture on the dresser and unfolded the newspaper article. It was faded and bleached, as though it had been left out in the sun too long. Most of the words were obscured, but she could make out the heading: "Mystery Fire: Mystery Man." Then, underneath, "Manhunt Begins After Suburban Inferno Kills 8." Fiona's breath froze in her throat. Was Micah that 'mystery man?' Was Kaleb? Her mind reeled. Had Micah been responsible for 8 deaths? Were there more fires? More deaths? Why had he kept this article? This photograph?

Instead of satisfying her curiosity, Fiona's clandestine visit to Micah's room only stoked it. It wouldn't surprise her to learn that Micah had a sinister past, but what *did* surprise her was that despite that knowledge, she still wanted him, lusted after him. What did that say about her? There was yet another question she couldn't answer.

She carefully refolded the photograph and the newspaper article and placed them back in the box; she then settled the watches back on top. Pulling the door closed behind her, Fiona smelled burning.

The cinnamon toast, she said to herself as she raced back up the stairs. As much as she tried to forget about the article and the photograph, she couldn't. Possibilities spun in her head like a manic carousel. Why couldn't she just do what everyone else told her to do: just accept the situation and stop asking questions?

Why was that so difficult? She decided that she would try harder to quell her curiosity. What did it matter anyway? She was here, indefinitely. There was nowhere else to go. She needed to just accept that truth and move on, regardless of who Micah and Kaleb really were and what they wanted her for. This was her only path.

Chapter Seventeen

After a particularly long day of training, Fiona was exhausted. But there was pride there too, mixed with the exhaustion–pride at her emerging ability to harness whatever condition was inside of her. She displayed some control today–of both her flame and her emotions. And that was surely progress, right? She was shocked to feel that sense of contentment stir within her. And not only contentment, but pleasure. How was it that she could like the feeling of burning? It was new and welcome.

She trudged down the steps after an early dinner. Rhea, Maya, Spence and Fiona ate an entire pizza along with a salad and 12 garlic knots. Her appetite had returned as the dark circles under her eyes packed their bags and left. She found that she was developing a sort of companionship with the three housemates–was that what they were? Maya's No Bullshit attitude was refreshing. There was no guessing or games with her. And Spence had an easy-going goofy nature. She hadn't had much alone time with him–or with Rhea for that matter–but he didn't push her and always included her in the conversation, or tried to. Rhea didn't talk to Fiona much, and she wasn't overly warm or friendly, but she seemed to accept Fiona with a simplicity that was in itself comforting. Spence and Rhea often went out to "do their own thing" as Maya put it, and Fiona still wasn't sure exactly of what their roles were, but she assumed that they were important. Micah wouldn't keep them around if they weren't.

As for Micah, he was rarely around. The photograph and newspaper article remained etched in her mind. "Mystery Fire: Mystery Man." That phrase rolled around in her brain. Was Micah the "mystery man"? She wished the article was legible. She thought about asking Micah about it, but what would she even say? "Hey Micah, I was snooping around in your room the other day and I found a picture and an article. Can you tell me about it? Did you kill 8 people in a 'Suburban Inferno?'" There was no way she could broach the subject with him–frustrating, but true.

Once Fiona asked him where he went everyday; his answer was something like, "I'm out working every day." Fiona didn't push, partially because Micah didn't seem like one to budge, but mostly because frankly, that man did something to her. Her blood seemed to pump wildly in her veins when he came close, and she was sure he could hear her heart hammering against her rib cage. There was no denying that he was handsome–gorgeous actually, but the way he commanded the attention of everyone, the sureness of the way his feet were planted on the Earth, drove Fiona mad. There were times when she would hyperfocus on a single aspect of him–his hands, or his chin, or his lips, and imagine vividly what that part would feel like or taste like. And the worst part about it was that her longing was so obvious. He would catch her staring and give her a small smirk. Fiona couldn't help but think he liked it.

So Fiona was surprised when there was a light knock on her bedroom door and when she called "Come in," it was Micah who stepped across the threshold into her small space. He looked so large standing there, his hair and complexion so dark in contrast with the white panelled walls. She felt her face flush immediately and that heat inside her began to rise. Using some of the breathing techniques Maya had recently taught her helped her to at least fake composure.

"Can I sit?" he asked, indicating the bed.

"Ummm, yeah," Fiona said, standing up to frantically toss the clothes strewn on the bedspread into the hamper so there was room for him.

He sat, fully at ease, while Fiona ran fingers through her tangled hair. She didn't know what to do; she felt awkward and clumsy in her own space. And flustered. Aside from a few moments here or there, she hadn't really been alone with Micah since the car ride to Plattsburgh. She thought a lot about how his hand felt enclosed in hers. That was the last time she even touched him. So, she stood before him, shifting on her bare feet that suddenly felt clammy against the tiled floor.

Micah laughed at Fiona's obvious discomfort–the sound was surprisingly warm and throaty–and ran his own thick fingers through his mahogany curls.

"Maya tells me that training is going well," he said.

His teeth were so straight and white; God, when he smiled, Fiona almost couldn't take it.

"It is," she said, feeling like she should elaborate, but not knowing exactly what to say.

"And she tells me that you have been coping well with the change of scenery," he continued.

Fiona just looked down at her feet, toenail polish chipped–the only remnant of her former life. Had she been "coping well?" Not really, if she was being honest with herself. When she was working with Maya, maybe. But the second her mind was unoccupied, too many emotions came crashing back. Guilt. Sorrow. Desperation. Anger–yes, even anger. Anger towards the way her life had shifted. But despite all that, on the outside, she had been able to fake it. Fake it til you make it, right? That was something her mom always said.

When Fiona didn't answer, Micah said, "I'm proud of you."

Fiona's heart swelled a bit at the compliment.

"Proud of me?" Fiona asked. "Why?"

Micah stood up. "Come here," he said. Not a question.

Fiona listened, even though her knees knocked and her breath hitched in her throat. Standing right in front of him, she could openly drink in his appearance. His dark eyes met her own. They were bottomless, those eyes. And he saw her. Really saw her, and knew her. Fiona bit her lips as her gaze traveled from his eyes to his neck, to the bit of smooth chest visible at the top of his v-neck shirt, and finally settled on his mouth.

Placing a finger underneath Fiona's chin, Micah raised her face so she was staring into his eyes again and said, "Look at me, Fiona."

Fiona obeyed.

"You know I'll always take care of you, right?" Micah asked, his breath warm and sweet against her flaming face.

And in that moment Fiona believed him and trusted him. Hell, she needed him. More than she had ever needed anything else. He was her life raft. Her savior.

"Yes," she responded.

Micah brushed the pad of his thumb over her lips. "Beautiful," he said, pushing his thumb slightly inside her mouth and tracing the ridges of her front teeth.

Fiona gently scraped her tongue against his skin; he tasted masculine and earthy. Fiona wanted more of him, wanted to know what the rest of him would taste like and smell like.

"I think you're ready," he said–whispering it in her ear.

The vibration of his speech so close sent shock waves of chills through her body, and suddenly she couldn't stop trembling, her voice shaky when she said, "Ready for what?"

Before he answered, he scraped his teeth against her ear and Fiona let out an audible moan as he sucked her hot flesh into his mouth. She wanted to touch him, but she couldn't seem to move her arms; she was paralyzed against him.

"I think you're ready for your next fire," he answered.

The sentence made Fiona recoil slightly, and Micah sensed it.

He pulled her closer, his hands firm on the small of her back, fingers tracing the sliver of exposed skin above her shorts. Part of her knew this was coming, expected it. Why else was she here, training? The rhythmic rubbing of his hands against her back paired with the sensation of his tongue ghosting against her throat rooted her to the floor. At that moment she would have agreed to anything. And Micah knew it.

"What fire?" Fiona asked, voice shaky with need.

He moved his face up and traced the bow of her mouth with his soft, skillful tongue before parting her lips to give her the kiss she yearned for. The feeling of him in her mouth, his tongue, his lips–it broke open the dam and she couldn't get enough of him. Need and raw hunger crushed her underneath their powerful weight and she pressed her chest up against him, needing to take him further, deeper. He gave her what she needed as she explored his mouth with her own.

He pulled back gently and answered her last question, "The one you're going to start in Nina Bradley's penthouse."

Before she could even think or process what he had just said, his lips were back on hers and his hands had dipped below her shorts, caressing the smooth curves of her ass. She could feel his fingers tracing the elastic lines of her underwear covering her most intimate area, and she desperately wanted him to touch her there– right in her centermost place. But he didn't give her that. Not yet. First, he required acquiescence.

His fingers teased her while he asked, "Will you?"

She couldn't even think about what agreeing to this would mean. What it would cost. She needed him with an urgency that terrified her. Why wasn't her fire raging? Maybe she really was getting better. Or maybe she just didn't have time to think about it. Maybe just knowing that she didn't have to hide her true nature calmed her condition. She could ponder all that another time. But she desperately needed his fingers on her, in her.

"Yes, Micah," she said, arching her body into him to give him better access.

Finally, his fingers reached inside the thin fabric and found that sweet spot between her legs. When his skin touched her there, she couldn't think of anything at all. She rocked her body against his hand while her head rolled back, totally consumed by the feeling of her rising need, her body desperate for release. She was so close; her body was clenched tight and she could feel her thighs begin to tremble. Ragged breathing escaped her parted lips and she could feel Micah watching her, studying her while she came apart. Normally that would have made her self-conscious, but her unadulterated need for the man took over and her body kept driving her towards a sweet peak that seemed just over the horizon. Sensing that she was just a few touches shy of falling over the edge of the abyss, Micah slowed his movements, began to graze his fingertips lightly over her sensitive skin while she whimpered, wishing that he would just give her the climax she needed.

"Promise me that you'll do what I ask," he said as his movements slowed to a torturous pace, fingertips moving in slow circles, just enough to keep her hovering somewhere outside of herself.

She gasped when he inserted a finger and then pulled it back out, a promise of what he would do once she agreed.

"Yes," she said. "I promise."

Did she even know what she was saying? It was hard to tell when he was touching her like that. Making her body feel like sunshine was radiating out of her core, that doves were fluttering around inside her quaking ribcage.

"Look at my face and tell me," Micah said, still keeping his movements torturously slow.

Lifting her eyes up to meet his, she saw an intensity burning there—an intensity mixed with curiosity and genuine amusement. Whatever game he was playing, it was clear that he liked it.

"I promise Micah. Please, just—" she murmured.

She couldn't finish her sentence, because at the word *please* Micah's fingers—which seemed to already know exactly what her body craved–touched that spot again and she shattered into a million pieces in Micah's hands.

It wasn't until after Micah left her room, after she stopped shaking, after her breathing returned to a normal cadence, and after her heart stopped dancing in her chest that she thought about what she had just agreed to, about what it meant. She guessed at the symbolic nature of the act–burning down this stunning apartment that had taken over so much of her past life, and it made sense why Micah requested it. Or had it been a request? Not really. It was an expectation. One she signed on for when she agreed to go with Micah in that field those weeks ago. Then Fiona thought about Nina–Nina Bradley and her beautiful apartment. Thinking about her brought her back to high school graduation–which if she really thought about it, was the start of everything. And then she thought about that apartment–that beautiful penthouse she knew by rote–and of course she knew it by rote; she had designed every square inch of it.

Chapter Eighteen

PAST

The remainder of high school, graduation—it was all over in the blink of an eye. Fiona walked across that stage in her blue cap and gown and received her diploma with her mom and Noah looking proudly on. She was 18 years old now, and it seemed as though real life was unfurling all around her. Prom was behind her, and it was now time to look forward.

Summer bloomed and with it came the bittersweet feeling of change in the air. Once the yearbooks were signed, and final good-byes were said, all of the pomp and circumstance that accompanied the end of senior year faded into the background. Life simply plowed forward, like a freight train.

Even though Fiona didn't have a summer job—she didn't think she could manage with college racing towards her as fast as the speed of light—July wasn't relaxing. There were so many errands to run in preparation for the upcoming school year and she tried to spend as much time with her family as she could. Even Jenna was preoccupied with her own college shopping. She proudly told Fiona that she decided on animal prints for her dorm room decor and purchased a leopard-patterned area rug, a zebra-inspired comforter and frilly hot pink curtains.

She never confronted Jenna about what she overheard from

the bathroom stall at Prom, but the words her friend said still rang every so often in her ears and Fiona was never truly able to look at Jenna the same. But that, like everything else, was in her past now.

And then there was Jared. In the weeks after Prom, their little–relationship...or whatever it was, dwindled. Maybe he was too busy with his own college preparation. Or more likely, he sensed Fiona wasn't fully open to having him as a boyfriend...if he sensed that, he would have been right in his assumption. She liked him...she did. But the way her body responded to him scared Fiona. She would have been lying if she said the whole prom fire hadn't traumatized her a bit, no matter how much she tried to convince herself otherwise. What if something like that happened again? What if her passion for Jared sparked a similar reaction?

He tried to kiss her again a few days after prom, and Fiona actually recoiled from his touch. Jared, of course, misinterpreted her reaction. Wouldn't anyone feel turned off by his girlfriend flinching at his advances? Fiona felt awful about it and tried to offer some shallow explanation, but Jared just shrugged it off. So, in early August, after an awkward phone call and a promise to come down and see her at FIT, Jared went upstate to move into the dorms. He was probably better off. No, not *probably*. He was *definitely* better off. Fiona was sure he would meet some amazing college girl and fall head-over-heels in love with her. Hopefully someone who could be the kind of girlfriend he deserved. She was briefly sorry about the whole thing, but she was also excited to move on with her own life, and she wasn't about to allow a rela-tionship that never really was in the first place, spoil that. FIT was a dream ever since childhood, and it was finally happening.

When Angela finally dropped her daughter off at college–and when the dorm room was all unpacked and set-up–Fiona was both shocked and grateful her mother's eyes were dry. She needed that. If her mother had been a blubbering mess, Fiona definitely would have been a blubbering mess too. And she got into trouble when her emotions weren't held in check–as evidenced by the "little situation" at The Piermont. For a while, Fiona was worried that her condition was worsening, but during that summer before she went off to college, unless she was feeling extremely sad, extremely nervous, or extremely angry everything remained relatively contained. So when Fiona walked into her dorm room for the first time, she felt buoyed up by a newfound confidence that her life was all going to work out for the best. She wished she had more insight into her condition. She knew it was tied to her emotions, and knew that lowering her body temperature helped control it. But she didn't understand why sometimes it rose up, and why sometimes it remained hidden away like a dragon snoozing in his lair.

Jess, Fiona's roommate, already settled in the day before, and she left Fiona alone with her mother and brother to say their goodbyes.

"Fiona Blake, I am so proud of you," her mom said, embracing her daughter in a tight hug. "I just know that you'll be so happy here."

Noah joined in and the three stood there for a moment, just holding one another, knowing that things were changing for all of them.

"I think so too mom," Fiona responded. And she truly believed it.

"Jess is cool," Noah responded. "I like her photos on the wall. Maybe she can help me learn to use a camera."

Jess was a photography major, and specialized in natural landscapes. Her work was incredible and she had some of her favorite pieces displayed above her desk.

"Maybe," Fiona replied.

"Ok," Fiona's mom said, exhaling an audible sigh. "I guess that's our cue. C'mon Noah. Let's let Fiona get settled in."

"Love you guys," Fiona said as her mother and Noah headed out of the dorm room, each casting one last fleeting look back.

"Love you more," Angela shot back like she always did. "Call me later."

"Of course. Bye guys."

Fiona couldn't deny she felt relieved when they finally left. She loved them so much, but she couldn't wait to start a new life at FIT. Design was always her passion and Fiona worked endlessly on her portfolio–meticulously plotting it out and revising it for this very moment. Plus, she was only about an hour train ride from Levittown–no cars were welcome or needed in New York City, so her little, red baby remained safe in the driveway at home. She was sure she would still see both her family and her car plenty.

Fiona looked around what would be her new living quarters with pride. A new room, new bedding, new fairy lights lining the desk area, and some new posters on the wall above her bed. A fresh start.

Jess came back into the room and plopped down at her desk. Although the two girls had never met in person, they spoke a bunch of times on the phone and had a good deal in common. Like Fiona, FIT had been Jess' dream ever since she was a little kid. Like Fiona, she came from a single-parent household. Like Fiona, she was from Long Island–Manorville. And like Fiona, she seemed relatively laid back and didn't pry too much–which was definitely a bonus. Jess was different from Jenna–more tomboyish in her dress and overall attitude, but Fiona found her refreshing. Real, in a way Jenna was not.

"It's 6 o'clock," Jess observed. "Wanna go find some food?"

Fiona's growling stomach approved of the idea; she hadn't realized it until this moment, but she was starving.

"Sure," Fiona eagerly responded. "I haven't eaten since 8 o'clock this morning."

The new roommates locked up, without as much awkwardness as Fiona anticipated, and left the building in search of the meal hall.

Looking back on it now, Fiona couldn't say how many times she and Jess shared a meal together over the course of the next 4 years that they remained roommates. Nor could she accurately report how many late night pizzas they ordered, or how many hours they spent studying together in the library or critiquing one another's work. Fiona found a friend in Jess that she didn't know she would. Jess knew that Fiona had her secrets and she let her keep them. And Jess never pushed for information when the room smelled a little bit smoky.

Both of their talents grew tremendously as they delved further and further into their coursework. Fiona knew Jess was headed towards a tremendous future; her talent was undeniable. She only hoped she would follow a similarly auspicious path.

Chapter Nineteen

The four years of college flew by, like high school, in what felt like a hazy blur. As Fiona lost herself in her classes, she had less time to think about her condition, and as a result, it appeared less often, or so she told herself. The work was more demanding than it was in high school, as Fiona expected it to be, so she didn't have as much time to dwell on what simmered inside of her. She was also, miraculously, able to get through those years without alerting her roommate–or anyone else for that matter–to what she could do. It helped that their classes for the most part put them on opposite schedules...it also helped that during sophomore year, Jess started dating Ciara. Ciara had a studio apartment and Jess spent many nights there. So, she wasn't in their dorm room when Fiona almost set her pillow on fire– good thing she dumped the half-full Poland Spring water bottle on it before the fire alarm registered–or when, towards the end of Junior year, Fiona singed the edges of her portfolio for Design Fundamentals. Those were really the only two instances when Fiona's fire couldn't be contained. It was still very much alive, but it seemed, for the most part, dormant. And Fiona was grateful, because Prom–though a fading memory–still appeared like a ghostly mirage in her mind every now and again.

Fiona attributed this dormancy to the hectic schedule and the intense coursework. But, she found herself feeling hopeful about it. Feeling like this flame was just a tiny piece of her, like any other personality trait, and that it didn't define who she was, or who she would be.

Fiona was even able to date a bit. Nothing super serious; she was too committed to her studies to consider a steady boyfriend, just a few late-night hook-up sessions. But during those moments, she still felt heat bubbling within, nothing like how she felt with Jared, but there just the same. Fiona still thought about Jared, and they spoke a few times on the phone during their college years; they even met up at a bar during one Christmas break for a drink and some catching-up, but he was staying upstate after graduation and their conversations were more friendly and nostalgic than anything else.

For a while, Jess and Ciara would try to hook Fiona up with random guys they met in their classes. When she refused, they would tease *Are you asexual or something*? Fiona would just laugh those comments off. Ultimately, after many failed attempts, they stopped trying. Despite her lack of a romantic life, Fiona didn't feel lonely. She loved spending time with Jess and Ciara; they always included her in whatever they were doing. They were adorable together and Fiona truly hoped they would remain a couple well after college.

An intense passion for design fueled Fiona during those years. Her love for sketching and textiles deepened into something like an obsession and she would spend hours in the studio running her fingers delicately along the skeins of fabric, relishing the way the canvases and silks and flannels felt on her skin. She was in the studio by herself one night during Senior year–all of her classmates were probably out bar-hopping–when Professor Fierro walked in through the double doors. Professor Fiero rarely made an appearance in the studio after hours, and her presence made Fiona feel flummoxed and clumsy, as though she had been caught red-handed doing something wrong. The professor walked directly up to Fiona.

"Fiona, I'm really impressed with your eye and attention to detail," she said.

Fiona was floored. Professor Fiero never complimented her students; known as a strict and critical instructor, she had an impressive career behind her, making her both feared and respected by students and staff alike.

"Thank you Professor Fiero," Fiona managed to sputter out.

"What are your plans after graduation?" she asked, her gray eyes studying her pupil.

Had she come to the studio just to speak to me? Fiona wondered. The thought made her nervous and a deep blush bloomed on Fiona's cheeks as she answered.

"I applied for a few internships; I'm still waiting to hear–"

She waved her hand in Fiona's face as if to dismiss what she just said.

"Dana Ferranti reached out to me. She's seeking an intern," Professor Fiero said.

Fiona almost couldn't speak, "Dana Ferranti as in–"

"Yes. Dana Ferranti. Head of The Ferranti Design Company. Have you heard of her?"

Had she heard of her? The woman was legendary in the design world.

"Yes. I have heard of her," Fiona responded.

The professor plowed on, "She asked me for an intern. I select you. Do you accept the position?"

It took Fiona a minute to register this information and she just stared at her professor, too shocked to speak. Fiona replayed what her instructor said over again in her mind. An internship? With Dana Ferranti herself? Did she just hear correctly? This would be the chance of a lifetime.

Professor Fiero spoke again, "Well? Do you accept the position?"

Shaking herself out of her stupor, Fiona replied, "Oh my God! Yes! Yes! I accept!"

She tried unsuccessfully to keep the excitement out of her voice; she didn't want to lose her cool in front of the impressive woman standing just two feet away.

"Good. I will send you the paperwork immediately. You begin directly after graduation," Professor Fiero responded matter-of-factly.

"Professor Fiero...thank you for thinking of me. Truly. I'm honored..and humbled–"

She interrupted Fiona, not one for gushing appreciation.

"There is nothing to thank me for," she replied. "I simply believe you are the best one for the position. This is an incredible opportunity. A career-making opportunity. Don't prove me wrong."

"I won't," Fiona replied, but at that point, she was speaking to the back of Professor Fiero's head as she walked away.

When the door of the studio closed behind her Fiona allowed herself a moment of celebration. "YESSSSSS!" She screamed into the air. The yell echoed off the walls of the empty room. Fiona was ecstatic. Beyond ecstatic. She felt the flush rise in her cheeks; her fingers tingled with the heat held below her skin. She put hands out on the table in front of her that held one of her latest sketches. Lowering her head, she took a few deep breaths, but that pulsing heat remained. *Calm down*, she told herself. *Easy now.* But before she could gain control, she watched as the edges of the fine sketch paper began to curl up and char from the tiny spark that radiated from her fingertips. Thin smoke tendrils drifted up from the table as Fiona used her hands to bat out the small flames. Luckily, the table was metal, and therefore did not catch. Just those drawings had been lost. *Close call*, Fiona said to herself, actively slowing her breathing. She refused to give herself the space to think about the what-ifs, or about the disaster that befell her senior prom. *No! This is a time for celebration...not tragedy.*

Finally, the heat abated. Her breath came easier and her shoulders loosened. Everything was going to be ok. She just scored the internship of the century. All of the hard work paid off. For someone like Professor Fiero to think she had what it took to work for Dana Ferranti. It was an incredible confidence boost and Fiona intended to deliver in a big way. She couldn't wait to tell her mom and Jess; they were going to flip out. The almost fire, slipped from her mind as excitement took its place. *Yes. It's time to celebrate*, Fiona said to herself again. And she made herself believe it.

For the first time in Fiona's life, she felt as though she was in the absolute right place at the absolute right time. She knew that once again, life as she knew it was about to change...in a big way. What she didn't know was that this change wasn't going to be at all what she expected. No. Not at all.

$$Chapter\ Twenty$$

True and real tragedy hadn't yet struck Fiona, as she prepared herself for that internship with Dana Ferranti. But it was lurking in the shrubbery of her life, unseen, but there.

As life seemed to fly by, aside from preparing for finals and putting the finishing touches on all the exit portfolios required for graduation, Fiona also had to think about packing up her dorm room. It felt like yesterday she was moving in...and now, college was over. Just like that. She looked around at all of her possessions tucked away in cardboard boxes and felt that bitter-sweet pang that accompanies all of life's endings. But this was also a new beginning for her. She just signed a lease on a small studio apartment on the Upper East Side, effective immediately. Fiona almost choked when the realtor announced the rent...such a small space for so much money, but Fiona was beaming with the promise of a budding career path. In time, she would figure out the finances.

The excitement of graduation paled in comparison to the eagerness she felt about starting the internship for Dana Ferranti. Fiona met with her the previous week and despite how nervous she was, she found her to be kind and down-to-earth, greeting

Fiona with a warm smile and expressing her enthusiasm for having her join the team.

"Thank you so much for this opportunity," Fiona said to her as she left.

"I'm always pleased with Lucy's recommendations," she responded, extending a handshake.

"Lucy?" Fiona asked in question.

"Oh, excuse me," she said. "Professor Fiero. Lucy is her first name."

Fiona laughed; she wouldn't have pegged the professor as a Lucy.

"I can't wait to start Mrs. Ferranti," Fiona said, taking her smooth, manicured hand in her own.

"Please. Call me Dana. I'll see you in a few weeks Fiona," she replied. "I hope you're ready to work hard."

"I am," Fiona said, taking in her appearance one more time before she left.

Fiona was starstruck just to be in this woman's presence. *The* Dana Ferranti. She was a legend–at least for those in the design world. Fiona remembered reading an article about her in the *New York Times* a few months ago–not typically a newspaper reader– while waiting for Professor Dooley to get his critique on some of her sketches. He was running late and as Fiona was waiting in a chair outside his office, she happened to pick up the newspaper sitting on the small table next to her. Plastered on the front cover was Dana Ferranti's face–her cropped black hair with a single gray streak lining her face and her signature black-rimmed glasses were unmistakable. Above her was a heading that read *Fierce Ferranti; Taking Over New York One Building at a Time*. The fact that she even met with Fiona in person, instead of having one of her underlings do the job, spoke of the pride and humanity with which she ran her company. She, like Fiona, came from humble beginnings. Fiona hoped one day, she could be just like her.

Fiona walked out of her office building and gazed up at the windowed facade. The day was warm and the sun reflected off of the mirrored surface. She had the distinct feeling that life was beginning again, and she couldn't wait for what was in store.

After the subway ride back to her dorm, Fiona found Jess and Ciara doing what she had already done: packing. Graduation was tomorrow and Jess and Ciara were headed off on a trip abroad with no certain return date. Both of them decided to defer the real world for a while in exchange for adventure. Part of Fiona envied them—their freedom—but she knew that she could never choose that path for herself; she needed order, certainty.

"How did it go?" Jess asked, as soon as her roommate walked in.

"Great," Fiona replied, still on cloud-nine from simply being in Dana Ferranti's presence.

"Was she a total bitch?"

"Farthest thing from it," Fiona replied.

Last night, the two girls microwaved a bag of popcorn and built up Dana Ferranti to be a cutthroat, calculating, Miranda Priestly type character...from *The Devil Wears Prada*. Jess mused sarcastically, *How else could a woman get to her position?* Thankfully, the truth was far more pleasant and Dana Ferranti in real life seemed more wonderful than Fiona could have hoped.

"I have a really good feeling about working for her," Fiona continued.

You deserve it," Jess said, as she engulfed her friend in a tight hug.

"I can't believe I'm not going to see you everyday," Fiona said, with tears welling up a bit in her eyes. "I'm going to miss you two."

"Don't get sappy on us," Ciara added, joining the hug.

"We'll be crashing on your floor when we get back," Jess joked, to lighten the mood.

"Oh yeah...In my HUGE new apartment," Fiona laughed. "I don't even think I could fit a hamster in my tiny little studio."

"It's perfect for you," Jess said. "I know you'll be happy there."

"I think so too," Fiona replied. "I really do."

"I think so too," Fiona replied. "I really do."

Chapter Twenty-One

Graduation came and went, Jess and Ciara went off to travel the world, Fiona moved into her little apartment–life moved on. The internship with the Ferranti Design Company consumed every waking moment of the week days, but Fiona was never bitter about it. Even though she wasn't technically doing much design work–she was more the errand girl–Fiona was learning so much and making connections.

Like college, Fiona was happy...no, wrong word. She was *thrilled* beyond words that her condition continued to lie mostly dormant. Aside from a few small hiccups–like burning the edges of a throw pillow on the couch and holding onto a cup of tea that suddenly got so hot the ceramic mug shattered in her open palms–Fiona caused no major catastrophes. She didn't know why her condition was behaving, but she wasn't going to look a gift horse in the mouth. And, she was proud of herself, really and truly proud of herself. She had grown up. Sometimes she looked around in amazement. Even though the apartment was small, even though she was barely making rent, even though her social life hadn't picked up speed yet, Fiona felt successful. She was 22 years old, living on her own in Manhattan, working at a dream internship that would hopefully, fingers crossed, lead to a successful career. She was on the up and up.

The year ended and Dana offered Fiona the chance for another internship–this time with a salary attached to it–a meager one, but better than before–which she of course accepted. Dana delivered on her promise that this next internship would allow Fiona to use her design knowledge and skill. Throughout the year, she found herself helping with design sketches and textile selection. One time, Fiona even got the chance to lead a small team of interns on a project for an office design. Dana had been impressed and at the end of that year, offered an actual position. Apprentice Designer.

"You're the youngest full-time employee I've ever hired," she confided in Fiona one day.

"I am so incredibly appreciative Mrs–I mean, Dana," Fiona responded.

It still felt awkward for Fiona to call her by her first name.

"Yes, the position is still considered entry level, but with hard work, I know you will move up the rungs," she explained.

"I'm so grateful for the opportunity. There's nowhere else I'd rather work," Fiona answered truthfully. "I won't let you down."

"I don't think you will, Fiona. There's fire in you for sure," she said, ending the conversation with a small smile.

For a moment Fiona was caught off guard by her mention of fire; had she seen something in her? But she shrugged it off, and accepted the complement for what it was. It was just a saying. The problem was that for Fiona, fire was never far from her thoughts. What was that phrase? Out of sight out of mind? Fiona learned that was definitely NOT true. Her fire had remained mostly out of sight...but it was never totally out of her mind. She waited with dread for it to rear its ugly head–never feeling fully secure or safe.

Fiona called her mom as soon as she left the office for the day to deliver the good news.

"Mom! Oh my God, you'll never believe it! Dana Ferranti offered me a full-time position!"

"Oh Fiona," she responded. "Of course I believe it. You're amazing! She's lucky to have you. I'm so proud of you. Congratulations! You've worked so hard."

Angela Blake–always her daughter's biggest fan.

"You and Noah should come in this weekend so we can celebrate,"Fiona said.

"Wouldn't miss it! Keen's Steakhouse?" she asked. "My treat?"

"Keen's is pricey mom," Fiona began, knowing that money was not something her mother had in excess.

"Don't be silly, Fiona. No price is too high to celebrate my talented, beautiful, gifted daughter. Plus, I've always wanted to try it."

"Ok mom. But I'm giving you money towards the check. Otherwise, we're going somewhere else."

"We'll talk about it this weekend," Fiona's mother retorted. "I'll make the reservation."

"Thanks mom. Love you."

"Love you more. Can't wait to see you," she said, and ended the call.

Fiona loved spending time with her mom and Noah, who seemed to be taller every single time she saw him. He was almost 12 already, and a few inches taller than Fiona.

Dinner was incredible, rich, thick steaks, creamed spinach, crispy hash browns, a glass of 20 dollar Cabernet. Keen's is a New York City staple and has been around since the late 1800s; that night with her mom and Noah, Fiona saw why. The service, the linens, the food–everything was impeccable. Angela even allowed her daughter to contribute 50 dollars towards the bill...shockingly. Not remotely enough to cover even half the hefty cost, but still something.

Over the course of the next few years, Fiona worked her butt off to prove not only to Dana Ferranti, but to herself that she had what it took to make it in the cutthroat world of design. Dana became something like a mentor to Fiona, and her belief in her talent helped buoy her confidence. As Dana told Fiona when she first hired her as a full-time employee, she moved up the rungs a bit, and finally, finally, she got hired...Fiona, for a solo project. It happened by chance, but she was grateful for the opportunity. Fiona just knew it was her time to shine.

Chapter Twenty-Two

Fiona remembered that day and that dinner with fondness. It seemed like both forever ago and yesterday at the same time. It's amazing how life can feel like that sometimes–old and new, near and far. What was that saying? The days drag, but the years fly by. At 27 years old, Fiona finally understood what that meant. She felt it...deeply, keenly. Especially when she saw her family. After working for months on her first solo project–which she referred to as her baby–and after running the final design plans to the architect, Fiona felt the tension in her shoulders ease. She had actually done it: gotten her first commissioned project approved. It was a dream job, and a dream client. *Too good to be true*, Fiona thought to herself. But it was true. It really was.

Her client was Mrs. Nina Bradley, the trophy wife of a high-end realty CEO. The only reason Fiona even entered into Nina's privileged orbit was because the barista at Starbucks got their coffees switched up. The orders were almost exact–except for the fact that Fiona's latte was made with cream and Nina's with almond milk.

Nina had tapped Fiona on the shoulder and said, "Are you Fiona? I think I got your order."

Sure enough, Fiona glanced down and read the name 'Nina' on the cup in her own hand.

Nina had probably seen the ink smudges on Fiona's thumb and the manilla portfolio clutched in her other hand and asked, "Are you a designer?"

"Well. I am but–I'm only a Junior Designer...I work for FD&Co," Fiona bumbled to her, cringing at how unconfident, how unsure of herself she sounded.

Even though she had been promoted from Apprentice Designer to this new role about a year or so prior, she was far from the top and didn't want to falsely inflate her achievements. It was still difficult for Fiona sometimes to promote herself to others, a skill she knew she had to work on if she was going to survive in this competitive world.

"FD&Co," Nina Bradley repeated. "That's the Ferranti Design Company right? Do you work for Dana Ferranti?" she asked.

"I do. She's my boss, and my mentor," Fiona responded.

"I've always admired her," Nina said. "May I?" she asked, indicating the sealed portfolio.

"Um. Sure," Fiona answered.

Standing at the small counter, Fiona tentatively opened the folder, revealing a sketch she was working on. Nina's eyes roved over the pencil lines, and the lightly-colored detail that Fiona slaved over for weeks and smiled.

"I'm redesigning my entire apartment," she had said. "I love your aesthetic. Do you have a business card?"

Fiona didn't even really know who Nina was when she handed over the freshly printed card. But the next day, Dana Ferranti herself called Fiona into her office to report that Nina Bradley was interested in setting up a meeting with her to help design an open-air living space in their 10th floor, 4 million dollar penthouse apartment in Tribeca.

"Fiona," Dana's always calm exterior split with a brilliant smile. "This is huge."

"I don't know," Fiona responded nervously. "I mean. Can I do this? I'm still only a Junior Designer. Am I ready?" she asked Dana.

"This is not an opportunity you can pass up," Dana answered. "It's time to take the plunge. You're ready. I'll help you. This could make your career. Everyone knows Nina Bradley. She's highly regarded not only amongst Manhattan's most elite, but throughout the entire country. Saying 'no' isn't really an option."

"Ok," Fiona sighed, exhaling an audible breath. "I'll take the job."

"Yes! That's my girl," Dana responded. "Call her and let her know."

And that's just what Fiona did.

Under Nina's careful, but kind scrutiny–and with Dana's supervision–it took a few months and about 12 meetings to finalize the plans. Nina was always changing her mind about some small detail or another and there were two times that they completely scrapped an idea and went back to the drawing board. Fiona found both her skill and patience tested at times–even though she bit back any frustration with a smile. It was all part and parcel of working with high-end clientele. Finally dropping the design plan off at the architect meant that the project was officially a go. They were going to move on to the next phases of implementation. Fiona succeeded in coming up with a design suitable for the discerning eyes of Nina Bradley. That thought alone was staggering.

On her way back to the office that day, Fiona took a detour through Central Park. The afternoon was warm and the bluffs were surprisingly empty. She took a moment to breathe while some of the tension in her shoulders drained away. She felt herself relax for the first time in a long time. The park was so beautiful in June. The fresh buds on the trees, the smell of cut grass tinged with the odor of straw from the bales of hay swung around the horses necks as they nibbled from the carriage baskets, their velvety noses wet and soft. It had been awhile since Fiona enjoyed the serenity of this oasis smack dab in the middle of the sprawling metropolis of Manhattan. Usually, she hurled through it on wobbly heels desperate to meet a deadline or make it to a meeting on time. But today, with those plans finally at the next stage of development, Fiona allowed herself a breather, a respite and she plopped herself down on a green bench and sipped her coffee–still warm–from the new black Yeti her mother purchased for her. A small smile crept to her face. *I did it*, she breathed audibly. She scored an A-list client, wow'ed both her and Dana Ferranti, and Fiona guessed she wow'ed herself too. It's not a sin to feel pride in one's accomplishments, right? She worked long and hard for this and she finally arrived.

When Fiona got back to the office she was greeted by the startling call of "Surprise!" The entire floor, including Dana, had prepared a small party to celebrate the accomplishment, complete with balloons, streamers, and a cake that read "Cheers to Good Taste" in pink buttercream.

"What's this for?" Fiona asked, still recovering her breath from the surprise.

"This is to celebrate your success," Dana responded. "And this isn't it. I planned a small get-together for you out in Long Island next weekend, at the Garden City Hotel. I know it's far, but I've been hosting my events there for years now. It does us all good to get out of the city every once in a while–especially in the summer. I reserved rooms for the entire design team. Unfortunately, I can't personally stay the night; I have a meeting early the next morning, but I will pop in and say hi. And, you will all have a marvelous time."

"I don't know what to say," Fiona uttered, the kindness of Dana's gesture floored her.

"Say yes," Dana replied.

"Yes," Fiona said, smiling. "Thank you, Dana," she continued, encircling her boss, her mentor...her friend, in a hug.

"I'm proud of you," Dana said before breaking the embrace.

This time, Fiona couldn't stop the tears from streaming freely down her cheeks while her co-workers clapped on in approval.

Chapter Twenty-Three

It was the day of the party and Dana spared no expense. She hired a limo to take all of the design team who lived in Manhattan to the Garden City Hotel. As a kid growing up in Levittown, Fiona knew of the hotel. One time she went to high tea there for a friend's Sweet Sixteen. The wait staff had served them tiny triangular sandwiches and decadently iced cakes on tiered silver trays. Fiona had never been anywhere so fancy. It was probably the swankiest hotel in Long Island, with white marble floors and crystal chandeliers that glistened in the sunlight streaming through the sprawling windows. Fiona never would have thought that she would ever have the chance to actually stay there. It all felt like a dream.

When she checked into the hotel, the woman at the front desk gave her a small white keycard, and said, "Your suite is on the fourth floor. You can take the elevators in the lobby, over there." She indicated the direction.

"Suite?" Fiona asked.

"Yes ma'am," she replied. "And Mrs. Ferranti left a gift for you. We took the liberty of having it delivered directly to the room."

When Fiona opened the door to her very own suite, she

couldn't believe her eyes. Up until that point, she only ever stayed at budget-friendly accommodations...and she usually had to share a full-sized bed with Noah, who would knee her in the back throughout the night. But, as she gazed around the space, complete with a separate living area and plush king-sized bed adorned with fluffy white sheets and pillows, Fiona couldn't believe the space would be hers for the evening. A bouquet of red roses sat on the dresser next to a bottle of champagne already on ice. A little folded up note card read:

> Dear Fiona,
> Congratulations on your well-deserved success.
> I hope you enjoy your celebration. Cheers to many more successful years at FD+Co.
> Sincerely,
> Dana

Bringing her nose down to the fragrant blooms, tears welled up in Fiona's eyes. She was truly touched by Dana's words. By the kindness, support, mentorship Dana provided throughout it all. She certainly spared no expense to celebrate Fiona's achievement, gratitude welled up in her chest, and she couldn't wait to express that appreciation at the party. In this cutthroat world of design, Fiona found a friend she hadn't expected.

The thought of the party sent Fiona into motion. She wanted to shower and curl her hair; it was already 4 o'clock and the festivities were scheduled to begin at 5. Fiona wanted to look her best. After all, she was the guest-of-honor.

Fiona took a final glance at herself in the full-length mirror in the bathroom before heading downstairs. She scoured the racks at Bloomingdale's to find the perfect dress. It hurt a bit to spend so much money on a single outfit, especially one she might never wear again–she was more of a TJ Maxx kind of girl–but Fiona splurged. The emerald silk clung to her body in all the right places, and her hair tumbled around her shoulders and down her back in soft waves. As a red-head, green had always been her signature color; her freckles stood out against her pale complexion and the new gold dangle earrings winked back at her when she caught her reflection in the mirror. She looked good: professional, polished...and sexy. The neckline of her dress plunged tastefully... not too revealing, and her bare arms and shoulders prickled with goosebumps. Fiona sent the heat that threatened to rise up back into the pit of her stomach–she was getting good at doing that– and prepared to publicly celebrate her well and hard-earned success. Slipping her feet into gold, strappy heels, Fiona closed the door to the suite behind her. Feeling the soft flutters of nerves, Fiona made her way to the cocktail room anticipating a great night ahead.

Clearly Dana told Fiona to arrive later than the rest of her colleagues because when she opened the double doors, the room was filled with friendly, familiar faces. Dana was the first one to greet her.

"Fiona," she cooed. "Our guest of honor!"

She thrust a glass of champagne into Fiona's hand while everyone clapped.

Dana continued speaking as the room quieted to hear what she had to say, "I'm so pleased you could all be here tonight to celebrate Fiona's success. Since I'm headed out soon, I'd like to propose an opening toast."

About 40 glasses went up into the air.

She continued, "Fiona came to me as an FIT intern about 8 years ago and as soon as I met her, I knew she was destined for a bright design career."

Some whoops echoed through the room. Fiona couldn't keep the smile from her face listening to Dana speak about her.

"Tonight we celebrate the completion of her first commissioned project that is sure to make the pages of *Design Time* very bright indeed."

Design Time was the premier interior design magazine read throughout the world. To be included in its pages was a major, career-changing opportunity. Fiona hadn't even thought that was a possibility until that moment.

Dana concluded, "Fiona, you have made FD&Co. and me very proud indeed. So, everyone raise those glasses, and let's all drink to Fiona."

Then Dana embraced Fiona in a warm hug and while everyone cheered and took the customary sips from their glasses, Dana whispered softly, "I cannot wait to see what's in store for us. Cheers to a beautiful future."

By the time Dana released her, Fiona couldn't suppress the tears welling up in the corners of her eyes.

"Thank you Dana," Fiona choked out. "Thank you for this opportunity, for this amazing party...for the incredible suite. Just...thank you for being you."

She was overcome by the emotion of the evening and the kindness shown to her by those glowing faces surrounding her.

"Don't mention it," Dana replied with a wink. "Now. enough with the sappy stuff. Let's have fun. Sound good?"

"Sounds great," Fiona answered, relieved the formality of the event was over.

Dana excused herself after another half an hour. Even though Dana was well-loved by her many adoring employees, when she left, the rest of the guests didn't have to worry anymore about being on their best behavior. When it came down to it, Dana was still their boss. The night flew by in a whirlwind. Away from the office for a night, Fiona's colleagues really let loose. Champagne and wine flowed freely in the dimly lit, wood-polished cocktail room of the Garden City Hotel. A DJ started playing dance music and at one point, Fiona kicked off her heels and actually joined her friends on the dance floor—she guessed that after a few drinks her reserved demeanor began to crack open a bit. The pride she felt in herself allowed her to briefly shed that rigid, controlled exterior...if only for a little while. Fiona couldn't remember a night she enjoyed more thoroughly. The whole event felt extravagant and Fiona couldn't believe she was the reason for such a celebration.

As the time ticked on, people began to head back to their own hotel rooms and before Fiona knew it, she sat alone with an unfamiliar co-worker at the shiny lacquered bar to close out the evening.

"Shall we end the night with a shot of tequila?" he asked with a smile.

"Um," Fiona replied, her head spinning a bit from the alcohol she consumed. She wasn't much of a drinker, and even though she had been careful to take it easy, Fiona was feeling those few glasses of champagne.

Looking at the man sitting next to her, Fiona said with a laugh, "What's your name anyway? You don't look familiar."

He smiled back at Fiona and let out an easy-going chuckle.

"That sounded rude," she backtracked with a blush.

"Not at all," he replied. "We met when you were first hired. I work in the accounting department. Gio." He held out an extended hand for a small shake.

"Gio," Fiona repeated back. "I do remember," Fiona lied.

"No you don't," he replied good-naturedly. "That's ok. Accounting doesn't always mix with the design team.

"Then what brings you to the party?" she asked.

"I'm here tonight...at *your* party," he emphasized the word 'your' and Fiona giggled. "...because anytime money exchanges hands, Dana calls me," he explained. "And since she couldn't be here to handle the check, I'm here in her place. Besides, I live in Garden City. Just 5 minutes away."

"Oh," Fiona said. "Well...thanks for handling all that. The party was really great."

"Well unfortunately, I cannot take responsibility for the details...that is all Dana. If you saw my poor excuse for a bachelor's pad, you design people would laugh your asses off."

Fiona wondered if he used the phrase 'bachelor's pad' to clue her into the fact that he was single.

"I'm sure it's not that bad," Fiona replied, finding it easier and easier to talk to him as the moments progressed.

"My IKEA furniture begs to differ."

His eyes shone when he spoke and his laugh was rich and deep. He wasn't conventionally handsome, but his shaggy brown hair and matching chin stubble were charming nonetheless–in a school-boy kind of way.

"I have nothing whatsoever against IKEA," Fiona replied with a chuckle. "...except their instruction manuals."

"There you go...lying again," he said, regarding her with his blue-eyed stare and simple smirk.

Is he flirting with me? Fiona thought to herself. *Yes. He is definitely flirting with me.*

After a minute, he spoke again, "So. What about that shot of tequila?"

Not only was Fiona not much of a drinker, but the thought of tequila sent a shiver down her spine. Once at a local college bar that boasted 2 dollar pints on Tuesdays, Jess had convinced her to take a shot of Jose Cuervo. It was lukewarm–bartenders catering to the college clientele can't be bothered chilling low-grade liquor–and it lit a fire down her throat as she swallowed. Even the dash of salt that she licked off her wrist beforehand, and the lime wedge she sucked on afterwards, couldn't quell the nausea. Fiona had raced to the bathroom, vomiting up the entire contents of her stomach.

Gio saw the hesitation and asked with a chuckle, "Not a tequila fan?"

"I had a bad experience in college with Jose Cuervo..."

"Well Don Julio is much better. Want to give it a shot?" There were those sparkling eyes again.

Swallowing her hesitation, Fiona thought to herself, *Oh, what the hell? Live a little Fiona. You have a right to celebrate. And what better way to do that than with a cute guy?*

So she said, "Sure. Sounds good. But only one."

"One. I promise," Gio said, holding a hand up to his heart in emphasis.

He turned to the bartender and ordered, "Two shots of Don Julio please."

"I'm just going to run to the bathroom," Fiona said. "Excuse me for a minute."

Fiona hadn't had even a minute to use the restroom since she left the hotel room...suite...hours ago, and she was bursting at the seams. After washing her hands, she took a glance at herself in the mirror. Her hair shone and her complexion boasted a healthy glow. Reapplying a coat of sparkling lip gloss, Fiona started to think this life suited her, and she briefly hoped for more parties such as this in the near future. Tossing the paper towel into the wastebasket, Fiona walked out of the restroom and back to the bar where Gio sat with two filled shot glasses on the bar in front of him.

Sitting back down on the bar stool, Fiona felt Gio's eyes studying her.

"You're pretty beautiful," he said, causing his cheeks to burn pink.

"And you're pretty...fun to hang out with," she teased.

"Thanks," he said through his laughter.

"Shall we?" Fiona said, indicating the shots before them.

"Let's do it," he said in response.

They each picked up a small glass containing the crystal clear liquid and clinked them together.

"To your career," Gio said.

"To new friends," Fiona replied.

Closing her eyes, she upended the glass. The alcohol burned as it slid down her throat and into her stomach; she felt its downward path. It wasn't as bad as that time with Jess, but she wouldn't have described the taste as pleasant either. When she put the empty vessel down again on the bar, Gio had slid in closer. From then on, the world got fuzzy. Fiona felt his leg press against her own bare thigh. His blue eyes had such thick lashes surrounding them.

"Fiona...Are you ok?"

"Fiona..."

"Fio..."

Then blackness.

Chapter Twenty-Four

"I don't think I can do it Micah," Fiona said in the car. "I don't think I can destroy that apartment."

Tears and raw emotion made her words come out stilted and jumbled. How had she gotten here? How had she come this far to be seated inside Micah's Range Rover a few blocks away from Nina Bradley's penthouse? It was like her life was a video game and someone else was controlling her avatar. But then again, she had been complicit. She knew what she was supposed to do, but she felt paralyzed by the reality of it. Yes, she had trained. Yes, she had gone along with it all–even enjoyed parts of it. But what was she doing? Doubt, fear, and regret snaked their way through her soul, making her question the very essence of who she was.

"Yes you can," Micah said simply. "Go. Do what you trained for." He was all business. Cold, curt, insistent.

"Micah–" Fiona began again, but before she could say anymore, she felt his warm hands on her neck, turning her face towards him.

"This was the agreement Fiona," he said. "This is what your training was for. This job is proof that you are on my team. That you're with me."

"What if I say no?" she asked simply. "What if I say that I changed my mind?"

"You don't have that choice," he responded.

"There's always a choice Micah," Fiona said. "What if I choose to say no?"

"If you *choose* to say no?" Micah repeated. "If you choose to say no, Kaleb won't be happy. I couldn't guarantee your safety."

"Are you saying he'd have me killed?"

"I'm saying I don't know what he'd do."

"And you're ok with that?" Fiona asked, never having weighed the reality of walking away from this life.

"It's not a matter of being *ok with it*," Micah said. "It's a matter of doing what has to be done. Sure there are always choices in life. But when you *chose* to come with me after the Garden City Hotel...that *choice*, that's what led to this. And now, you're out of options."

Fiona looked at Micah, really studied his face. He was so beautiful. And she loved him. The admission thundered through her soul. God, how could she have fallen so hard so quickly? So was walking away really a choice for her? Not in the face of love. Not in the face of death.

She leaned in and brushed her lips softly against his. Then, she turned away and opened the door. Her footsteps echoed through the night as she walked on towards Nina Bradley's apartment.

Part Two

Chapter Twenty-Five

Fiona found herself standing around the Tribeca building with a gaggle of onlookers, watching the fire rage. Wisps of orange and glowing red embers poured out of the top floor windows of the penthouse loft, licking the stone exterior, turning the facade black and ashen. Billowing gray smoke made its way skyward as the crowd shifted their eyes upward to take in the spectacle. Pulling her hood up, Fiona tried to blend in with the crowd, which had become easy for her—second nature. In fact, her life at that point demanded it. She couldn't afford to be noticed.

Honestly, it was pretty remarkable that the building still stood in 2023. Most of the art-deco style architecture around Manhattan had long been replaced by more modern construction, boasting open floor plans and lots of glass. It gave Manhattan a made-over, glossy feel, clinical even. When classic establishments such as Carnegie Deli and the like are forced to close their doors, when rent is so high that history itself gets brushed under the rug, residents and tourists can't help but feel as though they have been cheated out of something...cheated perhaps of the storied New York City—the one that features in imaginations only. A city of a bygone era replaced with the tawdry replicas of a modern age.

Maybe that was why this building, the one Fiona stood

before, was so sought after by New York's most elite—well at least the elite priding themselves on valuing character and old-world charm over modern convenience. Fiona supposed Mrs. Nina Bradley was one of the few blessed with that discerning eye, considering it was her penthouse—the one that Fiona herself had meticulously designed over the course of many months—that was ablaze.

Aside from a few residents being treated for smoke inhalation, the NYFD firefighters made quick work of evacuating not only this property, but the surrounding structures. Currently, they were extinguishing the remaining flames and dousing the neighboring buildings and businesses with water so the fire couldn't spread—an impressive display of efficiency and cool-headedness.

Fiona could have helped them in their work, at least tried to. She could have attempted to suppress the roaring flames, redirect them—her past few weeks of training provided her with more control over her condition than she ever had before—it was still hard. This job almost depleted her and it wasn't without error, but it was done. And why would she have helped the workers extinguish the fire? After all, she was the reason it started in the first place. Her first mission. An initiation of sorts. Fiona never thought that she could learn to value this ugliness burning inside of her.

Just as she was about to leave the scene, she noticed the pale, thin profile of Nina Bradley herself standing about twenty feet in front of her, engulfed within the flock of spectators still congregating in the street. She wore a sparkling, ruby-colored, fitted gown and clutched a black, lace shawl against her throat. She looked as though she had just returned home after some glamorous event reserved only for society's very rich. Her normally smiling lips turned down at the edges, and her bleary eyes threatened tears. Looking at her in the dim cast of the street lights, Fiona wished that she didn't like her so much. It would have made this easier to stomach.

Nina hadn't noticed Fiona among the throng. That would

have ruined everything. Blown her cover. If Fiona was being honest with herself, staying was a risk, yet she couldn't resist it.

Nina was standing next to another woman, perhaps a friend or neighbor. The women looked to be closely acquainted, as they huddled together for comfort. Even though Fiona knew she shouldn't, she was drawn to them like metal filings to a magnet. Pulling her hood more fully over her head, Fiona crept closer so she could hear their conversation over the din, knowing that the smoky evening and bystanders would hide her from their view.

"God," Nina uttered with a quavering voice. Her gaze shifted upwards to take in the fire fighters hovering near her penthouse window. "After all that work...after all that planning. How could it just burn down like that?"

"It must have been faulty wiring," her friend replied, tilting her head upwards to take in the plumes drifting into the night air. "It's an old building."

If she only knew the truth.

Nina responded, "Didn't those inspectors check that? It cost over ten grand to update the fuses and all of the electrical outlets. It's hard to believe they made such an oversight. You really think this huge fire is a result of old wiring? It seems more like arson to me. But who would–"

Nina's words trailed off into the hazy air.

The other woman spoke with calm reassurance, "I'm sure the police will investigate, but these 1920s Art-Deco buildings weren't exactly built up to code. I mean, you see the newspapers... it seems like there's another fire every month. It's one of the reasons developers are gobbling up all these old structures–to build new, safer ones."

"God I loved that apartment. Gary and I were on a waiting list for five years to be able to buy in that building. And now, look at it," Nina gestured with her outstretched palm, her anger bursting forth unchecked.

"Nina, where *is* Gary? He should be here with you," the friend offered.

Nina's slim shoulders rose into a shrug, "I'm used to being on my own. Gary's a busy man. He had a work event last night... some corporate gala. I actually would have been there with him if I didn't have that charity event for FEMA. Glad I wasn't inside when the fire started. When I finally got a hold of Gary on the phone, I must have sounded like a raving lunatic. He was so calm...didn't even seem rattled. But I guess he never loved this place like I did. He's a Brooklyn boy when it comes down to it, and would have preferred to move to one of those new luxury condos in Dumbo. I guess now, he may just get his wish."

"We all handle things differently. And don't give up hope. I'm sure it can all be rebuilt...in time," her friend said.

Nina went on, "I suppose." She remained silent for some time, studying the scene before her and then said, "Gary rented us a room at the Four Seasons. I guess I'll head over there soon."

The Four Seasons, Fiona scoffed in her mind. God, how easy it must be to be the Bradleys. To have such posh accommodations to retreat to. Such wealth must make any tragedy appear as trivial as a blip in the radar. Fiona liked Nina, she did. But the woman was completely out of touch with reality–as were most of the truly elite.

Then Nina added with a sigh, "It was just so perfect–the design. It's so sad to see it all up in flames. I worked with a really talented young designer..."

At the mention of herself, Fiona thought to herself sarcastically, *Yup. That's me...a talented designer. I guess I'm a talented destroyer too.*

Nina continued on, "I didn't even get to enjoy it...not really. It's only been about two months or so since the construction ended."

"I know, sweetheart," her companion replied, consoling. "I'm so sorry this happened, Nina. And you're of course welcome to come stay with me for a while. I have lots of extra space since Randy passed, and I'd love to have you and Gary."

Nina didn't respond, she just cast another fleeting look

upward. She almost turned around, and Fiona stepped back a few paces and pulled her hood tighter around her face in anticipation, but the distant voices of the firefighters captured Nina's attention, and she turned her gaze forward again.

Fiona felt a twinge of guilt needling her, and she turned to go, but stopped when she heard Nina speak again.

"I'm relieved I hadn't yet moved all my personal items in... photos and stuff. It would have been awful to lose those. Silver linings I guess."

Fiona couldn't help but view Nina with a bit of disdain at this point. *Rich people*, she snorted to herself. They can afford to be calm and collected in the face of anything...even when their 4 million dollar home is burning in front of their eyes. Money definitely softens the blow of tragedy. It might not buy happiness as that cliche suggests, but it certainly buys stability. Wealthy husbands also help. They always do. Nina would turn out just fine; she would eventually look back at all this destruction and maybe sigh about it, maybe use it as a feather in her hat, a sticking point to relate to society's less fortunate. An experience to make her seem less remotely rich, give her more credibility at her many speaking engagements. Maybe it would even give her another cause to fight for, another committee to spearhead: Women Who Survived Fire. Who could tell how the city's elite would decide to spend their fortunes or their time. What causes they would invent to give their lives purpose, meaning.

Nina's soft voice interrupted Fiona's pessimistic musings when she said, "...and, it doesn't appear that anyone is truly hurt. That would have been even more tragic."

The fact that there were no injuries was Fiona's top priority. It was the thought that allowed her to come to terms and accept what she had done, and what she would continue to do. It hadn't gone totally as planned–nothing regarding her condition ever did, but close enough. And with further practice, she was hopeful she could ultimately achieve mastery: whatever that would mean. Fiona was nervous for a while when the fire spread to the rooftop.

She hadn't accounted for the shrubbery up there, nor the green-house–the apartment building came complete with a mini Central Park on the sprawling roof as a draw for buyers. Many of the residents flocked there, thinking that the open air would be a deterrent for the raging fire on the up-most, penthouse floor. Fiona's nerves gave her only a shaky control of the trajectory of the fire and she couldn't quite take the steering wheel as she hoped. If she was being completely honest with herself, a lot of tonight's success was due to straight up luck–wind speed, building materials, etc.–a force she couldn't rely on if she were to continue in this line of work. But ultimately the fire department arrived before any major injuries occurred–another stroke of luck–so now Fiona was finally able to breathe a sigh of relief. But it was a close call.

She had wavered in her resolve to torch this apartment, but it was necessary. Fiona was tested and she passed. Yeah she still had a long way to go to master her abilities, and things *almost* spiraled down a dark path, but overall...it all worked out. She only recently gained enough control to even attempt to pull off this job. Imagine what she could do with continued training. She could be unstoppable. But Fiona's true wish was simply to move on. And hopefully now, she could–now that she knew what she was capable of. Dwelling on the past was exhausting.

The other woman spoke, "Maybe you can work again with that designer? Maybe she could make you something even more beautiful? Something even better."

Nina tried for a sarcastic laugh, but it escaped her throat as a choked gasp, "Her name was Fiona at the Ferranti Design Company...over in Midtown. Didn't I tell you how I ran into her at Starbucks?"

"Oh, yes. I do remember. You did tell me. You were smitten with her work."

Smitten, Fiona rolled her eyes to herself. *Only rich people use that word. Who speaks like that these days?*

"She had an incredible eye," Nina replied, picking up the thread about Fiona's former life.

"Well, I'm sure she would be happy to work with you again. Working for you and Gary would do wonders for her resume," the friend continued.

Fiona thought about her *resume*. About the hours she spent agonizing over it, crafting it, editing it. How useless it all was now. Her design career seemed to have come to an abrupt end before it even really began. It had gone up in smoke–now there was a fitting metaphor. Fiona wondered what her resume would look like now. In the "Job Experience" section, maybe it would say: Arsonist. She almost laughed at the thought. Maybe it would be littered with words like: ignite, burn...conflagration, that was a good one.

Nina responded to her friend's suggestion about working with the same designer to rebuild, "I thought I told you. Fiona died suddenly. There was a tragedy. Ironically, another fire. Out on Long Island. I don't really know all the details. From what I do know, it was at a work event and..."

Fiona didn't stay to hear the rest of Nina's sentence. She definitely didn't need to be reminded of what had happened. Of her "death." Of the work event–the tragedy. Of the upheaval that changed the course of her path in life. It's funny how life can change on a dime like that. How what you wanted all along can suddenly feel pointless and dull. Despite Fiona's prior aspirations, being a high-profile interior designer figured very low on her list of goals at that moment in time–something she never expected to feel...especially after all those years of college and internships.

Pulling her dark, hooded sweater more snugly around her shoulders, Fiona turned around on her heels and headed down Murray Street towards the corner deli. The weather was too warm for such clothing, but she couldn't risk being noticed. She had already taken too many risks tonight. And anyway, her ride should be there by now.

Walking down the pavement, the sulfurous smell of the fire

started to dissipate, as did the sirens and flashing lights. Aside from the sporadic crowds of people headed home from The Brixton or Belle Rev after a night of drunken revelry, the city was quiet, or at least quieter than it would have been on a weekend night. It was one-am on a Tuesday...well technically a Wednesday. Maybe, contrary to the cliche, New York actually did sleep sometimes.

Nearing the corner, Fiona saw the vehicle she needed: a sleek, black Range Rover with tinted windows obscuring any view inside. She opened the passenger side door and swung herself inside.

Chapter Twenty-Six

Pulling the door of the Range Rover closed, the overpowering scent of leather invaded her senses and Fiona could no longer smell the smoke that lingered in her hair.

"It was a mistake to stay," said Micah as soon as she sat down. "You could've been caught. Could've blown your cover...our cover. If Nina Bradley would have seen you–"

"Well, she didn't. No one suspected a thing," Fiona shot back, leaving out the details of the conversation into which she had eavesdropped.

"Your control wasn't good enough. You got lucky. If the winds weren't working in your favor, if the fire department hadn't shown up," Micah continued in that same critical tone. "That rooftop–"

"I know," Fiona interrupted. "That rooftop could have been a disaster. But it worked out. My condition poses risks. Always has. You knew that when we started. And you know that now."

"You have a long way to go Fiona. You need to seriously commit to your training," Micah added, as though Fiona didn't know that.

"I am committed. Haven't you seen that these past weeks?" Fiona's anger rose.

Micah was infuriating sometimes; well, more than sometimes. That phrase from the newspaper article tickled the edges of her brain as she sat there in his car: "Mystery Man." That's exactly what Micah felt like in many ways–a mystery. And then there was that subtitle, "Suburban Inferno Kills 8." She wished she knew the true story of the man sitting next to her, maybe then she could wrap her head around her life with him.

With a sigh of frustration, she averted her gaze and noticed a steaming cup with a string coming out of the sealed lid nestled into the center console. This was odd, because Micah never allowed food or drinks in his car; it went against his meticulous nature. As Fiona looked at the cup, the telltale string, and the label attached to the end, gave it away.

"You stopped?" she asked.

She was referring to the boutique tea shop located in Midtown that she discovered what felt like a million years ago–in some former life.

"Lavender tea. From Infusia. Still hot," he replied automatically.

Lifting the cup to her nose, she inhaled the fragrant scent. Taking a delicate sip, her insides felt immediately warmed, as if a down blanket had been wrapped around her heart. The sensation could have been from the tea, but it also could have been from the fact that Micah had actually listened to her stories, and had paid attention–at least to one small detail. It seemed as though whenever she was at her wit's end with the man, he would go and do something thoughtful and sweet–like buy her the very cup of tea that she had been craving for months. The push and pull was enough to drive her insane.

"Taste good?" he asked.

"So good. Thank you."

"Well you can repay me next time, when you exhibit more control over your condition," he responded.

Fiona rolled her eyes; she was sick of being told what to do by him, especially since he had just come into her life. Sometimes, like right now, her annoyance with the man superseded the raw desire, the yearning she felt for him–the need that had intensified since that time a few weeks ago when he walked into her bedroom and took her by surprise.

"Yes boss," she replied. Anything to avoid the subject.

"I'm serious Fiona," Micah said, unwilling to drop the subject just yet. You have to be more careful in the future. Don't let your pride get in the way of doing what you have to do."

"Pride?" She couldn't conceal the edge in her voice. "You think I'm proud of what I did?"

"Yes, Fiona," he replied, expertly maneuvering his car away from the curb and out onto Broadway. "I do."

Fiona couldn't let the comment drop; she was too angry, "I spent *years* studying design in college, working my ass off in internships while all my friends were out partying like normal 20-year-olds. Months of my life were dedicated to designing that apartment. All that work, up in flames. All to prove my loyalty to you. To this *Kaleb* that you speak so highly of. Proud of myself? That's the last thing I feel."

Micah didn't miss a beat before responding to Fiona's comment, "On some level, didn't it feel good to watch that place burn? After everything that happened to you because of it? I'm not the one you should feel angry at. I didn't try to hurt you at that party. I was the one there to help you...to get you out. The one that offered you a new path. Working that job only brought you pain, in the long run. One day you'll see that. And no matter what you say out loud, I saw the triumph in your eyes when you stepped into the car–despite the little..." He searched for the word, "mishap."

Fiona glared out the window as the lights whizzed by. *Mishap*, Fiona thought to herself. *Great word choice.* It wasn't that she didn't agree with what he said. She knew she messed up–and that things could have turned out badly. But he was the one who told her that she was ready to even take this on in the first place.

But something else nagged at her about what Micah said–about feeling pride in what she had done. Was he right? Was there a part of her that felt proud of her *condition*? She viewed it with disdain for so long, concealed it from everyone–at least she tried to.

When she met Micah for the first time, over a month ago (was it nearing two months already?), when she woke from a drugged slumber, naked, and surrounded in flame, he told her that he knew about her for quite some time; one day, Fiona decided, she would force him to be honest with her about that. Make him tell her the truth about how or when or why she had been put on his radar. Why exactly he had been at that corporate party with her that night. Why his face was the one she saw when her consciousness pulled her out of sleep. Fiona had been so thankful for an out, for a savior, so broken and needy, she didn't insist on details, didn't ask the necessary questions. At the time, Fiona acted on impulse without any true concept of the fact that this incident would take her away from her family, and change the course of her life. Now that she was here, now that she was Fiona Smith, now that she had fallen for him, Micah didn't really need to give her the information she craved. And he knew it. He held onto it, like bait.

Up until that party, Fiona had been so careful to blend in, to suppress those embers pulsing deep inside her–suppress the emotions that caused them. But now, being out in the open–at least with Micah and the others–now that it was useful, even for the sinister purposes for which it was being used, was there a bubble of self-acceptance forming within her? Fiona didn't know. *Was* it pride she felt? Pride in being needed...being wanted...being accepted? It was difficult to tell. Whatever emotions she felt about her role here, it was better than the abject sorrow she felt when she was at her lowest point about a month ago. After the *tragedy* that Nina spoke of to her friend. After her "death." That darkness was unsustainable. But over time, Fiona began to heal...well, maybe not *heal*, but cope. And that was good. And she also couldn't deny the pleasure that burning gave her. Pleasure that she never acknowledged before.

She glanced over at Micah and took in his angular jawline and dark hair, those impossibly brown eyes–so deep; Fiona fell for him the minute she saw him, she just didn't realize it at the time. Maybe all of the sadness, melancholy, guilt, depression she felt metamorphosed into lust. Into need. Maybe it was a survival mechanism–a bodily escape from the abyss. Fiona didn't know. But had she not experienced those intense feelings towards Micah, she didn't think she would have ended up here, with him and his people. Not that she really had much of a choice; not when it came down to it.

"Whatever," Fiona said. "I did it. It's over. Now what?"

"Now, Fiona," he replied with a small smile creeping to his mouth. "Now on to the next one."

"And what might that be?" she asked.

Micah's hand went to her knee; Fiona could feel his warmth through her thin jeans.

"You'll see. You must be tired. Close your eyes and try to get some sleep," he said. "We have a long ride ahead."

Chapter Twenty-Seven

Fiona was on the rooftop of Nina Bradley's apartment building. Residents crowded against the barrier separating them from tumbling headlong into the abyss of the New York City nighttime sky. Nina Bradley was up there too, mouth agape. Fiona ran toward them, trying to speak. Trying to tell them it was all alright, that she would control the fire–she would protect them all. But no words escaped her lips as they huddled together–a squirming mass of bodies terrified by what approached. Fiona turned around, searching for the source of horror, expecting to see roaring waves of flame licking her heels, but there was no fire. In fact there was nothing at all.

Fiona blinked her eyes open, but the images remained. She tried to replay the rapidly fragmenting dream, but while most of the nightmare faded as consciousness overtook her, what stayed there, what lingered at the edge of her mind, was the open mouths of fear. For a moment she couldn't understand why they were afraid–there had been no fire...only a starry sky. But as Fiona woke to the new day she realized that in her dream, they weren't terrified of being burned by fire. In their minds, there was a far more dangerous threat. And that threat was Fiona. They were terrified of *her*. Suddenly Fiona didn't want to think of that nightmare anymore, and she certainly didn't want to psychoanalyze its meaning. So often we ache to grasp onto the fleeting remnants of our dreams, but they elude us–like bygone lovers sweetly fade into the background of our identities. But this one didn't elude Fiona–even though she desperately wished that it would.

The sound of the chirping birds stood in stark contrast to the crackling roar of last night's fire. Fiona woke up to the soft ticking of the car turning off and to the gentle crunching of the gravel driveway beneath the tires of Micah's Range Rover. She wiped the sleep out of her eyes with the back of her forearm, ran fingers through her tangled hair and checked in the visor mirror to make sure there was no drool hanging off her lips. Running her tongue over her teeth, they felt gritty and the desperate need for a toothbrush superseded all else. It felt as though she had been asleep for days, when in reality it had only been five hours since she first climbed into Micah's truck. Five hours since they pulled away from that New York City curb. Five hours since she turned her back on her lifelong dream of being a designer. Five hours since she officially severed any semblance of normalcy her life had possessed. Yes, in truth, Fiona's former life had ended significantly before last night, but that fire was the final nail in the coffin.

Her sweater smelled of smoke–how is it that that scent could be so appealing when it came from a campfire, but so nauseating when it reminded her of what she did just a few hours ago? Yes, she consented to go along with all of it, she had to. It was a non-negotiable to prove herself, her allegiance, her commitment to the future–to this small group she joined. But thinking about it, Fiona guessed she hadn't really considered how she would feel in the aftermath. It was all a jumble in her head. She would need time to sort through the debris.

The images of last night crashed back into her mind with a force she hadn't anticipated: the mental map she was able to visualize of the electrical wiring of the Bradleys' penthouse, the tiny spark she was able to summon, the tiny spark that intensified when it came into contact with the foamy, pink insulation and then intensified again as the embers spread inside the walls until they could be contained no more. And then the unplanned spread of the flames to the rooftop gardens–where many residents huddled together like kindling. That last part was what her mind latched onto. It was a reminder that she hadn't perfected her ability–by any means; she was close. Closer than she had ever been, but she needed more work. She couldn't count on luck. Again, she tried to remind herself that no one got hurt–she tried to force her mind to acknowledge that immutable fact; afterall, that was the thing that mattered most. Wasn't it?

It had been desperately draining to control the trajectory of her flame, and she never could have done it without the past weeks of training. And even with that training, her control was sub par. But she thought that with a bit more persistence, she would get better…stronger.

A large part of Fiona was amazed she actually pulled it off. Up until last night, the plan had been merely theoretical, and dependent on her ability to control her condition. But Micah believed in her, and that simple fact made Fiona believe in herself.

Micah's dark eyes studied Fiona as she took in her sleep-worn reflection in the car visor. Sometimes the intensity of his gaze put her on edge. It took her a minute, but eventually she met his stare.

"Are you going to say anything?" Fiona asked simply.

"What would you like me to say?" he retorted without a beat.

"I don't know. Something. Anything," Fiona tried to force a laugh, but it sounded shallow in her throat.

Micah didn't say any of that; all he said was, "We'll debrief with the others when we go in."

Even though they were sleeping together, when they spoke about their work, Micah was infuriatingly formal and cold. She shouldn't have been surprised by the cool detachment of his tone. It was always that way with him, and no matter how much Fiona pushed for more, Micah wasn't going to budge. Many times she wondered how it was that she even fell for him in the first place. Yet, there was that empty cup of tea in the center console. No matter how small the gesture, that did mean something. Besides, if one were to look at the scenario from a psychological perspective, Fiona's feelings towards Micah really weren't all that surprising. Not considering the circumstances by which he entered her life. She should probably stop trying to change him. Fiona exhaled an audible sigh and unbuckled the seatbelt. He placed a hand on her forearm, gently stopping any movements, forcing her eyes to return to his.

"I'm proud of you," he said. "You didn't think you could do it and you did it."

Surprised by the sentiment behind his comment, Fiona responded, "I'm not looking for validation." But she couldn't ignore the swell of warmth in her chest that his words evoked. "I'm looking for honesty. Transparency. I feel like I know so little about what we're doing here...what *I'm* doing here. I feel like I know so little about you," she said.

Fiona tried to count the facts about Micah that she did know: She knew he grew up just across the border in Canada, that he formed the group about three years ago and that he took instructions from and reported directly to his overseer who he referred to simply as Kaleb–likely a false name. But Fiona longed for the smaller details. His favorite color, his favorite ice cream flavor, his most beloved book or movie or song. Any time she asked those questions, she was met with a sigh or some sarcastic quip aimed at evasion. Fiona hoped that maybe in time he would open up–especially since he knew so much about her, but that time hadn't come just yet. Patience was what she needed.

"You know enough about me Fiona. I'm not that complicated of a person," he responded.

"I don't believe that at all," she shot back. "And what about what we're doing here? How do I come into play?"

"It's obvious isn't it? You provide invaluable means for us to do what we need to do. And you are virtually untraceable. You leave no evidence behind."

His blunt words hurt a bit. Is that all she was to him? A useful tool? A personified matchstick?

He read the hurt in Fiona's down-turned eyes and said, "Maybe I misspoke. You're more than that to us. You're more than that to *me*."

That last statement stopped her breath.

"Oh yeah? What am I then...to *you*?" she sputtered out.

"You're my spark," he replied.

He leaned in and brushed his soft, full lips against Fiona's. An inferno bloomed within her at his touch and when he broke the kiss she saw the heat within her reflected in his eyes, in the crimson of his cheeks.

"It's time we went in," he said, breaking the kiss. "They're waiting for us."

Chapter Twenty-Eight

Micah and Fiona walked up the gravel driveway to the front door of the single-story, brick, ranch house. From the outside, it looked like any family home—complete with garden gnomes interspersed between the well-manicured bushes, blue shutters, and an American flag billowing in the wind from the flagpole attached above the one-car garage. The whole property screamed wholesome and whispered *nothing to look at here, carry-on*. No one would suspect a group such as this to reside in the suburban community outside of Plattsburgh, New York.

It was early when they walked inside. Fiona glanced at her phone screen to read the time: 6:48. In her former life, she would have undoubtedly still been snug beneath her soft comforter at this hour, with her childhood teddy bear looking happily on—her mom downstairs, brewing her daily herbal tea, her brother just down the hall. A life in order. It's bizarre how things change. Despite the early hour, everyone inside was awake and bright-eyed, waiting for the two guests-of-honor to return. The scent of brewing coffee drifted through the air—along with the stale smell of cigarettes, thanks to Rhea. Fiona wished that Rhea would at least put off her first smoke until later in the day. She hadn't gotten used to that acrid odor that clung to her clothes and hair no matter how much Febreeze she used. It didn't seem to bother anyone else, so Fiona kept her thoughts on Rhea's habit to herself. She wasn't looking to make waves. Plus, Rhea had been here long before Fiona—she had seniority, so to speak. And that mattered here.

Spence sat at the kitchen counter typing away, his glasses illuminated by the light coming from the screen while Maya wiped down the granite countertop, wearing yellow rubber gloves—the spray bottle containing the purple Fabuloso flanked her elbows. She loved the clean smell of the disinfectant. This was it—these three people, plus Micah and now Fiona guessed that she was included too. They reported to Micah, and Micah reported to the elusive Kaleb. Fiona had no idea as to the actual amount of fires they had been responsible for since they formed their little unit. But she guessed a lot. Maybe one day they would tell her their stories—even though she wasn't sure she really wanted to know. Maybe she would learn about the 8 hinted at in the article.

"Hey!" Spence called to Micah and Fiona as they walked in. "I guess it was successful! Fifi for the win!" he joked, giving her a mock salute.

Fiona had to roll her eyes at Spence's nickname for her. It was a game they played; Spence would call her Fifi, and Fiona would pretend like she hated it. But Fiona would have been lying if she said that she didn't sort of enjoy the term of endearment. Spence knew it too, which was why he kept it up. She had never been given a nickname before. Certainly not one that sounded like some spoiled Persian cat lapping milk from a silver saucer. The moniker couldn't be further removed from her true personality, but it was sweet nonetheless.

Spence turned the laptop screen around so that all the eyes in the room could drink up the images. Fiona cringed a bit as the footage reeled before her, wrapping her arms around her abdomen to quell the rising nausea. The fire looked larger, more formidable on screen than it did in person. Red and orange wisps of light danced in windows as the video-camera zoomed in to give the viewer a closer look. The camera angle didn't capture the rooftop–nor the people huddled there. That was an image for Fiona's mind only, for her dreams. It was difficult for her to believe she had caused such a fire–her most public one, by far.

The screen cut to an anchorwoman dressed in blue seated in the newsroom. She said into her headset:

What you just saw was footage of a blaze that consumed the entire top floor and part of the rooftop garden of a Tribeca apartment building last night. Authorities report that the fire started at about midnight and by about 2am FDNY finally had it mostly subdued. The penthouse belonged to billionaire Gary Bradley, the president and CEO of the realty development firm, The Bradley Corporation. Although it appears that the blaze was a result of faulty wiring and possible negligence on behalf of the building inspectors, authorities have not yet ruled out arson. Luckily there were no casualties, and aside from an elderly couple being treated for smoke inhalation, no other residents sustained any injury.

Spence closed his laptop, ending the news report. Aside from Micah, Fiona felt closest to Spence. Maybe in some ways she felt even closer to Spence than to Micah; he was certainly easier to get to know. The two had formed a sort of friendship since she folded herself into the group, and his goofy energy and outgoing personality brought Fiona comfort. He was kind, and brilliant; no one would ever suspect that underneath the beloved *Simpson's* hoodie was a tech genius. He could hack into anything with a modem. He studied Fiona for a minute and rose from his seat with his hand extended out for a high-five.

"That's my Fifi," he said, a smile beaming across his lips. "I told you you could do it," he continued as Fiona gave him a tentative hand-slap.

"Well–it wasn't perfect. I almost–"

"Almost doesn't count," Spence said in his reassuring tone. "You got it done. Told you you'd be fine."

She smirked back at him and said, "I guess I'll never doubt you again."

"Damn right," he said with his signature light-hearted tone as he enveloped her into a tight bear hug.

That hug made the "almost" fade into the background of Fiona's mind. He was right. Or at least Fiona hoped he was. Maybe "almost" doesn't count.

Over the past few weeks, Spence gave Fiona numerous pep-talks about believing in herself. About harnessing grief and guilt. When the others doubted her, Spence remained constant in his belief. Micah probably would have been angry to learn that Spence filled Fiona in on a prior group member, some guy named Derrek. Apparently, the cops caught Derrek after he ignited a fire at Grumman, a military facility in Long Island. Caught red-handed so to speak, he never ratted on the others, but it put every-one, including Kaleb, at terrible risk. They were forced to lay-low for a whole year before they resumed activity. It was at that point that Micah found Fiona. She was the golden ticket; after all, as Micah said before, she was virtually untraceable.

Micah interrupted the embrace, "All right, all right. No use gloating. It's time to debrief."

Did he always have to be so damn practical? Fiona guessed that he did; it was a trait that allowed him to do what he did.

The group members all took seats in the living room. Rhea lit up a cigarette and sat down on the arm rest of the couch. Fiona couldn't help but feel a bit surprised when she whispered, "Good job girl," to her as the others congregated around. Rhea was the house-member Fiona felt most distant from.

"Ok," Micah began. "It worked. Fiona was able to do what, with our help, she practiced. There was a bit of a hiccup, but I'm confident that with further training, we can eliminate any of those in the future. Fiona, will you fill us in on the specifics?"

Four sets of eyes fixed on Fiona as she spoke," Um, sure. I used the visualization strategy to set off a small spark in the wiring of the Bradley apartment. With a little bit of mental coaxing, I helped it spread enough to engage the insulation inside the wall. At that point...it didn't need me anymore. It just did its own thing."

Fiona thought to herself, *It's "own thing" almost amounted to spreading to an entire building–injuring however many people it came into contact with..maybe even killing people*. But that's always the way with fire. It has a mind of its own–even her fire. And this was Fiona's greatest fear.

But she didn't voice any of this. All she said was, "I guided its course, but it didn't really need me once it got going."

"Awesome," Spence said in open admiration. "Our little Fifi... a true badass!"

Fiona wanted to laugh at Spence's assessment, but she couldn't help herself from adding, "But then...I guess I got nervous and–"

Micah cut her off, "You don't need to go into that. Just focus on what went well."

Fiona didn't know if her explanation made any sense–she was still trying to process it herself–but the others nodded. Even Maya looked impressed, and that said something.

Micah continued to stare at Fiona, asking her with his eyes to say more.

She continued, "At first, I wasn't sure I would be able to do it. It felt a lot different from the practice sessions, higher stakes, more pressure. It took me a while to be able to see it enough to make it happen. But I used some of the breathing techniques Maya worked on with me and was able to get myself in a headspace to make it happen."

"This was a big step for you, Fiona. A big step for us. You proved that you could be trusted and that you belong. Kaleb agrees," Micah added.

Micah's comment about trust set her on edge. *Last night, I set my whole world aflame, Fiona* thought to herself. *Of course I can be trusted.*

Fiona didn't know what emboldened her to ask the next question, but she sputtered out, "Who is this Kaleb? And no way that's his real name, right?"

"Unfortunately, that is above your paygrade," Micah chuckled.

"Eventually, you'll stop caring about that and just take the paycheck and say thank you," Rhea said, through an exhale of gray smoke. "That's what the rest of us do."

"Well," added Spence, "the money is nice."

"And now you're on the payroll," Maya chimed in, looking at Fiona pointedly. "You should be happy."

That word: *happy.* Was that what she felt? Fiona hadn't really discussed any specific financial incentive with Micah; honestly the paycheck wasn't the reason why she ended up here, but he nodded his head in agreement.

Even though the promise of money was attractive, Fiona wasn't satisfied. Paychecks. Payroll. They spoke as if they were a legally recognized corporation.

"What is our purpose exactly?" she asked.

"We send messages to people. People who need some...shall we say, motivation," Micah explained.

"And these *messages* come from this Kaleb? What kind of *messages* are we sending? Are they political?" Fiona pushed on.

By the tilt in Micah's gaze she knew she guessed right—but she also knew he wouldn't satisfy her with a direct response.

He answered the question with his usual evasion, "Don't worry about the motive. That's between me and Kaleb. Your job is simply to execute. And trust me when I say this, the less you know, the better off you are."

That last part, Fiona did believe. It was the case in every single crime-thriller she ever read or watched. The less the person knew, the less culpable he or she was. So, even though there were many more questions swarming around inside Fiona's head, she stuffed them back somewhere deep down with the intention of saving them for another time.

Maya asked, "Do you feel more confident that you can replicate it, now that you did it successfully the first time?"

Fiona thought for a moment about that before answering. The truth was, yes, she did feel more comfortable. More confident. Her skill wasn't perfect–no, not by a long shot. But she thought that in time, it could be. Before she came here, before she met Micah and the others, her condition was even more erratic, and heavily tied to her emotions–as evidenced by the tragedy that remained etched in her mind indefinitely. As evidenced by her "death." Prior to that, for a time–for a long time–she thought her ability was becoming dormant, that it was fading as she got older. Maybe that had simply been a wish, a hope that she could attain some level of normalcy. Sometimes she could summon a spark, sometimes nothing happened for months. These strangers helped Fiona to harness whatever odd ability she had hidden away inside. They didn't make her feel like a monster, or a freak. Only needed. And it felt nice to be needed.

"Yes. I definitely need more practice, more training. But, I'm pretty sure I could do it again," Fiona answered Maya after a few moments of quiet contemplation.

The air in the space shifted, and the approval radiated off the people crammed into that living room. It was at that moment that Fiona truly believed that she had finally found a place in the world.

Chapter Twenty-Nine

"So," Fiona said, turning her attention to Micah. "What's next?"

Micah seemed caught off guard by the question. She hadn't exactly been the easiest of pupils over the course of the past weeks–bombarding him with questions, concerns, doubts. Had even shed quite a few tears to put it mildly, wavering back and forth like a pendulum about her resolve to explore the flame residing inside of her. Hell, Fiona had wavered in her resolve about actually even trying to do what she had just done last night. A part of her, a very real part, was still attached to that apartment. The soft gold touches in the kitchen, the burnished bronze switchplates, the Italian glass light fixtures. It was so beautiful, so perfect. Yet, all that perfection was tainted beyond repair that awful night all those weeks back. Just thinking about it made Fiona shiver. The disgust threatened to creep in and take over again and she swallowed it down to prevent the onslaught.

Micah just needed to give Fiona the final push, and when he said, "You know, Fiona, if I start a fire, or if Maya or Rhea or Spence does, there's no telling how many people could get hurt. Fires can rage out of control very easily...you know that. But you. *You* could control it–ensure that no one gets hurt."

He knew that was Fiona's Achilles Heel: that concern for others. And, he was right. Fiona *could* do that. If all went well, that was. Yes, last night's fire spread more than she wanted it to–was that downplaying her error? Perhaps. But unlike last time–the incident that landed her here–there were no casualties, but it had been close–too close. But like Spence said, what was the benefit of dwelling on "almost"? There was room for improvement–a lot of it. But she exhibited more control than ever before. And that was saying something. It was saying a great deal.

So when Fiona asked Micah, "What's next?" she suggested compliance. She was telling him that she was in–an official member of the group. Not that she really had many other prospects. Not after everything. It hurt Fiona to think about that–a scab that couldn't seem to heal. But either way, last night was the official initiation. If she could pull it off, she was in. She was too afraid to ask about the possibility of failure.

But, despite it all, Fiona hadn't failed. And now here she was. She was well aware that her actions were at best shady and at worst sinister; morality was a matter of perspective after all, and from Fiona's perspective, it was her only avenue of pursuit. What is morality in the face of necessity? Not much. Yet, Fiona felt that if she could prevent innocents from being put in harm's way, there was some redemption in her choice. And sometimes, it just felt damn good to burn. She was at a point where she could finally admit that to herself. Rationalization is a human's best trick–perhaps it is a survival mechanism that developed a long time ago, allowing us that personal vindication for which we so often thirst.

Despite his surprise, Micah didn't miss a beat.

"What's next," he said. "...is another assignment. Your first *real* assignment."

"Was last night not *real*?" she asked, knowing fully well that it was merely a test of her ability and resolve.

Despite that truth, it certainly felt real to her. She torched her old life. What could be more *real* than that?

"It was real for you, Fiona. But it didn't have anything to do with our mission here. It didn't send any messages. This next one will," Micah explained.

Fiona swallowed the anger that simmered inside at his words and tried to concentrate on what would come next. Rhea, Spence, and Maya leaned forward in their seats, their eyes trained on Micah.

"What's our target, boss?" Spence asked.

"Kaleb has his eyes set on a branch of Planned Parenthood over in Washington D.C. It's one of the larger clinics attached to corporate offices...a good way to make a statement," Micah explained levelly.

A jolt of unease rippled through Fiona. It was one thing to burn the apartment of some billionaire realty guy, but it felt different to go after desperate women looking for help. Hearing that they would target an abortion clinic made it clear to Fiona that whoever this Kaleb was, he was definitely tied to politics. Whether he was trying to "send a message" to Pro-Choicers or Pro-Lifers, she couldn't really say, but abortion was a hot-button political topic for sure. She thought that maybe she should start to pay more attention to the news if she wanted to learn more about their purpose.

Spence, Maya, and Rhea began chattering incessantly, their excitement palpable, but Micah sensed a trepidation in Fiona's demeanor.

"What's on your mind?" he asked while the others prattled on.

"I don't know, Micah. I don't know how I feel about this one. I mean, one less New York City billionaire is one thing, but burning down a Planned Parenthood? People depend on those clinics. I believe in–" Micah cut her off.

"I'm going to stop you there, Fiona. You're putting too much emotion into this. This isn't personal. Nor is it a reflection of your own beliefs. Look at Spence over there...he's the most liberal guy I know. It's not about that. This is just a job," he said.

"Well, what if someone gets hurt? I don't know if I could–"

"No one will get hurt," Micah assured her. "Not with you in control. You can make sure of that. If you dedicate yourself to your training, you remove the risk."

"I almost hurt people last night–and I've hurt people before," Fiona responded, unable to hide the shame from her voice. The mere reference of that event turned those raging emotions into swirling eddies in her stomach.

"I know that you've hurt people before, Fiona. I was in Long Island. I was there. And I know you. You're better now. You're already more controlled. And like I've been saying...with more training, you can do it."

She looked over at Micah and then glanced at the others, who were watching her with open curiosity. She thought fleetingly about the pain her mom and brother must have felt when they lost her. She hoped that they had also found an outlet for their hurt, their sadness–a means of coping.

"Well?" Maya asked, interrupting her thoughts. "Are you in or out?"

Did she really have a choice? With or without her help, that Planned Parenthood was as good as gone, and if she didn't use her abilities, there was no telling how many people could get burned. She thought about that article she found in Micah's room, the indication that 8 people had died in a fire, presumably a fire caused by Micah. She hadn't been able to discover anything else about the people she was surrounded by, least of all Micah. She never ventured into Micah's room again, but she had tried to log into Spence's laptop; it was, of course, secured by a password. She tried to search for the article by typing the title into her phone and couldn't find anything either–not like her phone had full access to the web yet, Micah had instructed Spence to put restrictions up. She wasn't fully trusted yet. Her search was unsuccessful. She couldn't access anything without paying for subscriptions and registering for websites, none of which she could do at this point. She recently decided that she'd stop trying, what was the point anyway? Either way, at that moment, all eyes were on her. She had to say something–and there really was only one acceptable some-thing to say.

Fiona exhaled a deep breath and answered Maya, "I'm in."

Micah's eyes danced with a fiery heat as he regarded Fiona and for a moment she wondered if her life would have been different–better perhaps–had she never laid eyes on this man in the first place. But then she would have probably been dead. Or in jail. So there really was no alternative.

Fiona shook off those thoughts, those feelings of apprehension and for the first time since she had been there, to feel the spark of feverish anticipation rise within her. She hadn't truly been excited for the Tribeca fire; it was more that she went through the expected motions, for the sake of her future. For *a* future. She was willing, but not passionate about it. Her emotions had been like a twisted elevator ride since she arrived here—up and down, and then up again. But sitting in this living room, with Micah, Rhea, Spence, and Maya, Fiona found a place she belonged. These people accepted her, needed her. And on top of that, she would make a fair share of cash...enough to not worry about money anymore–at least for the foreseeable future. Enough to maybe, somehow, help her mom and brother. Enough to swal-low–at least for the moment–the doubt and reservations she felt about pursuing this path. That compiled with the paradoxical thought that she could actually save people. Micah was going to start fires regardless of her participation; at least she could lessen the possible human casualties.

"Alright," Micah said, breaking the trance. "We have a lot of work to do."

"Well, then," Fiona replied. "We better get started."

Chapter Thirty

The group talked about their next assignment for hours, deep into the evening. Fiona wasn't part of the planning stages for the Bradley Job–which was what Micah called it–she was too consumed with grief–so she was unaware of how much thought was required. There was way more to it than simply showing up and burning something down. The thoroughness and efficiency was impressive. She finally saw how the group worked together and how each one played a fundamental role.

They talked about timing, location, the best place to maximize impact, the news exposure they needed, just to name a few of the key elements to consider over the next few weeks. They even discussed the weather: the direction of the wind, rain forecasts. Fiona's head spun with details, every single aspect a choreographed dance. Spence dealt with the technology: research, city grids, surveillance cameras, internet blasts. Rhea was in charge of logistics like maps, floorplans, and traffic patterns. Maya was to tap into her vast media contacts. Micah wanted every person in the world to see what they were going to do. He was fond of saying: *What's the use of sending a message if it's only seen by a million people? Let's get a billion people to tune in. Let's really make Kaleb appreciate what we do here.*

As for Fiona, she was supposed to continue to practice. She was told the next job would be bigger, more nuanced. She would need an even stronger grasp on her condition. It was odd to discuss her talents–Spence's word, not her's–so openly. It was certainly a change from all those years of hiding. At times, Fiona felt like a star pitcher, discussing the specifics of a shoulder injury on public television. Her roommate in college loved to watch ESPN and every time Fiona watched athletes open up about their medical diagnoses, it always struck her as an invasion of privacy–like their bodies weren't their own. They owed the public an explanation. And now Fiona felt the same.

Maya agreed to continue working with her on those relaxation techniques and once Rhea had floor plans and maps, they would work on visualization strategies. Fiona now knew that her efficiency and control was contingent upon both her visual understanding of the target and her emotional control. It would've been nice to have these people to guide her in the past. Maybe if they had been there, things would have turned out differently.

It was midnight when Fiona trudged down the basement stairs to her bedroom, followed by Micah. The others knew about their evolving relationship, but aside from a few sarcastic comments about "odd" noises they heard in the nighttime hours, no one mentioned it. Fiona perceived that there was also something going on between Rhea and Maya, but when she asked Micah about it, he just shrugged his shoulders and said, "Who cares what people do behind closed doors?"

Micah insisted they maintain separate bedrooms, and even when their nighttime *activities* ended late, he always strode out of her room at some point between when her eyes closed for the evening and when they opened in the morning. And they never met in his room, only her's–probably so Micah could control his own leaving. Even on nights beginning with the two of them together, Fiona always found herself tucked alone, in her own bed, plagued by nightmares about her mother and Noah–her brother. Fiona supposed he felt that he needed to maintain a degree of separation, considering he was in charge and intent on maintaining an air of professionalism. Anytime Fiona asked about it he just replied, "What we do is no one else's business."

Micah followed Fiona into her bedroom at the end of the hallway and closed the door softly behind him. Even though she was exhausted–the five hours of sleep she got in his car last night hadn't cut it–she felt a heat roil in the pit of her stomach as she regarded him, leaning against the door. It wasn't fair; he was always so cool and calm. Even being in his presence made Fiona's blood pump wildly in her veins. He was impossibly handsome: a swimmer's build–broad shoulders with ropy, muscular biceps. His veins popped out as they traversed the length of his forearms and hands. Even in a t-shirt and jeans, he commanded attention as his dark eyes glittered with mischief and desire. Fiona's mouth went dry as he walked towards her, his long strides making quick work of the distance between them. Her five-foot four-inch stature paled in comparison to his height; he had to be well over six-feet. She couldn't help but back up a few steps as he closed in, but he hooked his thumbs into the front belt loops of her jeans and pulled her close. She let him. Fiona turned her gaze up to reach his. Pressed up against his chest, he drew his thumb across her jawline, and pushed her wayward hair behind her ears. When he touched her like that, it became too difficult to focus, too difficult to even breathe. It was in these moments where Micah made the most sense to her–all of his broody intensity and sporadic acts of sweetness converged to invoke an irresistible attraction deep inside Fiona's fluttering heart.

"Always so warm," he whispered, his breath minty cool against her burning face.

Fiona flushed with embarrassment; it was impossible for her to hide that raw desire; it always had been, but for some reason, with Micah, Fiona felt more exposed than ever before. All pretenses lay bare before him. Probably because he knew the truth of who she was, *what* she was.

"You could probably burn me alive," he continued.

"And why would I want to do that?" Fiona responded feeling out of breath.

He didn't answer as he pressed his lips against the soft skin of her throat, his fingers reached down and slid underneath her tank, exposing the smooth skin of her stomach.

"You did well today," he whispered against her burning flesh.

She wanted to say "thank you," but suddenly she couldn't find the words.

"Think you could do it again?" he asked when she didn't answer, pausing in between each word to give a gentle nip to the spot directly behind her ear.

The act made her quiver; all Fiona could do was nod her head yes against him.

His fingers trailed upward, slowly leaving fingerprints of fire along her rib cage as he deftly removed her shirt. His mouth moved to her shoulder, and then Fiona perceived the gentle scraping of his teeth brushing against her collar bone as the straps of her bra slid down.

"Touch me," her breath hitched in her throat, twisting the soft waves of his hair with her fingers. "Please," she added breathlessly.

Micah continued to tease the sensitive skin of her chest as he unhooked her bra.

"Please Micah," Fiona said again in a breathy whisper.

She could feel his mouth pulling into a grin as he sucked the tender skin just above her breast. He liked it when she begged, and no matter how much she resisted giving him that satisfaction, she always caved. Always. Even like this he insisted on being in control. Even in intimacy he couldn't submit. Sometimes Fiona wished that he would allow her to take charge, but at that moment, the raw need she felt for the man overpowered all other logical thought. She would do whatever he wanted, say whatever he wanted; her body was on fire for him.

"Micah," she said again, pushing up against him, the need in her voice nearly palpable.

She couldn't resist shamelessly grinding her hips against him—anything to satisfy the yearning she felt between her thighs, the ache making her insides shudder and tighten in anticipation.

Finally he listened, swirling his tongue around her nipple, he took her into his mouth. The sensation evoked a gasp and she dug her fingers deeper into his hair. His teeth scraped against the delicate skin, his mouth warm. Fiona felt her back meet the wall and watched through heavy lids as Micah sank to his knees before her, his lips leaving a line of kisses.

He looked up at Fiona, one hand poised on the button of her jeans, the other lightly caressing the exposed skin of her belly and hips. The triumph in his eyes shone in the dim light and Fiona felt frustration blend and swirl with the desperation she felt. His eyes always looked this way when he finally succeeded in reducing her to this—to a trembling, begging disaster.

"You're driving me insane Micah," Fiona gasped, looking down and meeting his gaze.

In response he blew out a small breath right below her navel, eliciting immediate goosebumps, despite the heat coursing through her.

"Driving you insane?" he asked, kissing her hip bones and unbuttoning her jeans, slowly, torturously.

"Yes Micah," Fiona's voice came out thick, her longing as obvious as a red rose amongst daisies; he continued to tease.

"What do you want Fiona?" he asked.

"You know what I want," she said, trembling under his mouth, his fingers brushing lightly against the tender flesh above her zipper.

How was it that she was coming totally undone while he remained calm and even?

"I want you to tell me what you want," he said. "I want to hear you say it."

"Please, Micah," she said again.

Fiona glanced down and watched Micah's mouth against her, his fingers poised at her zipper. She couldn't resist anymore.

"I want you. Take off my jeans. Let me feel your mouth against me," she said.

"Say please, Fiona."

"Please, Micah. Please."

The zipper felt cold against Fiona's blazing skin as Micah slipped the jeans down over her hips. The cotton thong she wore was saturated with her arousal as he moved it aside and plunged his finger inside her. Every nerve ending clenched around the sweet invasion. He added another finger as he massaged her from within.

"So wet," Micah said as he watched her face break, fingers stroking the warmest and most intimate places.

"I want your mouth," she said.

Fiona reached a place where she was beyond embarrassment; her mind was in the stars. Her insides fluttering like butterfly wings, without any logical thought.

Micah slung one of Fiona's legs over his shoulders and Fiona threw her head back against the wall thanking whatever power lay in the heavens above that he didn't make her beg for a second time before he acquiesced. She honestly didn't know if she would survive that torment.

Fiona rocked against his face, feeling the rough stubble of his jaw against her most delicate places. Vibrating and pulsing uncontrollably, Micah steadied her with one hand gripping her thigh and the other pressed firmly against her stomach, pinning her in place. His mouth knew exactly where to go and his tongue knew exactly what she needed as he drove her toward a peak that split her brain in two. The onslaught of sensation radiated outward from her core echoing through her limbs and chest. Her climax tore through her body ripping her away from the earth while raspy cries escaped from her parted, raw lips. When the rolling waves of pleasure subsided, she was breathless.

As Fiona trembled in the aftermath, Micah rose to his feet and removed his shirt, his pants. While gasping for air, Fiona openly studied him—appreciating the ridges on his abdomen, the definition of his chest. God, he was like a sculpture. Perfect. Looking at his naked form stoked the fire inside of her afresh and that need coursed through her even more powerfully than before. Her eyes traveled lower, and his arousal was obvious.

"How can a real life person look like you?" she asked, admiring the size of him. "It's just not fair."

With a small chuckle, Micah eased Fiona down onto the bed and pulled the ruined thong down her legs and slipped it off her feet.

Kneeling between her thighs, Micah said, "Open wider for me."

Fiona did, eagerly; she didn't need to be told twice. Micah's smirk told her that he approved of her quick compliance, of the hunger she felt for him. In one swift motion, he was inside her and the edges of her consciousness blurred and darkened with the sweet friction he created. The flames roaring in her head drowned out the sound of his deep moans as he pushed himself into her over and over again. Swollen and sensitive, Fiona's body was no longer her own. It was his, and she couldn't help but admit she liked it that way. Still shaking from the pleasure Micah's mouth had given, the sensation of being filled by him—utterly and completely—was almost too much to take.

Fiona dimly perceived the two candles on the old wooden dresser flare, the flame gradually rising higher as the pleasure they created mounted. She called out his name as he brought her to a second climax and for a short while she didn't think of anything at all, she only felt. Micah in between her thighs, her heart racing, her lips, chapped and ragged, her fingernails rasping down the smooth skin of Micah's back. It was exactly the escape she needed. It always was; every single time with him. She wished it would never end. But it always did, and when she floated back to Earth, tired and depleted, her mind resumed its relentless racing as if some higher power clicked "play" on the remote that controlled her brain.

The intensity of their love-making stood in stark contrast to the cold distance Micah established between them during every other moment of their shared existence. In his arms was the only time Fiona glimpsed the passion that hid under his stone exterior. The lion that lay waiting in its den.

In the aftermath, Fiona closed her eyes and snuggled against his chest. She didn't expect to feel his arms encircle her; he had made it clear that he was not a cuddler. Minutes, or hours later–as usual, Fiona lost track of time in Micah's presence–through drooping, heavy eye-lids Fiona felt him disengage her arm from across his shoulder, and dimly perceived the bed shift as it was released from his weight. The floorboards creaked as he made his way out of the room.

The spark within her dimmed, leaving her with the blurry images of her recurring nightmare: her mom and brother's faces calling out to her in the darkness. Angry red blisters on smooth little-boy skin. A charred Nirvana t-shirt. She heard her name across the vast space of nothingness. She could feel the desperation rising from their panic. Tears slid down Fiona's cheeks every time she had this dream, which was often. She didn't wake up, she never did. Her consciousness never extended that mercy to her. When daylight came, she acknowledged the damp wetness on the pillow beneath her head. The dreams consumed her psyche as she lay there paralyzed under the downy blanket barely able to catch her breath.

Chapter Thirty-One

The weeks passed quickly as the group meticulously plotted out their course. Even though Fiona was officially part of the group, her role in it all felt lonely. Micah was a machine, the rotors always spinning. While their nightly activities continued with fervor, during the day, they barely interacted. Micah was preoccupied with making sure everyone in the unit stayed up-to-date and well-informed. With each new tidbit of information, Micah printed up detailed instruction pamphlets to document their preparation, and they de-briefed on the nights they were all home, which happened about twice a week. All of the out-dated materials were burned in the firepit in the backyard. The neighbors must have thought them so wholesome, sitting around chatting beside a campfire; no one would have expected that these innocent s'mores roasts were a front to dispose of subversive content.

On most days, Micah left early in the mornings to meet with Kaleb, who apparently demanded frequent updates on the group's progress and who had his own list of expectations. He had a few non-negotiable stipulations. One: The fire should begin at 5:30 am sharp on a Monday morning towards the end of July—

he would defer to them on the exact date based upon traffic and weather patterns. Two: The fire should completely level the structure, but should spare the corporate offices, which were smack dab in the center of the structure–a tricky request. And finally: The fire and ensuing damage must be untraceable. This was where Fiona came in. Micah mentioned these stipulations could be amended at any moment as Kaleb saw fit and that they were not to ask questions, even though Fiona found it so desperately difficult to swallow those that buzzed around in her head. Questions like: Why did it have to be on a Monday? Why 5:30am? What was the purpose of sparing the corporate offices and torching a clinic that sought only to help others? She had some ideas as to the whys: possibly to maximize exposure, cause a larger disruption, make those in charge look responsible or negligent or both? But those were just guesses. She had no real insight into Kaleb's head, so she tried to take Spence's advice. Keep her head down, take her paycheck, and be thankful. And most of the time, that was just what she did.

Rhea and Spence would disappear for days at a time–off doing surveillance in DC, which even with Spence's lead foot was an 8-hour drive (at least) from Plattsburgh. They would return home for a bit and then Micah would express dissatisfaction in some aspect of their reconnaissance and send them back. They never seemed to resent all the hours they dedicated to their research, nor the time they spent behind the wheel of Spence's Audi. They made the round trip at least 4 times in the 5 weeks leading up to the job.

Before Fiona arrived, she had no idea how large New York State truly was; coming from Long Island, and spending her college years in and around the metro campus of FIT, upstate was simply upstate. When she was little, in her naiveté, she envisioned a single road leading straight from Long Island to Canada. She never accounted for the breadth of it, especially because it looked so small on a map. Unlike Fiona's high school friends–aside from the one family trip to Lake George–most of the time her mom took her and her brother south for vacation: Florida, South Carolina, even one memorable experience at Dollywood in Tennessee. Thinking of her mom, her childhood brought a tightness to Fiona's throat. It seemed as though nothing made the absence any easier, any more bearable. The pain snuck up on her sometimes when she didn't expect it. Fiona wondered how her mom was? Did she miss her? It seemed like ages ago Fiona faked her own death...disappeared from life as she knew it. Disappeared from her brother's life. Fiona never would have thought such a thing was even possible–outside of the movies of course. Never would have known that real life had such darkness tucked away, where a person could and would actually choose such a route. Well...she *had* chosen that route. Not that there had been much of a choice–not when it actually came down to it. Fiona shivered at the recollection.

She often wondered when her life had become so much like a movie. Loneliness can do that to a person, force her to consider those she loved, those that made her feel whole. And Fiona was lonely, despite the fact that she was surrounded by the rest of the group. But those making up this group–Maya, Spence, Rhea, and Micah too–sometimes felt more like movie characters than real people. Stars and co-stars of the action movies Fiona loved as a child–of those suspense thrillers she used to drink up, one after the other. She was never one for the Disney princess movies her friends watched with zeal. Instead of a lunch box featuring the pale face of *Snow White*, Fiona's boasted a glossy photograph of Sylvester Stallone as Rambo, holding an oily machine gun strapped across his heavily muscled chest. Yes, the movie was technically before her time, but she loved it anyway. Her mom used to cringe as she snapped the latch shut and handed it to her as she walked out the front door to go to the bus stop. *How about a My Little Pony Lunchbox*, she would say. *Nope*, Fiona would reply. *Rambo is so much cooler.*

As a kid Fiona would sit on the couch tucked next to her dad, drinking up films like *Terminator*, *Predator*, *Die Hard*. Her mom used to yell at her father, saying she was too young and impressionable to have her mind filled up with such violence. But that was before her father left. Before he turned his back on his family. That was the first loss Fiona's mother and brother had to cope with. But at least then they had one another to lean on. Looking back on it now, Fiona realized how astounding her mom's strength had been. She was just a kid at the time. Fiona wished she'd had the chance to tell her mother how miraculous, how beautiful and selfless she had been. But now it was too late for that. Mom and Noah didn't know then that years down the line, they would also have to endure the loss of a child...of a sister. A second loss. The loss of Fiona.

After the incident leading Fiona here, she spent a significant amount of time thinking of her life as a before and after. Before, her father was around. Before, she had a simple life and a home and a mom and a brother. Before, she didn't have control of her condition, but it was weaker–still developing. And then there was the after. After the incident. After she altered her reality. In the after, Fiona's life emulated those very plotlines that played out on the television glowing before her childhood eyes. The one difference was that in real life there was much more waiting, much more boredom, much more downtime than in fiction.

The downtime in Plattsburgh wasn't good for Fiona. Her mind traveled down dark paths and sometimes, the urge to call her childhood telephone number, just to hear her mother's voice say "Hello" into the receiver was so great she had to go for a walk to prevent her itchy hands from doing something she would regret. They were better off without her anyway. That had become her mantra since everything happened. They were better off without her.

Once, when Fiona felt particularly lonely, she asked Spence, "Can I go with you guys to D.C.? I mean, it might be good for me to at least see the location."

"That's Micah's call, Fifi," he had replied.

The fact Spence hadn't immediately denied the request buoyed her spirits and she ran to ask Micah about it.

"No," he said simply.

"But why?" Fiona pressed. "I'm the one who has to execute it. Shouldn't I at least have a direct visual?"

"A few days before the job, Rhea will take you there. It's important she has the logistics right first. We can't risk you being seen. We only get one shot at this," he explained.

It was a fair point, but Fiona sensed an underlying subtext. Micah was afraid she would change her mind once she saw the women coming in and out of the clinic. This was the topic of more than a few conversations since they got the assignment, and even though Fiona remained resolute and determined to perform the expected role, she would be lying if she said there wasn't a hint of unease lying dormant inside of her. Those "close calls" in her past played on the edges of her mind...as did that one terrible event floating in the back of her periphery. The one she desperately tried to push from her mind.

With Rhea, Spence and Micah gone all the time, Maya and Fiona spent more time together. Even though Maya had her own responsibilities that took up the majority of her time, Fiona saw her the most. She came to look forward to their morning coffee together, before Maya shut herself in her bedroom or ventured out for the day on the various errands needed to sustain the household. Fiona was never permitted to accompany her, lest she be recognized. Even though Fiona cut and dyed her hair, changed her last name, and lived hours from her old life, Micah was cautious.

Last time Fiona asked him about the time-frame in which she could possibly resume a certain level of life outside the home–she wasn't asking for much–he replied, "Fiona, we have to take precautions. I would imagine in a few more months, you could begin limited outside activity. Assuming you take the proper steps to ensure anonymity."

Months just sounded so unbelievably long. Interminable. So, Fiona tried to be content with the few people closed within the small ranch in Plattsburgh. And even though her mind still drifted to the soft curve of her mom's cheek, and to the smattering of freckles across her 12 year old brother's nose, she succeeded most of the time.

Chapter Thirty-Two

A few weeks later Rhea and Fiona sat in the small, black BMW in front of the Planned Parenthood in the DC metro area. The parking lot allowed them a full view of the front of the building along with a partial view of the east side.

"Wow. Nice building," Fiona said to Rhea, admiring the impressive structure.

The building that Fiona stared at through Rhea's soft-tinted windows looked nothing like the Levittown clinic, with the crumbling brick facade. This one was large and modern. It looked more like a luxury condo complex with its boxy structure and beveled edges. Morning sunlight gleamed off the rows of windows, reflecting a blindingly blue sky. That uneasy feeling crept over Fiona again. Was she really going to torch this building? It was so beautiful. So meticulously designed, right down to the friendly cherry blossom trees lining the walkway—wasn't D.C. known for those trees? *Stop being stupid*, she said to herself. *No one will get hurt. It's not like I'm torching the place while people are inside.* No matter what reservations she had, there was only one path: forward.

She had limited experiences with Planned Parenthood, never visited one: thankfully. There was a clinic near her childhood home in Levittown, and Fiona remembered passing it at least once a day when she lived at home. She remembered how protestors would line up along the sidewalk holding signs boasting images of dismembered fetuses with sayings like, "Jesus is Pro-Life," or "Hitler Killed Babies Too." Whenever she and her mom drove past them, her mom would say, *Don't these people have anything better to do than make the decisions these poor women have to make even harder than they already are?* Once Fiona's mother even cursed under her breath. *Fucking despicable*, she had said. Fiona had asked her who she was talking about and she had responded, *I'm talking about these people Fiona. These people who think they have the right to cast judgment on what other people choose to do.* Her mom hadn't even apologized for saying the f-word, which she never used around her children.

Rhea pointed out some of the features, "That tall annex over there is the Straub Center, a brand-new state-of-the-art clinic built last year after an anonymous donor pledge of 5 million dollars."

"Amazing someone would actually do that, just hand over 5 million dollars," Fiona responded.

"Focus Fiona," Rhea responded. "We're not here to marvel at philanthropy. Plus, nothing is done in this world without selfish purposes. I'm sure the donor had a very specific motive in mind."

Rhea's pessimism was jarring and Fiona wasn't sure she was fully ready to adopt such a worldview, but Rhea was right in one regard. Fiona did need to focus. Admiring the possible humanity of the structure certainly wasn't going to make burning it down any easier.

Fiona picked up the conversation, "What's that section over there?" Pointing to the area to the left of the Straub Center she continued, "...that section with the shrubbery covering the base."

Rhea answered, "Those are the corporate offices–the one section that is to remain in-tact."

"It's right in the middle of the structure. You're saying that everything above, below and around it is supposed to burn?" Fiona asked, concern lacing the question.

Rhea must have sensed her hesitation because she spoke with precision, "It *is* a much more nuanced scenario than the Bradley Job. But you can do it. Micah thinks so too. You nailed it last time. Well, for the most part."

Rhea's hint at the near-catastrophe didn't fill Fiona with confidence, and she must have picked up on the doubt that crept into Fiona's eyes.

Rhea continued in what she intended to be a reassuring tone, "You're stronger this time. More controlled. And that's why we're here. To practice. I have all of the floor-plans and now you have a visual. We can work on the techniques you've been mastering. And there's no rush. Nothing happens until you're ready."

Fiona exhaled a slow breath. It helped to know that Rhea believed in her. She just needed to believe in herself.

"Are you ready to start?" Rhea asked.

"I'm ready," Fiona responded.

Rhea reached into the back seat to retrieve a large piece of paper, rolled up and secured with rubber bands. Spreading it out on the dashboard, Fiona saw the floorplan of the structure laid out before her, including the emergency exits, electricity pathways and most importantly, the fire safety precautions. Those would have to be disabled first.

"How did you get this?" Fiona asked.

"What did you think Spence and I were doing during all those trips here? Visiting the monuments? We've been taking meticulous notes. Going undercover to get inside. Spence was even able to get a screenshot of the architectural plans. He's a damn genius in some regards. Once we had all our ducks in a row, I drew up this finalized sketch."

"I'm impressed," Fiona said, admiring the pin-straight pencil lines and the crisp angles.

Rhea didn't acknowledge the compliment. Instead, with her

pointer finger, she drew Fiona's attention to a spot on the map marked in red.

"What's that mark?" Fiona asked.

"Where the fire should start," she responded.

Fiona studied that section on the floor plan. It was the rearmost area of the lobby of the Straub Center. The 5 million dollar addition Rhea spoke about. Fiona tried not to imagine the women who had sat in that lobby, squirming in their chairs, ready to make choices that could potentially change the trajectories of their lives forever. Maybe their hands clutched their still-flat abdomens pondering the life fluttering beneath their skin. How many women had this place helped? How many women could it continue to help? Fiona tried to squash these uncomfortable thoughts as they erupted in her mind. She thought to herself, *They'll rebuild. Some other billionaire will donate tons of money to put his name on a new clinic. Maybe this time there would be a 10 million dollar donation. 20 million dollar donation. Maybe future women would even be better off because the rebuild would be newer...more modern–if such a thing was even possible.*

Rhea interrupted her thoughts and said, "Earth to Fiona. You really need to focus on the task at hand."

Shaking herself free of the images dancing through her mind, Fiona replied, "Ok. I'm ready."

"First, I want to show you a video clip of the lobby; this way we can be discerning about specifics. It would have looked too suspicious to walk around recording, so I had to be discreet about it. The video is short, but it will give you the general idea, which, combined with the floorplan should be enough."

Placing her cell phone in Fiona's hand, Rhea directed her to press the 'Play' button. The swoop of the video included a vast waiting room with blue-upholstered chairs inhabited mainly by women; some were accompanied by men–probably boyfriends or husbands. Fiona couldn't discern the expressions on their faces, but the hunch in their shoulders and the restless tapping feet told her enough.

Rhea must have seen something in Fiona's expression because she said, "Fiona, stop looking at the people in the video. You should be focusing on the layout."

She was right, so Fiona pushed the sympathy to the edge of her consciousness, and trained her attention on the details. There was a large reception desk against the far wall and even though the space was orderly, the file folders and shelves of stacked paperwork etched themselves in her mind. Giving Rhea her cellphone back, Fiona compared the images she just viewed with the sketched floor plan.

"There," Fiona said pointing.

"The reception desk?" Rhea asked.

"Look at all that paperwork; it will help spread the flames. And it's far from the windows...tucked away against the other sections of the building. It will take some manipulation to make sure the corporate offices stay safe, but I think I could do it."

"That's exactly what I wanted to hear," Rhea responded. "Now close your eyes and start the visualization techniques. I'll help guide you through it."

Fiona spent the remainder of the day committing the space to memory. Traveling through the passageways of the building, tracing the course her fire would take–if all went well. And it would go well. It had to.

Chapter Thirty-Three

Once Rhea and Fiona returned from DC, the days went quickly. Plans were finalized, weather patterns checked, the job confirmed with Kaleb, and then confirmed again. A thousand checks and balances. Their thoroughness felt clinical, as though they were about to perform surgery.

A week later Fiona found herself trying to force herself to fall asleep at 1 o'clock in the afternoon, because they would be leaving in 7 hours–8pm–to begin the drive to DC. This was it. What all that training, all that preparation was for. Even though it seemed difficult to conceive, the time had come and Fiona was jittery. She knew she would perform better with even just a few hours of deep sleep, but she couldn't seem to find the Power button in her mind. The small windows in the basement bedroom helped hide the daylight gathered around their house, but her nerves made her feel as though she was teetering on the edge of an abyss. Sleep felt impossibly far out of reach. The onslaught of thoughts left Fiona feeling wired and jumpy. *What if I can't perform? What if last time was a fluke? What if I can't control the fire effectively? What if it spirals out of control, hurting innocent people in its wake? What if I disappoint Micah?* Questions ricocheted off the walls of her subconscious and no matter how exhausted she was, sleep remained elusive.

Fiona thought about the Bradley Job, which seemed like it occurred ages ago. She was definitely in more control now, but the stakes were higher, the pressure intensified. There were so many moving parts. Fiona knew she had the whole team behind her, but just Micah would accompany her to DC. That was the plan. *It's too big a risk to travel with more than two people*, he explained yesterday when Fiona tried to convince him that Rhea should join them.

A light rap on Fiona's bedroom door scattered her thoughts, and Micah's large frame entered the space. Why was it that the very air shifted in his presence, like electricity radiated off of him? Fiona looked up from the maps and floor plans laid out before her on the desk and regarded this man who came into her life and uprooted her from the reality she had known for almost 28 years. The fire within her pulsed dimly, but taking in his high cheekbones and the muscles rippling beneath his thin shirt, the flame rose unchecked into her cheeks. Fiona knew she was blushing, she could feel the heat radiating off her in waves.

His gentle speech didn't match his smoldering eyes as he said, "What are you doing? You should be resting."

"I wanted to spend a bit more time looking at the floor plans," Fiona replied, feeling–as always–foolish in his presence.

"You don't need to do that anymore Fiona. You're prepared. You've studied the plans and maps. You know the building by heart. Sleep is what you need."

Fiona's temper flared a bit, as it usually did when he dictated what she *should* be doing and she replied, "And how do you expect me to sleep? I can't just turn myself off like you can–like there's a light switch behind my head." And then she added tentatively, "What if I screw it up? What if I'm not ready?"

"You *are* ready. This is our one chance to get it right," he answered. "...and I wouldn't take that chance if I had any doubts."

"You mean this is *my* one chance to get it right. *I'm* the one that is expected to perform. *I'm* the one with the weight on my shoulders."

"That's not entirely true Fiona," Micah responded sitting down on the side of the bed facing her. "We're a team. If we fail, it's not just you that looks weak. It's all of us. And that's one thing I will not accept. Weakness. Failure...the failure of myself or the failure of this team."

"Wow, Micah," Fiona said, sarcasm dripping. "You sure know how to make a girl feel less stressed."

"I don't want you to feel less stressed," he responded. "I want you alert. Which is why you need sleep. You can't be at your best without ministering to the needs of your body."

"I can sleep in the car, you know."

"Car sleep is not deep sleep," he said. "Here," he continued, reaching into the front pocket of his jeans.

Fiona took what he held out to her in his open palm, and brought the item closer to her eyes for inspection. It was a rough-cut stone, smaller than a golf ball, but solid and weighty. It was uncut and raw, with edges and imperfections; an opaque milky white hue, veined with slashes of vibrant orange and crimson. It looked like the stone bled from the inside. When held up to the light, it emanated a soft glow.

"It's beautiful," Fiona said, mesmerized by the way it shimmered in the muted lamplight.

"It's a fire quartz," he responded. "I saw it in the window of a small shop in town. It reminded me of you."

"I've never heard of that stone," Fiona replied, flattered that Micah had thought about her.

When Fiona was a child, her mother loved shopping for crystals. Fiona would accompany her to Moon Child, a small boutique in a neighboring town and admire the enormous slabs of Amethyst that shone like jewels against the black velvet tablecloths; one time her mother bought her a small piece of polished rose quartz and explained how it would help Fiona to balance her emotions. Fiona walked around with it in her pocket for an entire year; sometimes she could have sworn she felt it vibrating. Micah didn't seem like the type to believe in the healing powers of crystals, so this gift surprised Fiona.

"Are you into crystals?" Fiona asked him.

He let out a small chuckle in reply, "No. But I thought you might be."

Again, the gap between what he knew about her and what Fiona knew about him stood in stark contrast. Fiona wouldn't even know where to begin had she the need or occasion to shop for Micah. Was there a store that specialized in black, tight-fitted tee-shirts? Yet he had Fiona pegged from the get-go. She didn't know how he saw through her so clearly, as if she was transparent. Upon their first introduction, he hinted that he had "done his homework" about Fiona–he called her his "hobby." But Fiona couldn't guess what kind of homework would have keyed him into her propensity towards spirituality. Or what he meant by the word "hobby."

"I did some research for you," he continued. "The fire quartz clears away anxiety, fear and doubt...if you believe in that sort of thing. And I figured it might bring you comfort in the task at hand."

The stone felt jagged in Fiona's hand, but its mass did bring a sense of relief. It fit snugly in her grip, and her mind was drawn to its cold, cratered surface, which warmed gradually in her grasp.

Fiona didn't know if it was the power of the crystal, or the warmth in knowing that Micah actually thought about her when he was outside of the house that brought her solace, but when he closed the bedroom door behind him and Fiona laid down on the bed, her eyes drifted peacefully closed.

Chapter Thirty-Four

Fiona woke up to Micah shaking her awake.

"What time is it?" she asked.

"It's 7 o'clock. Time to get ready."

As soon as he spoke those words, Fiona sat bolt upright, no trace of lingering sleep anywhere in her body. Her heart pounded in her ears and her face felt flushed and hot.

He must have seen the panic in her eyes because he said, "You're fine Fiona. You have time for a quick shower. Try to relax."

Relax, Fiona repeated in her head. She took a slow inhale and let it out, just as she learned to do during all those hours of breath training.

Without another word from Micah, Fiona grabbed a towel and headed down the hallway towards the bathroom. She turned the shower knob as far to the right as possible and let the warm water roll down her taut neck and back. Again, she breathed deeply, In and out, in and out, in and out, using the relaxation strategies Maya helped her master over the course of the previous weeks...or was it months? Time sometimes stood still in this house. Inhaling the balmy moisture, Fiona thought to herself, *This is it. Don't screw it up Fiona. If you can't fit in here, there's really no other place for you.* And as ominous as those thoughts were, they were true. This was Fiona's chance. Yes, she proved herself with the Bradley Job, but this job...this one, was real.

Wrapping the towel around her chest, Fiona tramped back to the bedroom leaving a trail of wet footprints behind her down the tiled hallway. She dressed quickly in the outfit Micah prepared: dark jeans, plain navy, fitted tank and black converse sneakers. Simple clothes selected for the purpose of anonymity. Running fingers through her damp, tangled hair and securing the strands into a tight bun at the top of her head, Fiona glanced at herself in the full-length mirror behind the door.

Unlike many women, Fiona could admit she was pretty. And she didn't feel self-conscious nor ashamed of this admission. As far as she was concerned, women needed to stop being so critical of themselves, so sorry all the time, and boldly embrace their beauty. Too many women tried to play demure, humble, thinking they would sound conceited if they admitted their worth.

Fiona refused to be like that—at least with her physical attributes—but she hadn't always been this way, hadn't always felt this empowered about her physical appearance. It took her years to adopt this mindstate. When she was younger, she used to be embarrassed by the freckles, which danced fearlessly across her nose and forehead and down her slender arms. One time, Fiona's brother tried to count them, but gave up after he reached 500. *There are just too many*, he had said. *I don't think I could even count that high.* Fiona's mom always tried to tell her that these markings made her special, that she should view them as a super-power of sorts, little dots that made her unique, beautiful. But like most young girls, Fiona desired the tan even skin tones of her peers and hated the way those auburn markings became even darker in the sun's unforgiving rays. On top of the freckles, her red hair made her obtrusive, when all she longed for at the time was to blend in. Ginger, Carrot-top, you name the insult, she heard them all. Kids can be cruel when it comes to the physical appearance of others—a fact that no amount of anti-bullying campaigning is ever going to change much.

But once the awkward years of adolescence melted away, and Fiona became a curvy, green-eyed, fire-haired, freckled 15-year-old, she embraced the fact that she stood out. Her peers didn't tease her about her freckles or that bright red-hair once she got older. And the stares she received from boys turned from critical to admiring. Fiona began to feel comfortable in her own skin for the first time. It was other aspects of herself–namely her hidden condition–that drew her scrutiny, her shame.

Taking in her appearance, Fiona felt as though she was still in high school. Like most of us, it had always been difficult for her to conceive of the passage of time. And maybe her lips had filled out a bit, and perhaps she had come to dress differently than she had as a teenager, but that red hair and those freckles blazed fiercely on. The irony wasn't lost on Fiona... fire-haired girl with the ability to make fire. The freckles on her face looked like embers in the light. And who knew...maybe the fire within her marked her outside appearance. Almost like her insides couldn't contain her condition, and it seeped out to influence her outward semblance. But for better or worse, fire was stamped in Fiona's DNA, and now she was expected to put it to use.

"Fiona," Micah called from upstairs, his voice muffled through the floorboards. "Are you ready?"

"I'm ready," she called back.

Fiona flipped off the lights and ascended the creaking basement steps. Before reaching the top landing, she realized she forgot something. Hurrying back down and into the bedroom, she grabbed the item that had remained grasped in her hand overnight, leaving an indelible imprint on her palm. The fire quartz. She placed it on her desk when she went to shower. Fiona wasn't sure why, but she felt as though she needed its cool company on the journey to DC. A talisman. Maybe it would ease that self doubt and bolster her belief in herself. Pocketing the item, Fiona left the bedroom again and with a renewed sense of confidence, headed up the stairs a second time.

Chapter Thirty-Five

The drive to DC was much shorter than expected. Driving through the night meant reduced traffic and Micah took liberties with the speed limit when he deemed it safe enough. While there was some idle chit-chat, most of the ride was quiet. Soft acoustic music emanated from the speakers; at one point Fiona remembered hearing Kurt Cobain's gravely voice singing a melodic rendition of "Where Did You Sleep Last Night" from the the MTV Unplugged album, and she drifted in and out of slumber while the highway unspooled beneath them.

She opened her eyes in time to watch the sun rise over the Washington Monument. The long, pencil-like structure seemed to scrape against the bruised hue of the sky as morning bloomed, warm and bright, over Washington DC. It's impossible to visit this area and not feel in awe of the nation's capital. The White House, with its double line of windows set off by four ridged columns in the midst of the emerald expanse of the great lawn is a noble site, and Fiona remembered a time so many years ago–another lifetime ago–when she toured the structure on a school field trip in 8th grade. But now, in the still silence of 5am, the area bespoke a stately majesty as it welcomed in the dawn of another day. But it wasn't just another day for Fiona. Soon the cerulean sky would be tinged gray and the faint scent of honeysuckle in the air would be shrouded in smoke. And, it would be Fiona's doing–her mark on this serene cityscape.

The two drove on in silence down Pennsylvania Avenue; Micah pointed out the Treasury Building and Ford's Theatre. Fiona almost wished he hadn't drawn her attention to these historical relics. Their presence made the knowledge of their goal here much more ominous, much more sinister. She sent up a silent prayer of thanksgiving to whoever was up there listening that her mission was not to destroy one of these landmarks; she didn't know if she could have set aflame a place with such meaning held within its stony walls. But did the National Planned Parenthood Clinic, with its 5 million dollars worth of upgrades and technology, hold any less gravity than The Pentagon or Freedom Plaza? Fiona had to tell herself that it did.

They turned left on 18th street and pulled directly into the parking lot she had sat in for all those hours with Rhea, studying the floor plans and maps–all for this very moment. There were no other cars in the narrow, lined spaces around them; the clinic wasn't scheduled to open for another 4 hours or so and the tick of the cooling engine and the sound of the gulls in the distance brought a sense of calm that contrasted with the pounding she felt in her chest.

Micah studied Fiona for a moment and then asked, "You ready?"

Fiona turned in her seat and faced him. She allowed herself to openly drink in his face–the dark stubble on his angled jawline, his thick brows and lashes lining his deep mahogany eyes that gave so little of himself away, the sliver of chest that poked out above his t-shirt. Questions ricocheted off Fiona's brain, *Am I ready? Can I do this? What about those women?* Was there really a question as to what her response was expected to be? The goal was clear. She had a role to play. This is what she signed up for when she made her choice in that field all those months ago. After the tragedy that she tried so hard to forget. It chased after her unfailingly, like a shadow. Was it only months ago that her life had imploded? Or was it a lifetime ago? She hadn't known it then, shivering in shock on the crab grass beneath her, watching the smoky tendrils curl up in the distance, but she was complicit. And Fiona came to learn that in her current situation, complicity was as good as a binding contract.

"Yes," she answered, with an effort to keep the quaver out of her voice. "I'm ready."

"Let's go then," Micah responded. "We have to be in and out. Spence has virtually disabled the security features, but we still only have a small window."

In response, Fiona unfastened her seatbelt and stepped out of the car. No use delaying the inevitable. With Micah following a few feet behind her, she positioned herself so she had a direct view of the entire structure. The gleaming glass windows, the main walkway lined by cherry-blossoms that already experienced their run for the season, the fringe of shrubbery obscuring the base of the complex, the cement facade so meticulously crafted, the peaked Straub Center that housed all that high-tech medical equipment to help those women who sought refuge and aid within its walls. It didn't matter that Fiona didn't fundamentally agree with what they were about to do...what *she* was about to do. When she first learned about this job, she rationalized her role in it all by telling herself that she could control the situation enough to protect any innocents from harm's way. She told herself the same thing as she stood there in front of the structure, about to set it aflame. She inhaled a breath so deep it burned the base of her throat. Then she let that breath go. Micah didn't say a word as her eyes traced over the edges of the building; he didn't know that in her heart, Fiona uttered a brief apology for what she was about to do.

Pulling the fire quartz out of her back pocket and clutching it tightly inside her sweaty palm, Fiona closed her eyes as the tepid breeze ruffled her hair around her face. She concentrated just like she did in the Bradley Job, just like she practiced the past weeks. She tried to force her flame to life. But nothing happened. Nothing at all. Her heart rapid-fired in her chest and her breaths became shallow and raged. *Come on*, she said to herself as sweat gathered at her temples. *Light. Spark.* Nothing. What would it mean if she couldn't perform? What would the rest of her life entail if she was ejected from this one group of people who wanted her? The what-ifs became a swarm of maggots teeming over her brain.

"Work, Goddammit," the words were stiff though her lips as her frustration began to boil over.

But still, nothing. She opened her eyes and glanced back at Micah, who stood silently a few feet behind her. He was calm as ever, but when she caught his eyes, she could tell he saw the turmoil about to explode from within her.

Fiona spoke again, "I can't do it." Her voice trembled with anxiety. "It's like I'm broken or something. I can't make a spark."

Micah stepped towards her and instructed her, "Turn back around."

"I can't!" she screamed, her voice laced with panic. "It's broken. I'm broken."

"You're not broken," he said, never losing that composure.

"I am. Nothing I've practiced is working."

Fiona jerked away, making a beeline towards the car. She felt Micah's strong grip on her arm.

"Don't touch me," she choked as she tried to shake his fingers off her, but his grasp was like a manacle.

Micah turned her around and with his free hand, tilted her chin upwards until she was forced to lock eyes with him.

"Breathe," he instructed.

Fiona listened. In. And out. In. Out. The breath flowing in and out of her lungs steadied a bit.

Tears rolled down Fiona's cheeks as she said, "I can't. I just can't do it. You should have let me burn with the rest of them."

"You're better than that, Fiona," Micah said soothingly.

Fiona exploded, "This thing...this condition I have. It's so fucked up. Why is it that fire happens when I don't want it to, yet when I want it to come, I can't make it? What the fuck is wrong with me?"

Micah didn't miss a beat, "Nothing is wrong with you. You're amazing. Powerful. And you're better than you were. I know that you are. You know it too."

"I don't know that," she responded without emotion.

"You can do this. You did it before. You can do it again," he said.

"Yeah, but I fucked up last time. It was all luck," Fiona said.

Admitting this aloud cost Fiona a great deal, but it was time for honesty.

"You're better now," Micah said. "Stronger. I believe in you."

Fiona studied this man in front of her. His dark eyes, full lips. She could feel her very soul gripped tightly around him; God, had she ever needed someone so much?

He spoke again, "Turn around Fiona."

This time, she listened. She could sense his presence on her back, feel his breath on her neck. His cool fingers brushed the hair away from her neck as he whispered into her ear.

"Look at the building in front of you," he extended a hand over her shoulder to point. "See it. Really see it. You can do this," his voice was barely audible. "You've done it before. Think of your training. Think of your past. Visualize the fire. And then, make it happen."

Maybe it was because Micah was so calm, so firm in his belief; whatever the motive, Fiona mustered the courage to try again.

So Fiona did what Micah advised. Holding the fire quartz between her two palms at heart-center, as though she were in prayer, she thought about Nina Bradley, Rhea, Maya, Spence. She thought about the passion she felt when she was alone with

Micah. She thought about her past and the damage she caused... and the damage she almost caused. She thought about the haunted event that resulted in her being here. The emotions simmered over as tears streamed down her cheeks.

She could feel the heat generating inside of her, the crystal in her hands absorbed the warmth too. Lowering her head in reverence, she blocked out everything around her until she was engulfed in silence. Not even the early morning cicadas permeated her thoughts. She was focused. And alert.

In the corridors of her mind, Fiona walked through the front entryway and into the bright lobby. She heard the squeak of her shoes against the polished floor. There it was–the reception desk, with all the file folders behind it...with the displays of pamphlets, glossy magazines, multi-colored flyers all containing the message to patients that *You are Not Alone*. That Planned Parenthood cares about *Your Body and Your Choices*.

Then, Fiona visualized the spark. It fluttered to life. A tiny thing, starting deep within one of the filing cabinets. It didn't need much coaxing to engage the surrounding papers. She pushed it softly with her mind towards the second cabinet, then to the mountain of paperwork and then to the room of medical records located just on the other side of the wall. Studying those floor plans helped her chart the trajectory. She dimly perceived the whoosh as the flame caught and magnified, turning the lobby into a blistering inferno. The new paint curling off the walls resembled the trunk of the Shagbark Hickory tree that grew in Fiona's very own childhood backyard. On a controlled course, the flames spread through the narrow throats of the hallways, into the expertly-designed patient rooms–consuming the flimsy rolls of medical paper that the nurses used to line the exam tables. The windowless sonogram rooms came next, the machines with all their knobs and buttons and the accompanying monitors melting from the relentless beating heat. Fiona had a dim sense of her physical body–standing outside the building–and she could feel that heat in her cheeks too, flushed and sweaty from the searing temperature radiating outward from deep inside her.

When the fire reached the central area containing the corporate offices, Fiona guided its path up into the second floor, which held spare equipment and closets upon closets of medical supplies. All of it burned easily, fully: complete and total destruction. At its peak, it was almost blinding in its brightness. Whiter than White. Beautiful in its brilliance–its molten fluorescence dancing in the still silence of the early morning. Only when nothing except the first-floor row of offices remained, when the walls, and the plaster crumbled from the blaze leaving only the steel skeletal remains of what once was the premier outpost of Planned Parenthood in this great Nation, did Fiona begin to quell the flames. Placing a mental blanket over the last few flashes of orange and yellow and red flickering from deep within the ashes, she brought the fire to a close. There were a few remaining groans and pops as the crackling flames quieted to smoldering ashes. It had been sated. Fiona's job was complete.

She opened her eyes to Micah's firm touch on her shoulder, shaking her out of her trance. Before they could utter a word to one another, the sound of sirens in the distance set Micah and Fiona's legs moving and they raced back to the waiting car. Fiona hadn't even fastened her seatbelt, and Micah already maneuvered his Range Rover out of the parking lot and back onto Pennsylvania Avenue. A line of fire engines passed them going towards the scene, their flashing lights searing into Fiona's brain sending reflections dancing on the insides of her eyelids, the siren wails piercing her eardrums with their shrill cry. Fiona cried too, but only a little. Maybe they were tears of relief, maybe tears of guilt. She couldn't properly label the feelings colliding against one another, emotions like turbulent waves crashing through her mind in relentless, rhythmic beats.

Once the two arsonists were on the highway, Fiona's heart finally began to slow and Micah spoke for the first time.

"You did well," he said, the hint of a smile playing on the corners of his lips.

"How long were we in front of that building?" Fiona asked, still a bit dazed.

She completely lost track of time as she visualized the flames spreading out from the lobby, the way veins carry blood away from the heart.

"Less than 25 minutes," Micah answered.

"Less than 25 minutes," Fiona repeated with incredulity. "I did all of that, in less than 25 minutes?"

"You did, Fiona. Well done. After your initial issues, you were efficient and controlled. Traceless. I bet next time you could even beat that time."

Next time, Fiona thought to herself. She had no idea what Kaleb had in store for them in the future, but she couldn't focus on that now. She needed to process what she just accomplished. After the Bradley Job, Fiona was horrified when Micah mentioned the notion that she felt proud about it. Then, Fiona denied those feelings of triumph. But now, sitting in Micah's cool car, seeing the plumes of smoke swirling up into the morning sky through the rearview window, she couldn't ignore the pride swelling within her. It was there, raw and unadulterated. A raven among doves in her subconsciousness. Fiona couldn't deny it. And if she couldn't deny it, what other choice did she have but to embrace it? She succeeded. Was it perfect? No. The ignition phase was hard...really hard. Controlling her emotions was even harder; she would need more work. But she had made major progress since last time.

Maybe this life with Micah and Rhea and Spence and Maya wasn't the life that she would have chosen for herself. But now that she had cemented her path, it was the only life available. Sometimes, you don't choose your course, it chooses you.

Looking down, Fiona realized she was still gripping the jagged stone. The fire quartz. With an effort, she unraveled her fingers and stared down at the object that lay glittering against her skin. It was only when she secured it firmly in her front pocket that she noticed it left an imprint on her pale flesh. The skin directly in the center of her open hand was bright pink, and there was a tiny blister bubbling up from the life-line running down the center of her palm. When she scraped at the blemish with a chipped fingernail, the sore opened and a small stream of water trickled down towards her wrist. Wiping the liquid on her lap, Fiona continued to stare out the window as morning raged brighter over Washington.

Chapter Thirty-Six

Micah and Fiona drove through the day and got back to Plattsburgh at about 5pm. The traffic was much worse on the way home than it had been on the way to DC., and aside from a few quick stops to use the bathroom or to pick up some snacks at a highway rest stop, Micah insisted that they keep on driving.

"We need distance," he kept saying. "Each passing mile makes us that much more protected."

Fiona should have been exhausted. She used her condition with much more intensity and focus than ever before, but she didn't feel sleepy in the least. She felt wired, alive—her nerves smoldered and sizzled, like embers.

"Why didn't Kaleb want those offices to burn?" she asked, unable to restrain her curiosity. "He must want to make a statement. It won't look very good for those administrators of Planned Parenthood when the public gets wind of the fact that the entire clinic is gone except for those offices. They might even look like they are the ones responsib—"

Micah cut her off, "Look Fiona. You're wading into confidential territory here. Yes, you were successful. I mean, you need to really hunker down and work more on the ignition phase, and controlling your emotions. But, you pulled off a job that would have taken all four of us to complete single-handedly, and without leaving so much as a matchstick in your wake, but as to the whys and hows, that's simply not for you to know."

"I know my role here Micah," Fiona replied, annoyed by his lack of enthusiasm. "And Spence lectured me about just closing my mouth and accepting my paycheck, but I just can't help wondering about the meaning behind it all."

"Wondering will only lead you to more questions," Micah replied. "And the last thing you should be doing is asking questions. That is and always has been your position here," he responded coldly.

And even though Fiona still had a million more questions swarming around in her mind, she knew that uttering them aloud would get her nowhere. Micah was a locked box when it came to this topic. When it came to anything, really. So instead, Fiona stopped asking. Taking Micah's advice, and Spence's advice, and Rhea and Maya's advice, Fiona swallowed her raging curiosity.

The only other question she asked Micah on the drive home was, "So. How much do I get paid for this?"

"Now that's the right question," Micah replied. "Your cut is 75k. Cash."

The number was shocking. Staggering. Fiona expected the price to be high, but $75,000 was *really* high. Again, Fiona wondered who this Kaleb was that he could afford to pay out such a hefty sum. But that again, remained an unasked question; it was above her pay-grade.

When they walked through the front door of their Plattsburgh headquarters turned home, Fiona was greeted with a small round of applause. Spence stood on one of the kitchen chairs pounding his hands together enthusiastically, glasses gleaming in the kitchen light, while Rhea and Maya stood next to one another wearing matching smiles on their faces. Rhea even put down her cigarette to come greet Fiona with a squeeze on the forearm.

"Great job, Fiona," Rhea said, those hazel eyes peering into Fiona's soul. "It's been all over the news. You nailed it."

Fiona smiled. She was never one to relish in the compliments of others. Accepting accolades always felt awkward to her—and to be applauded for the deed of destruction made it more strange. But for some reason, with these people, she didn't feel self-conscious—and could actually feel herself beaming in their presence.

"*We* did it," Fiona replied, not because she was trying to exude humility, but because it was the truth.

Without Rhea, Maya, Spence, and yes without Micah too, she would not have been able to pull this off. They were a team, each with a role to play.

"Let's see the reports," Micah cut in, always pragmatic.

Spence hopped off the chair and typed maniacally into his keyboard for a few moments. He turned the screen around so they could all absorb the newsreel.

A harried CNN anchorman wearing a white-collored shirt with the buttons mis-aligned spoke into a microphone.

Early this morning, the recently renovated Planned Parenthood in the DC metro area was consumed in flames. Authorities believe that the blaze originated in the state-of-the-art Straub Center, built with the generous donation of philanthropist Joseph C. Straub. Since construction ended earlier this year, the clinic has helped over 20,000 women explore pregnancy options and family planning with the safety and security of leading medical experts. As you can see, ruins *is the only word that can be used to describe the scene behind me.*

The camera panned out to provide a display of the collapsed facility. The destruction appeared even more complete as Fiona watched it from all those miles away on the screen of Spence's laptop, and for a moment she couldn't comprehend that she had been the one responsible for the charred boards and debris piled in a gigantic heap on the concrete, like an anthill for mutant insects.

Investigators are still trying to discover the cause of the fire, but with so little of the structure remaining, I'm not sure they will be able to fully distinguish the source. Some speculate that this was intended as a political message, considering the Central Wing of the building—the section housing Planned Parenthood's corporate offices—remains completely in-tact.

CNN presented aerial drone footage. The Central Wing, with its unmarred white exterior, stood in stark contrast to the rest of the building. The row of pristine offices, with their dazzling floor-to-ceiling windows, glistened like a diamond in the blazing July sun and stood in antithesis against the blackened, charred wreckage surrounding it on all sides.

It appears unusual that the fire would have completely consumed every other area of the structure leaving those offices untouched, but authorities have refused to comment upon this anomaly. Hopefully we will learn more as the story develops.

In response to the anchorman's report, Fiona thought, *Fat chance of that. We were traceless.* Again, that word...traceless. Micah's word. The news reporter continued:

The one silver lining is the fire began and ended hours before the clinic opened, and aside from one woman currently being treated for respiratory damage, who prefers to remain anonymous, no significant injuries were sustained.

"Wait, pause that," Fiona interrupted. "I didn't see anyone there. Who's the woman?"

Maya reported, "Apparently some woman was waiting by a back entrance somewhere. She was sleeping in the vestibule. Some homeless lady, waiting for the clinic to open. I have sources in the George Washington University Hospital. She's going to be fine. She'll just have to find somewhere else to give her that abortion."

Micah must have seen the worry lining Fiona's features or heard the near-panic in her voice, "See." He turned to her, "No one got hurt."

"I had no idea that anyone was even there. I should've sensed it. Someone was almost hurt," Fiona corrected.

"*Almost* doesn't count. Don't let this temper the fact that you were successful. Extremely successful," Micah said.

He was right. Fiona remembered the anchorman said "silver lining...no sustained injuries." The anxiety faded as Spence pressed the 'play' button allowing everyone to view the remainder of the broadcast. Five sets of eyes greedily drank up the footage before them. The more Fiona studied the video images, the more she heard the man on the screen report about the lack of any evidence pointing the police in their direction, the more confident, the more successful, the more competent she began to feel. Elation swelled up inside of her like a balloon, rising to the edges of her being, pulsing softly throughout her core. Fiona's skin buzzed with it. And for the first time since she arrived, she looked forward to what would come next. She looked forward to the next mission.

Chapter Thirty-Seven

S wathed in the muted glow cast from the sparkling light fixtures, Fiona sat at a small corner table with Maya, Rhea, and Spence at Bouillon Bilk, one of the swankiest restaurants in Montreal. Her crushed velvet dress felt cool against her legs and the skin on her exposed shoulders and arms prickled in gooseflesh. Micah declined this celebratory dinner claiming that he had work to do, but Fiona suspected the real reason for his absence was the stolid vigilance he demanded of himself.

Maya suggested the idea a few days ago, after the group's most recent success–a celebration of sorts. This restaurant, this city–it was the only acceptable location for the group to cut loose–according to Micah that was. They had secure Canadian identities, and Micah had "people" in and around the city that he trusted. Fiona imagined that Micah understood the need of his employees for an outlet at times, so he allowed for it in a way that gave him the needed control–and protected their anonymity.

"Come on, Micah," Spence had teased. "You can take a night off, you know. Live a little."

"You guys go," he replied. "I have some documents to review."

Maya pushed, "We deserve to celebrate all our successes. We've been killing it lately."

"I'm out guys. Have fun," Micah said coldly.

"You never join us when we go out. You'd have fun," Maya continued.

"I doubt that," Micah responded.

No one else had anything to say.

So, without Micah, Rhea planned a sumptuous night out in Montreal, which was about 50 minutes away from Plattsburgh over the Canadian border: dinner at Bouillon Bilk, followed by some live music and dancing at Club Soda, then a luxurious night's stay at The Ritz. This was always the routine for the group, it had to be—Micah insisted that they never deviate from what was safe and acceptable—but it was Fiona's first time.

The Cabernet was rich and flavorful on Fiona's tongue—a far cry from the boxed wine she used to drink in her tiny Manhattan apartment—and the glass felt so thin between her teeth that she thought she could bite out a neat slice if she just closed her lips a bit. The only thing preventing Fiona from downing the glass completely was the opulence of their surroundings. Classy ladies didn't chug their $50 glasses of wine. They sipped them. It was hard for Fiona to believe she was really here, and her mind drifted as Rhea, Maya, and Spence's casual conversation hovered amongst the delicate clinking of silver against China in the hushed reverence of the place.

It had been eight months since the Planned Parenthood job. And over the course of those eight months, their little group of arsonists performed three more jobs for Kaleb. They all started to blend into one another and it became difficult for Fiona to distinguish between them. After Planned Parenthood, there was a state-of-the-art urbanized vertical farm located outside of Chicago, and then a high-rise building containing a bunch of corporate offices for some organization in Albany Fiona never heard of, then some tiny nondescript home about which they received absolutely no information in terms of the occupant. She stopped trying to find out about Micah and Kaleb, even though the tiny article she found still rolled around in her mind sometimes; instead, she just accepted her role. She found a place where she belonged; that was enough.

The three jobs totaled a salary of over 200 thousand dollars—so much money without much use. Fiona planned to gift a hefty portion of this to her mom and brother, but hadn't yet discovered how to do so anonymously. She promised herself she would continue to investigate this matter further over the following weeks. Providing some financial relief to her family could possibly ease some of the guilt gnawing away at her whenever her mind drifted far enough into the past to allow it.

And aside from her growing finances, with each one of those jobs, with each success, Fiona gained more mastery over her condition. More confidence. She didn't need to work with Rhea anymore on the visualization techniques, nor with Maya on relaxation strategies; she internalized them. They became a part of her, woven into the very tapestry of her DNA as a result of repetitive practice and complete dedication. She threw herself into this new role with fervor and enthusiasm, much the same way she had thrown herself into establishing a design career in what was now thought of as a former life.

The flickering candle inside of Fiona remained subdued unless she needed it to flare. And more importantly, she was able to remain true to that promise, her vow, of keeping innocents safe from her flame. Yes, it was a close call with the Planned Parenthood job, but since then, Fiona took immense pride in the fact that she hadn't singed a hair on another human's head. This knowledge alone allowed that awful tragedy, which caused that complete upheaval in her life, to fade to the periphery. She would have been lying if she said it didn't still haunt her dreams at times—that awful work event turned massacre: the Garden City inferno she had single-handedly created. A man named Gio sprang into her mind—his soft eyes that had so deceived her. Even in this celebratory mood, that single name remained un-uttered on her tongue. If she let it, the thought could overtake her. But, she got better at pushing the ugliness aside. And for the most part, she moved on.

It was harder to suppress the sorrow she felt over abandoning her mother and brother. Knowing they were still living in her childhood home–or at least she assumed they were–and that contacting them would be so easy, was torturous at times. But then again, logically she knew there was no life for her there–not after what occurred all those months ago. They were better off without her. There was that mantra again. And Fiona had a new family now.

Sometimes, with her new look to protect her identity should she encounter someone from the past, Fiona didn't recognize the person gazing out from the mirror. After the Planned Parenthood job, Micah insisted that if Fiona wanted to venture out of the house, she had to alter her hair color. The red was just too vibrant, too recognizable. And even though the thought was distasteful at first, she desperately wanted more freedom. She wanted to go to the grocery store, take a walk along the sprawling lake in the next town over, hell...go to Target. So, in the small bathroom, with hands enclosed in clear plastic gloves, Fiona dyed her hair a deep brown. Dark Coffee Brown was the name of the hue on the box of Loreal gel-dye. Unlike her high school classmates, who experimented with all manner of highlights, and glazes, and tints, Fiona never colored her hair before. There was never a need nor the desire to do so. The bright copper color with flashes of lighter strawberry was Fiona's trademark, and once she finally learned to embrace it, she never would have dreamed about changing it. But now, with the darker hair, Fiona blended in, attaining the necessary anonymity. She needed to be just another face in the crowd; she needed to be Fiona Smith. The last thing anyone in this small unit needed was to stand out. And even though Fiona cried the first time she caught a glimpse of her new brunette reflection in the mirror, she understood that the change was necessary.

"Earth to Fiona," Maya called, bringing Fiona back to reality.

"Sorry," Fiona replied, taking another sip of wine to hide the flush in her cheeks.

"Are you almost ready to head out? I hope you're ready to party Fifi," Spence added.

Three pairs of eyes gazed back at her. She couldn't help but notice how Maya and Rhea acted differently around her now. Before Planned Parenthood, they never really sought out her advice, nor her company, unless they were explicitly training together. But now, they seemed to hang on Fiona's every word. And even her relationship with Spence shifted. Yes, he still treated Fiona with his friendly kindness and warmth, but he seemed a bit more reserved with her lately. A fact Fiona mourned sometimes. The whole dynamic of the group changed–shifted. Fiona attributed this change to the simple fact that she had drastically grown in importance. Instead of being Micah's little peon, with each success, she became almost his equal. Not completely equal–she didn't *yet* have any face-to-face contact with Kaleb–that was still reserved for Micah alone, but they exchanged emails through an untraceable account that Spence set up for this purpose, and Kaleb consulted with Fiona directly for matters such as location and time. Fiona had hopes of meeting him in person one day, and sharing Micah's role in a 50/50 split. Micah looked on approvingly as Fiona gained more of a voice, and even though much of what they did–what Fiona did–remained shrouded in mystery, she relished the idea that she would learn more and more as time passed. Fiona found a place in the world–a little corner in which to exist–even though she never thought she would have.

An hour later the group walked through the mirrored, prismatic entrance of Club Soda. Fiona's appearance reflected back at her a thousand times–shoulder-length dark hair in stark contrast with her pale, freckled complexion. No amount of dye or make-up could cover up that smattering of auburn markings on her face. At least she still had that.

The upward tilt of her chin bespoke a confidence she hadn't realized was there, the slant of her eyes echoed a hardness she hadn't seen before. *Who even am I?* The thought beat over and over again in time to the bass drum. With pulsing music reverberating in Fiona's ribcage and hazy darkness hanging in the air, her image in the mirror looked like a stranger as she glided into the open space trailing behind the others.

When they reached the bar, Spence turned around and thrust a triangular martini glass at her, filled with a blue cocktail that seemed electrified with an other-wordly glow.

"Thanks," Fiona screamed back at him over the drum beat blaring from the overhead speakers.

"Cheers," Maya said, clinking her glass against the other three.

"To us," Rhea followed.

Fiona downed the contents in a single gulp; she didn't think decorum was expected here. After another two cocktails, Fiona felt her body loosen. Rhea, Maya, Spence and Fiona were engulfed by the accepting crowd and her body swayed to the sounds vibrating through her ribcage.

They stumbled back to the Ritz when the sun was beginning to rise over the Saint Lawrence River. Fiona walked barefoot, holding her heels in her hand as Spence held her up with a tight, supportive arm around the waist. She couldn't remember the last time she was this drunk. On second thought, she didn't think she had ever been this drunk before. The alcohol sloshed around in her belly, and the lightness of the evening was replaced by the daunting reality of a wicked hangover. After Spence deposited Fiona in her own room and then shut the door behind him, she peeled off her dress and climbed into bed naked. Twisting herself up in the lush bedding, wishing that Micah was there with her, Fiona fell into a fitful sleep hoping the pounding inside of her aching skull and the tumbling inside her stomach would subside soon.

Chapter Thirty-Eight

Life went on. Job after job after job. Paycheck after paycheck. She learned to use her condition efficiently, and keep her emotions in check. It wasn't always perfect, but it was close. Really close. Sometimes Fiona scared herself with her skill.

Fiona's life gained a rhythm she didn't know she needed. It was because of this steadiness and structure that she stopped trying to dig for information. Digging gave her anxiety, fear, doubt. Maybe that sounded stupid and naive, but after everything she went through, Fiona wanted stability. As oxymoronic as it was, that was exactly what she found with Micah and the others. She relished in that, and tried to keep the little voice of her conscious on the back-burner as much as she could.

Three months later, Fiona found herself standing with Micah outside of yet another job. This time, the target was back in New York City, Brooklyn actually–a brand new building that was advertised as the first "completely green, eco-friendly apartment complex, an architectural feat located in the heart of Park Slope." She briefly wondered if Gary Bradley–Nina Bradley's husband and realtor extraordinaire–was involved in the property at all; she certainly wouldn't have been surprised. Even in Plattsburgh, the news channels were talking about the solar and wind technology used to power the structure along with the expansive garden lining the structure's ample roof.

The group went through all of the planning, reconnaissance, and analysis over the course of the past few weeks and this was the final phase of the job–the part where Fiona would officially step in and do what she had come to almost enjoy: burn.

It was 2 o'clock in the morning on a Sunday in early June. Despite the spring breeze, Fiona felt the fire spark from deep within her. It pulsed like a pilot light, ready to ignite and spread at her command.

"Ready?" Micah asked, his typical question.

As the jobs rolled on, less pomp and circumstance was needed. The last two jobs felt like business transactions–neat, orderly and precise.

"Yes," she responded to his question, closing her eyes and gripping onto the fire quartz that became her good luck charm since Micah first gave it to her all those months ago.

"You know," he said. "It's been about a year since I found you."

The thought hadn't escaped Fiona, but she was surprised Micah mentioned it.

"So I guess this marks my anniversary," Fiona responded with a smile tugging at her lips. "I can't think of a better way to celebrate."

She meant it too. A year of burning. And Fiona emerged from the ashes. Changed, but unharmed.

Fiona closed her eyes again, holding the stone at heart-center, her signature position. Like a yoga practitioner, she lowered her chin to her chest, getting herself mentally prepared to begin. Blocking out Micah's profile, blocking out the night stars, blocking out the faint rumble of trucks racing by on the Brooklyn Queens Expressway in the distance, she focused her energy on what she was about to do.

Mentally, Fiona entered the building. It was void of inhabitants; construction ended a month earlier and even though it was fully furnished and ready, buyers weren't permitted to move in until the 1st of next month, making tonight an opportune time to torch it to the ground. No bodies meant no one could get hurt.

Her eyes locked onto the source: the sleek, navy-blue, velvet upholstered sofa gracing the polished bamboo floors of the lobby. When she saw it on Spence's video, she knew it would be the perfect target. She could imagine the plush stuffing of the pillows smoldering easily and fully, spreading with fervor to the gold-foiled wallpaper and the chic gray valances icing the windows like a wedding cake.

Just as Fiona was about to conjure the first spark, a sharp jerk on her arm pulled her out of the trance. Opening her eyes, Fiona's gaze darted over to Micah's face, worry etched in thin frown-lines surrounding his mouth.

"What the fuck?" she blurted out, annoyed at the interruption.

"Someone's here," he whispered, and with that ominous news, nerves made Fiona's blood dance in her veins; a trickle of sweat slid down between her shoulder blades.

"What should we do?" Fiona asked, trying to keep the panic from rising, trying to subdue the heat that flared through her chest.

"Head towards the car Fiona, quickly," he instructed.

Fiona pocketed the stone and began to speak again, "But–"

Micah cut her off, "I'll meet you there in 5 minutes. I need to clear the area."

Fiona wasn't sure what he meant when he said *clear the area,* but she could only imagine what he would be compelled to do should he find the person or people that encroached on their sacred space. When it came to work, Fiona didn't put anything past Micah. No measure of ruthlessness was beyond his reach. Fiona shuddered at the thought.

The car was parked at the south end of the building and Fiona walked briskly in that direction, eyes straining against the darkness for any glimpse of Micah—or for an outsider. *Please let Micah be wrong*, Fiona thought to herself. Micah certainly could be paranoid at times. Praying this was just another example of his neurotic vigilance, Fiona's breath quickened in her throat.

Just as she spied Micah's Range Rover twinkling onyx in the distance, Fiona felt a presence behind her. Risking a glimpse over her shoulder, she perceived someone a few feet behind, and closing in quickly. Fiona couldn't make out the features, and didn't have time to try to discern the specifics. She ran. *If I can just get to the car*, Fiona thought to herself. But with each step, she felt the person behind her inching closer, gaining distance. Fiona thought about using her flame, but without any visualization or knowledge regarding logistics, her skill was inaccurate, clumsy. Relaxation was a key component to attaining that control—and a state of relaxation was far out of reach. She veered to the right, but the person behind was undeterred. There was nowhere to go, nowhere to hide.

Fiona tried to scream "Mic–," but a hand clamped around her mouth.

Cool fabric replaced the hand, blurring Fiona's vision. She could feel herself coming undone. The acrid scent of fire invaded her flared nostrils as whatever was around her head burned. Smouldering fabric, heat around her ears. When was the last time Fiona's emotions roamed so unchecked that her fire burst forth unwarranted? But then again, someone was attacking her. Fiona wouldn't have control of her condition for much longer and she feared for the destruction she knew she was capable of. Once unleashed it would consume everything. Where was Micah?

A sharp sting on Fiona's right shoulder was the last perception she felt before sinking into a pit of mind-numbing darkness. In that darkness she remembered the horror that landed her with Micah, the memory that when she had control of her facilities she could keep at bay. But when your mind is no longer your own, the thoughts flow like water over every wrinkle. And the water that trickled over Fiona's brain in that slumberless slumber was awash with the macabre hue of tragedy.

Part Three

Chapter Thirty-Nine

I promise not to scream. Fiona said the words inside her head and hoped her eyes conveyed the message. If only she could have said them out loud. Mumbling didn't work either; she tried that already. The bandana was tied so tightly around her mouth that her cheeks and lips ached from being pressed so taut. Her throat burned with thirst, and her tongue felt dry and rough—like sandpaper. Swollen and foreign it scraped the ridges on the hard palate of her mouth. Her eyes stung; probably from the tears mixing with mascara lining her lashes. She hadn't been able to wipe them for the past five hours. Not since her hands had been tied behind her back, not since her feet had been bound and tied to the metal radiator that sat on the far windowless wall in this empty room.

A year ago, those tears would have been the result of fear, of sadness—a byproduct of weakness. A year ago, Fiona was an entirely different person. Time and her experiences with Micah and the others had hardened her. But the tears that sprang forth from the corners of her eyes as she sat there restrained in the unfamiliar space—though tinged with anxiety—were a direct result of frustration, from raw desperation, and yes, from rage too. But she certainly wasn't going to explain her emotions; she thought that perhaps letting him think she was afraid would work in her favor. By this point in life, Fiona knew that women were often under-estimated.

The room was empty except for the clock, taunting from the small bit of wall above the thick-paneled wooden door. Fiona wondered if the door was locked. If she could race through it and free herself from this ridiculous predicament. Where did it even lead? All those thoughts were theoretical. She couldn't even reach her shoes, nonetheless get to that door. Not with these tethers shackling her to the floor.

The sluggishness inside her brain told her she had been drugged—unfortunately she was no stranger to that feeling. And, she was shivering. The air-conditioner must have been set to 50 degrees—maybe even lower, there was an additional free-standing unit in the far corner of the space, plunging the temperature to an even colder degree. Her teeth chattered frantically. She tried to summon some warmth from within, from buried deep in her core where the fire resided, but she couldn't do it. The drugs and frigid environment definitely didn't help things either. All her senses were dulled, numb—especially her spark.

The first three times this strange man came in, Fiona's frantic movements deterred him from removing that insufferable rag from her mouth. He didn't trust her not to scream. Fiona couldn't blame him. For a while, she wondered if he would even come back a fourth time. Or if she would be left to decompose and rot—eyes rattling around in her skull like those creaky Halloween skeletons you can buy in the pop-up stores that open at the end of September. But he did come back—just as calm as ever—regarding her with those cool, unfamiliar eyes.

So now, with *her* eyes, Fiona tried to convince him that she could be trusted to remain calm. That he should remove the rag from her mouth. As crazy as it sounded, she actually was calm. Maybe her body had simply shut down…overheated.

"If you scream, Fiona, the rag goes right back on. And you'll be left here even longer. Nod if you understand," he said.

She nodded, eyes never leaving his. They were dark. Emotionless.

"Ok. Good girl. I believe you."

That phrase *good girl* set Fiona's teeth on edge. It was so condescending, so demeaning. She clenched her jaws together to quell the anger simmering deep within. She was trying to play the damsel in distress anyway; an explosion wouldn't help the scenario. Fiona couldn't even summon a flame in this dampened state, nonetheless an explosion– something she hadn't even learned to summon on the best of days.

He reached both hands behind her head and began to undo the knot, her face pressed into his chest. He smelled earthy, masculine. He felt warm against Fiona's cold, upturned face. She didn't scream, even though she wanted to. In some ways this felt like an awful case of deja vu.

Finally, the bandana came off. She felt exposed in a way, naked. He stared at Fiona with curiosity and opened up a Poland Spring bottle. He held it to her lips and Fiona greedily slurped the tepid water, trying to will her gaze to appear soft and demure. Some of the liquid dribbled from the corners of her mouth and this man...this stranger, wiped it roughly away with the pad of his thumb. It was the first time Fiona didn't flinch when he touched her. The action felt paternal, surprising and intimate.

"Better?" he asked.

Again, Fiona nodded.

The two stared at each other for a silent moment, taking in one another's appearance. It might have seemed odd to others that Fiona had the wherewithal to analyze this man, especially considering her situation, but she had grown used to this type of thinking. Fiona was crouched awkwardly against the radiator in black leggings and a tank, he was towering over her in clunky, tan work boots, faded blue jeans and a non-descript gray hoodie. He wore a Carhartt winter cap–which would have seemed out of place this time of year had it not been for the frigid air pumping through the grates in the ceiling. Thick tawny hair poked out the sides, falling over his ears. A beard covered most of his face and Fiona couldn't make out his eye color, not from that angle anyway. He could have been 25 or 40 in the dim light of the room.

"If you think you can behave, I can take you somewhere a bit more comfortable," again, his patronizing tone grated against Fiona's sense of independence.

No matter how much she didn't want to admit it, fear ignited in her mind, churning in her stomach. She almost perceived a tiny flame kindle inside, but it winked out.

Unable to control her temper, Fiona spat out, "Who are you?" But due to the fading drugs her words came out slurred and stilted.

When he didn't respond she tried again, "What do you want with me?"

Infuriatingly, he responded, "Those are questions for another time."

In an increasingly clear voice she said, "Well, I'm not going anywhere with you. I want to go home. My boyfriend'll find me soon enough. You can't just keep me here. And, take these–whatever they are, off and let me go."

Fiona intentionally played the boyfriend card. Was he even her boyfriend? She supposed the label didn't really matter anyway. She hadn't really *needed* Micah in quite some time, not for protection anyway, she had that covered–but at that moment, it would have been nice to have some assistance.

Now that her faculties were returning, Fiona's attention went to her shoulder, where she felt a bitter sting and a throbbing; the ache was probably an indication of how the drugs–or whatever they were–entered her system. She briefly remembered getting the flu vaccine a few years ago and experiencing a similar sensation.

Wracking her brain she thought to herself, *What is the last thing I remember before sitting in this room?* Brooklyn. That apartment complex. *The first eco-friends apartment complex.* Standing with Micah. Getting ready to make it all burn. Micah...where was he? He saw someone. Someone had been following them. "Meet me at the car," he had said. But Fiona hadn't made it to the car. There was someone there. Someone waiting for them... for her. This man was there, the person that now stood before her; he knew about them, somehow. Despite how careful they had been to protect their anonymity. A dull ache. Fiona winced as she moved her arm to rub the sore spot.

Her teeth chattered? For a moment, Fiona was surprised she couldn't see her breath on the exhales. What the hell? She wasn't some pawn to be played with and controlled. Not anymore anyway. She was drugged once by Gio and look at what that led to. Even thinking about that name, Gio...that man, brought a flood of disgust up into her chest–shame too. And now it had happened again. Even though she swore to herself that she would never let anything like that happen to her...ever again. Fiona tried to summon the spark, but her mind was too muddled. And she was too damn cold. She felt useless and alone. Alone, except for this stranger standing before her. Her heat seemed just out of reach, like when she used to catch fireflies in her backyard as a child; they always slipped through her fingers, their yellow glow eluding her again and again.

Fiona thought, *If this guy just turned off the air-conditioner and the drugs wore off fully, I could help myself.* At least she thought she could. But again, if she feigned helplessness, maybe she could catch him off guard.

"Please," Fiona tried again. "Just let me go."

"Can't do that," he replied to the suggestion.

"I don't understand," she pushed.

Those angry tears threatened to overflow and Fiona had to blink them away. She was not going to allow herself to cry again in front of this psychopath–wasn't going to give him the satisfaction.

"Are you going to behave, or not?" he asked again; it was the same question he had posed the other times he tried to reason with her.

She gritted her teeth in response.

"Ok. Suit yourself," he said without emotion. "We can do this all day."

He advanced towards her with the bandana. *No*, she thought. *Please not again. I'll go crazy if he puts that thing on my face again.*

"Wait. Please just wait," Fiona managed to stutter out through tight lips.

But he didn't wait. He knelt down in front of her. His eyes were hazel. She could see them now. And was there some guilt in them? Fiona thought so. He moved to put the rag back in place.

Fiona spoke quickly–hating the desperation that hung in her voice, "Ok fine. Fine. I'll behave. Please don't tie that thing on my face again."

It cost her a great deal to use that word, *behave*, but she had to play whatever game this was. Whatever hand she had been dealt–and she *had* to keep that rag out of her mouth.

He stopped mid-motion, assessing.

"You will cooperate," he said. More of a statement this time than a question.

"Yes," Fiona whispered, she knew she had to play the game if she had any chance of getting out of here.

"I didn't hear you."

"Yes," louder this time.

"Good girl."

She flinched when he pulled the knife from his pocket, and when he saw that jerky, involuntary movement, a victorious smile crept to his mouth. *Asshole*, she said in her mind. *Is he enjoying this?* But she settled down once she realized that he wasn't going to slit her throat. If he wanted to kill her, he could have done it already–easily. He wanted something else. But what?

He sliced through the thick rope binding her hands and feet and stepped back, allowing Fiona the space to stand up on her own.

"Look," he said on an exhale. "This is me showing you that I'm trying to work with you here. I could keep you tied up, but I'm not going to do that. I'm really not a monster."

Yeah right, Fiona said to herself; this was the first time he had shown any indication of humanity. *If the shoe fits.* But she didn't allow her lips to betray those thoughts.

Her legs were shaky as she stood, so he put a steadying hand on her elbow, which she shook off once the dizziness subsided. Her Doc Martens were discarded in the far corner of the room; he went to retrieve them and then handed them over. Fiona didn't put them on, but instead held them tightly in her grasp, staring at the stranger before her, trying to puzzle out his motives.

"Can you at least tell me your name?" Fiona asked as he led her from the room.

This time he wouldn't allow her to shake off his hand gripping the upper part of her arm. It remained there, firmly in place and insistent. She supposed that he was trying to make sure she didn't try to run away. Not that she would have even known where to go. Where to run to. Her sense of direction was completely off.

"Don't worry about my name, Fiona," he responded. "There are too many other things to worry about."

That statement sent a fresh bout of chills rolling down her spine and she had to work hard to still her trembling hands. She didn't know what the hell she was in for, but she definitely didn't want to find out. At that moment, all Fiona wanted was to go home.

She thought again about Micah. Was he worried about her? Was he looking for her? Would he burst in and bring her back to the small, brick ranch in Plattsburgh that had become her home? Fiona didn't know the answers to those questions. For now, the only person she could rely upon was herself.

$$Chapter\ Forty$$

They walked through the door and into a small hallway of what looked like an apartment building. He led Fiona down a flight of stairs and stopped at another nondescript, white door...but this one had a padlock on the outside. Fiddling in his pocket, he pulled out a set of keys, opened the door and firmly nudged his captive inside. A flip of the lightswitch brought the room into focus and Fiona tried to take in her surroundings, but her captor spun her around.

Fiona tried to fight again when he grabbed her arm and pulled a syringe out of his back pocket.

"Stay still," he said.

"Don't do that. I promise I won't be a problem," Fiona pleaded. "Just let me go home."

Her protests hadn't worked. He was stronger than Fiona, bigger. The thought of being drugged...again...brought back memories of that work party with Gio. Other memories too, but those were even more painful–more tragic. Fiona swallowed those over the lump rising in her throat.

"Please," she said again as he advanced towards her. "Don't do this."

The stranger must have seen something in Fiona's gaze,

because his eyes softened a touch as he said, "This won't knock you out. It's a lower dose...to control things."

He tried to explain with a patience that was in itself jarring, but all Fiona saw was a swirling haze of fear and confusion swimming around in her skull.

"Control what?" Fiona demanded.

But he didn't answer. And there it was again–a brief sting, then the release of his gripping fist. When Fiona looked up from the tiny bead of blood that bubbled from the injection site, he was already closing the door behind him.

Sitting alone in that room for hours was torture for Fiona, mostly because her mind couldn't be distracted from thinking about her past. The incident at the Garden City Hotel rolled over and over in her brain like those television jingles that replay endlessly in one's subconscious. The facts ricocheted off her skull, washing over her like a tidal wave.

Fiona killed 12 people that day. 12. She tried to pull her eyes away from the news reports and media coverage following the *Garden City Inferno*–as the CNN news anchorman coined it–but she couldn't. She absorbed every single word until her heart bled. Kayla Fowler. Herman Goldberg. Jessica and Robert Ortiz. Bill Bloomenthal. Fernando Aquilla. Jamie Graff and her 5 year old son Joseph. Arman Singh. 13 year old twin girls Luna and Layla Richmond. A 4 month old baby named Elijah Wykowski. And finally, Fiona Blake. 12 deaths. Even though in the physical sense she was still very much a member of the living, Fiona died that day too...but in a different way than all the others. The names played like movie credits at the end of a horror tale. Fiona felt every single one of those lost lives. They were tally marks inside her head reminding her of her purpose. Never again. And despite it all, despite all of her work with Micah and his group, the work she had done for Kaleb, the things she burned...she never hurt a living soul again. Fiona made a new life for herself. Not the life she dreamed of or envisioned. But a life nonetheless. Even though she would always bear those scars of that awful event, she healed, sort of—felt accepted, wanted. Fiona had a new family to replace the one she had lost. Micah, Rhea, Spence, Maya. Did they pale in comparison? She couldn't allow herself to think that way.

Shaking her head to clear those gathering thoughts, Fiona now faced a new captor—another stranger who came into her life. Standing in this bare room, rubbing her wrists that had just been freed from their tethers, Fiona contemplated her next move. There wasn't much she could do. Fighting failed. Screaming failed. It seemed like the only thing that would get her out of this space was to play nice. So that was what she set out to do. But how could she possibly do anything when she was behind yet another locked door?

Chapter Forty-One

When it became clear that the stranger wasn't going to come back, Fiona looked around the room and took in her surroundings. There was a tiny bathroom to the right—the door had been taken off the hinges, so she could see the white walk-in shower and toilet from where she stood.

Walking over to the far wall, Fiona laid down on the twin bed that had been clearly made up for someone...probably her. *Who else has slept here?* She thought to herself. She was exhausted; all those emotions left her reeling with that awful feeling of defeat. The stranger was right about the drugs; they weren't all-consuming, but they brought on a dull lethargy...and Fiona was unable to summon her fire, which was clearly their purpose. At least she was still able to think, a concept she took for granted up until that point.

Even though the blanket beneath her was thin and the light from the fixture above dim, it was definitely an upgrade from the radiator room. The walls were still bare and white, but there was a navy blue throw rug on the ground and a dresser in the corner. As Fiona got up to explore, she saw that there was a variety of clothing held in the drawers, all about her size. The oddness of this was striking—was it a coincidence her captors knew her approximate pants size?–but at the moment she didn't complain. It felt good to change out of her old clothes and feel the warmth of the jeans and baggy t-shirt enveloping her body. Even though it was June outside, it felt like winter here. Fiona was sure that the temperature was purposeful. The air-conditioner blew out frigid air that smelled slightly stale and there were no windows; the low ceiling felt almost like the basement in Fiona's uncle's house.

Nerves humming beneath her skin, Fiona knew she needed to do something. It had been hours since this stranger left, promising to come back around dinner-time with some food, and time felt slippery here. With a growling stomach, Fiona walked over to a large bookshelf against the far wall. *How nice,* she thought sarcastically in her head. *They at least left me with something to do to occupy the time.* The shelves were filled with titles: there was *The Great Gatsby,* and *Tale of Two Cities* along with three other Dickens' stories. *Outliers* by Malcom Gladwell, *Gone Girl, 50 Shades of Grey,* and probably about 100 other titles, some of which Fiona knew and others she didn't. Certainly something for all types of readers. Despite it all, Fiona laughed when her fingers grazed over *Wine Tasting for Dummies.* Such an odd collection. She wondered where all of the books came from. Continuing to scan the titles, her eyes were drawn to a worn paperback copy of Stephen King's *Firestarter.* She pulled it off the shelf and admired the cover–the silhouette of a woman outlined in fire.

She read *Firestarter* when she was in 6th grade. The spine stood out to Fiona as she ran her fingers against the books snuggled up next to one another in their vinyl jackets on one of the Fiction shelves in the public library. She couldn't have said she was looking for it specifically; she vaguely remembered watching a scene from the movie when she was much younger. Snuggled up to her father, one scene stuck out to Fiona's childhood eyes: the scene where a young version of Drew Berrymore stood outside, her hands outstretched in some field with a fire raging behind her, a scream ripping from her open mouth. But in the library that day, the book caught Fiona's attention nonetheless.

Instead of bringing it up to the circulation desk for check-out, Fiona shoved it in her knapsack and walked out of the library. She wasn't sure exactly what sparked this embarrassment–there was nothing overtly shameful about expressing a desire to read a best-seller. Maybe the title reminded her of her dad, and his leaving did feel somewhat shameful sometimes, as though she and the rest of her family were somehow not good enough, that they were defec-tive in some way. Or, maybe Fiona just didn't want the questions, or the stares, or the librarian's recommendations for what she believed to be a more suitable read for an 11-year-old girl. At the time, whatever the reason was, Fiona felt that the matter was a personal one, and she should keep her reading interest to herself.

It took Fiona four days to read that book; it was harder than she thought it would be and she had to pause to look up some of the longer words in the dictionary in order to fully comprehend some of the sentences. But Fiona remembered breathing a sigh of relief when she finally flipped to the last page and read the last words. She wasn't like Charlie at all, not really. Or at least that was what she told herself at the time. Charlie was explosive. Scary. A liability. Fiona was just...herself. Just Fiona. An 11-year old, 6th grader at boring old Nassau Elementary School. Sure, she could *do* things–make things happen. But she wasn't involved in some government conspiracy or crime ring. The thought had given her comfort at the time. Solace.

But now, she *was* involved in...something. That anger and fear welled back up inside of Fiona threatening to drown out any rational thought and consume everything. Even though her captor injected her with an additional dose of some drug–prob-ably a lesser version of the one that got her here in the first place–the dullness and haze were less pressing and her thoughts were clearer. But there wasn't a damn thing she could do about it. She already pounded on the door, screamed at the top of her voice. The only thing those attempts succeeded in doing was getting her a harsh reprimand from the other side of the door. "If you don't cut it out, I'll knock you out again and put you back in the other room," a loud voice shouted. Fiona didn't want that to happen. So she quieted down.

Taking *Firestarter* back to the bed, Fiona laid down, trying to lose herself in the story and not see the awful parallels that played out in the back of her conscious mind.

Chapter Forty-Two

The clock on the wall told Fiona that three hours passed before she heard a light knock on the door.

"Come in," Fiona said, feeling foolish.

The stranger clearly did not need her permission to enter, it was strange he even bothered to knock. Fiona stood up; for some reason she didn't want to be seen lying down on the bed. She felt as though she needed to be on guard.

The stranger entered carrying a brown paper bag which he placed down on the small table next to the door.

"What's in the bag?" Fiona asked, noticing all of a sudden she was hungry. Gurgling sounds issued from her stomach, and she felt almost embarrassed that this stranger could hear them.

"A sandwich, drink, and a bag of chips," he answered matter-of-factly.

"Thanks," Fiona said, still rooted to the floor in her bare-feet.

"I guess the clothes fit ok?" he asked.

"They do," she responded, itching to ransack the contents of her meal.

The two looked at one another in silence. He still wore the winter cap, but he had changed out of the clothes he was in earlier and was instead wearing a faded green Champion sweatshirt and gray sweatpants. His eyes were softer somehow and he gazed at Fiona with open curiosity. She wondered what he saw. A skinny girl with dark hair in clothes that were not her own. Did he see the trepidation? The latent fear?

His eyes flicked towards the bed, where *Firestarter* was lying open and face down on page 215.

With a brief nod in that direction he said, "Interesting reading choice."

Fiona perceived a slight smirk on his lips and she could feel her face redden under his scrutiny. She didn't respond to his statement.

Instead she asked, "Where am I?"

Surprisingly, he answered, "In our headquarters about an hour north of New York City."

"That's pretty vague," Fiona responded. "In what town? Who is *our*? Are there others here? How did I get here? Last time I checked, I was in Brooklyn."

"Lots of questions," he observed.

"Umm...yeah. When you wake up to find yourself tied to a radiator in a freezing cold room, you can get pretty confused," Fiona shot back sarcastically.

"Hopefully we can turn down the air-conditioner once we have your full cooperation," he said.

"I'll never cooperate with you."

"Then you'll be pretty cold."

Fiona snapped her mouth shut before speaking again.

After a beat, she asked, "Well what about my other questions?"

"You mean about who *we* are and how you got here?"

Jeez this guy is infuriating, she thought to herself.

"Yes," she answered, trying to subdue the rising frustration, the urge to burn this guy to the ground...if only she could.

"Well," he began. "I injected you with a light tranquilizer and put you in my car and drove you here."

The way he explained himself, with such calmness...documenting how he took someone against her will, with such calculated coolness, it made Fiona's temper flare even higher.

"Light tranquilizer?" she responded. "It knocked me out for hours."

"Had to be done," he said casually.

He was so different from Micah in every way. Even the lightheartedness in his tone when talking stood in stark contrast to what Fiona had become used to.

"Ok," Fiona said. "Why did you take me? And who are you?"

"I'm Adam," he answered, simply. He extended his hand. When Fiona refused to shake it he retracted it, putting his hands in his front pocket.

He looked like an Adam. Soft brown hair, fair complexion, light eyes that changed colors...gray, to hazel, to brown.

"Well Adam," Fiona said over gritted teeth. "Can I get more detail? Why did you inject me with drugs–"

"Tranquilizer," he corrected. *Was he enjoying this?*

Fiona started again, "Why did you inject me with a *tranquilizer* and bring me here?"

"I,–along with my group–have a problem with what you've been doing. And we decided to stop you," he answered levelly.

"You have a problem with what *I'm* doing," Fiona repeated. "How the hell do you even know what I'm doing? How the hell do you even know about me?"

"I've known about you for a while, Fiona," he said.

The statement was scarily reminiscent of what Micah had said in that field near the Garden City Hotel. How was it possible that this was happening again?

"How?" she asked.

"Well. I, we... have been following your path of destruction. We don't like it. We don't like Micah or Kaleb. What they are doing is criminal and interrupts the natural course of the way things should be. We want you to join us and stop them," Adam concluded.

His answer reverberated through her mind as question upon question floated to the surface of her consciousness. How did this guy–Adam–know about Micah? ...or Kaleb for that matter? Micah was always so careful. So serious. So focused on anonymity. On being traceless.

"Why do you care about 'the natural course of the way things should be'? Why don't you just mind your own business?" Fiona responded bitterly.

"Because it *is* my business. It's everyone's business. How much do you know about what you've been doing?" he asked.

Did he sense Fiona's reserve before she answered? She hoped not. This guy was starting to grate on her last nerve.

"I know enough," Fiona said with feigned confidence.

"Then I guess you're ok with tampering with the democratic process. With forcing one's selfish political campaign upon the unsuspecting public?" he pushed.

Fiona didn't answer, just stared at her feet going cold and clammy beneath her.

When she didn't speak, Adam said, "I bet you have no idea what kind of people you fell in with Fiona. And I think that once you know, you'll feel differently."

Fiona changed tactics, "You can't just steal someone. I'm a person. You can't just shoot me with dru–I mean tranquilizers, and expect me to be ok with it."

"I saw what you did on Long Island," he said.

Fiona's breath stopped.

He continued, "I was there at that party."

The revelation struck Fiona with the force of a freight train and she just stood there, unable to respond. That familiar shame crept back in.

Finally she sputtered out barely above a whisper, "Why were you there?"

He and Micah. Both there? How was this possible? She could feel the tears hovering in her eyes. She dared them to fall.

"It was by chance. My best friend was getting married that weekend and we also happened to be staying at the Garden City Hotel that night. I made a wrong turn and opened the doors of the cocktail room right as your boss was making that toast. I saw you. Your red hair stood out like a flame. I read the sign on the door that said, "Celebration for Fiona Blake/ Ferranti Design Co." I knew that you were Fiona Blake. I remember thinking you were pretty and that you looked happy."

Hearing this story from Adam's perspective made Fiona feel like she was living in the Twilight Zone.

She was silent as he continued, "I was there for the fire too. The would-be-groom died that night. He splurged on one of the suites...probably just a few doors down from yours. I was lucky enough to escape with only this scar."

He rolled up the left sleeve of his sweatshirt to reveal a bumpy, pink patch of skin that marred his inner forearm.

Seeing the burn, seeing the deformed section of skin on his arm was almost too much to take. Fiona had come so far to get past that awful night. To move on. Now, here it was staring her in the face.

"Arman Singh," she said, the name slipping out between her tight lips.

She read all about Arman in the gushing obituary written about him in the *New York Times*. She had hidden the publication under her pillow so Micah wouldn't know she had it; he hadn't approved of her obsessive need to learn all the details about her victims–he didn't think it was healthy, and he was probably right. But she *had* read about all of them...every single one. Including herself. It didn't take long for her to scour her still-fuzzy memory to find all that information she had tried to bury about Arman Singh. Born and raised in Queens. Graduate of George Washington University. Aspiring thoracic surgeon, working towards his degree in medicine at the University of Chicago. Scheduled to be married to Farah Narjawa in the ballroom of the Garden City Hotel. Too bad for him that Fiona had been there also. That she stole what would have undoubtedly been his happily-ever-after. Fiona wanted to ask Adam how he had known Arman, but she stifled her curiosity. It didn't matter now...nothing did. Instead she remained silent, waiting for the rest of Adam's tale about that fateful night all those lifetimes ago.

Adam continued, "I was standing outside the hotel, pacing, waiting for my friends to come out–hoping they would. I saw Micah carry you out of the building. I saw your red hair. In some part of my brain I knew that you were Fiona Blake. It was hard to process, but I knew you didn't die. I remember feeling relieved that you survived."

"What are you trying to say?" Fiona yelled back at him, her emotions morphing into rage as the defense mechanism kicked in.

"I knew you escaped. So when I saw in the papers that you were one of the victims, that you had died, when I saw the information about your funeral...I was confused. I followed the story... felt like I had to. I guess my mind latched onto you while I was dealing with the loss of my friend. I don't know. But, I went to your funeral, Fiona–"

"Stop. Please," Fiona begged, no longer able to harness the emotions.

"I sat 6 rows behind your mom and bro–"

"Stop talking! Just stop!" she begged, feeling as though she would rip in half if he didn't.

She wanted so badly to ask about her mother and brother. How they seemed. What their reactions were. But she couldn't ask those questions. She had the image built up in her mind; hearing the truth would just break her further.

Despite Fiona's pleas, Adam didn't stop. "There wasn't a body to bury. Each victim's family was given a small urn of ashes. Did you know that? They divided up the remains of that fire among the 12 families–to give them something tangible to hold and mourn over."

She did know that. She had read about it when she first came to Plattsburgh. Fiona could barely breathe listening to Adam recount the sordid truth of the situation.

"Please stop," she said, almost breathless.

Adam changed tactics a bit and spared her the rest of the gory details, "After that, I continued to follow you. Maybe it was grief. Maybe it was curiosity. I'm not sure what it was. It seemed as though I was the only person who knew the truth. It wasn't until much later that I knew what you could do. That I knew what you were capable of."

Fiona sank to the floor as that reservoir of tears burst open. The worst moments of her life, the ones she thought she alone kept locked in the subconsciousness of her frantic brain...there was someone else who knew. Someone besides Micah. Someone else who witnessed it all. The shame, anger, and crushing depression rushed back tenfold.

He forged on, "I was there in Tribeca, I was there at Planned Parenthood...I was there at the others too."

"Why didn't you turn me in? Why didn't you reveal who I am?" Fiona asked.

"For a while I wanted to. But you fascinated me. The fire you learned to control. For some time, I hated you for taking away my friend. But as I watched you, I came to realize you're not a monster, Fiona. You didn't intentionally hurt those people. Micah took you and manipulated you after a traumatic experience–"

Two men who had known about Fiona long before they entered into her life. Micah who had known about Fiona in her past life somehow–the details on that were still hazy. And Adam who had learned about Fiona as her old life burned to the ground.

"Micah gave me a new life," Fiona responded, repeating those very words he had said to her as she sat there, crumbling in that grassy field.

"He gave you the wrong life," Adam said back without missing a beat. "I'm going to help you find the right one."

Before Fiona could answer, Adam backed out of the room.

She could hear the lock on the outside of the door engage. She didn't know how long she remained there, heaped on the floor. She didn't look once at the clock. All she saw was her own past playing like a movie on the inside of her eyelids, and the news photo of Arman Singh as he smiled unabashedly back at the camera, as she sank once more into a fitful slumber.

Chapter Forty-Three

"I'm sorry for your friend," Fiona said when Adam came back into the room.

The clock on the wall read 7:10...and Fiona was pretty sure it was 7:10 in the morning. It was hard to tell when there were no windows or natural light in this room, and her sleep pattern had been erratic. She opened her eyes an hour prior and remembered the brown bag left on the table. She gobbled down the turkey and cheese sandwich in record time and washed it down with the Peach Snapple that, due to the temperature of the room, remained pretty cold. She hadn't eaten the bag of Lay's potato chips; for some reason she thought she should save those in case Adam never returned and she was left to starve in this room. Maybe this was all a ruse to punish her for the death of Arman Singh. Maybe she deserved it. In any case, the small bag of chips wouldn't do much in that scenario, but something was better than nothing. .

"I appreciate the apology," he said. "But it's unnecessary."

Fiona felt like she had to explain, "I was almost raped by some guy who roofied my drink. His name was Gio–if that was even his real name. And I guess I couldn't control my emotions. When I woke up from the drugs, everything was on fire."

"I figured it was something like that," he responded. "I didn't think you just started that fire for no reason. I'm sorry that happened to you."

"Thanks," Fiona mumbled back.

"I don't want to have to drug you again," he said. "But I need to know that you won't use your fire against me."

"I won't," Fiona lied.

The second she felt like herself again, she planned to torch this place to the ground. Adam didn't seem so bad, but she was not going to be held here against her will. She wanted to get back to Micah. Thinking about him made the yearning even more intense. He had been Fiona's safety net, her security...she didn't know how to function without him.

"Unfortunately, I don't believe you," Adam responded.

Adam extended his palm to Fiona. In the center was a small white pill.

"I am not taking that," Fiona said.

"We can do this one of two ways," he explained patiently. "You can take this pill. Or I will inject you again. This pill is much milder and should allow you to function relatively normally. The injection...not so much."

Fiona didn't doubt his ability to hold her down and stick her with another needle. He was bigger and stronger. And if what he said was true, which she thought it was, as she still felt the effects of the injection–even after all those hours had passed–she needed her faculties to figure out how to escape. It sounded like the pill was the best option–one of the few choices she was actually given.

"Fine," she responded, reaching into his hand.

She swallowed the tiny tablet; it left an acrid taste on her tongue. She opened her mouth to show she had indeed swallowed it.

"Good girl," he said, that awful phrase.

"Please don't say that," Fiona responded back.

"Say what?" he asked.

"Good girl," she answered. "It's demeaning."

"Ok," he said simply. "I didn't mean it that way."

"Now what?" Fiona asked.

"I'd like to show you around," he said.

"Show me around where?" she asked.

"I'd like to introduce you to my people and tell you a bit about what we plan to do, and how you can help us," he answered.

"I already told you. I'm not going to help you. You're wasting your time. You might as well let me go."

"Well, I'm not going to let you go, Fiona. So you might as well humor me," he said smiling. "What else do you have to do? Finish reading *Firestarter*?"

"I finished it a few hours ago," she said.

He laughed at that response. Really laughed. It lit up his whole face and Fiona had to suppress her own smile.

"So then, you have nothing else to do," he said.

"There are lots of other books to read," she countered, pointing to the bookshelf crammed with titles.

"That's true," he responded.

"Those are all your books?" Fiona asked. "Have you read them all?"

"Yup," he answered.

"Any recommendations for which one I should read next?" she replied sarcastically.

"How about this... How about you let me show you around, and then you can have all the reading time you want," he suggested.

A pause.

"I'd like to shower first," she responded.

"Ok. There are towels in the bottom drawer and soap and stuff already in the shower," he instructed.

"Ok," Fiona responded awkwardly. "Well, since there are no doors on the bathroom, do you think you could step out and give me some privacy?"

"Absolutely. I'll come back at 8," he said.

"Is it morning or nighttime?" Fiona asked, feeling silly she didn't know the answer.

"Morning," Adam answered as he once again walked out the door.

Fiona was surprised to learn the shower offered warm water, not hot–that would have been counterintuitive to Adam's need to suppress her flame–but warm enough to wipe away the chill that nudged itself into every crevice of her body. She tried to summon her spark, but the pill was doing its job and even though she didn't feel the lethargy that the injection caused, she could sense that her condition was dulled–as though it was on a dimmer switch stuck in the down position. If only she had these pills throughout her childhood and early adulthood. Things would have certainly turned out differently.

Heading over to the dresser with her hair wrapped in a towel and a bathrobe tied around her waist, Fiona felt a jolt of pain travel up her leg from her foot. Looking down she saw that she stepped on the fire quartz. It must have fallen out of her pocket at some point. Picking it up, she inspected its fiery shine in the harsh fluorescent lights overhead. Just rubbing her thumb over its cratered surface made Fiona feel closer to Micah. Stepping into a fresh pair of jeans, Fiona placed the crystal in its rightful place, the front pocket. Maybe it would offer some luck as she figured out how to get herself the hell out of here.

There was no hair dryer in sight, nor brush, so Fiona used her fingers to comb the tangles out of her hair as she inspected her appearance in the mirror. It had been some time since she had dyed or cut her hair and even though it was still much shorter than how she used to wear it–in college, the red tendrils almost reached her waist–she was able to see some strawberry and copper highlights shining through the brown. And her roots were starting to show.

Fiona sat back on the bed to wait until Adam came back. She wouldn't have said she was anxious for his arrival, but she would have been lying if she said she wasn't just a bit curious. She was sure at some point along the tour she'd been promised, she would be able to hatch an escape plan. If–that was–Micah didn't find her first.

Chapter Forty-Four

Adam came back at 8 o'clock as he said he would and led Fiona out the door of the room–or maybe prison cell was the more accurate word. The two walked down the long hallway.

There was a row of fluorescent lights overhead and the corridor was lined with closed doors. The floor was tiled with large green squares that looked like they came directly out of some classroom, and the whole place had a stark, clinical feel to it.

"What kind of facility is this?" Fiona asked, looking around.

"Pretty retro, right?" Adam responded. "It's actually an old bunker, probably used during Vietnam or something. It was abandoned before we got here, but in mostly good condition. We had to repaint and refinish some of the rooms, but it's been home for the past 5 years or so."

"You've been living here for 5 years?" Fiona asked.

"Yup," Adam replied.

"But that means–" Fiona began.

He guessed at her thought, "I didn't just come here once I found you Fiona. I haven't dedicated my entire life to tracking you down. I've been here way before that."

"Then what have you dedicated your life to?" she asked,

genuinely curious. She thought about Arman and said in a softer voice, "How does someone like you come to know a thoracic surgeon who was about to get married at the Garden City Hotel?"

It took a moment for Adam to answer, but when he did, he said, "Arman was a buddy from grade school. We never lost touch, even though our lives went in, how should I say it?... different directions."

Fiona snorted at that, "*Different directions* is putting it mildly."

"And to answer your question about what I have dedicated my life to... well, I've dedicated my life to doing the right thing," he continued cryptically.

"You can get down now," Fiona retorted.

"Get down?" Adam responded quizzically.

"From that high horse," she finished the quip.

Adam just laughed in response. "Good one," he said. "I'm sure you'll find out all about me, in time. And all about our organization...when you decide to stay."

"Don't count on that," Fiona responded.

"We'll see," he said with that infuriatingly calm tone.

They walked on in silence.

"This place doesn't feel much like a home," Fiona said.

"It's not so bad."

"What's behind all these doors?" she asked.

"A lot of them are empty," he answered. "My room is actually the one directly next to yours," he responded. "And the others have their own rooms in different hallways."

"Others?" Fiona asked.

"Yup. You'll meet them all in a few minutes."

Fiona couldn't imagine what the "others" could be like. Could they be anything like Adam?

"Are we underground?" Fiona asked.

With Micah, she spent so much time studying structures and buildings, it was difficult for her to not impose that critical eye. It was dark here, without natural light. Hanging ceilings, older fixtures.

"Yeah. Can't you tell by the low ceilings? It would be nice to have some windows, but this place definitely wasn't built up to code."

"Where are we going now?" Fiona asked.

"I'm going to show you the command center," he laughed." You ask a lot of questions."

"Wouldn't you ask questions if you were kidnapped?"

"I guess I would," he responded.

He pushed open two double doors and they stepped into what looked like a high school cafeteria. All the tables but one were folded up along the far wall. The one set up had 8 connected stools. They walked past the table, through another door, and into an industrial kitchen. The sounds of friendly conversation echoed off the walls as they continued through the space lined with steel countertops and shelves. Walking around a huge pantry that could probably hold enough food to feed an army, Fiona saw a small group of people congregated around another steel island. In the center of the countertop there was an enormous box of Cocoa Crispies and a hearty stack of pancakes. The scent of coffee filled Fiona's nostrils. Everyone stopped their chatter as Adam and Fiona entered the space.

"This is Fiona," Adam said, introducing her to the group.

She was surprisingly greeted by friendly gazes and a few "Hey Fionas." She was puzzled by their warm welcome. Wasn't she the enemy? Their prisoner? She expected to be bombarded with questions and skepticism, but instead Fiona was met with good natured warmth.

"Hungry?" a man wearing flannel pajamas and a gray sweatshirt asked as the others picked up their conversations.

It took Fiona a second to realize that he was talking to her.

"Um. I kinda just ate," Fiona replied, thinking about the turkey sandwich she scarfed down about an hour ago. "But I would love a cup of coffee."

"Take a seat," he said. "I'm Bryce," he extended his hand. "That's Josh," he said, pointing to a guy sitting on the countertops across the room. Josh smiled and waved at the sound of his name. "And that's Erin and Andrea," he said, nodding his head to two girls engaged in a lively conversation near the refrigerator.

"Hey Fiona," they said in unison.

Bryce continued, "And the chef extraordinaire over there, is Chelsea."

The petite, blonde standing at the stove turned around for a quick wave. "I make killer pancakes," she said, wiping her hands on the yellow checkered apron tied in a double band around her slim waist.

Chelsea handed Fiona a steaming cup of coffee and asked, "Milk? Sugar?"

"Sugar please," Fiona responded.

Reaching over the countertop, she pushed a ceramic bowl over to the new guest.

"Thank you," Fiona said, trying to push down the awkwardness that bloomed inside her.

It felt odd sitting in that enormous, clinical kitchen with these strangers who talked so easily with one another. They looked like ordinary people, civilians. Suddenly Fiona felt curious about the identities behind their sunny faces. They clearly built their own family here, and their laughter came readily and easily. It was obvious they enjoyed each other. It reminded Fiona of her own little found family in Plattsburgh—except Micah, Rhea, Maya... even Spence, didn't laugh or talk like this. Not often anyway.

Bryce did his best to include Fiona in the conversations, as did Adam and Chelsea, but she remained mostly quiet. Adam referred to this as the *Control Center*; was he being sarcastic? Fiona felt her mind spinning, *What do these people do here? They seem so wholesome to be involved in anything sinister. What exactly do they want with Micah and the rest of us? How are they planning on stopping us?* It seemed to Fiona that Micah and Kaleb could destroy these people. But then again, Adam succeeded in grabbing

Fiona...in drugging her and taking her here. That was definitely a feat in itself. *Maybe I shouldn't underestimate this guy*, she mused.

Fiona couldn't restrain herself any longer and blurted out, "Ok. So you all seem nice and everything. But are we going to talk about what you want with me? What I'm doing here? I already told Adam I'm not interested in helping you bring down Micah. My loyalty is to him. So am I just going to be held captive? Or are you going to let me go? Because you'll have to kill me before I decide to work for you."

All eyes turned towards Fiona, and none of them reflected anger...only curiosity mixed with amusement.

Adam spoke first, "Anyone care to explain?"

"I will," Chelsea said. "We know about you Fiona. We admire you. What you can do, is–well, pretty amazing–"

"It's not all that amazing," Fiona replied back. "I've hurt people before."

"That may be true," Chelsea pushed on. "But we don't think you're going to hurt us. And we think that once you understand the type of person Micah is, what he used you to do, you'll change your mind and join us."

Her anger flared a bit, "Micah has not used me. I chose to join him, and I chose to do all those things. And what kind of person is Micah? Someone who drugged me and took me here against my will? Someone who continues to drug me so I am powerless against him? Oh wait–" the sarcasm edged into Fiona's voice. "That wasn't Micah who did those things. That was you guys."

Bryce interrupted, "I get why you're angry Fiona. I do. None of us wanted to do those things to you. But we did what needed to be done to get you here. Once you accept the truth, you'll make the right choice."

"The right choice," Fiona repeated.

"Yes," Adam cut in. "The right choice is for you to stay with us and bring down Micah and Kaleb."

"I told you already. I'll say it again. That. Is. Not. Going. To.

Happen," Fiona shot back, emphasizing each word so they might possibly sink in.

Why did no one look convinced by her words, or worried? Why weren't they scared of her? Were these people so certain in their knowledge? In their unfailing righteousness that they were on the right side, and that Micah, and Rhea, and Spence, and Maya were on the wrong side? How comforting it must have felt for them to feel that sense of security.

"Why don't we save this conversation for another time," Adam suggested, sensing the fruitlessness of having the discussion when Fiona was clearly not open to do so. "For now, why don't you just get to know us."

"And then will you bring me back to my room?" Fiona asked.

"It's a deal," Adam said. "But you have to make an effort. You have to at least try to hear us out."

"Fine," Fiona replied, trying to calm the rage she felt. She continued sarcastically, mimicking the voice of a teacher, "So class, why don't we all go around the room and share a bit about ourselves. Like we used to do in elementary school."

Her tone was bitter and sardonic, but that was exactly what happened for the next hour. And despite it all, Fiona found herself listening and learning about these strangers who sat before her with such open faces. What a stark contrast they were compared to Micah and Rhea and Maya, who shared virtually nothing about themselves—where every admission was like finding a pot of gold. Yes, it might have been true that Spence was more forthcoming, but even he harbored secrets.

Fiona wouldn't have admitted it then, she was too angry and far too broken, but despite her resentment, she even found herself liking them.

Chapter Forty-Five

"I've always been a bit of a hippie, which was probably why I ended up going to college in the Adirondacks," Bryce said light-heartedly. "Sophomore year I joined this environmental group called GREEN. Actually, I think it was an acronym, but I can't remember what each letter stood for. We spent a lot of time in nature...hiking, camping. I got hooked really quickly. Partly because I really did believe in the causes GREEN promoted...partly because the hottest girl I had ever seen was the one in charge of the group."

With that last reveal, he glanced over at Chelsea with a wink; she smiled back. Fiona knew right away that Chelsea was the "hot girl" Bryce fell for. She couldn't blame him; Chelsea was absolutely stunning.

Bryce continued, "I changed my major to Environmental Law and really dedicated my time to GREEN. Chelsea and I spearheaded a movement against deforestation; we've done great work in the past for the local forests...or at least we tried."

Chelsea's smile faded a bit as Bryce spoke.

"We tried to stop a pharmaceutical company from building their corporation. They had their eyes trained on 50 acres of land just outside of Lake Placid," Bryce trailed off.

Chelsea picked up the thread, "We couldn't stop them. No matter how much man-power, no matter how much protesting, picketing...writing letters to useless politicians. Nothing worked. They had government backing. Ultimately, no one cared about the trees that would be destroyed, the wildlife that would be uprooted."

Bryce walked over to Chelsea and planted a kiss on the top of her head. Fiona could see their defeat, their feelings of failure in the tilt of their eyes. But despite all that, the warmth and genuine love they exuded towards one another moved Fiona in a way she hadn't anticipated. The way Bryce looked at Chelsea–as though the Earth turned just for her...Fiona thought that it would be nice to be looked at that way. With a pang of regret, Fiona wondered if Micah ever gazed upon her with that raw emotion on his dark face. If he had ever shown unguarded emotion. She didn't think so.

When they didn't continue speaking, Fiona asked with unmasked curiosity–despite her reluctance, she was drawn in, "So...then what? How did Adam come into your lives? Did he drug you and kidnap you, and drag you to this compound?" Fiona couldn't keep the edge from her voice.

Bryce just laughed at Fiona's flaring temper and said, "Not exactly. I finished school. You might not know it from looking at me, but I am the area's premier expert on environmental litigation and water safety." His chest swelled with feigned arrogance and then he added, "And Chelsea and I stayed together."

The two laced their fingers together in solidarity, and Chelsea continued, "Adam came to us for legal advice a few years back. After getting to know him and after learning about his whole vision, we decided to join up."

"Just like that?" Fiona asked. "You left your practice and came here?"

"We were getting frustrated by all of the legal red-tape. It felt like we were fighting a losing battle...and our biggest adversary was the U.S. government. It's hard to win that fight. Impossible actually. The government is a bulldozer; if you don't agree, it will plow you down without the slightest reservation. Coming here allowed us to be more productive…to make more of a difference."

The thought that these two people *chose* to come here on their own free-will floored Fiona a bit. She couldn't imagine abandoning a promising legal career for an uncertain future. But actually, when she thought about it more, she did that exact same thing, hadn't she? Sure her circumstances were different. Sure she felt cornered, trapped. But she made her choice as well…just like Bryce and Chelsea made theirs. And they seemed genuinely happy with their choice, happy to be here…with Adam. No matter how much Fiona tried to fool herself, she couldn't say she felt as content with her own life choices.

Fiona risked a glance over at Adam to find him gazing down in quiet contemplation, silently sipping his coffee. The steam from the styrofoam cup rose up into a hazy halo, hiding his mouth and jaw. When he felt her eyes upon him, he looked over and gave her a tiny smile, the corners of his mouth barely turning up at the edges.

Turning her attention back to the couple seated across from her, Fiona asked, "You say you're more *productive* here. What do you mean by that? What exactly have you *produced*?"

"Well," Bryce responded. "Chelsea and me….our primary interest is taking care of our planet. Cheesy as it sounds, we believe that it's worth saving. Global warming and stuff is real, and it's taking a toll. With Adam and everyone else's help, we have been able to save some land, help limit some fossil fuels from being released into the ozone, things like that. I can give you more specifics if you want them. But we're proud of what we've achieved…and we still have so much more we want to do."

Fiona thought about that vertical farm she helped destroy. She thought about that eco-friendly apartment building in Brooklyn. The two facilities certainly could have done much good for the environmental realm in which Chelsea and Bryce were so interested. How had they felt when they saw the news reports showing those structures consumed in flame?

Bryce interrupted her musings, "And we're also always up to help with other causes. To fight the good fight as they say. Sitting around this table you'll find a bunch of like-minded people. Maybe Chelsea and I are the nature nuts, but Josh over there..."

Josh waved a hello at the mention of his name.

"Josh over there," Bryce repeated. "...has a passion for social rights. He's former CIA. Got bogged down by all the bureaucracy of the government. Has a ton of connections that help us do what we do. Erin and Andrea, they're sisters: Andrea is a veteran who worked her way up to the Army Counterintelligence Unit–"

Fiona couldn't restrain her incredulity, "And they left those prestigious positions to come here? No offense or anything, but this place just seems...not as exciting."

Fiona chuckled with the assessment that issued forth from her lips. "Not as exciting" was the first phrase that came to mind.

Fiona glanced at Adam and watched him give a small shrug, "I guess the lack of red-tape and the freedom from government expectations has some perks."

"I guess so," Fiona responded.

Bryce picked up, "And Erin–she's an expert in security. She's our eyes and ears."

Fiona spared Erin an admiring gaze. "Damn," Fiona said. "A bunch of bad-asses."

Bryce continued, "Now these two badasses..." He indicated Erin and Andrea with a nod of his head, "dedicate a lot of mind-power to women's rights. The Me-Too Movement, Reproductive rights...that sort of thing."

"We'd love to show you some of our contributions to the cause," Erin volunteered. "I could ramble on for hours...I won't... I promise, but I could. I'd love to tell you all about it sometime."

Fiona just gave the tall brunette a good-natured head shake. As much as she also loved female-inspired causes, well at least she had in her former life, she didn't think she could bear hearing about one more altruistic story. All of these people made her feel dirty, ashamed in a way she hadn't felt in a long time. To compensate, Fiona raised the tilt of her chin slightly; she was definitely not going to broadcast her conflicting emotions.

While gazing at Erin's open smile, images of the D.C. Planned Parenthood flooded Fiona's mind. Out of all the jobs she had done, out of all the fires she had ignited, that was the one that Fiona could never quite put out of her thoughts–and she tried, desperately. All the women who received care from the medical staff there sometimes danced on her closed eyelids. Erin and Andrea must have known what she had done, yet they looked at her with friendly eyes and warm smiles.

Fiona swallowed her emotions and turned to face Adam directly. "And what about you?" she asked.

"What about me?" Adam replied.

"Don't play dumb. What's your story?"

"I'm not nearly as impressive as everyone else," he began.

"Bullshit," inserted Josh. "Don't be modest."

Adam laughed. "It's true. I'm a former private eye. Before that, I was a detective...counter-terrorism stuff. But I got frustrated. I felt like every time I got close to something, I was told my methods weren't *appropriate for a government official*."

Fiona noticed that his tone changed slightly as he spoke those last few words.

Adam continued, "I guess I felt like I could just make more of a difference if I went out on my own. And that's what I did. And I believe I have made a difference...just in another way."

"I'm definitely going to need to hear more about that. And your organization," Fiona responded, unable to restrain her curiosity.

Chelsea picked up with a laugh as she stood up to lean against the counter. "We each have our own story, as does our little organization...and we each have our own reasons for being here. There've been others too, others who have moved on to different things. Some stay for a year, some for 2...some for a few months. People go, and they come. Just like you, Fiona."

Fiona thought about the fact that all of these people came here on their own accord. Most of whom left promising careers. All of these people *wanted* to be here. All of them except her. Her hand was forced. She had no say in the matter at all.

Some bitterness crept into her voice when Fiona said, "Well, unlike all of you, I didn't come here by choice. I'm being held here against my will. I'm your captive. Doesn't that kind of contradict your *vision*? You all think you're so much better than Micah? You're exactly like him. Worse even. How does the fact that Adam kidnapped me–and that you are all complicit in it– mesh with your *noble* purposes?"

To this question, Adam responded, "We aren't proud of the methods we used to get you here...or the methods we're using to keep you here. But it's the only way you'll give me...give *us* a chance."

Fiona rolled her eyes in feigned frustration. *Feigned*, because, much to her displeasure, and as much as she tried to hide it and force her thoughts to rebel, she liked Bryce and Chelsea...and Josh and Erin and Andrea. And was she starting to like Adam too? Despite it all? They were so damn earnest, had such conviction, were so true to their beliefs. Traits Fiona lost long ago. Sitting among these strangers made Fiona feel incredibly old, incredibly jaded. Tired and worn out.

She didn't want to hear any more of those do-good stories. They made her feel something she had long tried to suppress...shame. Shame in who she was and what she had become.

So without truly acknowledging Adam's justification for her kidnapping and the drugs, she said, "I think I'm ready to go back to my room now."

In response to her request, Adam stood up and walked towards the door. Fiona followed him. They didn't speak to one another as they walked down the long corridor towards Fiona's room, and Fiona was appreciative of the silence. She felt tired all of a sudden and weary. She knew she had much thinking to do, especially if she was going to make that escape plan. *Escape.* The word sounded so huge, so dramatic. How would she ever pull it off with these people guarding her all the time. She needed time to inspect her surroundings. There had to be a way out...there just had to be. Fiona promised herself that she would find it. She just had to think.

Chapter Forty-Six

A week passed in a similar manner. Every morning began with the small white pill offered on Adam's outstretched hand. She stopped protesting; she preferred the round tablet to the indignity of a forced injection. Once she swallowed–it never stopped leaving a chemical taste behind on her tongue–she would walk with Adam to have breakfast in the cafeteria. Fiona listened to the friendly banter between Erin and Andrea, observed the small loving gestures exchanged between Bryce and Chelsea. Josh was quieter–more reserved–but always greeted Fiona with a warm wave and smile.

Despite her better judgment, Fiona sometimes participated in their lively conversation, always careful, of course, to avoid revealing too much. They already knew so much about her; she didn't want to give them anything else. Sometimes Adam would stay; sometimes he would go. Fiona had no idea where exactly he went or what exactly he did. She assumed that, like Micah, as the head of this group his responsibilities would take him elsewhere at times.

On the third day, Fiona asked him, "When you leave, where do you go?"

To this, Adam replied with a smirk, "How about this...once you decide to stay, I'll tell you."

"*Decide* to stay," Fiona responded, emphasizing that first word. "When have I ever been allowed to decide? None of this has been my choice. You know that."

"That might be true. But my goal...*our* goal...is for you to want to stay. To *choose* to stay on your own volition," he explained.

"That's not going to happen," Fiona said quickly.

Fiona knew her refusal to cooperate was the one bit of leverage she had. No one could force her to use her fire, and Adam knew that. And as long as those little pills were used to subdue that fire, she was essentially useless. *There's one silver lining*, she thought to herself...*The fact that I only work when I want to work.*

Adam responded to her rejection with his typical smirk, suggesting he didn't, not for a minute, believe her. It infuriated her when he reacted that way, as though her mind could be changed, as though she could be so easily manipulated. There was no way she would ever *choose* to remain here, when she knew in her heart she belonged with Micah.

Just thinking about Micah made Fiona's heart ache. Logically she wondered if he was searching for her; she assumed he was–she was shocked actually that with his thoroughness and resources, he hadn't yet discovered her whereabouts. But emotionally, she wondered if he missed her the way she missed him. If he longed for her. If his body ached for her the way hers did–especially when she finally curled up in bed and closed her eyes at the end of the day.

Even though she knew the pills would continue to dampen her condition, she never stopped trying to summon her spark. If she could just force it back into action, she could use it to her advantage. But, it didn't work. During that week she wondered sometimes if she had simply forgotten how to use it. Aside from her college years, she couldn't ever remember a time where she went so long without using the heat raging inside of her. She almost didn't recognize herself anymore.

After those "family breakfasts"–Bryce's phrase, not hers–Adam would give her the choice of either remaining to socialize or returning to her room. In the beginning, she always chose the second option, but boredom could be a powerful tool, and oftentimes she found herself sitting in a starkly furnished living room watching Netflix on a television propped onto a wobbly dresser, with whoever chose to sit with her. It all felt so normal sometimes, especially on those evenings when they would gather together to watch the newest episodes of *Stranger Things* or *Criminal Minds*. Sometimes Fiona had to remind herself that this...none of this...was normal. Not at all. She was a prisoner, despite it all.

Fiona was never left alone, which was likely purposeful, but usually during that nighttime time together, in front of that television, or when she found herself engaged in a heated match of checkers with Adam or Josh, the normalcy of their routine almost tricked her into thinking that she belonged.

She was surprised to find that, since she arrived–or at least when she was present–the group hardly ever discussed their plans, their future, any upcoming jobs, nothing.

One time after her first week concluded, she asked Chelsea, "Do you guys ever *do* anything? Or do you just sit around and hang out all day?"

Chelsea laughed good-naturedly at the question and responded, "Oh we usually always work. There are lots of things on our to-do list, so to speak. But for now, we are in a holding pattern."

"Holding pattern," Fiona repeated. And even though she knew the answer, she asked, "Why?"

"Well," Chelsea began. "We're waiting on you."

"Well," Fiona responded sarcastically, aping Chelsea's response. "You should stop waiting."

Chelsea sighed. It was the first time Fiona ever saw her demeanor exude anything but chipper and positive energy.

Chelsea said with a seriousness Fiona didn't expect, "Come on Fiona. Open your eyes. See the truth about Micah...about what you've been doing. We're giving you a chance at a meaningful life here. A meaningful future. A future that will allow you to *create* instead of destroy. Don't you want that?"

Chelsea didn't often speak to Fiona like that; those conversations were usually reserved for Adam, and for a moment, Fiona was stunned silent by what Chelsea said. Wasn't that what Micah offered eons ago in that dreaded field? A path? A *meaningful* life? Fiona didn't remain silent for long.

"What I want," Fiona began. "...is to go back to Plattsburgh. You people don't even know me, not really. You think you do, but you don't. And as far as leading a *meaningful life*. I have one already. And it's not here."

No matter how much Fiona tried to hide it, Chelsea saw the tears that welled in the corners of Fiona's eyes. Saw the hurt gathered there.

"Fiona–" Chelsea began.

Fiona cut her off, "I'm going to get a drink of water. That's one *meaningful* thing I can do."

Getting up in a huff, Fiona knocked the television remote on the floor in her haste. Chelsea rose from her seat in response.

"I guess you'll follow me, right? Like you always do? You want me to trust you and you don't return the favor?"

To this, Chelsea responded reluctantly, "I want to trust you Fiona. Can I?"

"Yes! Where am I going to go? This place is like Fort Knox. And besides, I think I'm old enough to get my own damn drink of water. What do you think...I'm going to burn the place down? Oh wait...I can't do that. Because you're drugging me."

Despite her better judgment, Chelsea didn't follow Fiona. After all, Fiona was right, wasn't she? Trust is a two-way street. For the past week, Fiona had been agreeable. She had shown some progress...some promise. Chelsea didn't want to undo all of that by shadowing her every move. So while Fiona stomped her way next door to the kitchen, Chelsea waited on the couch thinking she had overstepped, that she should have left the convincing and recruiting to Adam. She felt guilty for pushing too hard. Next time, she decided, her tactic would be softer. She liked Fiona, when her guard was down, and Chelsea hoped to see more of that inner self living beneath the glossy veneer.

Chapter Forty-Seven

Seething, Fiona swung the metal double doors open and stormed into that huge industrial kitchen, the one she had become so accustomed to over the past week. She was surprised Chelsea hadn't followed her, and aside from when she was locked in her bedroom, this was the first time Fiona had been alone in any of the "public spaces" this compound boasted since she arrived. It made her feel almost human.

She knew it had been difficult for Chelsea to allow her to go without an escort–even though the living room was just next door; the doubt was written clearly in those blue eyes. But, Chelsea was trying to show Fiona that she trusted her...she was trying to give her just a tiny bit of leeway, a tiny show of faith, and even though Fiona hadn't liked the words Chelsea spoke, she appreciated the gesture. She needed a minute to think, to clear her head. Each of Fiona's footfalls echoed through this cavernous space; the air felt alive with movement and sound.

The scent of the tacos Chelsea made for dinner still lingered in the air. Fiona closed her fist and slammed it into the steel island before her. The sharp sting of the impact reverberated through her arm and shoulder. The blow rebounded through the air and bounced off the metal fixtures. Hot tears stung her eyes. The futility of her situation was maddening. She felt so damn helpless—so useless. The last time she felt this way was in that field with Micah a lifetime ago. She had sworn to herself that she would never feel so weak ever again. And yet, here she was.

What Chelsea had said played over and over again in her mind like a worn out song. *Meaningless.* The word flew about through her conscious thoughts. *How dare she presume to know anything about me*, Fiona thought to herself as she grabbed a clear bottle of Poland Spring water from the 24-pack on the counter. *Why do I care what Chelsea thinks? Why do I care what any of them think?* Fiona didn't want to answer those questions. She was too afraid of what they would reveal...what truths would bubble up to the surface. It was so much easier to feel that simmering anger. She knew all about anger. Anger, at least, was safe.

Unscrewing the plastic cap, Fiona emptied half the contents of the bottle in one gulp. Even though it was only room temperature, the liquid felt cool running down her raw throat. Bringing it up to her mouth again she finished the rest. Taking a few deep breaths, Fiona got her rage under control. She used one of the relaxation techniques she mastered with the help of Rhea all those lightyears ago. Inhale—One, Two, Three. Exhale—One, Two, Three. And again, Inhale...and Exhale. In. Out. She felt her chest rise and fall, her belly fill and empty. Each exhale expelled that troublesome emotion impeding her ability to think and reason. Level-headedness was her only chance here. Without it, she had no hope of getting out.

With a glum sigh, Fiona realized it was probably time she headed back to Chelsea—before she came looking for her. Picking up the cap to the water bottle she left carelessly on the island, she gave it a quick toss towards the trash can. It sailed swiftly through the air towards the target. Score. But the action gave her no satisfaction.

She walked back down the hallway and stopped at the entrance to the makeshift living room. Peering in , she saw Chelsea in a conversation with Bryce; they were so involved in one another, that they didn't notice Fiona lingering. With her heart in her teeth, she continued down the hallway. Slowly, then more briskly. She knew exactly what she was looking for; the exit. There had to be one in this godforsaken place, right?

Eyes darting around her wildly, she fluttered down the hall-way, softly opening doors and glancing down hallways. In a near run, Fiona cringed at every squeak made by her shoes, but remained undeterred. Finally, she saw a sign: Emergency Exit. Her heart leapt. *Yes! That's it.* She stumbled into a small room and saw it immediately–a door.

Her ears felt hot and her pulse hammered in her throat; her breathing increased. She approached the thick, metal door. Gingerly, Fiona turned and pulled the knob; it felt cold in her palm. At first, it wouldn't budge, and Fiona's hope sank. There must be some sort of lock preventing its opening, but then as she applied more force it sprung open with a slight pop, and stood gaping before her.

It was as if Fiona moved in slow motion, not fully believing her luck. Since Micah, everything in her life had been meticu-lously planned, and this unexpected turn felt perplexing and frag-ile. She knew she had to capitalize on it.

She was surprised to feel an inkling of hesitation as she studied the open door–the passageway leading her back to freedom. *Don't be stupid*, she said to herself. *You don't belong here.* And with that bit of encouragement, she inhaled a deep breath, and took her first step. A trickle of fear ran down her spine, along with those pesky 'What-ifs,' like Shel Silverstein wrote about in that poem. But she swallowed that along with her hesitation, doubt, and even those misplaced feelings of guilt.

Just as she was about to take those next few steps towards free-dom, she felt something–or maybe the more accurate term was *someone*–grip her forearm. The hold was firm, strong. And then she heard her name, "Fiona."

Chapter Forty-Eight

S hit, Fiona thought to herself. *It's Adam.* She tried to shake his fingers off her arm, but when his grip remained firm, she backtracked and re-emerged into the small room. Adam was standing next to her, his hand still affixed. Boldly, she met his gaze. His eyes studied her—green and brown with flecks of gold; there was a sadness there, a defeat she hadn't seen before.

Despite the severity of the situation, Adam said simply, "Hi."

Fiona didn't take the bait and instead said, "You're hurting my arm."

Releasing his fingers, Adam said, "Sorry. That wasn't my intention."

"I think your *intentions* are pretty clear," Fiona shot back.

"I guess they are," Adam replied.

The two sat there silently in front of that open door, staring at each other. Both calculating one another's next move. Calculating their own next moves.

Fiona broke the spell when she said, "So now what? Are you going to force me back into my room? Lock me up? Give me more drugs?"

It took many seconds for Adam to reply—seconds that felt like an eternity. Fiona could see him grappling with himself, struggling with what to do, how to respond, what to say. Fiona guessed she finally stumped him. Fiona knew Adam didn't want to be the kind of guy who forced a woman to remain somewhere against her will–she saw the hurt in his eyes when he gave her the pills to keep her in compliance; he had done it simply because he had to. He made it clear on numerous occasions that he was uncomfortable with the way he treated her. And at that moment, she forced him to confront that fact. She contemplated running for it, but something held her in place, and she wasn't sure exactly what that was.

"Well?" Fiona asked again. "Are you going to stop me from walking out that door? Because I'm going–whether you want me to or not. You'll have to force me to stay here...and I will fight back."

Adam gazed at her with hurt in his eyes. "No," he finally said quietly. I'm not going to stop you."

"No?" Fiona repeated, the question hanging in the air above them.

"I'm not going to stop you," Adam said again. "If you want to...if you really want to, just go."

"Just like that?" Fiona asked.

She didn't know why she questioned his decision, why she didn't simply scamper ahead unchecked, but she was stumped, and needed answers.

She continued,"You're just going to let me go? After all that? After keeping me here for a full week? After shooting me with a needle and putting a sack over my head and dragging me here... against my will?"

Adam responded earnestly, not acknowledging the nastiness in Fiona's tone, "I thought that if you got to know us, saw we have good intentions, that we are good people, you would realize how misguided your actions have been–"

When he saw the temper flare again in Fiona's eyes, he continued on defensively, "...I don't blame you. I don't think you're bad, or evil. I truly think there is goodness inside you Fiona. A sense of decency. Morality–"

"I don't have to listen to this," Fiona interrupted, but she asked for this, didn't she? She opened up the floodgates, "If you're going to let me go, just let me go already. Spare me the lecture."

Adam stood up and reached into his pocket to remove an object. In his outstretched hand lay the fire quartz, glittering in the harsh fluorescent lights overhead.

"I found it in the hallway just now. I know it's important to you. It must have fallen out of your pocket," he said.

When Fiona didn't move, he spoke again. "Take it," he said.

Fiona took the stone, which felt warm from being enclosed in Adam's palm. Placing it into her front pocket, Fiona looked up at Adam. She was surprised to feel no anger, only a dull aching in her chest she couldn't explain. In another time, in another life, they could have been friends. It was clear that he was still grappling with his decision to let her go. He knew it was a risky choice. But despite the risk, it contended with his humanity; he couldn't be both a hero and a monster. And he would choose to be a hero. Every. Single. Time.

"Thank you," Fiona said quietly.

"That door will put you out near Route 87. I imagine you can find your way from there," Adam said, holding out a fifty dollar bill.

"I can't take that," Fiona replied to the offer of money. "I don't need your help."

"You don't really have a choice," Adam said with a forced laugh. "How else would a broke girl like you get anywhere?"

Fiona hated that he was right.

Pocketing the bill Fiona said, "I imagine you're going to come after me again? That you're going to come after Micah, and the others?"

"I can't force you to change, and I can't force you to join us. You have to want it. I want you to want it, and I believe that you'll come back. In time. I think that you'll realize the truth about

Micah," he said. "But until then, I guess it's just time we part ways."

His answer shocked Fiona. Could he be lying? Maybe. But his gaze was so open, so grave that Fiona thought he spoke honestly.

"Aren't you scared that I'll come after you? That Micah and I will burn this place to the ground?" Fiona asked.

"I trust you Fiona," Adam replied. "Like I said…I don't think you want to hurt anyone. Despite it all, I think you like us. And I think you're a good person. I don't think you would hurt any of us."

If Fiona was going to challenge Adam's character, he was going to challenge her morality. How could he know her so well, see inside her so clearly after only knowing her for a single week? The fact was uncomfortable for Fiona. So she didn't tell him he was right in his assumption. Hurting people was the one thing she simply wouldn't do. Not again. She wasn't going to hurt Adam, or the others. They both knew it.

With a final look, Fiona turned away from Adam and ascended the stairs behind that door. The last thing she heard before she began her journey back to Plattsburgh was Adam's reassuring voice saying, "I'm not giving up on you yet, Fiona. Come back when you're ready."

Chapter Forty-Nine

As she ascended those stairs leading to the outside, Fiona couldn't quite swallow the feelings of guilt–that paralyzing emotion weaseling its way into her subconscious. It has the power to quell all of life's enjoyment, to expose the fragility of peace. Ever since she was little, guilt had always been a dominating presence in her life; she guessed she inherited it from her mom.

Stop it, Fiona, she said to herself. *You have no loyalty to those people. Those* being the key word. She wasn't one of them. But...

But they treated her with kindness. Yes, even Adam displayed a sense of care and concern for her that she never would have thought he was capable of. Adam, who had been systematically drugging her. Why weren't those the immutable facts that stood out most prominently about him? How could she overlook the simple fact of what he did to her? *But he let me go*, said a tiny voice in the back of her skull. Then Fiona thought of Chelsea and Bryce. Of Erin and Andrea–two women who fought so courageously for what they believed in. Even Josh's kind brown eyes loomed large in her mind.

Whatever, she thought as she walked on. *None of that matters now. Now, I can get my life back on track. Now I can get back to Micah and forget all about this past week.*

After a long train ride, and then a 15 minute cab ride, Fiona finally made it back to Plattsburgh the following day at around 2 in the afternoon. She was exhausted; seated on the hard, faux-leather Amtrak seats, she slept fitfully. And she couldn't get these new people–who popped into her life with such suddenness–out of her head.

The fact that Adam let her go was staggering to Fiona. He had actually allowed her to go. He trusted her with such openness that he didn't fear retaliation. Would Fiona be able to honor this trust? Especially under the barrage of questions she would certainly face from Micah? Fiona didn't know the answer to that, but in her heart she knew she couldn't allow Adam to be harmed...or the rest of them. They seemed to have parted ways amicably enough.

Without a cellphone, she hadn't been able to alert anyone to her escape, and she wondered how surprised Micah, Rhea, Spence and Maya would be to see her show up at the house. Would they be happy to see her? She thought they would. She hoped they would.

She felt nervous as she stepped out of the cab and onto the familiar paved pathway leading up to the front door of the single-storied ranch. She briefly wondered how the house could possibly still look the same when she felt like so much time had passed. The past week aged her in so many ways; it almost felt like she was a completely different person now. But she guessed that this was just the way of life. One person can go through major changes, but the rest of the world...it just keeps spinning.

The American flag hanging to her left waved cheerfully to Fiona, as she pushed the familiar numbers into the keycode. She noticed Spence's Audi parked neatly in the driveway, but Micah's Range Rover and Maya's BMW were absent. She wondered where everyone was. Was Spence even home? Or had he gone somewhere with Maya, as he typically did?

Fiona's hands trembled as she turned the knob to let herself into the house. Immediately, the familiar scent of coffee and ciga-rettes embraced her and she felt, for the first time in a week, a sense of relief wash over her. The living room was empty, so was the kitchen. She walked to the refrigerator and pulled the cold handle. As usual, there was an entire shelf filled with gatorades and bottles of Fiji water. She grabbed a lemon-lime gatorade and twisted open the orange cap; she hadn't had a single thing to eat or drink since that bottle of Poland Spring.

"Anyone home," she called to the open space.

She didn't expect anyone to answer, and just as she was about to open the door to the basement and trudge down to her bedroom to await everyone's return, Spence's pale face emerged from the back office room. Without thinking, Fiona raced over to him and enveloped him in a warm embrace. It took him a few seconds to respond to the action, but Fiona felt his arms encircle her waist. Tears flooded her eyes and when Spence released his grip and held her at arms length to inspect her, they coursed freely down her cheeks.

Fiona studied Spence's face and when he didn't speak, she said, "Well, I'm back! Aren't you happy to see me?"

Where was the goofy Spence she had come to know? Where was that smile that provided comfort when she needed it most? Had she shocked him so thoroughly with her surprise arrival he couldn't process her return?

When Spence didn't speak...or smile, Fiona continued, her grin melting off her face with each passing moment, "Umm... Spence? This wasn't exactly the greeting I was expecting."

When she was met again with only a sheepish side-glance, Fiona felt her temper rising. She spoke again, "Spence...you honestly have nothing to say to me? I've been gone for a week. Don't you want to know where I was? How I am? If I'm ok?"

Spence seemed to shake himself free from whatever spell he was under and finally, he said, "Of course I'm happy to see you Fiona...I'm just–"

He trailed off and Fiona picked up the thread immediately,

"You're just…what? You better start talking Spence, or I'm going to scream."

With a deep breath, Spence began, "When Micah came back and told us what happened, we were all devastated. Micah was freaking out about blowing our cover; we actually took off to Canada for two days, just in case."

"Just in case what?" Fiona pushed on, growing more and more agitated. "Just in case I ratted you all out? Just in case I told them where you could be found? Do you really think I would do that?"

The fact that Micah's primary concern was being discovered, not her safety, struck Fiona with the force of a severe blow.

Spence answered quickly, "*I* knew you wouldn't do that Fiona. But precautions are precautions. We had to make sure our operation was safe."

"Yeah," Fiona responded sarcastically. "Who cares if *I* was safe?"

Fiona knew she was being childish; their work was definitely the priority, but it still hurt to hear Spence speaking so matter-of-factly about it.

"Come on Fiona," Spence replied. "Don't pretend you don't know how things work around here. After those first two days, they tried to find you. Literally, they exhausted all our resources."

The word '*they*' stood out like lightning. *What the hell does he mean by the word 'they'?* Fiona thought to herself.

Fiona couldn't hold back, "*They*? What about *you*, Spence? Did *you* try to find me?"

Fiona couldn't quite shake that bitter resentment weaving its way through her as Spence spoke.

"Don't be like that Fiona," Spence said, clearly exasperated by the trajectory of the conversation.

"Do you even want to know where I was? Do you even care?"

"Micah will care…and so will the others."

"But what about *you* Spence?"

"I do care, Fiona. But I don't want to know where you were?"

"Why? Stop being so damn cryptic, Spence, and tell me what's on your mind!" Fiona screamed it out loud, unable to restrain herself any longer.

Spence's words flew out of him unchecked as he buried his hands in his pockets, "Because I was happy you were gone. Because you don't belong here. Because you should run away from here so fast. Go somewhere far away. You're better than this. Start a new life, away from me...away from Maya and Rhea. Away from Micah most of all."

The words bit physically into Fiona and a sense of confusion dulled the anger pulsing in her ears.

"What are you saying?" Fiona responded. "I don't understand."

"I knew where you were the whole time," Spence confessed. "And I know all about Adam. I wanted you to stay there, stay with him. I made sure Micah couldn't find you."

"You know he drugged me, right? Adam did. Yet, you think he's a *good* guy?"

"He had to do that Fiona. Don't you see that?"

Fiona couldn't even acknowledge that concept, "*You* allowed me to stay missing? Stay abducted. I thought you were my friend. You could have helped me? This whole week? But you *chose* not to?"

"I did," Spence answered with a sadness that consumed his whole face.

None of this made any sense to Fiona. How could Spence betray her like that? What had she ever done to cause him to turn against her? All she had been was his friend. Or so she thought. The weight of the knowledge was heavy on her, and she felt the beginning of a headache pulsing deep inside her skull. It drained her of all emotion. Betrayed. By everyone it seemed. How was she so gullible? So weak? So trusting. Was her ability to form accurate opinions on others so flawed and broken? Was *she* so flawed and broken that she couldn't see the blinding truth blazing before her eyes? It was as if she was trudging tragically behind everyone else, unable to catch up—as if she was losing some metaphorical race.

Again, all Fiona could ask was, "Why, Spence? Why?"

Chapter Fifty

"Fiona," Spence began, running a hand over his face. "I'm trying to protect you. There's so much you don't know. So much–"

"Spence, instead of being vague about all the things I *don't know*, how about you just tell me exactly what it is I need to know. Wouldn't it be easier that way?"

Spence took a deep breath as if to steel himself and said simply, "Ok. It's time you knew the truth."

"You're scaring me a bit Spence," Fiona replied, taking in the pallor of his complexion and his solemn eyes. She had never before seen him so serious, so stoic. Even when they were preparing for a job, Spence retained his good humor, but at that moment, he appeared a shell of himself. Devoid of that charismatic spark that made him simply, Spence.

"I'm just going to start from the beginning ok?"

"The beginning is always a good place to start," Fiona replied tonelessly.

So Spence began, "When Micah told us about you last year, I couldn't believe it. You were our magic ticket. I was already making plenty of money, but now...I stood to increase that sum exponentially, and so much of the risk would be gone. We had some close calls in the past. But now, with you...it seemed like a slam dunk. I'm not even totally sure how he and Kaleb knew about you. Apparently, Kaleb has tracked you since you were a kid, but Micah has always been pretty close-lipped about it."

Fiona knew Micah had been tracking her, but she didn't know Kaleb was also involved. The idea was staggering to her and she wished Spence had more details. Tracking her since she was a kid? How? She decided she would demand answers as soon as Micah walked through that door.

Spence continued, "We were all so excited to recruit you, that when Micah told us about how it would all go down, none of us hesitated. I think Rhea was the only one who voiced any objection at all, but ultimately she was overruled by the rest of us."

Fiona broke in with a question, "I'm trying to follow you Spence, but I'm confused. What do you mean by *how it would all go down*?"

"This part is hard for me to tell you about Fiona. I've come to really care about you, your friendship."

"Please just spit it out Spence," Fiona interrupted.

He went on, "I guess you deserve that. Ok. Micah said that in order to secure you, we needed to start a fire at the Garden City Hotel. That we were going to make you think you did it. That this was the only way to gain your cooperation and protect your identity."

Spence stopped talking when he saw Fiona's expression. Her eyes wildly searched his face for a hint that this was all just a joke, a big, fat joke...that it wasn't true. But when she detected none of that, when he saw her body shaking, he reached out to steady her. With a violent shudder, she shook his hand away. Realization, acceptance had not been fully reached; it was still hovering on the horizon like some terrible storm in the distance.

"*I* started that fire," Fiona said with ferocity, trying to correct him...convince him, convince herself of the statement's truth. "Not you. Not Micah. Me. I did it. *I* killed those people."

"You didn't Fiona. We did."

"No no no no no no. Gio, he tried to rape me. My emotions took over. I lost control. I killed so many people. 11 people. I don't believe any of this. I don't believe you!"

"I'm telling the truth Fiona. Why would I lie? What do I have to gain? Micah would literally kill me if he knew I was telling you this. We have all been sworn to secrecy. Listen to me! Micah hired Gio. He gave Gio the roofies to put in your drink. *We* started that fire Fiona. *We* killed all those people. Not you. Think about it logically. Why would Micah have been there? How would he have known? It was all planned. Perfectly orchestrated. And it worked. We recruited you," Spence spoke glumly, apologetically.

Fiona struggled to keep up, to process all the thoughts spinning around in her jumbled mind.

When Fiona didn't speak, Spence continued, "I wanted to tell you so many times. This guilt, it's eating me alive. So when you got taken last week, I was glad that–"

"All this time. All this time, I thought it was *my* fault...that *I* hurt all those people," Fiona began.

But then a thought just as terrible occurred to her, "You were the reason I had to fake my own death, why I had to leave my family. Why I had to uproot my life. It was YOUR fault...YOU made me believe I had no other choice...my mom lost a daughter, my brother lost a sister...all because of you."

Fiona looked up at Spence, her chest heaving, tears of sadness, anger, frustration, bitter bitter betrayal streaming down her face unrestrained. All these years of guilt, shame, self-hatred. This new life she built. It was all a giant illusion, a facade to acquire her commitment and loyalty. To force her hand. These people played with her life on a grand scale as though it had no more worth than a simple child's toy...played with the lives of those she loved: her mother, her brother. They killed 11 innocent people! It was almost too much to take. Had it not been for Micah, Fiona could have gone on living her life...with her family...and a career. All those people would still be alive.

"How could you just kill all those people Spence? Take all those innocent lives?"

Then another thought came to Fiona, the article, she had to ask, "Did Micah kill 8 people in some 'Suburban Inferno?"

She saw puzzlement in Spence's face, then a dawning understanding, "How did you know about—"

"Don't ask me *how* I know about that. Just tell me the fucking truth. Did he kill 8 people in some suburban fire?" Fiona was almost screaming.

"Fiona–" he began and then let out a shaky exhale. "It wasn't just Micah involved in that. All of us played our part in that—that..." he almost couldn't finish, but he took a breath and finished the thought–his slumped shoulders told her all she needed to know, "...we all played a part that fucking disaster."

She wanted more details, but couldn't bear to ask. She had been living among monsters...had become a monster. Her rage was directed as much as herself as everyone else.

Clutching the neckline of her shirt, she sputtered accusations, "How could you just...hurt so many people? How could you manipulate me like that? What kind of a person are you?" Fiona sputtered out, flailing to and fro, unable to control the movements of her body.

God! She burned down Nina's apartment...burned it to the ground along with all the hard work that went into it. And that fucking Planned Parenthood! Rage overtook Fiona. Blind, red rage.

Fiona felt her fingers begin to smolder; the first inkling of fire simmered softly inside her. Not nearly as strong as it could be–the fading drugs still kept it in check–but for the first time in a week, she felt heat return, giving her life–fueling her.

"I'm trying to make up for it now," Spence responded. "By telling you the truth. By giving you an out."

"You think you can make up for destroying my life? ...for killing all those people? You think you can make up for any of it?"

"I don't, Fiona. I know what we did–what *I* did–is inexcusable. When you were taken by Adam, I was glad you were gone. He's a decent guy...unlike us. I was glad that maybe you could find another path. I know I can't give you back what we've taken from you. Or bring back all of the innocent lives I've helped end. I know that. But I'm telling you to leave. Don't stay here. I won't tell anyone I saw you, that you came back. You can get out."

"You know Adam wanted to take you down, right? All of you? Micah and Kaleb too?" Fiona tried to reason.

Without missing a beat, Spence replied, "Maybe I wanted him to. Maybe I'm sick of all of this."

Fiona tried to think rationally, but the emotions collided so violently within her she still wasn't sure she fully processed all of what she learned. She felt terribly used. Terribly broken. A tendril of smoke curled up from the rug beneath her feet; if her condition hadn't been tempered by those pills, she would have probably burned the house to the ground. And maybe she should have. Momentarily she wished she could. If her senses hadn't been dulled thanks to Adam, Fiona thought she would have turned that small ranch into a flaming hellscape. And she would have enjoyed watching it go up in smoke.

"Where would I even go? I have no place...no one."

But as she spoke those words to Spence, in the back of her mind, Fiona knew exactly where she would go. There was only one option, really.

"I know you'll find your way Fiona," Spence responded.

He tried to embrace her, but Fiona couldn't endure the feeling of his touch. Not after what he had done. There are just some things that are unforgivable, and this was one of them. She thought about Rhea and Maya; she thought about Micah–she had loved him. Was that love still there? Despite it all, it was. And Fiona hated herself for it. Hated herself for briefly contemplating just pretending she hadn't had this conversation with Spence. Wouldn't it have been easier to just forget about it all and go downstairs, take a nap in her bedroom. To sink into blessed ignorance? To wait until Micah got home and fall back into that same old routine that had occupied the past year–more than a year–of her life?

No. She couldn't do that. She couldn't un-know Spence's confession. And if there was any hope for her at all, any scrap of dignity left in her body, she needed to follow Spence's advice. She needed to get out...now. While she still could. At that moment, Fiona had no idea how to reconcile this new version of herself with the one she worked so hard to establish...how these new pieces would fit into the puzzle she had thought complete. It would take her a long, long time to come to terms with it all. To come to terms with herself.

Stomping out the smoldering rug fibers, Fiona raced out the front door. Spence let her go.

<h1 style="text-align:center">Chapter Fifty-One</h1>

The knowledge Spence imparted weighed heavily upon her, and she felt as though she had a boulder strapped to her back. She couldn't breathe and her fingers itched with the power harnessed beneath them—power that had only recently returned. She collapsed against the wall of the train station, relishing the cool feel of the exposed bricks against her back. It was 5 o'clock and the sunlight filtering through the leaves of the trees cast shadows on her tear-streaked face.

Fiona worked to calm her breathing and to get control of the heat rising so forcefully below her skin. With the drugs fully out of her system, she could feel that ignited flame. *I'm here*, it seemed to whisper. *...and I'm ready to burn the whole fucking world to ashes.* Inhale. Exhale, 1-2-3. Again. Inhale. Exhale. *No*, Fiona told it. *No more destruction.* It took quite a few minutes for Fiona to subdue the fire roiling within her, but she finally beat it into submission.

"Are you ok sweetheart?" a voice interrupted her thoughts

Fiona looked up to see the dark, concerned eyes of an elderly woman peering down at her.

"Um," Fiona began, unused to being approached by strangers at the train station. "Yeah. Yes, I mean. Just resting."

"You're crying," she observed.

Fiona swatted at her tears with the back of her palm, and replied honestly, "I was just thinking of something sad."

"It's all going to be ok," the woman continued, placing her hand on Fiona's forehead. "Oh my, you're very warm. Shall I help you to the walk-in clinic, just across the street?"

"No thanks, " Fiona responded quickly. "I really am ok. Thank you for your concern though."

"Go home and get some rest. Chicken soup always helps," the woman said moving along. "Oh actually," she continued, rooting around in her enormous purse. "Here's a granola bar. I always carry around snacks for my grandkids. You look like you could use something to eat."

Fiona took the offering and smiled up at the woman's back. Kindness from a stranger, and at exactly the moment when Fiona truly needed it.

The temporary distraction helped Fiona get herself under control, and she rose to a standing position. Glancing at the screen overhead, she saw that a train would arrive in approximately 20 minutes. She didn't know if it was the correct train exactly, but it was headed to Albany, which was at least in the right direction. She didn't want to wait any longer. She had to get out of Plattsburgh; suddenly, she couldn't bear to be there for another minute. How funny. She couldn't wait to get here...now, she couldn't wait to leave.

Searching through her pockets, she found the remaining bills that Adam gave her yesterday. Was it yesterday? It felt like ages ago. She thought it would be just enough to get her to where she needed to go. She sat down on the wooden bench to wait and the thoughts slammed into her with a force that almost doubled her over. So many lies. So much deception. The memories burst forth as the floodgates opened; Fiona let them wash over her.

She had been happy once–with her mom, and Noah. Working for Nina. Yes, her condition inhibited her. But, she was able to live with it. It turned out she was able to control it more than she gave herself credit for. And she hadn't committed that awful act–that massacre in the Garden City Hotel. The names of those 11 people scrolled through her head–those never-ending movie credits. This last bit of knowledge, both awful and beautiful in its raw unadulterated truth, was the hardest for Fiona to accept. She thought of herself as a monster for so long. But maybe, just maybe she wasn't a monster. Micah orchestrated the whole thing. *He* was the monster. And there had been so many more lost lives–8 more that she knew about. But how many others? *He* made her believe she was so broken, so out of control that she had to make an impossible choice. A choice that took her away from everything she loved, everything she held dear. She had accepted the choice, without asking the necessary questions–naively, dumbly. And then there were all those choices that followed. All the burning, the destruction, the ashes leaving a trail of breadcrumbs through her subconscious, shaping the way she thought of herself, her life. They shaped her very identity. Micah and Kaleb stole her family from her, her job...but hadn't they stolen her very sense of self too? And wasn't that the most egregious crime?

On top of that, Fiona loved Micah. God, even still, she loved him. But now that love was tinged with hatred, growing like a weed in her heart. How can two opposite emotions be woven so intricately together inside one person? Maybe it's true what they say, that within all love is a kernel of hatred as well, that one cannot exist without the other, like an evil twin vying for attention. Fiona would have a long time to ponder the nature of life's complicated emotions, but now, she needed to make one more choice. What would she do with this knowledge? With this truth spewing forth like lava, oozing forth, destroying everything in its wake? This time, she would choose correctly.

Chapter Fifty-Two

It was nearly morning when Fiona showed up back at Adam's compound. It felt strange to arrive there on her own free will. She spent a whole week trying to get out. How the tables had turned. Now that she was there examining the structure, she marveled at it. The vastness of the underground complex was completely hidden and the only above-ground portion was a double, free-standing garage–the home of the very door she had used to escape. Nothing would hint at the life that thrived below the soil.

Looking at the door, she saw that it was held in place with a large pad-lock. Adam must have affixed it after she left–which also meant that there had to be another exit somewhere. Upon examination, Fiona discovered that the entry-code was a 10-digit number. She didn't even know they made locks so large.

Rattling the lock in her hands, she discovered there was no wiggle room; it was secured tightly. Spence could probably figure out how to pick it, if he was there. The thought brought with it a fleeting pang of sadness. The betrayal was so raw, so new, Fiona hadn't fully realized its breadth yet.

She closed her eyes, felt her breathing steady, her heartbeat slow. It was amazing how much those relaxation techniques worked. How easily they allowed her to gain control of her condition. And she remembered how long it had taken her to master them. Those afternoons outside on the grass with Maya. The endless practice. Now she would put all that to use, but this time for her own purposes.

She visualized the lock. Large. Brass. Heavy. In her mind she traced the way the mechanism wove through the holes on the door. The way the numbers felt as they spun on their axles embedded in their metal bed. Fiona closed her eyes. She felt the air enter and exit her nostrils, her lungs. Lips relaxed. Tongue relaxed. Shoulders relaxed. *Melt*, she commanded. She pictured the metal turning into liquid, slowly dripping into the crevices of the door and sliding to the floor. *Melt*, she said it again inside her mind.

She felt a familiar heat flare inside of her; it pushed against the insides of her ribcage and skin. It felt good to use her condition intentionally again after a week of dormancy. So good. She opened her eyes to see the job was done; the lock was a puddle of metallic shine on the floor at the base of the door. There was still residual brass leaking off the hasp.

Without the lock fastened in place, there was nothing preventing her from opening those doors and descending into the compound. Was she ready to take such a step? To join forces with the people she had come to know? She could just run away...from all of it. From Micah. Adam. Maybe go live somewhere else. Travel the world. Then another thought: could she go back home? Show up on her mom's doorstep, *Surprise guys! I'm not dead.* That was an impossibility. She couldn't just return from the dead. How would she explain what happened that night? Or what happened thereafter? Where she had been. That life, that old life, burned to ashes on the night Micah made his appearance at the Garden City Hotel.

She looked at the door, still closed. Should she open it? After her encounter with Spence, her feet lead her here, instinctively. This was the only place her mind could think to go. But maybe there were other options. Fiona thought for a minute. Was she being impulsive? All of the other alternatives formed a sort of list in her mind...and she crossed each of those ideas off systematically as they popped into the logical part of her brain. What did this new life look like for her? A life with Adam and Chelsea and Bryce, and the rest of them? Fiona didn't know the answer to any of those questions buzzing around her head, but she decided to let her gut make the decision for her.

The door squeaked as she opened it. Without fear, she took the first steps down the steep set of stairs, excitement and a fair bit of nerves welling up inside her. Listening to her own internal voice was a new experience for Fiona; it had been quelled for so long, overpowered. But she couldn't ignore the sense of rightness she felt bloom within her as each footfall followed the last. She still couldn't see the bottom, but maybe that was as it should be. Maybe she just needed to trust that once she did reach solid ground, the floor would hold her up.

Part Four

Chapter Fifty-Three

Finally reaching the bottom of the stairwell, Fiona looked around. Even though she had just been there the day prior, the space felt foreign.

Walking down the hallway, she passed the common area serving as a living room and wasn't surprised to find it empty. It was a little after 3 o'clock in the morning; of course everyone was still asleep. No one was expecting any visitors. She was surprised no alarms blared. There were definitely security cameras and other surveillance devices around. Maybe they had been disabled somehow.

More closed doors greeted her as she continued her walk down the hallway, until she reached the small bedroom that she inhabited for the past week. That door, of all of them, was standing open as if inviting her in. Briefly, she contemplated rapping on Adam's door, but she didn't think she was ready to face him just yet. Her head was cloudy with thought. So instead, she walked into the bedroom...her bedroom, and sat down on the bed. The room was swathed in shadows; in fact the only source of light came from the red numbers on a small digital clock on the bureau, but she bent down when she felt her foot brush against an object on the floor. When she sat back up, even in the darkness, she was able to perceive a book in her palm. Bringing it up closer to her face, she could make out the title, *Firestarter*.

Clutching the book to her chest, she curled up in a fetal position on top of the bedding. The pillow felt soft under her head, and she was so very tired. The exhaustion seeped into her bones, her heart. Paired with the bitter pangs of betrayal, Fiona was completely depleted. Her feet ached, her head pounded, her throat was raw from emotion. Everything hurt. How easy it would be for her to just torch this place. She imagined that the thin corridors would look like glowing arteries and veins as they carried her amber flames through the cavernous space. But she didn't want to burn this place. Not anymore.

Her weariness allowed her to shut off her thoughts, and she drifted into an uneasy sleep. In her mind's eye, she thought about Spence, Micah. She thought about her mom and Noah. She tried to reason out how things had gone so horribly wrong. But when Fiona's subconsciousness finally took her away, her breathing evened and the fire sheathed itself. At least for now.

Chapter Fifty-Four

"Hey," said a familiar voice.

When Fiona didn't respond, the voice spoke a bit louder, "Fiona. Time to open those eyes."

The voice was friendly, warm.

Blinking her eyes open, the artificial light pierced her retinas, causing her to squint up at the face looking down at her. Propping herself up on her elbows, Fiona allowed her vision to adjust and glanced over at those red numbers once again. 11 o'clock–she assumed it was in the morning, but couldn't be wholly sure. Without natural light, time felt rubbery. She felt as though she had slept for days.

"Is it 11 in the morning? Or 11 at night?" she asked, reminded of a similar question she asked when she first arrived here the week prior.

"Morning," Adam answered with a small smirk.

He sat on the end of the bed, wearing a navy blue sweatshirt and faded blue jeans. Fiona openly studied his profile, the tawny beard and shaggy hair. His contemplative hazel eyes. The smirk would have irritated her to no end a few days ago, but now it felt comforting and welcoming.

When he didn't say more, Fiona spoke, "How did you know I

was here? It's not like you could see my bed from the hallway. And it's dark as hell here."

"You triggered the silent alarms when you came in. I watched you on the cameras...and you left the door to the stairwell open," he said honestly.

"Is that how you knew I was going to escape yesterday?" Fiona asked without humor.

"Yup," Adam said simply. "And when you didn't come into my room to kill me–" he chuckled at that and then picked up, "I figured you needed some rest."

"I did need rest," Fiona responded quietly, stifling a yawn– and stifling the embarrassment she felt at being perceived so unaware.

The sadness, the bitter feelings of betrayal, the shame and embarrassment at the deceit she lived under for so long came back to her tenfold as she tried to meet Adam's steady gaze. She tried to force her emotions under control, but a salty tear slid down her cheek and into the corner of her mouth. Brushing it away angrily, Fiona sat fully up and folded her legs beneath her.

"All your drugs have worn off," Fiona said. "Do you have a pill hidden in your hand somewhere? To prevent me from burning this place to the ground? Because, my condition...it's back. And I could do it if I wanted to."

"We already are *in* the ground," Adam countered.

"Ha Ha," Fiona said in mocked laughter. "You know what I mean."

Adam simply opened his hand to reveal an empty palm, "No drugs. I trust you."

He was so earnest and so genuine in that simple admission that Fiona allowed her tears to flow more freely. And she allowed Adam to see them.

Adam took Fiona's hand in his own and the two sat in silence for a moment. Fiona allowing Adam to absorb all the emotions coursing out of her, and Adam accepting them freely and without judgment.

When the tears abated, Adam asked, "What brought you back?"

Fiona thought for a moment before she answered him. She didn't know if she wanted to reveal the truth, but she didn't want to start with lies either. Not again. Lies were what got her here—starting with the fabrication of her death all that time ago.

"I don't know if I'm strong enough to tell you why I'm back," Fiona responded honestly.

"Don't underestimate yourself, Fiona," Adam responded. "I won't judge you. You *are* strong. Tell me."

Fiona inhaled a deep breath. Revealing the story, the real, full, true, ugly story to Adam would expose a level of vulnerability Fiona hadn't shared with anybody in a very long time. But at that moment, Fiona felt tired of being strong. She wanted somebody to listen to her, to validate her thoughts. To help her sort through the torrent of tragedy she experienced in her life. To feel her betrayal.

So she told Adam. Everything. Beginning with her high school crush on Jared, through her years in college and at her internship. Her on-again, off-again condition. Gio, and the awful lie she believed about herself. The lie that had come to define her as she walked away from everything she loved and valued. The lie that allowed her to work for Micah and wreak all that destruction. Her training. And finally, she revealed the truth as Spence told her just the day before. It all came rushing out of her like an uncontrollable geyser. By the time she was done, she was gasping for air, and the blankets beneath her were clenched tight in her fists.

Adam didn't comment nor ask for clarification. He just listened, with those patient eyes.

Finally he said, "I'm sorry."

"Please don't tell me you're sorry," Fiona shot back. "I absolutely cannot deal with your pity."

"Ok. I won't. But I will tell you that despite it all, you're a survivor," Adam said.

"Well sometimes I wish I wasn't a survivor. Sometimes I wish that I really did die in that fire...along with your friend."

Fiona hadn't felt like that in a long time, and she certainly hadn't admitted that to anyone other than Micah. But she didn't feel ashamed by the admission, nor did she regret telling Adam what was in her heart.

"I'm glad you didn't die," Adam said simply. "And I'm glad you came back."

Fiona didn't respond, but instead she asked, "So what do you want me for? What are you going to do with me?"

"You don't have to do anything you don't want to do. If you just want to stay here, and then take off once you get back on your feet, that's fine by me. I'm not going to insist you stay here...or work for me. I'm not going to use you," he replied. "I realize now I made a mistake in taking you like that. It was wrong...and I'm sorry."

"It's ok," Fiona responded, and despite it all, she actually believed it was.

"Why did you come back?" Adam asked again.

"I just told you that," Fiona answered. "Where else would I go? I don't have any sort of life anywhere."

"You could have gone anywhere Fiona. Anywhere in the world. But what I want to know is why you came back here. What do YOU hope to accomplish here?"

Fiona realized he was right. There was a reason why she came back; her subconscious knew it, but it wasn't until that moment she was able to put it into words.

"I want to make up for what I've done. Everything. I don't want to allow Micah or Kaleb to get away with strong-arming people in order to get what they want."

Fiona thought again, fleetingly, about the Planned Parenthood. About the women she imagined needing such a facility. And when she spoke again it was with much more force.

"I want to stop them. They've gone too far; the cost has been too high."

"I agree," Adam replied.

The two looked at each other, and their gaze solidified a bond that could never have existed had Fiona remained there as a prisoner. They were no longer captor and captive, but friends... unlikely friends, but friends nonetheless. United in a common goal. This was the first time in a long time that Fiona felt she made an actual and honest choice. She made it with both her mind and her heart–and deep down, she knew that this would be one she wouldn't live to regret.

Chapter Fifty-Five

Two days later, Fiona found herself sitting around the cafeteria table with the rest of Adam's group. She looked around and saw the eyes of Chelsea and Bryce, Josh, Erin and Andrea, the eyes of Adam, studying her with good-natured interest. They all gave her some leeway over the past two days, figuring she needed some space, some time before opening up. And she did need that space...that time. But before she fully opened up about her past, she needed to know more about this organization she now found herself a part of.

"Ok," she began. "So I know you all have impressive resumes–"

Resumes. Now there was a funny word to use. In her former life as a designer, she thought so much about crafting her resume, her portfolio–making herself appealing to possible employers. Over the years she added to that resume...but not at all with the experiences she predicted as a young intern, eager to make a name for herself in the cutthroat world of interior design.

Fiona finished her thought, "...but aside from your past experiences, I'd like to know more about your group."

"What do you want to know?" asked Andrea.

"Well...everything," Fiona replied. "Do you guys call yourselves by a name?"

"We refer to ourselves simply as The Committee," Josh answered. "Everything else sounded cheesy. This name kind of formed organically...from our breakfast *committee* meetings."

"The Committee," Fiona repeated, testing out how the words felt in her mouth. "Who funds you? Are you affiliated with the government?"

Now it was Adam's turn to chime in, "We do get some funding from the local precincts...much to their chagrin. We have a love-hate relationship with the authorities, but they can't deny our usefulness to them. Sometimes we take on private commissions when we agree with the cause–that helps us to stay up and running. We can't offer the type of monetary incentives you were probably making with Micah's group. We're simply not in it for the money."

Fiona thought about that for a minute. "I'm not in it for the money either. Not anymore," Fiona replied honestly.

Bryce put in, "We're a mish-mosh of people with a variety of backgrounds. But, we all share a common goal."

"So, you're a vigilante group," Fiona said with finality.

Chelsea picked up, "We don't like the word 'vigilante.' It sounds— I don't know—"

"Overdramatic," said Bryce finishing her sentence.

"Yeah," Chelsea said. "Overdramatic. But in essence I suppose that's what we are. We fight for causes we believe in, in ways that the government and authorities can't because of all the red-tape. Politics free from manipulation. Environmental causes. Human rights. We can't fix everything that's wrong in this world, but we try to fix what we can. And we're proud of the small wins we have made–they were hard-earned. Can you get on board with that? With us?"

"I think I can," Fiona said.

And now, with the general details of the people in front of her–along with a steaming plate of pancakes, bacon and eggs courtesy of Chelsea–Fiona was finally ready to tell them her story. To let them see her...really see her. To know her, even though she didn't really even know herself. Fiona felt as though she lived a million different lives, been a thousand different people, yet here she was embarking on yet another path. The prospect was scary, yes. But knowing she chose this of her own free will, took the fear down a notch. It was like she was taking her life back–cathartic and so very needed.

With the fire quartz gripped in her sweaty palm, Fiona unraveled her past–without even editing out the most painful bits and pieces. She wanted them to know all of it. She was surprised to find that she wanted to tell it, even those jagged parts that made the tips of her soul bleed when she thought about them. She was sick of denying who she was, denying her past, burying her head under the sand of delusion and shame and justification.

Fiona found the more she revealed, the lighter she felt. That weighted backpack strapped to her shoulders felt less heavy, less daunting. For the first time in a week, she could breathe again. In for One, Two, Three. Out for One, Two, Three. The air she inhaled felt clean and unadulterated.

When she was done, she felt momentarily terrified. Terrified of judgment, but more so terrified of pity. She had built up such a thick and stony wall around her, had guarded all of those pesky emotions that made her feel vulnerable with such vigilance, that pity, sympathy...she couldn't bear. No one had spoken a word since she opened her mouth, not even to ask a question. They let her ramble and stutter, and choke it out. When she had nothing left to say, she pulled her gaze upwards, and met those of the people surrounding her one at a time. She didn't see sorrow in their eyes, just acceptance. Just gratitude.

Chelsea reached over and grabbed Fiona's shoulder as a sign she was there, a sign she heard her and recognized her.

"Damn girl," Chelsea said, and Fiona laughed.

"*Damn* is definitely an accurate assessment," Fiona replied.

Once Fiona regained her humor—and her composure—the air in the room shifted.

Fiona turned once again to Chelsea. "I'm sorry," she said simply.

"For what?" Chelsea responded with a puzzled look scrawled across her adorable face.

"For escaping on your watch."

As an answer, Chelsea merely swatted the air in front of her. "You're here now," she said. "And that's really all that matters."

"I *am* here now," Fiona responded to her with a smile. "Thank you for having me back."

"Ok," Erin interjected, wiping a single tear from her cheek. "Can we just stop with the formalities and sentimental bullshit?"

At that, Fiona laughed out loud. "That's the best idea I've heard since I came back."

In her bare feet with chipping black toenail polish, Chelsea stood up and walked over to that enormous economy-sized refrigerator.

Her voice was muffled as the cavernous appliance enveloped almost her entire body. As she rooted around she said, "I propose mimosas."

Erin and Andrea's faces lit up, but Josh spoke for the first time all morning, "Gross. Heartburn in a glass."

"Oh Joshy," Chelsea said with light-hearted affection. "Next time I'm at the store, I'll buy stuff for Bloody Marys."

"Even worse," he mumbled, not without humor.

As Chelsea poured the Prosecco into seven red Solo Cups, Fiona said, "Shouldn't we be talking about our...I don't know... our plans?"

"Let's save that for tomorrow Fiona," Adam replied. "For now, let's just have some fun."

Fun, Fiona thought to herself. That was definitely something she could use. As she took her first sip of the sweet, tart, bubbling, and slightly acidic cocktail set before her, Fiona felt her body relax. Her mind followed soon after.

Chapter Fifty-Six

"So Micah and Kaleb are planning a forest fire in Derby Line, Vermont. Up by the Canadian border," Adam told the group when they were seated around in the living room the following evening. "There's 300 acres of unclaimed forest there. 45 degrees North and 72.1 degrees West is the epicenter of the land plot. That's where the fire will originate."

Fiona did a double take; Adam dropped this metaphorical bomb unexpectedly and without warning. She almost thought she imagined it. They had all been nursing massive hangovers after yesterday's breakfast mimosas progressed into late afternoon revelry. Fiona's head still felt the after-effects of too much booze. She was headachy, woozy, and totally exhausted. Adam's statement jolted her out of her stupor and she felt a flush creep to her cheeks.

Adam spoke with a gravity that Fiona hadn't seen before, and all eyes in the room went directly to him. Bryce and Josh looked up from their chess game, where a check-mate was about to be issued. Chelsea looked up from the newspaper grasped in her hands and put a mental bookmark at the sentence on which she left off. She leaned eagerly forward. Erin stopped painting Andrea's nails a deep shade of cobalt, the polish dripped off the brush in a crystalline shimmer that briefly caught the shine of the overhead fluorescent lights. The reactions reminded Fiona of when she used to play freeze-dance as a child. When the song stopped, you had to pause mid-action, and wait for the music to start up again. Even if you were in an impossible position, that was the one rule. If you were caught moving, you were out. Simple as cake. The silence, the way everyone just froze, would have been comical, if it wasn't so serious. Fiona briefly wondered if all of their jobs began this way. With the quiet, almost militaristic intensity of anticipation.

Bryce said, "A forest fire? That's not really his style. What's the play?"

Adam responded matter-of-factly, "There's a political group called EarthJustice, throwing some pretty heavy monetary incentives at a few different politicians that have serious sway in some upcoming elections. They want to claim the 300 acres as protected land. Micah's group is working to...make them less of a threat."

Fiona's gaze dropped to her trembling hands clasped together in her lap, and her breath felt ragged as it hitched in her throat. It was odd hearing Adam and Bryce and the rest of them speak about Micah and his...*activities*. It reminded her just how much this group knew about her, how long they followed her movements and...*contributions*. The word *contributions* felt sarcastic and hollow, but it was the only one that crept to her mind. Fiona forced her eyes to focus on Adam and found he was looking directly at her, a question in his calm, steady eyes.

The thought that Micah and the others were planning another job, this time without her, made Fiona's emotions flutter around inside of her, like a flock of caged birds. Jealousy at being excluded was one of those feelings—no matter how ridiculous that sounded it was still there, a flash of red feathers in her mind. It was reckless of them to plan such a large fire without her...but then again, she hadn't always been there with them. And they had been successful enough before her arrival. Then there was fear—the notion of actually working to stop him was stark and terrifying; he was too strong, too meticulous. But more colorful than all the rest was anger–raw and unadulterated. Could she take down Micah? Could *they*? Did she want to? Yes. She did. Even though she wanted him. Even though she loved him...did she though? Did she really love him? Or was that emotion tied to the man she once thought of as a savior, as a path, as an only option? Micah was none of those things to her anymore. He was a monster. A murderer. A villain. Yet it was still hard for her to reconcile all of the shifts her subconscious tried to process. His deep mahogany eyes played on the edges of her mind.

Adam broke her thoughts and said, "Fiona, if it's too soon. If you need more time–"

"I'm ready," she said without hesitation. "It's time to stop Micah. It's time to stop all of them."

Suddenly, she was talking about Rhea and Maya too. Their complicity was just as damnable. Spence too. Even though he had told her the truth. Can "I'm sorry" always make things right? Fiona didn't think so. "I'm sorry" is a band-aid. When it comes off the skin, leaving a red rash behind, the festering sore is still there.

Her agreement marked a shift in the room and Fiona could almost feel the air become electrified, tense. Fingers twitching with subdued fire, Fiona stood up and walked over to the side of the room, just to give her jittery body something to do. So this time she wouldn't be the one starting the fire, but instead the one stopping it. The one controlling its trajectory. The one to smother it. She hadn't explored that part of her condition. She could easily control the fires *she* started, but controlling fires started by someone else? She would have to prepare. Practice. If it was even possible in the first place.

"When is the forest fire scheduled to happen?" Fiona asked, suddenly worried, daunted by all she must do to ready herself.

"Three weeks," Micah answered. "It doesn't give us much time to prepare."

It certainly doesn't, Fiona thought to herself as her mind raced with all that was to be done.

Adam continued, "My information is often delayed. I wish we had more time, especially considering the fact that the location is so far away."

Three weeks! She thought about the months of planning and reconnaissance and visualization that went into the prior jobs she had been part of with Micah and the others. And now, she needed to tap into a completely different part of her condition. All in just three weeks. The others must have seen the look of sheer panic cross onto Fiona's face because Chelsea stood up and walked over to Fiona immediately.

"Together, we can do this. We can be ready. Let us help you. This doesn't all rest on your shoulders," Chelsea said, placing a reassuring hand on Fiona's arm.

Fiona had no knowledge of the previous jobs this group was part of, but she did know they had no idea what they were up against now that they selected Micah and Kaleb as Enemies Number 1. And as much as Fiona appreciated the kindness of Chelsea's offer of aid, she also knew that most of this would rely on her own abilities. When she thought about what she could do as an *ability* in that moment, she was momentarily surprised. Maybe it wasn't a *condition*, but a power...an *ability*. Maybe. The idea sent a jolt of pride down her spine she couldn't quite ignore.

"Ok," Fiona said, exhaling a long shuddery breath. "What do we do now?"

Adam answered this question, "Now, we start planning."

Chapter Fifty-Seven

About an hour later, after everyone had already gone to bed with an aim to begin the discussions the following day, Fiona found herself alone in the kitchen with Adam. She went to grab another bottle of water before she herself called it a night–still feeling dehydrated from all of yesterday's champagne–and saw he was already there. He sat on a stool with his back to her, alone at the large, steel island, staring off into nothingness. He was so lost in thought he didn't even hear her enter. Fiona studied the back of his head, the way his ears tucked in close to his scalp, the slump in his shoulders, and found herself wondering about him. She knew so little about this person in front of her. Yes, he had told her the story about his friend at the Garden City Hotel, but what about his family? Did he have one? What brought him here, doing this type of work? He clearly wasn't receiving the paycheck Micah was. If not money, what was his incentive? Could it be genuine morality? The honest desire to do what was right in this world? Did such nobility and selflessness truly exist?

Fiona leaned against the counter and one of the cabinet doors banged shut behind her, causing Adam to turn around and face her. His eyes were curious, unguarded, and there were small crinkles forming in the corners. *Smile lines*, her mother used to call them. *That's a much kinder word than wrinkles*, she used to say.

"Hey," he said. "You're still awake?"

Fiona felt nervous all of a sudden, and she could sense the scarlet flush creeping to her cheeks.

"Thirsty," she said, grabbing a bottle of Poland Spring from the package and raising it towards him in a gesture of cheers.

"Champagne will do that to you," Adam replied.

All of a sudden, Fiona found it difficult to meet his gaze.

"You ok?" he asked, sensing some shift in her emotions.

"Yeah," she replied. "You know–I'm not some magic wand," she continued. "Yes, I have an ability to create fire, but it's not easy. I can't just burn on demand. Not for a job this big. Also, I don't even know if I can be successful with this. I can create and control my *own* fire...but controlling someone else's? I've never tapped into that aspect of myself."

"I know you can do it Fiona. I believe in you," Adam said simply.

"Well, I hope I don't let you down," Fiona spoke her fear aloud.

"You could never let me down," Adam replied, standing up and moving towards her.

Trying to ignore the sensation of his close proximity, the earthy, masculine scent of him, Fiona continued, "There are things I need," Fiona told Adam tentatively. "...in order to ensure success. For a job this big, I can't just go in blind. I need maps, pictures...since the target is a forest, drone footage would be helpful. I also need to see the location in person."

"I'll make sure you get what you need," he responded. "We might not look like much, but don't underestimate us. We are thorough and organized. You'll see."

"But we only have three weeks to get it right. Makes me nervous," Fiona said.

"We've been in time crunches before," Adam said reassuringly. "I think we can pull it off."

"I hope so," Fiona responded honestly. "I really do. What's the end-goal with Micah and Kaleb...and the others?"

"Well I guess we all have to discuss that. And a lot of that decision rests on you," he answered.

"What if I don't know what I want?" Fiona asked.

"We have three weeks to decide," Adam replied with a small smirk.

Does this guy take anything seriously? Fiona asked herself. But she supposed he did. She supposed his smirk was a defense mechanism or something he built up. Maybe one day she would see him without it. Fiona exhaled a breath, but the tension was still there, palpable.

Her breath hitched as he placed his hands on the counter behind her, one hand on each side of her so she was enclosed within the space of his arms. Suddenly, he was all she could see. A handsome face–so much softer and more direct than Micah's. There was openness and honesty in his gaze, but something else too. Desire. He leaned in and she felt his full lips brush softly against her own; she felt heat rise up from within her and guessed her own desire was written in red across her cheeks where her freckles danced like cinders across her nose and forehead. For a single moment, Fiona allowed herself to taste Adam, to enjoy him, but that was all she allowed.

"I can't," Fiona said, turning her face slightly to the side to gently break their contact. "I need to be my own person. I need to know myself before I let someone else in."

He let out a deep breath and looked down at the floor between them trying to collect himself.

"I get it," Adam said without rancor. "I'm sorry. I never should have done that. It was wrong of me...wrong of me to assume."

Adam looked sheepish for a moment, and he ran his hand down his face as if to shake himself free of the lustful thoughts racing through his mind. His grin told Fiona he wasn't angered by her rejection...he didn't even view it as such–he understood.

"It's ok," Fiona said, and she meant it.

Adam pushed himself up, but remained facing her.

Fiona felt a momentary pang of disappointment for not allowing herself the pleasure Adam surely offered, but when she was able to catch her breath again, she knew she made the right decision. Micah consumed so much of her, she was not going to allow herself to be consumed again, even though Adam's intentions were likely much different than Micah's. She wanted to embark upon this new path without being led by a guy. She was ready to do her own leading for a change. So as much as she felt a fleeting loss for what could have been with Adam, she relished in the thought of taking her life back. Once and for all, she was determined to be her own person and even though she didn't yet fully know who that person was, Fiona knew she was in there somewhere, buried in the depth of her psyche–and she couldn't wait to meet her again.

Chapter Fifty-Eight

F iona expected awkwardness over breakfast the next morning from Adam, considering what had occurred the night before–or maybe it would be more appropriate to say what had *almost* happened the night before. But she was pleasantly surprised by his good-natured smile. She exhaled a breath she didn't know she had been holding and sat down next to him. She was glad there was no tension or strain between them after last night's broken kiss; she had begun to value Adam as a friend and knew she needed his help if they were going to stop Micah and the others. What exactly that meant still remained a jumble in Fiona's mind; she needed to talk out the possibilities and come to terms with whatever they collectively decided.

The spare space echoed with conversation as noise bounced off the steel cabinets and tiled floors. Chelsea and Bryce were engaged in a heated conversation about the daily *New York Times* Crossword Puzzle, while Erin and Andrea teased Josh about his goofy sweatshirt, featuring a faded Bugs Bunny underneath the famous question, "What's Up Doc?"

"Leave me alone, ladies," Josh said light-heartedly. "You know you're just jealous you don't have my eye for fashion."

Erin and Andrea looked at each other and laughed. "Is that

sarcasm Josh? Are you feeling ok?" Andrea said through stifled giggles.

"Yeah, no offense Joshy," added Erin. "But you're not usually one for humor."

For a moment, Fiona was a bit concerned by their nonchalance. She thought to herself, *Aren't we planning a major operation? Shouldn't everyone be a bit more subdued?* How different this group was from Micah's. But Fiona checked her judgment. Everyone is entitled to some down-time, right? Even during times of stress.

As she watched the members of The Committee–it still felt weird to refer to them as such–interact, Fiona had to smile at the easy way they had with one another. They had formed a little underground family here, and Fiona's heart leapt a bit at being the newest addition. Chance had landed her with Micah, but choice landed her here. The two scenarios felt worlds apart in her mind as she sipped her cup of coffee.

Adam broke the lively banter when he said, "I think we need to get down to business and talk specifics. We don't have much time, and with Fiona's abilities, we have some things to add to our planning."

Fiona was surprised–and relieved–to see attentiveness steel over everyone's faces. It was like a switch flipped. The ease disappeared, and in its place was a fierce concentration. Chelsea, Bryce, Josh, Erin, Andrea–they all stopped their conversations and settled down around the kitchen island. For a minute, all Fiona heard was the irritating sounds of stools scraping against floors, the shuffling of feet and the creak of elbows as hands propped faces up to listen. It was evident that this was their routine, their dance–Rhea, Maya, Spence and Micah had one, and now she was seeing a new one, with these new people.

Adam got up and wheeled over a school-sized movable white board with dry erase markers of various colors lined up like cars in traffic on the thin metal tray underneath. All eyes watched as he wrote in red: Derby Line, Vermont.

"This is what I know," he said, taking the cap off the marker. It made a puckering sound as the seal released.

He wrote in neat block letters underneath the title as he spoke. Each point received its own bullet and line. With each swoop of a letter, the marker emitted a tiny squeak as it sent out its chemical aroma around the room—that squeaking and the calm drone of Adam's voice were the only sounds at all. Fiona and the others sat at rapt attention trying to absorb every detail.

49th parallel, Adam wrote and said, "49th parallel is a line of latitude that forms a nominal border between the United States and Canada from Lake of the Woods to the Strait of Georgia."

The next bullet point he wrote was, *The Derby Line–Rock Island Border Crossing/Interstate 91.* "The first is a road that connects Derby Line with Stanstead–a town just over the border in Quebec. Interstate 91 is the main thoroughfare and intersects with Quebec Autoroute 55. We have to familiarize ourselves with these roads to plan the best entry and exit routes for our purposes."

Derby Line Vermont Forest, was the third bullet point on Adam's list. "The forest consists of just under 57 square miles of pine, cedar, maple and hemlock trees and houses a large concentration of animal species. My source believes the fire will originate in the EarthJustice outpost located just southeast of the central point of land. I don't have the exact coordinates yet. Josh...I was hoping you could provide detailed maps along with drone footage of the area and roadways. Also, information about forest density and weather patterns would be helpful."

"On it," Josh replied, breaking the spell of silence that seemed to have fallen over the kitchen.

He leaned down and rifled around in a backpack on the floor to pull out a brand new Mac Book of which Spence would have approved. He began typing away while the rest of them followed along with Adam's list.

Next, Adam added, *EarthJustice* to the list. "EarthJustice is the organization campaigning heavily to designate the Derby Line

Forest as national protected land. They are a powerful eco-organization with some heavy political pull. It seems however, that the politicians with whom they align, go against Kaleb's allies–which is why Micah's group has been enlisted to send a message. Erin and Andrea–this is your area of expertise. I need all the information you can possibly find on this organization and the politicians they align with. I want to cross our t's and dot our i's on this one."

"You got it," Erin and Andrea said in unison. Their echo produced a small burst of giggles from the two women.

"What angle do you want me to run, boss?" Bryce asked.

Adam responded, "I was hoping you could deal with the media and news coverage. I want you to use all your contacts. This is going to be big. I want Micah to have an audience for this one. I want to catch him red-handed...put a stop to them once and for all. He and Kaleb can't keep playing God with American politics."

"Yes sir," Bryce said with a smile, giving Adam a mock salute.

The four with assigned roles sprung into quick action. Josh was already typing furiously away on his keyboard.

"What about me?" Chelsea asked. "Want me to work with Bryce?"

"Actually, Chelsea, I was hoping that you could work with Fiona," he responded.

Fiona felt her temper flaring a bit. Did Adam think she needed help? Assistance? Did he think she needed a babysitter?

Adam must have sensed her emotions because he spoke quickly, "I know you don't need help Fiona...I know you are exceedingly capable. But I also know this is a bit of a new angle for you. Chelsea is patient and has researched your abilities for some time now. She is knowledgeable and reliable. I thought it might be nice to have some company. I figured that your role could be lonely sometimes."

Fiona thought fleetingly of how isolated she sometimes felt in Plattsburgh. How she longed for companionship...begged Micah for it at times. But she learned to live with the loneliness, the separation. Maybe it would be nice to have someone around–a partner. Plus, Fiona genuinely liked Chelsea. So she swallowed the irritation and nodded her head in agreement.

Chelsea let out a small squeal of excitement and Fiona was again surprised by her light-hearted demeanor. Sometimes it was difficult to believe that Chelsea had such steel in her. Her sweetness was deceptive, but genuine.

Turning to Fiona, Chelsea said, "I'm so excited to actually get to work closely with you. I promise I won't overstep."

"I'm sure you won't Chelsea," Fiona responded.

Adam studied Fiona's face closely and asked, "Do you have any questions for me?"

"A few," Fiona said.

"Shoot."

"Well, I'd love to know about your source. Who is this person and how accurate is he or she?"

"I have a few sources. All of whom choose to remain anonymous, so it's not my right to expose them. But I can tell you that they have always proven to be honest and mostly accurate."

"Mostly," Fiona repeated.

"Yes," Adam replied. "Mostly. There have been a time or two over the years where they have gotten some small things wrong. But overall, I would trust them with my life. And I don't say that lightly."

"Ok," Fiona said, wishing that she felt more reassured.

"Anything else?" Adam asked patiently.

"Yeah. So much. But I'd also like to know about the aftermath...assuming we're successful that is."

"Aftermath?" Adam questioned.

"Yes. What is the plan for Micah and the others? After we stop them I mean? *If* we stop them."

"I wanted to talk to you about that one. I know that you have developed relationships with them. With Micah specifically," Adam said.

Fiona wondered how intimately acquainted Adam was of her *relationship* with Micah, but she didn't ask that. She just met his gaze head-on and answered, "Well there really are only 2 options, aren't there?"

"Yes," Adam replied.

Fiona continued, "If we stop them and just allow them to get away, they'll continue to do what they're doing. And that's not what you...or any of us, and I guess that now includes me...really wants. So that leaves us with either killing them–which I don't think is mine, yours or anyone else's idea of a victory. Or, turning them over for legal recourse."

Adam remained quiet for a moment and then said, "So there really is only 1 option...right?"

Fiona thought about the actuality of turning Micah, Rhea, Maya, Spence, Kaleb over to the cops. Of being the one responsible for their legal punishment. What would they even be tried for? Arson? Treason? Murder? And how long of a sentence did those heavy words carry? Probably years upon years. And while Fiona now knew that they needed to be stopped, there was still that nagging feeling of guilt–despite the fact that they had all betrayed her so intimately, so heartlessly. Just because they had hurt her, did Fiona want to go out and hurt them? No...that wasn't it. For the first time, Fiona was able to see clearly that this went far beyond any personal vengeance she may want. This was a matter of morality. Of right and wrong in the larger sense. And even though she didn't want to picture any of them rotting away in the prison system, it was really the only path available. Her choices had narrowed down to this tiny point.

So Fiona responded to Adam's question with confidence... with the only right answer that really existed, "Yes. There is only one option."

Adam just nodded at Fiona's reply with a grim set to his mouth.

He raised his voice and announced to the group, "Okay people. We have three weeks. We *are* going to take down Micah and his group. Failure isn't an option. Take the afternoon and evening to get yourselves situated. We'll have another meeting tomorrow morning to decide on the next steps and to address any concerns or problems that have come up."

"Ok boss," Josh said above his computer screen.

Fiona watched on with approval as everyone turned their attention back to the task at hand. She had certainly underestimated Adam and the people seated around her. They were better than she expected. Organized, meticulous...a well-oiled machine. She knew that she had her own tasks to attend to, so she gestured for Chelsea to follow her out of the kitchen and into the hallway. It was time to train. To prepare herself. To open herself up to someone new.

Fiona felt both nervous and downright terrified by the prospect of coming face-to-face with Micah again. He was not an enemy she desired. Not at all. But she felt ready too. Ready to confront the lies of her past. Ready to at least try to right some of the wrongs she had committed. It was too late for her to get her old life back, that was definitely true. But she could make this new life that she was given meaningful. And that was exactly what she intended to do. Step One–take down Micah and Kaleb. Step Two–the rest of her life.

<h1 style="text-align:center">Chapter Fifty-Nine</h1>

Holding the fire quartz in her sweaty palm, Fiona sat opposite Chelsea in the vast expanse of overgrown lawn outside of the compound. It was the first week of July and the grass was brittle beneath her, straw-like from lack of water and the summer heat that flared so relentlessly in this part of New York. There wasn't a cloud in the sky and the sun was aflame with hazy intensity.

It had to be at least 90 degrees outside and Fiona felt a small trickle of sweat trail down her neck and in between her breasts. She quickly wiped it away with the palm of her hand. Chelsea shifted her legs into a comfortable position and Fiona noticed a few pieces of dried grass stuck to her inner thigh as she moved.

The two women stared at one another tentatively. Chelsea, nervous about pushing Fiona too hard to display her condition and Fiona unsure of how to proceed and worried about scaring Chelsea off. It was one thing to study her condition on paper, but quite another to witness it first hand. She could feel eager anticipation rising off of Chelsea's being seeping into the charged air around them.

Fiona began, "So, I don't want to freak you out. It can be startling to see what I can do."

"I'm not scared of you Fiona," Chelsea responded immediately, and to prove it, Chelsea took Fiona's free hand in her own and gave it a gentle squeeze.

"Ok," Fiona responded, closing her eyes and exhaling a breath, feeling all the tiny muscles in her shoulders loosen and ease.

She thought about all the time she had spent with Rhea working on meditation and control. It had felt so different than it did with Chelsea. Rhea was so closed, so cold. Chelsea exuded warmth and openness.

Feeling a bit on-the-spot, Fiona closed her eyes. *One, Two, Three*, Fiona counted in her head. Visualizing the small space of earth between her and Chelsea. *Exhale. Inhale. Exhale. Inhale. Dry, tan grass. Scratchy. Lifeless. Straw.* She saw a tiny flash of light. A spark started at the root of a patch of crabgrass that looked like an outcropping of hair on a bald head. *Catch*, she told it. *Catch*, she commanded again.

A bitter pungent odor reached her nostrils as she opened her eyes and gazed down. The small patch of grass smoldered and smoked. Tiny flames erupted from the scraggly blades of grass and they hovered there, not moving, dancing almost invisibly in the harsh daylight.

She glanced up at Chelsea and saw her transfixed by the orange embers.

"Can you make it bigger?" she asked.

In response, Fiona closed her eyes and pushed. *Spread*, she ordered. *Nope, not too much. Just a few inches. Grow.*

"Wow," Chelsea said, watching as the contained fire glowed slightly brighter as it spread out another 2 inches in diameter—until it looked like a campfire fit for a Barbie Doll.

Fiona was impressed Chelsea didn't move back nor flinch as the flames licked the ground a few inches from her exposed legs. Chelsea trusted Fiona; despite it all, that sense of assurance was there. Chelsea believed Fiona wouldn't hurt her. And this unearned conviction, along with the small pyre before her, warmed Fiona's heart.

"I'll make it stop now," Fiona said to Chelsea, feeling more empowered. "Watch."

Stop, Fiona told the fire. *No more. Dim.Calm.*

Fiona and Chelsea watched as the flames grew smaller and smaller still, until only a few glowing embers resembling shimmering rubies remained alight. And after a few more seconds, even those sparkling bits faded into a paltry pile of gray ashes.

The two women gazed at one another–Fiona's green eyes met Chelsea's blue blues good-naturedly. Neither spoke for a minute, each engulfed by their own swirling thoughts.

Finally, Chelsea broke the silence, "That's pretty cool."

Fiona considered her comment. "I guess it is," she finally said. "It took me a long time to realize that. But it is...cool, I mean."

"How long did it take you to gain that much control over your ability?" Chelsea asked.

Fiona responded, "It wasn't until Micah found me and I spent time training and honing my condition that I got my confidence with it. And after each..." Fiona couldn't settle on the right word. "Job..." she finally decided on. "After each job, I got better and better. It's second nature now. I'm not worried about losing control anymore, or hurting people–"

Fiona broke off and Chelsea grabbed her hand again. The gesture didn't feel awkward or forced, just genuine. Right.

Chelsea said, "I know about the hotel. I know about those people who died in that fire. I also know it wasn't your fault. Those deaths aren't on you."

"I didn't kill those people, you're right about that," Fiona responded. "But even though I didn't start that fire, if I wasn't there, those people would still be alive. I'm indirectly responsible."

"That's bullshit Fiona," Chelsea said, surprising both of them with profanity. "If it wasn't there, it would have been somewhere else. If not those people, it would have been others. Micah was going to get you, no matter what you did…or where you were. You can't shoulder the blame. Those deaths are on Micah…and Kaleb and the others they work with. Sometimes I wish we could just show up in Plattsburgh and turn them in…but that won't work. We need to catch them in the act. It's the only way to stop them. They're too good. Too clean. No one would arrest them without proof. And hopefully, in three weeks, we'll get that proof."

"I hope so too," Fiona said. "I can't believe I've been so blind for so long. I feel so stupid."

"You're not stupid Fiona," Chelsea responded. "Don't even think that. You were brainwashed. Forced to believe you're something you aren't. They made you vulnerable. Took away your choices. I'm proud of you for coming here. It couldn't have been easy."

"Thank you," Fiona said, feeling those tears well up in her eyes. "I really needed to hear that, Chelsea."

Chelsea couldn't have known how much Fiona wanted, needed to hear these words, but their impact made the very air between them shift.

Wiping her eyes, Fiona spoke again, "Now. Let's see if I can control someone else's fire. Wanna help challenge me with something new?"

"Yes," Chelsea responded. "Let's do it. Just tell me what to do."

And Fiona did.

Chapter Sixty

For the next week, every day after breakfast–while the others worked on their various assignments–Chelsea and Fiona retired to the same patch of grass just outside the entrance to the compound. Sometimes to Fiona it felt like she could have been in a field in Iraq. The grass was straw-like, and aside from the small structure that housed the entrance to their underground headquarters, the flat undeveloped land stretched as far as the eye could see. How Adam ever stumbled upon this place was a mystery to Fiona, and she decided to ask him about it at some point. Maybe at a time when she was less stressed–stressed because even though it was the seventh day she found herself seated on the ground with Chelsea, she hadn't yet been able to gain control of a fire started from an external catalyst.

It took Fiona three days to feel defeated, and six to feel down-right hopeless. And now, on the seventh day, Fiona felt the hot pangs of anger simmer inside of her. On the first day of trying, Chelsea scratched a tiny wooden match against the course striking paper on the side of the matchbox. After a brief hiss of ignition a small flame sprouted at the end of the match. Chelsea lowered the small stick to the grass, which spread ferociously outwards as the brittle blades quickly caught. Watching the uncontrolled spread of the flame sent a panic through Fiona, and no matter how she had tried to calm her thoughts, to visualize the path of destruction and to mentally smother the fire, it didn't work. Fiona watched the panic settle in Chelsea as well as the grass continued to burn. Finally, Chelsea went scurrying inside the entry structure to unravel the hose in order to quell the rapidly growing blaze.

"No worries," Chelsea had said as the water splashed the dry ground. She tried to assuage Fiona's feelings of failure, "No harm no foul. It's the first day. Maybe we should've brought the hose out in the first place–you know, as a precaution. We'll try again, and we'll make sure we have a water source on hand...just in case."

And they *had* tried again. Three more times that day and endless times the days following. Despite Chelsea's unfailing belief and patience, Fiona found it exceedingly difficult to focus when the fire spread without her specific control and her feelings of defeat made any confidence she had diminish even further, sending her on a downward spiral that completely squashed any ability she might have had to truly master the task at hand.

"It's ok," Chelsea reassured Fiona again and again. "Is there something I can do to help you?"

"I wish there was," Fiona responded. "I really do. This is much harder than I thought it would be."

But it was more than that. Fiona knew their goal was completely dependent on her ability to tap into this aspect of her condition. And now, on the seventh day, Fiona tried to imagine the conversation she was going to have to have with Adam. A conversation centered on the fact that even though everyone else was doing their job with admirable proficiency, Fiona would not be able to do the same. Last night, when Adam and Chelsea had believed she wasn't looking, Fiona watched from the other side of the room, a tense conversation between the two of them. Fiona sensed that they were talking about her...about her inability to do what she needed to do and that Adam didn't want to put the added pressure on her by asking her directly. Up until that point, Chelsea had answered all of Adam's questions regarding Fiona's "progress" with optimism and cheer. But they were getting to the point where honesty was needed.

So now, Fiona said to Chelsea, "I can't do it. Maybe it isn't possible. Maybe my condition doesn't allow me to control external flames."

Chelsea pushed a sweaty strand of hair out of her eyes and said, "Stop calling it a *condition,* Fiona. You're not sick. What you can do...it's a superpower."

Fiona couldn't quite absorb the compliment, but it didn't escape her mind that she recently began to have that very same thought.

Chelsea continued, "And I don't believe for a second you *can't* do this. I think the pressure is holding you back. I know you can do this."

"Oh yeah?" Fiona asked, her frustration seeping through. "How do you *know* anything? You have no idea what this is like. What it's been like for my entire life. What if you're asking me to do something that's impossible?"

"Let's just try to use some of those meditation strategies. Maybe if you went back to the basics, it would be easier," Chelsea suggested.

Back to the basics, Fiona thought. *Before I knew that everything in my reality was a complete and total lie?*

Chelsea looked at Fiona with such earnest kindness it encouraged her to try again.

"Ok," Fiona sighed. "But if I fail again today, I have to break the news to Adam. It's not fair to have everyone working so hard on something I can't deliver on."

"Deal," Chelsea said. "But you have to really give it your all."

"I have been," Fiona responded.

"I know," Chelsea said quickly. "But you have to promise to try to control the anxiety and pressure you feel. If you can't do that, I don't think it's ever going to work."

Fiona sat down again on the ground and Chelsea sat right next to her, pulling that insidious matchbook out of her front pocket once again. Fiona had come to loathe the sight of those tiny wooden matches all lined up like sentinels.

"Tell me when," Chelsea instructed.

Fiona closed her eyes in concentration. In–One, Two Three. Out–One, Two Three. In–One Two Three. Out. In and Out. In. Out. She felt her breath fill her up and then leave her. Her heartbeat slowed. Her pulse slowed. She felt her shoulders settle down and the tension in her neck ease.

"Now," she whispered to Chelsea with her eyelids still drooping.

She could see a bit of light through her feathered lashes and heard the sound of Chelsea striking the match. She watched in slow motion as Chelsea again lowered the small flame to a fresh patch of grass and heard the pfft sound of the catching fire. It was spreading. Slowly at first, and then the burning embers picked up a bit of speed.

Calm, Fiona said in her mind. Did it hear her? It sounded like it did. Again, with more conviction, *Calm, Simmer, Slow.*

Fiona opened her eyes to once again see that the fire wasn't heeding her demands. It didn't care what she was saying...or maybe it didn't hear her. It burned recklessly forth making a small campfire before her as it greedily ate up the parched land. Fiona put her hands to the ground right in front of the fire and stared at it, begging it to hear her. To listen to her. Her face was inches from the flame and she could feel its relentless wavy heat batting against her cheeks and lips. It crackled laughter in her face as she felt its tentacles slide against her right wrist. She felt a burning sensation and looked down to see her wrist bubbling up with red blisters, the skin around them turning pink, almost translucent.

"No," she said aloud.

Chelsea was standing up next to her, pulling her up, "Fiona, step back. It's burning you."

The words were jarring to Fiona–foreign. As oxymoronic as it sounded, she had never been burned before, despite it all. But now, that the fire wasn't of her own creation, it seemed as though it *could* hurt her...and maybe it *would*.

But even though this new knowledge shone like a lightbulb in her mind, Fiona wouldn't stand. The firelight danced in her green eyes and she felt her own flame join those that were already engaged in a fiery gyration before her. In her mind she watched as her own fire formed a circle, a perimeter around the growing blaze–slightly more yellow in color, but powerful, strong. Her own. It was only then she gained a sense of control.

Condense, she told the small circle she created. And her fire obeyed. Slowly, almost agonizingly so, the circle constricted, forcing that outside fire inside its circle to do the same. Maybe now it was only 2 feet in diameter. Then smaller still. And smaller. Fiona clenched her fists together to coax her flame to subdue the unnatural alien entity it surrounded. And it worked. The circle diminished and shrank until only a single, minute, wisp of blaze rose up, casting smoky tendrils into the blazing daylight.

Fiona looked up at Chelsea with triumph in her eyes and saw that Chelsea was no longer looking down at embers sparkling in the grass. She looked directly at Fiona with a small smirk pulling up the edges of her adorable mouth.

Fiona closed her eyes once more and now she could see the remnants in her mind's eye. *Stop*, she said. And it did.

Once she was sure it was over, that the fire was fully extinguished, she opened her eyes again and raised her gaze to meet Chelsea's.

"You did it," Chelsea said. "I knew you could."

Fiona didn't say anything in response. She just breathed in a sigh of relief. She figured it out. Maybe she couldn't control an outside fire, but she could use her own fire to surround it...and vanquish it. With that knowledge, hope rekindled itself again inside of Fiona and took root, and for the first time since she came back to this place, to these people, she felt like maybe it was possible to take down Micah and Kaleb. Just maybe.

Chapter Sixty-One

"Ok people," Adam began. "It's been a week since we committed to do this. I'd like a detailed report from all of you so we can address the next steps."

"I'll go first," Josh said, pulling out his laptop and turning it around so everyone could see the screen. He clicked on a folder labeled *Vermont* on the home screen and then on another file. "This," he pointed, "is a map displaying the prominent buildings and roads in the incorporated village of Derby Line. It's an interesting place. Small town life. Charming. All that nonsense. The town extends into Quebec here," he said, indicating a darker border line on the map. "There are two streets that cross into Canadian territory without any checkpoints. Technically, any time anyone crosses the international line, they are supposed to report their whereabouts, but from what I see, no one's really checking. Traffic is fairly light here, and if you take this road, Maple Street," he pointed again. "...it turns into a thoroughfare that leads right into the forest. That's our best bet for both entry and exit...in my opinion. I have the coordinates and traffic maps in another document. I'm going to get everything printed out tomorrow afternoon."

Fiona and the others listened intently as Josh spoke about

road lines, coordinates, and traffic patterns. His attention to detail impressed Fiona and she realized how severely she underestimated every single person seated around this breakfast table. They were certainly a lot more than they appeared. But she guessed this was true about everyone. Would anyone suspect this pale, freckled, red-head to be capable of the type of destruction she was capable of? No way.

"What about the forest itself?" Adam asked.

"I'm still working on that," Josh replied. "I have a preliminary map of tree density and shrub layer on a gradient terrain map. I also have a general sketch on the EarthJustice outpost in the central region, but I need to work more on the details. It's not exactly as mappable as some of the other aspects. But from what I can tell, it makes sense to start the fire there...I mean, from Micah's perspective. I'm planning on working on drone footage this week."

"Great," Adam responded. "Let me know what you need and I'll arrange it."

Josh didn't answer. Fiona didn't know if he even heard Adam; he was already vigorously tapping away on his keyboard.

"What about any recon on EarthJustice?" Adam said, turning his attention to Erin and Andrea.

Andrea nodded at her friend to answer; Erin seemed brimming with excitement to reveal her intel.

"For an eco-organization, EarthJustice is pretty radical in their methods," Erin began as she plopped a large stack of papers down on the table before them. "I mean, it seems like their heart is in the right place, but they don't always practice what they preach. They've been involved in countless political scandals and are known to be pretty...aggressive if they don't get their way. Check this out," Erin said, picking up one of the articles in front of her.

She read aloud, "There was a well-executed assassination attempt on Senator Jamie Walsh for her role in the ban of the Fossil Fuels Emission Act. Luckily, the bullet–shot out of a Glock Pistol–only grazed the surface of the Senator's right forearm. Had she not turned around abruptly, it would have caused significant damage, much more than the flesh wound for which she is currently being treated at County Line Hospital. We are still searching for the culprits. Anyone who has any information is urged to contact local authorities."

"So?" Fiona asked.

"So," Erin picked up. "EarthJustice was responsible. No one has ever been able to link them to the assassination attempt. We even tried—briefly–but there was just zero evidence to go off of. Honestly we should have been contacted immediately...maybe then we could have helped. But by the time the police swallowed their pride and asked for our help, there just wasn't really anything we could do."

Bryce interrupted Erin and said, "Seems kind of crazy for Micah and Kaleb to mess with this group. I'm sure they know how dangerous they are...and I'm sure they know their track record."

"Truly," Andrea broke in. "And that's not the only story like that. There are countless others."

Fiona responded, "If you knew Micah, you wouldn't be surprised. He's not afraid of anything. And for as long as I've known him...he's never failed. Not ever."

"Well, there's a first time for everything," Chelsea offered, giving Fiona's arm a friendly squeeze.

Adam directed the group back to Erin and Andrea's research. Fiona and the others listened as the two women went on to provide an in-depth analysis of the organization's political affiliations, mission statements, and history.

In closing, Andrea said, "I'll print everyone up a thorough summary of what we just explained. We have more research to do, but we'll give you the notes thus far."

"Meticulous as always," Adam said in admiration. Then he turned his attention to Chelsea and Fiona.

"What about you?" he asked.

When Fiona didn't speak, Chelsea began, "It took us a little while, but Fiona's doing her thing. So far she hasn't been able to interact with fire that originates from an external source, but she has demonstrated an ability to use her own fire to subjugate...alien flames."

Fiona stifled a snort at that. *Alien flames.* It sounded like it could be the name of some cheesy action film.

Adam's expression mirrored her own and then became humorless again as he addressed Fiona directly, "Do you feel confident about being able to subdue Micah's fire?"

"Confident?" Fiona said in response. "No. Not yet." She looked over at Chelsea and said, more to her than to Adam, "But I will be."

Fiona gazed down at her wrist; it still ached, even though Chelsea cleaned it well and applied a layer of Bacitracin to the inflamed skin. For her whole life, Fiona spent so much time around fire, and yet, she had never received a single burn. Not until yesterday. Underneath the bandage, four angry blisters sprouted on the 3 inches of forearm the fire had marred. It reminded Fiona of her fallibility–a trait she didn't like to be reminded of.

Chelsea interrupted Fiona's musing, "We still have a lot of work to do. But I'm confident that Fiona will be able to do what's needed."

The positive news seemed to resonate well with Adam, and Fiona could see his shoulders relax a bit as he took a sip from his steaming mug of coffee.

"I'm going to need to make a trip to Derby Line," Fiona said. "Probably in about 3 more days, I'll be ready."

"I can arrange that," Adam replied.

Chapter Sixty-Two

Over the course of the next few days, Fiona practiced using her own fire to manipulate the contained blazes that Chelsea set for her. They started small: a match, touched to an area of dry grass, a metal trash can filled with old newspapers. Once Fiona mastered those, they worked their way up. And with each new task, Fiona grew stronger and more skilled as she tapped into this new facet of her condition. At times Fiona found she even stopped viewing what she could do as a "condition," which sounded like some rare disease–as Chelsea suggested–and thought of it as an *ability* instead. This positive thinking was a reversal from how she ever thought about this seed hidden inside of her.

The final task gave Fiona the rush of confidence she needed; the day prior, Chelsea took Fiona on a ride about ten miles north to an old, run down school in the middle of nowhere.

"When was the last time a child saw this place?" Fiona had asked walking up to the crumbling ruin and nudging a fallen brick with the toe of her sneaker. "Yikes. It's creepy here."

"It is, right? It's probably been at least two decades since anyone stepped foot in there...for the purpose of learning, at least," Chelsea answered. "There was a mill about a mile east that basically crashed and burned during the Bush administration. The collapse sent all the residents running for the hills. A few lingered for a couple of years, but ultimately this whole place became like a ghost town probably in like, the early 90s, maybe even earlier."

Fiona looked around. She had never seen a place so completely abandoned...so devoid of human life. It looked like something out of *The Walking Dead*, after the zombie apocalypse came and leveled the entire world.

"I found this place about a week ago. I knew we would need larger stakes and we can't very well just torch the compound. I thought it would be a perfect place to test your control," Chelsea explained.

"Looks good to me," Fiona said. "It almost seems like we'd be doing the world a favor by clearing all this rubble."

Again Fiona looked around, taking in the skeleton of what was once a learning institution. People had vandalized what was left of the brick exterior walls with graffiti in various colors and fonts, and the remaining windows were smashed in. The whole place had an other-worldly, dystopian feel to it that frankly gave Fiona the heebie jeebies.

"So," Fiona said, turning to Chelsea. "What did you have in mind?"

Chelsea reached down into her backpack and pulled out a small bottle of lighter fluid and a barbeque lighter. She held the items up for Fiona to see. Fiona laughed at the image. Looking at Chelsea, innocence radiated off her. Twinkling blue eyes, petite build. But she was much tougher than she appeared.

"Looks like we have a little arsonist in our midst," Fiona teased.

"Yup. That's me," Chelsea responded with similar humor. "Besides...you'll extinguish whatever fire I make, right?"

"I'll certainly try," Fiona said back.

"Ready?" Chelsea asked, her light eagerness contrasting with the task at hand.

"As I'll ever be," Fiona responded, closing her eyes.

Fiona pictured the image in her mind. Crumbling cement. Bricks scattered helter skelter. Gaping holes that used to be windows. A hastily written *Covid Sux,* scrawled in sloppy black spray paint. The slanted tilt of the sunshine reflecting off the shattered grass on the gravelly floor.

While Fiona added the nuances to that mental picture in her mind, Chelsea went to work dousing a section of rubble with lighter fluid.

"It should spread quick enough without this," Chelsea murmured. "It's so freaking dry and hot out, but a little help can't hurt." Chelsea liberally squirted the liquid about.

Fiona breathed deeply and took the pungent, chemical, kerosene scent of the fluid deep into her lungs. She let the inhaled air exit slowly through her parted lips. She heard the click of the lighter and felt an immediate blast of heat against her face. Without being conscious of the act, she reached into her back pocket for the fire quartz that had become a friendly talisman, perhaps the one constant in her life since Micah had given it to her all that time ago.

"Let it really spread before you start," Chelsea instructed. "Micah's fire will certainly be a big one. I know we can't match the scale. But let's just see how you do with a blaze that is less contained."

Fiona forced herself to wait, even though her fingers itched and her fire begged for release. She risked a glance and saw Chelsea's fire gaining momentum. The rubble of plaster and beams, the scattered sheetrock and remaining building material on the northwest side of the structure was aflame in a glaring blue, orange dance that lightly grazed the brittle scrubgrass that had sprung up through the cracks. It was beautiful in its intensity, its ferocity.

"Ok. Now," Chelsea said.

Fiona closed her eyes again and summoned the energy within her. She knelt down and touched the ground with her fingertips causing a trail of fire to spring forth in a controlled collision course with the one that already radiated forth. In the other hand, she held the stone. She remained there, transfixed in a crouching position until she could visualize her fire–like an obedient pet–surrounding the established flames.

Once it formed its glowing perimeter–as she practiced these past few days with Chelsea–she began to slowly close her fists. Dirt and earth was trapped within her palms as she told the fire to *Constrict, Smother, Compress.* And like it had finally begun to do late last week, it listened. It spoke in its own crackling language to the "alien flame"–that ridiculous phrase Chelsea used was more accurate than Fiona was ready to admit. And as the circle drew in smaller, the fire grew dimmer, and dimmer still, until only a pile of gray ashes with the occasional orangy-red glint winked forth into the afternoon.

"Holy shit," Chelsea uttered in admiration. "You're a beast."

Fiona knew Chelsea didn't mean that as an insult, it was quite the opposite as she gazed at her friend with awe and approval.

The heat in her cheeks faded and she hastily replaced the stone to its rightful home in her back pocket. She could feel its warmth radiating down her thigh. Taking a few more deep breaths, Fiona felt the fire within her dim and even though the day was humid and muggy, the small breeze felt cool on Fiona's skin.

When Fiona didn't speak, Chelsea began, "I think you're ready to see Derby Line. I think we should go the day after tomorrow. Now that you've mastered this, the more visualization and preparation you can get, the better."

"Agreed," Fiona said.

A slight breeze blew a tendril of hair across Fiona's eyes and she could see the coppery shimmer through the dull brown dye. It had been awhile since she colored her hair and it seemed as though the natural amber hue was more and more prominent with each passing day. And maybe that was as it should be. Fiona tucked the strands behind her ear and followed Chelsea back to the small gray Prius.

"I'll talk to Adam tonight," Chelsea said. "Tell him of our plan. I think Josh will want to come too, to get more of that drone footage. God, he loves his damn drone."

Fiona let out a small laugh and thought briefly about how much Josh would have loved Spence. How they could have been good friends, in another world, another life. Once the notion popped into her mind she couldn't clear it, no matter how much she tried. Why was it that she still thought of Spence with fondness? After all he had done to her? After all he allowed to be done to her? The conflicting emotions put a damper on her mood, and Fiona spent the 20 minute ride back to the complex barely responding to Chelsea's friendly banter. Fiona hoped all these pesky feelings wouldn't hinder her ability to perform when the time came. That was a possibility she couldn't quite move past in her mind. Emotions had always been her Achilles Heel. Always. Even from the time she was a child. It was time for her to use logic instead of emotions now. She just hoped she could do that when it came down to Micah.

Chapter Sixty-Three

It was a five hour drive to Derby Line Vermont from the compound, located just south of Albany. Fiona thought it would have taken longer, because when they spoke of the location it sounded like it was on the other side of the world, but all they really needed to do was head due north. Fiona, Chelsea and Josh passed the time in a mix of lively conversation and contemplative silence. Josh couldn't wait to try out the new high-tech drone he purchased for the occasion, and his enthusiasm almost made Fiona forget the seriousness of the mission.

Through the car window, Fiona admired the stark beauty of the mountains rising from the land around them in generous heaps. It was so green up there, and the fresh air brushed Fiona's hair back from her face as it streamed in through the open window. She held her breath in appreciation of the natural enchantment of this little pocket of the planet. If there was a God, and Fiona still wasn't sure what she believed about divine power, this was where he could be found. In the straight pines and the whispering leaves. In the gently braying cows chewing the grass in the fields to the left and right of her. In Lake Champlain that glittered below them as the sunlight streamed down through the wispy clouds overhead.

After a pancake breakfast at Dale's Luncheonette, with real Vermont maple syrup, it was a quick ride to the outskirts of town. The highway turned into a single-laned road, which then turned more meandering, finally ending up at a set of wooden posts with a sign that read *Derby Line Forest* written in green block letters.

Checking his map, Josh motioned with his hand, "This is the main entrance. The road leads right to the EarthJustice outpost and the ranger station. My intel says it's mostly unoccupied during the week. I think there are like 5 rotating rangers on staff, that's it. It's not exactly a tourist destination or anything...not like those big National Parks. We can park in the small lot there and then head in to explore."

Chelsea turned the car gingerly up the trampled dirt road, that was really not much of a road at all, and they slowly made their way inside the dense, tree-lined route. Errant branches scraped at the car a bit, making Chelsea cringe with the squealing sounds it made.

"Jeez, Bryce is gonna kill me if I bring the car back all scratched up," she said.

"If you stay in the center, you should be ok," Josh directed as Chelsea maneuvered the car into one of the three narrow spots outside the wooden house with EarthJustice Ltd. written neatly on the front door.

The structure was a ranch, with a small front porch housing a few rocking chairs and a standing rack holding an array of informational pamphlets about the land and forest written in a variety of different languages. Everything was dusty and cobwebs had formed in between the slats of the chairs. There was a sign propped in the front window indicating the office was closed on Mondays, which meant Fiona and the other two would be alone today–well at least alone in the sense that there would be no official supervision. They couldn't account for errant hikers, but there didn't seem to be any of those.

After parking, the three exited the car. Chelsea popped the

trunk so Josh could have access to the drone and Fiona took a deep breath in and looked around her admiringly.

"This place is so beautiful," she said. "How could anyone want to turn it into a pile of ashes?"

"I was just thinking the same thing," Chelsea said. "I mean, I've been to Yosemite and the Grand Canyon...and those are incredible places. But this...it feels like a hidden gem."

Fiona knew what Chelsea meant. The trees seemed to extend up into eternity and scraped against the turquoise summer sky while the sad notes of the chirping birds caught her ear on the gentle breeze. While Chelsea helped Josh get the drone situated, Fiona walked tentatively into the dense growth of trees. It was even cooler in the underbrush as the sun filtered down through the leaves.

Movement out of the corner of her eye caught Fiona's attention and she turned around in a semi-circle and came face to face with a tawny, white-spotted fawn. At first, Fiona was startled and took a tentative step back, but its glossy onyx eyes seemed friendly, curious. The creature advanced a single step, closing the gap until the two figures stood only two feet apart. Fiona had never been this close to any wildlife and the proximity nearly took her breath away, but she was undeterred. Extending her arm, she offered her open palm to the creature. She felt cool wetness as the fawn pressed its velvety black nose to her inner wrist, probably hoping for some morsel of food. Maybe it smelled the remnants of the maple syrup on her, but the sensation tickled Fiona's sensitive skin.

Just then, a crackling sound came from behind them and Chelsea's clear voice called, "Fiona?"

The deer leapt away with effortless grace as its spidery limbs carried it back into the trees. Fiona felt a momentary pang for the loss.

"I'm here," Fiona's voice echoed back, as Chelsea joined her.

"Josh is staying back by the outpost. It's easier for him to control the drone from there without all the trees blocking its launch," Chelsea said.

"That makes sense," Fiona responded.

"So," Chelsea began again. "Lead the way."

And Fiona did. The two women spent the next three hours hiking through the maze of trees and underbrush, getting a feel for the place. Every once in a while, they could hear the soft hum of Josh's drone overhead, making its methodical way over the land. Chelsea didn't utter a single complaint as Fiona led her across trickling streams and through thick growth, up steep terrain and between rocky outcrops. It was different this time than it was with Micah and the Plattsburgh group. She wasn't looking for the best means to start a fire. Rather she was trying to absorb the forest's heartbeat, hear its pulse, know its crevices and secrets. Puzzle out all its intricacies so she could keep it safe...or at least try to keep it safe.

When Chelsea and Fiona made it back to Josh, they were muddy and exhausted. Sticks, pine needles, and leaves had lodged themselves in their hair and clothes. But none of that mattered to Fiona. Her eyes...and her head were clear. But beyond that, she knew–knew with every ounce of her being– she couldn't allow Micah and Kaleb to destroy this sanctuary.

"I just need another half hour or so," Josh informed them. "I got most of it...I just want to do another lap around the perimeter."

Fiona watched as Josh fiddled with the remote and then checked his phone to make sure he was capturing the necessary footage.

"I want to take some time here also," Fiona said. "If this is where the fire is set to originate, I want to set it in my mind accurately."

"Need me to do anything?" Chelsea asked.

"Nope," Fiona responded. "I just need some space."

"You got it girl," Chelsea answered.

Fiona stood directly in front of the wooden structure so she could see it in its entirety. It would burn easily, that she knew. And she was sure Micah knew that too. It was a good place to start a blaze and if she were on the other side of the line, she would have had a clear vision of how to do so. It would have been easy. But she wasn't with Micah anymore. With her eyes, she traced each detail of the outpost: the buckled planks on the small set of wooden steps leading up to the entrance, the green lattice that hid the base of the structure from view, the brown window boxes with the peeling paint, the moss-covered shingled roof. Fiona walked slowly around the structure, examining each angle, each feature–no matter how tiny. After she made her lap, she closed her eyes. Yes, there it was. Brilliant and whole in her mind.

When she blinked her eyes open, she saw Josh and Chelsea studying her with interest. They didn't speak; they didn't want to interrupt Fiona in her work. Fiona thought she saw admiration flash in their eyes–and hope; that was there too.

It wasn't until after 6:30 that the trio exited the roadside tavern after dinner and got on the road back to New York. Despite the busy-ness of the day, Fiona felt a deep contentment rolling through her soul when she finally made it back to the compound. It was late, and she knew that she–for the first time since she made her way back to Adam and these new people– would sleep well. Maybe that's when a person is able to achieve the deepest relaxation, when she knows that she is finally on the right path. When the soul and the mind and the physical body are linked harmoniously in a healing path. And maybe that was what allowed Fiona's subconscious to feel at peace, despite the coming chaos. Despite the chaos she was supposed to stop. Was it redemption she was hoping for? Possibly? But perhaps it was simply the taking back of her life, her morality, her choices. And that was definitely something worth fighting for.

Chapter Sixty-Four

Fiona slept late the next day. It wasn't until the electronic clock across the room read 2:30 that her eyes finally opened. And this time she knew it was pm instead of am. She couldn't even remember the last time she allowed herself such indulgence, maybe high school...maybe not even then. She momentarily felt guilty for not setting an alarm. *Maybe if I wasn't sleeping underground, I'd be more attuned to the time.* There was so much to do, and they had so little time left–just one more week. *Relax*, she told herself. *You have everything you need.* But did she? Theoretically, yes she did...and logically she did, but she was still wading in unfamiliar waters. She thought she should schedule some extra practice time with Chelsea today to make herself feel more secure. Every time she felt her confidence swell, the next moment it dipped again. It was frustrating and out of character for her–this cycle of emotional upheaval. She didn't like it. Not at all.

She heard a light knock and, pulling her tank top down to cover her exposed belly, opened the door to see Adam standing there with a mug of coffee in his hands.

"Hey sleepyhead," he said lightly. "Are you going to grace us with your presence today?"

He was teasing, but Fiona blushed none-the-less as she took the warm cup from his offering hand.

"Yeah. I wouldn't want to deprive anyone of this gorgeous face," Fiona responded sarcastically.

Adam just laughed and leaned against the doorframe with his arms crossed across his chest; Fiona averted her eyes when she found herself studying the lines of his shoulder muscles, visible through the thin t-shirt he wore. How was it that he could be this at ease when there was so much at stake?

"Chelsea told me your time in Derby Line was a success," he said after a minute. "We debriefed earlier this morning."

Fiona let out a small giggle that came out through her nose like a snort. *God, Chelsea is efficient*, she thought to herself. *Does that girl ever sleep?* It seemed to Fiona that Chelsea must spring right up out of bed in the morning wide-eyed and ready to go. Her energy was unfailing.

"It did," Fiona replied. "It's such a beautiful place. I'm glad we have a role in protecting it."

"Me too," Adam said honestly. "But it's more than that... protecting a forest, I mean."

"I know," Fiona responded, looking down into the rich coffee. The hearty scent helped the exhaustion fade away.

"How do you think you'll handle seeing Micah again? Facing him and the others?" Adam asked, the question clearly in the forefront of his mind.

Fiona thought for a moment. "I don't know," she finally said softly. "I was hoping that maybe I would avoid seeing him. Maybe he will be long gone."

"You know this only works if he's caught in the act, right?" Adam said. "The point is, we have to face him. Otherwise he'll just retreat back into oblivion and keep doing the same thing."

"Yeah," Fiona sighed.

She had been kidding herself to think she could play this role in anonymity. That she could do what needed to be done without ever confronting Micah or the others. She felt anxiety creeping back up the back of her scalp again when faced with the reality of the situation.

"I know you have tapped into this other facet of your ability," Adam started again, and Fiona felt her heart swell a bit at his use of the word "ability." Not the word "condition" that Micah had used. Two similar words with such different nuances. Adam continued the thought, "But when the time comes, there will be intense emotions running around in your head. I know you've learned to exhibit extreme self-control, but this time…"

"This time, what?" Fiona picked up the thread Adam let drop. She wanted him to finish what he was going to say.

"This time," Adam began, eyes never wavering from Fiona's. "This time it might not be so easy."

Fiona thought about all the time she had spent in Plattsburgh harnessing those very emotions Adam now spoke about. She had become skilled at self-discipline, and at submerging those feelings floating around her into the pit of her being when she needed to. But Adam was right. This time, it would be different. Different because she was taking a stand against her friends–the fact that she still even thought of them as such troubled her. And she would be going up against Micah. A person for whom her feelings were far more complex. Even now those emotions swirled within her like the roiling tide during a summer storm. Like oil and water. The love, admiration and respect in stark contrast to the darkness of her ire and hatred. Unable to mix, yet existing together as one.

Fiona swallowed the lump rising in her throat and answered with more confidence than she felt, "I've harnessed my emotions before. I can do it again."

And she *had* harnessed them before; that wasn't a lie. She thought about Nina Bradley's sparkling penthouse. She thought of that Planned Parenthood outside of D.C. There had been emotions during those times too. Lots of them. She had mourned the destruction of each of those places. More so because she was the cause of their ruination. But now, she was in a position to save something. To do the right thing. The good thing. Her mind knew that. Why was it that matters of the heart are far more murky?

"I think you can too, Fiona," said Adam with genuine conviction.

Fiona briefly wished she believed in herself the way her new friends believed in her.

"We have one week," Adam continued. "One week to make our final preparations. Is there anything you need help with?"

"I'm going to plan more training time with Chelsea. And I'm going to want to go over all that drone footage Josh recorded yesterday. I want to make sure I have the whole area solidified in my mind. Now that I'm not the one manipulating the fire, I want to triple check I have it all right in my head. Especially because I can't fully account for what Micah's plan is, or the path the fire will follow. There are many more variables than I'm used to," Fiona explained.

"Whatever you need," Adam said in response. "But you can't do anything on an empty stomach. Let's go see what kind of leftovers there are."

"Sounds good to me," Fiona responded, slipping her bare feet into the pair of flip flops waiting by the door.

On their walk to the kitchen, they didn't talk anymore about the task at hand, but the weight of what needed to be done and the pressure of doing it right the first time–with no margin for error–hovered above them, an ever-present cloud of anticipation.

Chapter Sixty-Five

A week before the job, Fiona found herself sitting outside–as usual–with Chelsea. Her emotions were turbulent after a dream she experienced the night prior. The images of the nightmare were jumbled. First she was at prom–she could smell the sulfurous odor of the curtains as they danced with rolling flames against the picture windows overlooking the Long Island twilight. She had run away into the night, but instead of her mother's waiting car, she ran towards a swarm of people huddled together on the rooftop of Nina Bradley's Tribeca apartment building, their mouths frozen open in gaping holes. When Fiona turned around, she was no longer on the rooftop, but in the Garden City Hotel; Adam was there, crouching in the lobby, holding the blackened remains of his friend. He gazed up at her–piercing eyes full of blame.

Mercifully, she awoke after her brain concocted that final haunting image, but all of it, especially Adam's accusing stare remained with her. Her pillow had been soaked when she laid back down, and when she rubbed at her cheeks, she realized that her own tears were the culprits. Sleep eluded her the rest of the night, leaving her cranky and irritable for her training session with Chelsea.

"What's wrong, Fiona?" Chelsea asked, her brow furrowing with concern.

"Nothing. Just tired," Fiona replied, trying to keep her voice calm and even.

But Chelsea wouldn't let it go, "It's more than that. You're unfocused. And you have bags under your eyes."

"I'm fine, Chelsea. Please just stop pushing," Fiona's tone betrayed her.

Chelsea looked down at the ground as her fingers absently pulled at the scraggly grass.

The gesture made Fiona feel even worse. She hadn't meant to be short with Chelsea. As much as she didn't want to admit it, the nerves were kicking in—about the impending job, yes, but also at the thought of confronting Micah again.

"Chelsea, look—" Fiona began.

Fiona tried to quell those emotions, but they burbled forth unchecked and the next thing she knew, the grass around the women's feet pulsed with blazing ruby embers.

Fiona shot up and began to bat it out with her feet, but Chelsea was slower to stand, and the edge of her denim shorts caught and sizzled. Fiona lunged at Chelsea and using her hands smothered the last bits of stubborn flames.

Chelsea looked up at Fiona with shock and Fiona could tell that she was trying to downplay the pain that accompanied the pink puckered skin and yellow blisters that emerged on her upper thigh. It wasn't a large area of affected skin, but enough to turn Fiona's head into an angry mob of hornets. *Not again*, she said to herself.

"Oh my God, Chelsea," Fiona said, backing away.

"Fiona. It's fine. I'm fine," Chelsea said, taking rapid steps to close the increasing gap between them.

"It's not fine," Fiona nearly screamed it. "I burned you. I...I hurt you."

"You didn't. It's ok—"

Fiona didn't hear the rest because she was running, running, running as fast as she possibly could away from Chelsea.

Panic set in. *Oh my God. I'm a monster. There's no way I can pull off this job. I'm a fucking liability! I've been reckless all my life and I just continue to do it. I hurt her. I hurt her. I hurt her. I hurt her.* Thoughts slammed against Fiona's clogged brain as the sweat trickled down between her shoulder blades. When was the last time her emotions caused her fire to spring forth unchecked? What was happening to her? She was moving in reverse. She thought about the time she burned Maya...and even worse, the image of Noah's blistered hand surfaced with ferocity.

Finally, she stopped, and panting, slunk down to the earth, landing on her bare knees. The rough-packed dirt scraped against her skin as she hung her head and cried stormily.

She perceived a hand on her shoulder. Chelsea had caught up with her. Chelsea stood in front of her, so Fiona's eyes were level with the new burn on her thigh.

"Look at it Fiona," Chelsea said. "See. It's not that bad. Just a small burn. It's ok."

And then Chelsea knelt down so their eyes met one another.

Fiona spoke first, "It's not ok. I'm a mess. I swore to myself I would never hurt anyone...ever ever again–"

"But you never did hurt anyone!" Chelsea said. "You didn't hurt the people in the hotel. And me–I'm fine."

"You're not fine!" Fiona screamed. "I burned you. Look what I did. I can't be trusted. We have to tell Adam to call it off. I could really hurt someone–maybe you. And I couldn't live with that. I thought I was better. More controlled. But–I'm just not."

"Fiona," Chelsea began again. "You have got to have some grace with yourself. We all make mistakes. There is a lot of emotion tied to this...maybe more than you've ever experienced. It's understandable. You're human–"

"I'm not allowed to be human. And I'm not allowed to make mistakes. Not with this...thing..I can do."

She couldn't bear to call it an ability...not then. Maybe not ever again.

"Look at me Fiona," Chelsea instructed, placing a hand on her chin and guiding her face upward. "You are allowed to make mistakes. And I believe in you."

"How can you possibly believe in me? After what I just did?"

"Because I believe today was an anomaly. I believe today, your emotions got in the way. And I believe you would never really hurt me or anyone else. Not really."

"I'm so sorry," Fina said again.

"Don't be. I shouldn't have pushed you back there when you clearly didn't want to talk. You've been making so much progress. It's illogical to think there will never be any set-backs. And that's all this was. A tiny setback. Don't give up on me now. You've come too far. I know you can do this. We have about a week to work on it...work on those emotions. Just be honest with me about what you're feeling. We can work through it together."

Fiona was amazed by Chelsea at that moment. Her belief in her, her capacity for forgiveness and understanding. Her friendship...most of all, it was Chelsea's unflagging friendship that gave Fiona the courage to try again.

Chapter Sixty-Six

In Plattsburgh, Fiona thought she worked hard to control her condition. But the week after her "setback" with Chelsea, that week had tested her more than she could have imagined. Fueled by belief and hope, Fiona pushed the incident with Chelsea to the back of her mind. She began to achieve a sense of mastery over this new facet of her condition, and as the week wound down, Fiona felt almost as confident about controlling external flames as she did about creating flames of her own. She wondered what other aspects of her fire ability she could tap into if she tried. Maybe there were things she could do that her own imagination hadn't even conjured yet. That thought made her shiver a bit as she tried to eat her breakfast with a sense of normalcy.

The plan for the day was to eat breakfast, leisurely review the drone footage with Josh, debrief one more time with Adam, and then take a nap until dinner. They would eat dinner at 7 and then be ready to leave by midnight. That should get them into Derby Line by 5am...likely earlier with the relaxed overnight traffic patterns. On paper, it was all so meticulous, so easy. Would it be this easy in reality? In the actual moments when it counted most? Fiona didn't think so. Would she hurt someone? Chelsea maybe?

Even though she moved past that little accident during their training session, it lingered in the periphery. Chelsea did her best to hide the scar of the burn Fiona gave her, but Fiona knew it was there...underneath the blue denim shorts. It was a reminder that Fiona wasn't perfect–a fact she didn't like to think about. Despite her newfound confidence, she didn't want to make the mistake of naiveté. Anything could happen once they arrived in Derby Line. Anything at all. So many possibilities for error. Perhaps their intel was wrong and they received an inaccurate date. Perhaps the forest would already be leveled because they misjudged Micah and his pervasive efficiency. Maybe the cops wouldn't arrive on time. What if Micah got away? And then the biggest what-if: what if, once her emotions were flying wildly around, Fiona couldn't perform like she thought she could?

Fiona didn't allow herself to focus too much on that last what-if as she laid down to take her scheduled afternoon nap, but she still found it difficult to calm her turbulent mind as she closed her eyes. Sleep eluded her for quite a while, but eventually–Fiona couldn't be exactly sure of the time–her mind turned sluggish. She hadn't achieved restful sleep the night before, especially with visions of the fire quartz blazing in her mind. She was tired... exhausted, really. Slowly, her thoughts drifted to happier times. Her mom. Noah. Her apartment in the city. The elation that accompanied the time she was offered a real job by Dana Ferranti. And it was these happier visions dancing through her mind that allowed her finally to relax.

Chapter Sixty-Seven

It was midnight. The time had come. Every item on their itinerary had been checked off, well every one except for the last one. The big one. Fiona said goodbye to Erin, Andrea, and Josh. She didn't want to make it a big deal; she had never been good at goodbyes. But something about this one brought a fresh swell of tears to her eyes. It felt final in a way, and she tried to shake the terrible feeling of foreboding.

Bryce followed them up to the shed, where they placed their small backpacks in the trunk, and he lingered while they entered the car, never allowing his fingers to unwind from Chelsea's thin wrist. It was obvious he was nervous, unsettled. Maybe more so since Fiona accidentally burned Chelsea last week. Did he think the same thing would happen again? And on top of that, Fiona was told he usually accompanied his companion on these missions. That they were something of a duo. But today...today, he would be staying behind. Adam wanted only the three of them to go to Derby Line. *Four would be too many*, he said. *We have to keep it as simple as possible.* It must have been hard for Bryce to let Chelsea go.

Adam settled himself behind the steering wheel, and Fiona fastened the seatbelt in the passenger side. Through the window,

Fiona watched as Chelsea gave Bryce a kiss on the cheek and then watched as his lips mouthed, *Be careful*. He stayed there, rooted to his spot while Chelsea climbed into the backseat of the car and Adam maneuvered the vehicle out onto the road. Bryce's figure grew smaller and smaller in the rearview mirror, until Fiona could no longer see him at all.

The night was cool and peaceful around them as they drove on, miles upon miles of road unspooling beneath the wheels of Adam's Subaru Outback. Even though Fiona had made this trip just the week prior, it felt different now, in the dark. Somber, was the word her mind settled upon. It felt as though the air between the three passengers crackled with life. Fiona could perceive the nerves, the conviction, the anxiety, the resolve as palpable things as they each turned inward for reflection. She imagined that Adam and Chelsea, like herself, were running through the possibilities, the expectations, and the role they would each play once they arrived–trying to account for every tiny thing that could, would or should happen.

"GPS says we're an hour and a half out. We made great time," Adam informed them about 3 hours into the trip.

The way he said it was so nonchalant. As if they were headed towards a vacation destination instead of a... Fiona didn't know how to finish the sentence in her mind.

Fiona took in a deep breath to ease the panic that threatened to rise and she saw Chelsea wipe her palms against her pants in the rearview mirror.

"We've got this. I know we do," Chelsea said. "I believe in us." And then Chelsea tapped Fiona's shoulder, urging her to turn around in her seat and face her directly. The shadow of her eyelashes in the fading moonlight cast wispy patterns on her pale cheeks. "I believe in you Fiona. I'm so proud to have been there to help you these past weeks. But even more than that. I'm happy that you've become my friend."

Chelsea's belief in her, despite the scar marring the smooth skin of her thigh, inflated Fiona's heart. She wasn't used to such a genuine and honest expression of love from others and Chelsea's openness took her by surprise, as it usually did. But instead of closing up. Instead of doing what she always did with Micah and the others, she didn't hold anything back when she responded. What was the point in that anyway? She might as well be honest. If there was ever a time for the truth, now was it.

"I'm proud to have you as a friend too," Fiona said looking into Chelsea's wide eyes. "I wouldn't even be here, in this car, headed to confront Micah, without you."

Fiona's admission brought a smile to Chelsea's mouth and she settled back in her seat, tucking an errant strand of hair behind her ear, to study the road beside her. Adam picked up the conversation, reminding them of their purpose, of their mission. Of the necessity of success. After his little speech, Fiona closed her eyes again, not to sleep, but to engage in some mindful meditation and some breathing. She saw the forest emerge, vast and green in her mind. The sweep of the drone footage capturing the leafy foliage from the sky. The treetops snuggled together looked like rolling emerald waves.The wooden EarthJustice outpost with its rocking chairs and pamphlets. The way the shingles lined the roof in a toothy pattern of diamonds. The young deer with its inky, curious eyes.

From behind closed eyelids, Fiona perceived the early morning sunlight filtering in through the window, warming her face as it moved higher in its path towards the middle of the sky. Fiona couldn't tell how much time had passed, but soon a smell disturbed her momentary peace. It was a familiar smell and it invaded her nostrils, bitter and acrid. Casting her gaze out the window she scanned the horizon and looking north, perceived a gray haze hanging above the fringe of forest in the near distance. In the pre-dawn lightness that painted the sky, she saw billowing clouds of smoke curling upward into the not-so-distant air. Panic overtook her as she watched the thick plumes rise like steam into the atmosphere. This could only mean one thing. Micah was there. Somewhere. And his fire had already begun.

Chapter Sixty-Eight

"Are you seeing this?" Fiona sputtered.

But Chelsea and Adam were already looking out the window with horror streaking their pale faces.

At that moment a trio of phones pinged with an incoming message. Chelsea was the one to read it aloud.

"It's from Josh," she said. "He wrote, 'Alert. It's started. I repeat, it's started."

"I wonder why it took so long to alert us," Fiona asked.

"I bet we were driving in a dead zone," Adam said. "Tell him we are just about in position. He knows what to do."

"What's our ETA?" Chelsea asked, voice shaky with gravity.

"We're ten minutes out," Adam informed them, stepping harder on the accelerator. "The smoke is only coming from one small section. I think we're still early."

"I hope so," Chelsea said, tucking her thin legs underneath her.

"We anticipated that some acreage would take a hit. We're still on track," he added.

Fiona wondered if he honestly believed that, or if he was simply trying to convince himself, because she herself felt intense worry roiling in the pit of her stomach. Were things slipping out of their control? Fiona hoped not.

They made it to the entrance in 8 minutes. But those minutes dragged by at a snail's pace. Fiona's eyes remained glued to the smoke spewing forth in an increasing amount. It seemed as though it was spreading rapidly, consuming land at an alarming rate. At times, she perceived hints of orange and red between the trunks, licking the exposed branches with hunger. Fiona felt restless and paralyzed, her fingers drumming a soundless tattoo on her thighs.

Adam careened the car down the narrow pathway that Chelsea had so tentatively eased her own vehicle down the week prior. Fiona, Adam and Chelsea didn't see the other car that veered off the path into the woods to avoid a collision until it had already cannonned into a thick tree trunk just off the road. A screech and an ear-splitting sound of branches rasping across metal made them all look to the left.

And when Fiona turned her head to regard the other vehicle attempting to head out of the forest as her own car was heading in, she locked eyes with the driver through the shattered front windshield. The impact of the crash left the glass streaked with spidery lighting bolts of cracks on the top, but she still had a direct line of sight. The windshield belonged to a black Range Rover that was all too familiar. Aside from the damage to the windshield and a dented in front bumper, it was intact. Looking at it, she could almost smell the musky aroma of its leather interior. It was a familiar scent.

The eyes gazing back at her were familiar too. Cold, mahogany eyes fringed with thick dark lashes lanced into her soul–piercing her with their intensity. She would know those eyes anywhere. Fiona's breath turned to glass in her throat. They were the first eyes she saw when she awoke from the drugged stupor in the Garden City Hotel. They were the eyes that penetrated her own with lust and hunger in the throes of intimacy. They were the eyes that she had come to love, albeit with a tinge of fear. And at that moment those eyes stared back at her with a mix of surprise, assessment, and anger...yes, anger too. Fear took its stronghold on Fiona at that moment and her brain tried to process what she was seeing. Who she was seeing. It took a few moments for her to come to the conscious realization of what her mind already knew, what her heart already knew. The eyes fixed on her were eyes she had come to know intimately another lifetime ago. They were Micah's eyes.

Chapter Sixty-Nine

"Shit," Chelsea said, taking the words out of Fiona's mouth. Fiona herself couldn't utter a single word. Not after locking eyes with Micah. Her breath felt gravelly in her throat. She thought she would have been able to handle seeing him again. She told herself and convinced herself she could stay the course. That her emotions wouldn't get in the way. But now, that sense of confidence wavered as thoughts collided against her skull.

Adam turned the wheel sharply and the car came to a screeching stop.

"Fiona," Adam said, breaking her out of her trance. "Nothing has changed. Go do what you have to do. I'll deal with Micah."

What did he mean "deal with Micah?" Fiona thought to herself. Would Adam kill Micah? Shoot him while he lay defenseless in his shattered truck? And did Fiona want that to happen?

Adam continued, "The local authorities have already been alerted. And Micah crashing into that tree only helped us slow him down."

When Fiona didn't respond, he turned all the way around in his seat and yelled, "Go!" right into her eyes that were wide with terror.

Fiona dimly perceived Adam throw open the door and run back towards the scene of Micah's crash. Who else was in that car? Fiona knew that he certainly wasn't alone.

Focus, she tried to tell herself. *Breathe*. But she couldn't quite force her body to listen.

The next thing she knew Chelsea was at her side. She got out of the car and opened Fiona's door. She knelt next to her while Fiona struggled to disengage her seat belt.

Chelsea put a soft hand on Fiona's shoulder, halting her movement. "Fiona," she said. "You can do this."

Fiona continued to struggle. Something was wrong with her movements; she couldn't get her fingers to work.

Again, Chelsea's soft voice, "Fiona. Look at me."

Fiona did. And what she saw reflected back at her in Chelsea's sparkling blue eyes was friendship. And not just friendship, but belief, and confidence and hope. But then Fiona's gaze was brought behind Chelsea and she was astonished to see angry flames licking the trees, the shrubbery, and the roof of the EarthJustice outpost. The fire was spreading–rapidly. She could feel the heat on her face as she finally felt the lock release from her seatbelt.

Stepping out of the car the roar of the fire assaulted her senses. The crackling of the flames was deafening and the scent of burning pine was thick in her throat. She looked over towards where Adam had run off to and she perceived figures there...not just two...not just Adam and Micah, but someone else too. Or maybe more than one more person. But she couldn't focus on what Adam was doing. Or what Micah was doing. Even though she so desperately wanted to know.

"Chelsea, get behind me," Fiona shouted.

Chelsea listened with wide eyes and took a step behind Fiona, pinned between her and the car door. Fiona fixed her gaze on the treetops, trying to conjure the drone footage in her mind. This was way bigger than she anticipated. Way bigger than she had trained for. The doubt crept in, gnawing away at any shred of confidence Fiona felt.

That's when the panic rose. Fiona took in the inferno before her. If she didn't do something now, it would be too late. She had to act. Now. They could never outrun the wave of fire that blazed forth with intensity, licking its greedy lips as it gobbled up whatever stood in its way. This fire was angry, a whirling tornado in the still morning.

No, Fiona said, calming her breathing and closing her eyes. *In: One, Two Three. Out: One, Two, Three. In and Out. In. Out. It's not working.*

"Fuck. Chelsea. It's not working," Fiona said, turning around to find Chelsea's comforting gaze. But her eyes were wide and tinged with the same panic that threatened to destroy Fiona—Chelsea's pupils were so wide the blue irises looked like slivers around two gaping holes of fear.

"I can't calm my breathing. My emotions are all over the place," Fiona began to panic.

She thought about all those times where her spiraling emotions brought out the worst in her. Burning her brother. Prom. Nina's apartment. Planned Parenthood. Since then, Fiona had gotten her skill under such control. She learned to tame those emotions, temper them. Put them in the background. But now, in this situation, the anger, fear, sadness, pain...they all competed for space and caused paralysis. It was an onslaught, and Fiona was paralyzed.

"You can do this Fiona," Chelsea said, but her words were like echoes in Fiona's jumbled mind.

"I can't. I'm a mess! I can't visualize the fire. I can't sense its reach," Fiona spat out hoping beyond hope that Chelsea could come to her rescue. That Chelsea would have some words of advice...some direction.

She could taste salt as tears streaked down her face and settled into the crevice of her lips.

"I'm sorry Chelsea," Fiona said. "I'm so sorry. I'm such a fucking failure."

Fiona sank to her knees, the defeat settling heavy on her shoulders as the fire raged on.

It took Chelsea an entire minute to speak, which felt like eternity. Her pale skin shimmered in the growing heat.

Finally, Chelsea knelt down in front of Fiona and said, "Fiona. I know you can do this. I've seen what you can do. You're amazing. A failure? No way. Fiona, you're a gift. I believe in you."

"How can you believe in me?" Fiona asked. "I burnt you."

"Because you are more than your ability. It's not the fire that controls you. *You* control *it*. Your head. Your heart. Your goodness. Those are the forces that drive the flames. It's not the other way around," Chelsea spoke with passion and conviction.

Fiona gazed at this woman, this friend and saw that she was speaking from her heart. It gave Fiona courage, belief, conviction.

Turning around on her heels, Fiona faced the rapidly growing blaze. It illuminated the tendrils of copper in her hair and the warm rush of air blew her hair back from her heated face. Reaching into her back pocket she retrieved the fire quartz, which was already warm with purpose. Gripping it in her palms at heart-center, she lowered her chin and closed her eyes. A sense of peace rushed over the wrinkles in her mind, smoothing down all the doubt, the insecurity. She could do this.

See the fire, she said to herself. And suddenly she was above herself, gazing down at the forest. Watching the gray and red, and burning orange eating up the green waves of foliage. She saw its path. It looked like a blooming bloodstain on a paper towel, growing flower-like outwards. It already devoured many acres. Too many. More than they planned. But there was still a lot of life left. In her mind she saw the animals fleeing outward from the epicenter of chaos. She saw herself. A tiny speck of color in the chaos. It had to stop. It had to stop now. She was going to stop it. If it was the last thing she would ever do, she would stop this.

Even the knowledge of Micah's presence wasn't going to stop her from her mission.

Chapter Seventy

She transferred the stone to one palm and held it flat against her chest. Still crouching, Fiona touched the floor with her free hand, grazing her fingertips against the slivers of pine needles scattered about. The ground thrummed under her touch as she let out a final exhale.

The heat within her began to rise. It crept up slowly warming her insides from her toes to her knees, curling around inside her belly like a napping house cat. She could feel the purring vibrating through her limbs. It moved up farther and she felt it in her chest. Her heart–beating in sync with the pulsing energy that flickered inside her. Then the flush crept into her cheeks and if she would have opened her eyes, the casual observer would have seen firelight dancing in the depth of her soul.

Flames crackled out from her fingertips and traveled along the parched earth in a jagged formation to her left and right, spidering and splintering and shifting to engulf the flames that licked their greedy tongues against the trees and foliage. From above, it almost looked like the earth cracked to reveal molten glowing lava moving outward in a circular pattern, no thicker than a few inches, to surround the existing blaze. And Fiona watched it from above too. She was able to perceive her small crouching figure and trace the phosphorescent path of her fire as though she were a gull flying overhead. Slowly, agonizingly slow, she made a perimeter around Micah's fire...Micah's alien flames. And that fire *was* alien. She had laughed when Chelsea referred to it as such, but in that moment it was exactly that–raw and wild, it resisted being tamed. Fiona could sense that as if she could understand the crackling language it spoke. And she spoke back. The fire was big, too big. She couldn't imagine how many trees–how many animals–had been destroyed already, but she wouldn't let it take any more. When each end of her fire–slightly brighter than the one her former lover created–joined together in an enormous blazing perimeter, the brightness was almost blinding. But she had control of it now. Fiona could sense her power.

Dropping the fire quartz to the ground, she placed her other hand on the earth at her feet and clenched her fists together. *Clench*, she said to her fire. *Condense. Constrict.* It listened. She sensed it pressing inward. She could feel the resistance in her mind and her face burned with concentration and effort. This was nothing like the practice runs she did with Chelsea. This was more mental exertion than she ever expended in her entire life thus far and she could feel her body tiring. Weakening. *No*, she said as much to herself as to her fire. Fiona didn't know if her ability was a blessing or a curse, but she knew at that moment, at that moment, she was going to win out. She had to.

Again she spoke to her fire. *Close. Close. Smother. Listen.* She felt as though her mind was a fist trying to close around a bundle of hay that was simply too thick, too vast. Her mental fingers tried to condense the handful, her thumb and forefinger desperate to come into contact. The strain was immense. But finally, finally she sensed she had subjugated it. Slowly, watching from above, Fiona constricted the fire. A little bit at first, but she was gaining ground. As the fire receded, it left the land devastated of greenery. Charred remains of tree stumps and ashes only. The line between the emerald foliage of unharmed forest stood in stark comparison to the oily blackened and ashen remnants of trees and under-brush. But they could all study the devastation afterwards.

Fiona dimly felt Chelsea's hand close upon her shoulder in solidarity as the blaze continued to constrict, to weaken. The alien fire reversed as though someone had a remote control directing its course, but it was Fiona's doing. It was all her. 40 acres, turned into 30, which turned into 20. It was agonizingly painful for Fiona to keep up the concentration for so long. To keep her hold and control strong and powerful. But the fire sensed it had been bested. Somehow Fiona knew that. 10 acres. 8. 7. Finally just a single acre remained ablaze. And then even less than that. What remained of the fire at that point was dull and weakened. It was only half-hearted in its destruction and any remaining strength it had diminished rapidly as it ran out of fodder to consume to keep it alive.

Fiona opened her eyes and watched the remaining fire tamper itself out. In her exhausted state, she couldn't even feel triumphant. It was more so a feeling of contentment. A feeling of being sated. As a party host must feel after the last guest left smiling...only intensified, magnified by the weight of the world.

She couldn't relish that feeling for long because once she stood up, knees popping like fireworks, her mind returned to Micah...and what could have happened between him and Adam. Thoughts began to ricochet off her mind. Who else was in that car? What would become of Micah? The others? Had he gotten away? Where was Adam? Was Adam ok? Fiona had no doubt Micah would and could have killed Adam if it meant saving himself and his operation. Suddenly Fiona's pulse began to flutter again.

Turning around, her eyes searched for Chelsea in the acrid air. The smoke hung thick and redolent, stinging her eyes and throat. Tears streamed freely down her cheeks and Fiona couldn't tell if they were from relief, happiness, fear, exhaustion—or if they were simply the biological reaction to the fumes that lingered densely in the atmosphere.

And then she was looking into a pair of eyes, but they weren't Chelsea's. And this time there was no cracked windshield in between them. This time he was standing, facing her...Micah. Huge and intimidating in his black t-shirt and jeans, muscled biceps causing the thin cotton fabric to stretch over his sculpted chest and shoulders. God he was beautiful. But in that moment he was terrifying too and Fiona trembled as she beheld him.

His arms were held behind him in handcuffs and Adam had a firm grip on his forearm. How Adam managed this, Fiona couldn't even imagine. Micah always seemed invincible to her. Maybe colliding into the tree was Adam's winning ticket–the catalyst allowing him to be overtaken. Or maybe Adam possessed some hidden reservoirs of strength.

Fiona studied Micah's face. There was an open wound on his forehead–*probably from the crash*, Fiona assumed–and thick crimson blood oozed down the stubble on his cheeks and down to his chiselled jawline. Fiona's breath hitched in her throat as she stared into those mahogany eyes. But, there was not an ounce of love in that gaze–only steel, gravel, and the unmistakable flicker of anger there as she tried to make her mouth form her thoughts into cohesive words.

Chapter Seventy-One

Adam spoke first.

"The cops are on their way. Micah wanted to talk to you. I thought you might need this. I don't know...find some closure. Am I wrong?"

Fiona couldn't make her mind form words as thoughts bounced around. She was exhausted from the effort of controlling the fire that was, by that point, nothing more than a few feet of flickering ruby embers. And even though she sensed Adam was trying to do the right thing, she felt momentary hatred for him for forcing her to confront Micah. For not allowing her to take the coward's path and scamper away without having faced this human...this man, who had so drastically and aggressively changed the course of her entire life. But she couldn't deny that Adam was correct. She *did* need this. She needed to hear the truth from those painfully full lips that had known every inch of her body another lifetime ago.

Before Fiona could speak, Micah opened his mouth, "Don't do this Fiona. You and I. We're a team. Don't let this guy brainwash you."

"Brainwash me," Fiona repeated through lips that felt wooden and stiff. "He's not brainwashing me. That's what you've been doing. To think I trusted you–"

Micah cut her off, "I helped you Fiona. I gave you a purpose."

"Purpose?" Fiona asked. "You used me."

"I gave you a new life. A better one, someone like you…would never have been content living that bland life in Long Island. You needed more," he continued.

"That wasn't for you to decide Micah. That was MY life. Mine. And you took it from me. All those months ago, when you said that you knew about me, that I was your *hobby*…How? How did you know about me? It's time to answer those questions," Fiona demanded.

"Kaleb knew about you…*knows* about you. *He* gave me your identity, made you my hobby. Don't you see?" Micah went on.

Kaleb, Fiona thought. *None of this makes sense.*

But before she could ask more, Micah continued, "After you killed those peop–"

"I didn't kill those people, Micah! You did! You just made me think I did. You made me think I had no other option. You took away my options. Took me away from my career…from my family. And the worst part about it all…is that I let you do it. I fucking believed you," Fiona's anger exploded out of her, and the flames were back…itching against her trembling fingers.

Micah didn't miss a beat. He didn't even flinch when Fiona spit the truth right back in his face. Fiona wondered if in that moment, Micah realized he had been betrayed by one of his own. Maybe he knew that Spence revealed the truth. But it didn't phase him. Or at least he didn't show it. His countenance was like stone–not a single crack in the veneer. Smooth and hard and solid. Like always. Fiona briefly thought about the times they had been intimate…or at least she thought them intimate. But they weren't. Not really. Intimacy requires mutual trust, respect, doesn't it? It had all been one large ploy for manipulation. Micah's attempt to ensure that Fiona remained needy for him. He would make her beg, ask, plead with him to appease her desire.

The triumph and power that flashed in his eyes when she would submit to him, that was what he wanted. He never wanted her. And the worst part about it, was that it worked. *God, how blind I was*, Fiona thought.

Micah spoke, "So what if I manipulated the situation? You were a ticking time bomb. And you can't tell me you didn't like working with me. I saw the look in your eyes when you burned. You liked it. You still do...I can tell. It gives you purpose. Passion. I give you purpose and passion."

Fiona looked down at her feet and saw new embers alighting the dry ground, flickering against her sneakers. Micah saw it too and gazed back up into Fiona's eyes with a smirk that said, *See. You belong with me.*

"All of that might be true Micah. Maybe I did like to burn. And maybe I did care about you. But all that's gone. It was built on a foundation of lies. And I'm done with it. Done with Kaleb. And you're done too. You can't just go around toying with people's lives. This world isn't yours to control," Fiona said with a budding confidence.

Now there was another sound in the distance. The sound of sirens, and Fiona noticed the flash of lights through the depleted trees.

Again, Micah spoke, never losing that infuriating calm, "You and I can handle this Fiona. Use your condition. Help me escape. Let's be millionaires together. Don't let this guy think he can control you."

His use of that word "condition," sealed the deal for Fiona. It spoke of how he saw her...how he viewed her. And she wasn't going to define herself by that word anymore. Chelsea had been right all along. She didn't have a disease. No, not at all. What she had...it was a gift.

"It's not a 'condition,' Micah. And no one controls me. Not anymore."

As the police car made its way down the path Micah turned to Fiona one more time. Leaning as far in as possible so Adam couldn't hear, he whispered, "There's still something you don't know. Something that might change your mind."

"Oh yeah," Fiona said with rancor. "And what's that Micah?"

"Go see Kaleb. He's the one you need to hear it from. Once you talk to him, you'll see the error of your ways. Then you can come break me out of wherever they're going to put me, and we can pick up where we left off."

"Where is he? Where's Kaleb? He's the one who's going down next."

Micah just gave Fiona a wicked smile and replied, "Adam knows. He's about to tell the cops where he is. Don't let him do that until you go see him. It would be a mistake."

That was the last thing Micah said before the cop took over and assisted him into the waiting police vehicle.

Fiona quickly stamped out the smouldering pine needles at her feet. Even though her heart was pounding in her chest, she had control of herself now. Even in the backseat of the cop car, Micah looked composed and calm. He stared at her through the window, so sure she would do as he asked. And maybe he was right. She couldn't swallow the nagging feeling that she needed to confront Kaleb herself. She couldn't ignore the thought that Micah could possibly be right.

Chapter Seventy-Two

Breaking her gaze from Micah, Fiona tuned in to the conversation Adam was having with the arresting officer.

"Hey Dan," Adam was saying, and Fiona could tell the two men knew each other. She guessed they have worked together for years by the easy way they interacted.

"This is the guy you've been telling me about, huh?" the officer, Dan, asked.

"Yeah. This guy is bad news. He's destroyed countless properties and has meddled in politics for a long time."

"Well it looks like that ends today," the officer responded. "Thanks for the intel."

"No need to thank me. It's a team job. I'm just happy we could help out," Adam replied.

The officer went to get into the driver's seat of the vehicle, but Adam spoke again, "Dan, there's one more thing we need to discuss. This guy didn't work alone he–"

Fiona cut him off with a firm hand on his shoulder. Giving Adam a look and a slight shake of her head, somehow her meaning was conveyed. She needed to find out what Micah's game was. Then they could send the cops right to Kaleb's door.

"Come again?" Dan asked. "What were you saying Adam?"

"Nothing Dan. Never mind. Stay in touch please. And keep me posted on how this whole thing progresses."

"Will do," Dan responded as he closed the car door behind him.

Fiona, Micah and Chelsea watched the police vehicle pull gingerly out of the parking spot and make its way out of the forest.

Once Micah and the cop car were out of sight, Adam turned around to face Fiona, eyes full of curiosity. "What's up?" he asked, not even attempting to beat around the bush. "Why didn't you want me to reveal Kaleb's location?"

"Micah said something to me right before he was arrested," Fiona replied. "Does Kaleb know Micah was taken?"

"No, I was able to get the phone away from him before he made any contact," Adam informed Fiona.

She sighed a breath of relief. That gave them time...and discretion: the element of surprise. Even if Micah was wrong, they would still get him...once and for all.

"Ok. I'll tell you, but first I have to ask. Who was in the car with Micah?" Fiona asked, her curiosity getting the better of her.

"Rhea and Maya," Adam answered. "Once I got over there, Micah told them to book it. They ran off."

Fiona was momentarily surprised they listened. Adam would have been no match for the three of them. Fiona guessed Micah's pride did him in, in the end. He was probably so sure he could best Adam that he didn't want to take any chances with Rhea and Maya getting roped into the scuffle. Not when his precious operation was at stake. Always better to be safe than sorry...in Micah's mind at least.

"Rhea and Maya have no contact whatsoever with Kaleb, so they couldn't have keyed him into the fact Micah got caught," Fiona said. "But they could have contacted Spence. Spence is a genius and even though he doesn't deal with Kaleb directly either, he could probably locate him if he really tried. That kind of blows our cover with Kaleb. Don't you think?" Fiona asked.

Fiona tried to ignore the throb of hurt threatening to rise up within her at the knowledge that Rhea and Maya had been so close. She still very much felt that bitter sting of betrayal. But she could process all that later. Right now, she had to focus on the task at hand: being able to find Kaleb undetected. Learn what the hell Micah was talking about...and then turn him in. The end.

Adam had a small smile on his lips at the mention of Spence, and Fiona guessed at the truth.

"Spence is your informant," she said matter-of-factly.

Once the thought was in her mind, she knew it to be true. And if it was true. Spence wouldn't alert Kaleb. It meant he was on their side, on Fiona's side after all.

"Yeah," Adam answered. "Spence is one of my informants."

"Since when?" Fiona asked, shock written across her features.

"Since you escaped the compound to go back to Plattsburgh. I was shocked to hear from him at first, even though we've had some interaction over the years. He was genuinely concerned about you. He didn't go into specifics about the conversation you had; he told me it wasn't his place to reveal. But he didn't know where you were headed and wanted to let me know to look out for you."

Fiona was struck silent. She replayed the last conversation she had with Spence. The one where he revealed the truth about her past. She had doubted his intentions. Felt betrayed and hurt and angry. And he *had* betrayed her. There was no doubt about that. And he *had* kept secrets from her. But Fiona guessed he was being truthful when he said he cared about her. He hadn't lied about that. At least that was something. The thought brought a surprising warmth to her heart. And it wasn't from her heat. It was from knowing her friend was actually a friend...not an enemy like she suspected.

"Ok Fiona. I know this is a lot to process," Adam said, scattering her thoughts. "But I need to know why you didn't want me to give away Kaleb's location. Why the hesitation? Yes, we do have the element of surprise on our side...for the moment at least. But Kaleb is good. And he probably has his own informants. We need to act quickly. Start talking."

So Fiona told Adam exactly what Micah said to her. And Adam listened.

When she was done, Fiona said, "Thank you for trusting me Adam. I'm not sure why Micah wants me to come face-to-face with Kaleb, but I think I need to find out. I promise that once I hear what he has to say, we can alert the authorities and nail his ass."

"Ok," Adam said, and Fiona loved his willingness to listen to her. It showed a level of trust and respect that Fiona hadn't experienced in a long time. "I don't like it. But Ok. When I took Micah's phone, I was able to unlock his contacts. I got Kaleb's exact whereabouts. He's pretty close. Apparently he likes to lurk around in the vicinity of the jobs he commands," Adam informed Fiona and Chelsea.

Fiona briefly wondered if that was always the case. During all those jobs she had done, had this mysterious individual, this Kaleb, been somewhere close-by? Waiting for the news that all had gone to plan? The thought made her shiver a bit, despite the warmth of the day.

"Let's do this," Chelsea said, speaking for the first time in a long time.

Both Chelsea and Adam fixed their gaze on Fiona, waiting for her to make the next move.

"Ready?" Adam asked.

And Fiona was.

Before stepping into Adam's car, Fiona gazed around her one more time. There was significant destruction. The trees were charred and blackened and no foliage whatsoever remained in her sightline. It was like she was standing in a giant wasteland. But the smoke had cleared and the sky above her was blue and clear. Fiona knew that even though many acres were destroyed, that there were still vast expanses of trees left. She felt, in her heart, that new life could grow again. Maybe not this summer. Maybe not even next spring. But one day.

Chapter Seventy-Three

"This is it," Adam said, easing his car into a spot in the vast parking garage of a building that looked like it belonged in Manhattan as opposed to the styx of Vermont. Clearly Kaleb wasn't used to roughing it because he selected to hide-out in a modern condominium complex with a glass facade that sparkled like diamonds in the late morning sunshine. Most of the spots were empty and Fiona imagined that during the ski months these units rented out for thousands of dollars a season. But in the summer, clearly, people didn't opt to vacation in the outskirts of the Vermont/Canadian border.

"Penthouse apartment B," Adam announced, turning the ignition off. "How do you want to proceed?"

Again, Fiona felt that flush of love swell up inside of her as both Adam and Chelsea turned around in the car, regarding her with open trust. Fiona had been kidnapped by these people, drugged and held against her will. She escaped as soon as the chance arose. And yet...she came back. She was here. Fiona felt at that moment that maybe she didn't deserve their faith...their trust. Maybe she still had miles to go before she earned it. And yet it was there anyway. Blatant and clear like the North Star in the darkest of winter nights.

Fiona answered, "I think I need to do this by myself."

"I'm not sure that's the best plan, Fiona," Chelsea began, and by Adam's grimace, it was obvious he agreed. "You have no idea what you're walking into up there. Maybe someone alerted him of our presence. Maybe there's people with weapons...waiting for you. What if you get hurt?"

"I'm a bigger weapon than anything they have," Fiona replied truthfully. "Kaleb...and whoever else is up there with him–if there is anyone else–should be the ones who are afraid. Not me."

"I'm pretty sure Spence is tracking us," Adam interjected. "He would have alerted me if we were in any imminent danger. I'm fairly confident about that."

"Fairly?" Chelsea repeated. "No offense Adam, but I don't know if that's good enou–"

Fiona interrupted Chelsea, "Chelsea...trust me. Please. I need to see this through. Whatever it is. I owe it to myself. Maybe it will give me the closure I need. I'll text you when to call the cops."

Chelsea still didn't look convinced, so Fiona responded with finality, "I promise."

"We'll be right here," Adam said, holding up his phone to indicate that he expected that text. "I don't love this either, Fiona. But I'm going to trust you."

"Thank you. That means a lot," Fiona said.

"If we don't hear from you in 30 minutes we're coming up there," Chelsea added. "I don't care what either of you say. And calling the cops."

"Deal," Fiona said, giving Chelsea's shoulder a squeeze as she opened the car door to exit.

Fiona didn't look back as she walked towards the elevator. She didn't want to appear anything less than fully confident while Adam and Chelsea watched her make her way to this elusive man who, up until recently, had such a stronghold upon her. She wouldn't allow her friends to worry even more than they probably already were. But in reality her self-assurance was all a facade. Inside, Fiona felt jittery.

As she rode the elevator down to the ground floor and then stepped into yet another elevator that would bear her up to the penthouse level, she weighed what she knew about this person: Kaleb. She knew he was involved in politics...and Micah mentioned he had known about her for quite some time–before she even officially crossed paths with Micah. Fiona had exchanged emails with him, but nothing more than formalities about jobs to do and locations to burn. At that moment, Fiona desperately wished she had asked more questions, but she guessed that no matter how many times she voiced her curiosity, she wouldn't have gotten very far. Micah was closed-mouthed...and clearly Kaleb liked his identity kept hidden, which was why he went by a single false name. Micah's face materialized in Fiona's mind as she pressed the round button of the elevator. It lit up at the touch of her finger. Micah. She betrayed him...or helped to. But he betrayed her too–much more blatantly, much more coldly. Were they equal now? And if they were, why did Fiona still feel guilt heavy on her shoulders?

Stop it, Fiona said to herself. She didn't have time to think about Micah now...or Rhea or Maya, even though she desperately wondered where they had run off to. Those two couldn't take over the reins without Micah–they didn't have the connections or even the desire–but they were definitely survivors. Fiona thought how no matter where they went, they might possibly never materialize, at least not with their assumed identities. But again, she could think about them later. She needed to be present, focused. She was about to deal with the mastermind behind the entire operation–face to face–and she couldn't be thwarted with emotions.

She was alone in the elevator and used the ride up to close her eyes and breathe. *In-One, Two, Three. Out–One, Two Three. In and Out. In. Out.*

A soft ding told her she reached the top floor and that it was now time to step out of the elevator. Her heart hammered in her chest as she looked left and then right. Only two doors...two penthouses, one on either end of the hallway. Wasn't there some short story that sounded like that? Where there were two doors–behind one, a new wife...and behind the other, a tiger? Fiona wondered what she would find behind whichever door she selected. If she would even be permitted access.

She heard the faint closing of the elevator door behind her. In front of her, stood a slender table pushed up against the wall with a vase of red roses centered in the middle. Above the table was a gilt-edged mirror. Fiona's reflection gazed back at her from above the crimson blooms. There were deep purple circles under her eyes–the events of the day and night had finally caught up to her– and her emerald irises stood out like two chunks of raw tourmaline from her pale freckled face. The brown dye of her hair faded and the bronze streaks stood in stark contrast to the muted cocoa hue boasted about on the Loreal coloring box. But even though she looked tired...weak even, there were hidden reservoirs of strength coursing just below the surface. And something else was coursing under the surface too...pulsing like a pilot light in her veins, throbbing in her blood, and beating with each tremor of her heart. It was her fire. Silent and waiting. It gave her the courage and the push she needed to see this through.

Right, she said to herself. *Let's try the door to the right.* Her legs moved her hypnotically down the hallway, almost as though magnetized; she noticed that the rug beneath her feet felt plush and new. And as she stood in front of a door marked PH-B, she knew that she had chosen the correct direction. Above her, the black lens of a camera surveyed her and she gazed boldly back.

A tiny speaker on the wall, directly next to the door spoke, "Come in, Fiona. I've been expecting you. The door is unlocked."

Fiona went inside.

Chapter Seventy-Four

The first thing Fiona noticed when she opened the door was a huge window at the far end of the space with an unobstructed view of white-tipped mountains. It was remarkable that even in the dead heat of summer, somewhere on top of those sloping formations it was cold enough to keep snow from melting. The radiance of the picture took her breath away as she stepped farther into the room. She perceived the soft click of the automatic door closing behind her.

"Come all the way in, Fiona," a voice said, drawing her further down the hallway until she emerged into an airy living room with white couches and pale birchwood floors.

"Some view, huh?" the voice asked, and Fiona's eyes gradually settled on a figure reclining in a tan leather armchair that looked like it had come right out of an Olives Ateliers catalogue. "Those are The Green Mountains," the figure said. His voice was soft and precise. "Spectacular, right? I could sit here all day and gaze at that sight. Couldn't you?"

He uncrossed his legs and stood up with no more urgency than one getting out of bed in the morning.

"Are you Kaleb?" Fiona asked, not answering his question.

Fiona wasn't sure what she expected, but it certainly wasn't this *gentleman*. He did have a solid build, but his graying hair and soft wrinkles around his eyes didn't appear threatening. But then again, looks are often deceiving–Fiona knew that better than anyone. And despite his appearance, she knew of Kaleb's ruthlessness–his willingness to do absolutely anything to get what he needed.

"That would be me," he said, closing the distance between them with graceful strides.

The slanted sunlight cast odd shadows on the man's face and before Fiona could make out the nuances of his features she said, "What did you mean when you said you had been expecting me?"

"I meant exactly that. Before he was detained, Micah alerted me that you were on your way," he answered.

When Fiona didn't respond, Kaleb picked up, "I figured that now was as good a time as any to finally see you in person." He pressed one hand to his chest and extended the other with an open palm, inviting Fiona to take it, "I've been wanting to thank you for all you've done for me and officially welcome you to the family."

His calm, smug tone unnerved Fiona and without taking his hand, she responded quickly, "Thank me? I've come here to turn you in. Micah told me to wait. To come see you first, before I told the cops about you. But I think I was wrong to come here." She could feel herself recoiling, sinking into herself, "I've seen enough."

Fiona pulled her phone out of her back pocket to send that text to Adam. But before she could type anything into the keypad, she felt warm hands on her wrist, gently halting her movements. Fiona's gaze flickered up and she could hear the heat roaring just below her surface, louder than ever before. Why did she feel nervous? So out of control? Her brain was trying to tell her something, but the message wouldn't come through. It was as though the signal was interrupted, or the television was stuck on pause. His voice droned on; he spoke about loyalty and family, but she lost all focus on what he said. There was some revelation hovering on the horizon of Fiona's subconscious and her brain was desperately trying to push it into the forefront of her mind. But it was blocked. It was like she was trying to see through fog; something was there, but it was hazy and blurred.

Kaleb's face was close now, and the way he was angled, the sun was at his back, highlighting his features. This was why Micah wanted Fiona to go see this man in person. This was why Kaleb had known about her for all these years. Kaleb. Kaleb. Kaleb. Her mind flashed back to a memory that seemed odd and out of place.

Fiona was young, really young–maybe 5 years old, practicing writing her name on the large lined paper her Kindergarten teacher sent home with the students. Her handwriting was clunky, and it was endlessly difficult to keep the pencil inside the allotted space. She remembered her father's soft, firm hands closing over hers to guide her halting penmanship. *Where did this memory even come from?* Fiona wondered. *Why am I remembering this now?*

"I can't do it," she had said, tears welling in her eyes.

Her father had whispered to her as he gently manipulated her fingers, "You can do it. See? Fiona: F-I-O-N-A. Blake: B-L-A-K-E. Good job."

The letters of her first name came stiltedly, but they were there. Seeing the symbols gave her an immense sense of accomplishment.

Her father coaxed, "Ok, now the last name. B- One line all the way down, two loops. Good. You got it. Two words. 5 letters each. That lowercase e is tricky, huh? But it's an important one. Look at how many other words you can make with just those 5 tiny letters. Pretty cool, right?"

"What other words?" Fiona had asked.

"Oh. Lots of them. How about Beak? Or Lab?"

"Be," Fiona had added proudly.

"Yup. That's a good one," her father had said.

She still didn't know why the memory appeared seemingly out of the ether. But it stuck there, lodged in her head like a stone.

Then, all of a sudden, those letters swirled around in her mind. B-L-A-K-E. Just like her father had said, lots of other words from those 5 tiny letters: Bake, Bleak, Lake, Kale...Kaleb. Kaleb. What was that called? An anagram? An anagram of her last name? Kaleb. Blake. Her last name. His too. It was impossible in its simplicity...in the utter ridiculousness of it all. Fiona gazed into those eyes, and her mouth formed the words that her mind finally realized and acknowledged and understood as accurate.

"Dad," she said, staring into the face that was familiar and alien all at once. A face she dreamed about and thought about over the craggy rocks of time and space. She didn't even need to utter the title as a question, the certainty was startling in its white hot truth. After all those years, Fiona stared into the eyes of her father.

Chapter Seventy-Five

Before the man could respond, Fiona's entire world shifted. She felt off-kilter, as though the entire planet had shifted on its axis. Everything she thought she knew was a lie. The man she thought was gone, was here. Was right fucking here, and she didn't know what to say to him. He hadn't left. Not really. He had always been in her life, just not in the way any father should.

Her mouth opened, but the only word she could croak out was the one she had already uttered, "Dad."

Her voice didn't even sound like her own. She shook her head back and forth trying to make sense of it—images of her lost childhood, memories of her adulthood thus far, all spliced with flames. Hot tears sprang from the corners of her eyes and rolled down her cheeks.

"Dad," she said again, clearer, but still unable to form a cohesive sentence.

"Yes," he said, still holding her wrists. "It has certainly been a while."

Fiona pulled back from him and retreated, putting the couch between them as a barricade. She was trying to process it all, but she felt frantic and panicked. With a bit of distance between them, Fiona forced her gaze to take in his face. His eyes. Green, almond shaped–just like hers. People used to tell her that she had "smiling eyes," the way they crinkled at the edges. Well, her father had them too–even though he wasn't smiling. His salt and pepper hair was different from what she remembered. Her mind brought her back to that photograph she found when she snooped around in Micah's room. She couldn't be sure that the other man in the picture was her father, but the hair certainly looked like it. His nose was her's too–slender and turned up a bit at the end, like a ski-slope. And it wasn't just his physical appearance that solidified the connection. It was the timbre of his voice, the way he stood– his feet so secure on the ground as he leaned against the couch. All of it, familiar and yet alien at the same time. It was like seeing someone who had come back from the dead.

"All this time?" Fiona asked.

"All this time," he repeated.

The emotions were too much–so many she couldn't even identify all of them. The man had changed since he left. But those eyes...she could never forget them. After all, they were hers too.

"And...Micah?" Fiona didn't even know exactly what she was trying to ask.

"I've known Micah for a long time, Fiona. He's one of my best employees. I made you his mission." There was warmth in his voice, pride, "...and he succeeded. Brilliantly. And he helped bring us together again."

Wait. Fiona's mind made connections faster than lightning. Kaleb was her father. That meant he had been following her all these years. He played a role in torching her life. The Nina Bradley apartment–the undoing of her professional career as a designer. That fucking Planned Parenthood that haunted her dreams even though she tried to pretend as though it didn't. The deception of the Garden City Hotel. She died that night...along with those 11 other victims. Her mom organized a fucking funeral for her–over an urn of ashes that weren't even her own. And this man...her own father...he was the mastermind behind all of it. The maestro behind the orchestra of her life. He had conducted every horrible symphony. All of it. Every single awful thing she had done. He was the one who ordered it all–Micah was just a pawn in the greater game.

"You knew about me? You let all those things happen? You put Micah in my path? You had a hand in destroying my life? How could you do that to me? To Noah? To mom?" Fiona asked, unable to keep the anger from spewing forth.

As the shock sunk in, a bitter resentment was left–and it grew like wildfire in her mind. A bitter resentment and a scalding betrayal–worse than any of those she had yet known. Worse than Maya, than Rhea, than Micah. Because this betrayal was from her own father. Thoughts slammed against her brain as she sputtered out question after question–needing answers, yet terrified to know the truth.

"Fiona, these are questions for another time," her father began, batting his hand as though he was swatting at a gnat. He stayed composed, level, "What we need to think about now is becoming a family again. You belong with me, with Micah–"

"You don't care about me," Fiona clenched her hands together in front of her, desperate to grab onto something. "You don't care about family," she continued. If she didn't have something to cling to, she thought she might float away. Her body tensed and shook as she spoke, the words tearing through her throat as she released them, "If you did, if you truly cared about *family,* you wouldn't have walked out on us all those years ago. You wouldn't have played a part in destroying absolutely everything that was important to me. How dare you talk about family when you destroyed your own."

"Sit down. Calm down," he responded. He inched closer to her as he continued, "Let's talk rationally. I know I can make you understand my position."

Fiona's fingers itched with power, with heat. She leaned forward against the sofa to brace herself, the one item separating her from her father–he on one side, her on the other. Gripping the end of the couch, she felt the soft fabric under her fingertips begin to smoulder. She didn't even try to rein in those emotions. She let them rage. With no desire for restraint, she felt her fire bubble up. And she let it. Starting in the pit of her stomach, it blossomed outward, pulsing through her abdomen, flowing through her veins, pumping hotter with each beat of her heart, pushing against the inside of her skin. Insatiable and desperate.

Though the rage burned violently, she had to know the truth, "When did you first find out about me and where did you go when you left?"

"Ok, let's take one question at a time," he said with a purse of his lips. The arrogance in his tone made the welling chaos dance, "You were little when I realized what you could do...maybe six years old. I was watching you play with your baby doll...remember that Raggedy-Ann doll you loved so much? I saw you touch her head and then the yarn caught fire." He wagged his fingers at Fiona and smiled indulgently, "You were able to stamp it out with your little hand, but I knew then you were something special. I continued to watch you. Track you. I saw it all. You were amazing. Your mom thought I was CIA–it was an easy lie to allow me the freedom to do what I needed without her nagging."

"But you left us," Fiona said, chest heaving. "Why?"

"Well ultimately even the little CIA facade couldn't explain my absence. I grew in power and needed to devote my time completely to my work," he said with a shrug of his shoulders, as though this would excuse his abandonment.

When Fiona didn't speak, he continued, "But when I was still home, I saw you progress. And I knew you could have a place with me eventually–"

"So you just left us?" Fiona repeated again, unable to wrap her head around the warped logic. "And waited for the most opportune moment?" Fiona spat back, trying to get a hold of herself, but losing the battle.

"Fiona," her father began again, moving towards her. Fiona remained still, fingers digging into the plush material of the fancy sofa while her father continued his appeal, "You must see I never meant to hurt you. I gave you a better life with Micah. And I knew one day, when we all thought you were ready, I could make myself known to you again."

"So you and Micah conspired together to plan my future... and in the meantime, you figured you could use me to your advantage?"

"You're all twisted up, Fiona. Confused. We'll be very happy together." And then he glanced at the couch, the pulsing orange and blue embers spreading slowly. He continued, "Try to control your condition, you don't want to burn me? Do you?"

There was that word again. Condition.

"Maybe I do want to burn you!" Fiona said. The emotions were too much, too heavy; she felt weighed down by them–knees weak, and on the verge of collapse, her fire could no longer be contained. She continued with rising anger, breathy and insistent, "Maybe you deserve it. Actually. I'm sure you deserve it. You've been using me to make your millions, to tamper with what is supposed to be sacred and righteous in this world. You're disgusting! Evil! What you did...to me, to mom, to Noah–it's unforgivable. And I would never, never, never, never ever want to be part of your *family*."

And with that last declaration, the couch burst into white hot flames. Fiona's chest heaved with emotion, and with realization. She looked across at the terrified eyes of her father–watched him observe her fire touch the curtains, the throw rug, the decorative pillows. This was clearly not how he had intended their meeting to go; he truly thought that Fiona would join him. Panic whipped across his features.

He tried one last time, and Fiona could tell that he was trying to out-think her, find an angle that would force her hand; he was a smart man, "Fiona, you're my daughter. I'm the only family you have left. Don't do this. Let's find a way to use your fire the way YOU want it to be used." He slowly moved around the sofa and extended his hand towards Fiona as he continued to speak,

"Forget about Micah and Adam. Me and you. Just like it used to be."

Fiona stared at his hand, then moved her gaze up to stare directly into his eyes, "I know how I want it to be used. I want it to be used for good, and I don't believe there's a scrap of goodness in you." With each uttered word, she felt her confidence, her resolve, and yes her anger too, grow into something fierce and untamable, "And it was never just you and me. Mom and Noah are still alive. And even though you ruined that family for me, they're still out there. And I've found a place where I belong." She felt tears streaming down her cheeks, and a sob escaped from her mouth, echoing against the roaring flames as she concluded her thought, "...and I definitely don't belong with you."

"With Adam and those other loafers? The Committee?" her father said with a sardonic huff that transformed into a cough as the smoke thickened. The kindness in his demeanor cracking to expose the ugliness hiding like a serpent beneath his skin.

He glanced around the room and Fiona followed his gaze. She saw his eyes land on the fire extinguisher leaning against the wall. She hadn't noticed it earlier. He edged toward it.

"Yes, with Adam," Fiona said, positioning her body in front of him.

"Come on girl, you're not going to choose them over your flesh and blood are you?" There was fear in his voice now as the temperature climbed, and rasping coughs punctuated his speech, "Are you going to burn me alive in here? I thought that was against your code. You want to watch me burn?"

And as he spoke those words, the flames grew until the living room was a blistering inferno of heat and smoke. No need for the fire quartz now. Fiona allowed her emotions to roam free. He had thrown that last accusation in her face as a challenge. Face glistening with heat, he was daring her to harm him. And part of Fiona did want to see this man burn. Part of her truly wanted to bring destruction down upon him for everything he did to her... for every crime he committed against humanity. But despite it all, he was right. She swore she would never harm a living thing with her condition, her ability, no matter how much one might deserve it. And she wasn't going to start now. She wasn't going to compromise her moral compass for this human...even if he was her father.

"No. I'm not going to burn you. I'm not like you. You don't deserve to get the easy way out. You deserve to be held accountable for what you've done."

He ran to the door in an effort to escape, but Fiona followed at his heels. There was no way Fiona was going to allow him to get away. The air was thick with smoke and her father's face was shiny from the heat of the apartment. He was coughing and choking, trying to suck in any breathable oxygen from around him. He couldn't fight her much. Not now.

He desperately tried the doorknob, but Fiona grabbed him by the arm; she wasn't sure where her strength had come from, maybe from her fire. Or maybe her father was just too weakened from the heat and smoke. But she felt invincible as she barrelled him out of the room and into the elevator.

In between wheezy breaths her father said, "Just stop. Think about this." He could barely speak anymore, "You're making the wrong choice."

He fell to his knees, face red from exertion, tears streaming down his face, hands gripping the neckline of his shirt. She could hear his ragged breathing. Unable to even speak anymore, he looked up at her through eyes narrowed and swollen to slits, clasping his hands together in supplication. Finally his subconsciousness took hold, and he slunk down the rest of the way and laid quiet on his stomach. Rasping inhales, the only indication of life.

Fiona looked down at the unconscious figure before her. Her father. In the flesh. But she couldn't take the time to process it yet. There was another task at hand. She had to subdue the fire.

Her palms came together at heart center. In her mind, she visualized the penthouse apartment and could trace the fire. She had to put it out. There was no telling how many people were in the building. No one would get hurt. Not on her watch. *Smother,* she said to it. It resisted. Her emotions were tangled, scattered. She felt her control wander. She had to breathe. In. Out. In. Out. Her air felt warm as it passed through her lips and small beads of sweat gathered at her temples. *Smother,* she said. She knew it heard her; it was waiting, weighing whether or not it should respond. *Calm. Condense,* she spoke the words in a whisper. This time, it listened.

By the time the elevator door sprang open again on the lower level, the fire had been mostly subdued—at least enough to leave the rest of it up to the fire department. Three police officers and 2 EMTs were the first people Fiona saw, and she left her father's body to them as she stepped out into the lobby.

Seeing Chelsea, they embraced her in a fierce hug, "I couldn't wait for 30 minutes. I called the cops less than 15 minutes ago. They were just about to head in. Perfect timing. I was so worried about you."

Fiona couldn't even speak. Words wouldn't yet come. She gently disengaged herself from Chelsea's embrace to walk over to Adam, who was talking to the officer. She took in the scene before her as her heart hammered still against her ribcage, not quite over the shock of it all.

The EMTs had placed an oxygen mask over her father's face and handcuffed him to the gurney before loading him into the waiting ambulance. When she glanced at him, she saw that his eyes were open. His gaze was sad and solemn, and Fiona didn't know if it was because he was caught, or because he finally realized the error of his ways—Fiona suspected the former, and the thought made her feel the bitter pangs of melancholy and betrayal all over again. Micah and then her very own father.

The sound of sirens filled the air as she watched the ambulance and the police cars pull away from the curb. Adam stood on one side of her, Chelsea on the other, and despite the emotions that scattered most of her rational thoughts, there was an impending sense of peace there too. Peace at the knowledge that there were still people who would stand with her, even in the face of the immeasurable tragedy of her life. But was it a tragedy? Yes there were tragic moments, and yes there was bitter betrayal and loss and pain. But maybe it wasn't too late to start over again, with people who brought meaning and light to her life. Isn't that what a family does? Even if it isn't one joined by blood?

Adam looked over at Fiona's face and wiped a tear off her cheek with the pad of his thumb.

"Want to talk about it?" he asked her.

"No."

She had too much to process first. And that had to be done on her own. In time. But she *would* talk about it with him...with all of them. One day. One day she would talk about how her father had orchestrated the events in her life–without her even knowing. How he took advantage of the only daughter he had been granted and had turned her into a matchstick. One day she would talk about the feeling of the most bitter deception one can experience. About how she left a trail of embers and ash in her wake. But she would also talk about how she came back from those ashes. And one day, not today, but one day, she would talk about the pride she felt when she finally took her life back. Because despite it all...despite the ugliness, the darkness, the flames, and the burning, there was still a spark of hope left in Fiona, pulsing deep down inside of her. And she would never let that spark be extinguished again. Not this time.

Fiona stood on the quiet tree-lined street the following summer listening to the wind stir the cicadas full of life. The gentle hum made her think of her past. It was only very recently that Fiona could even think of her childhood with any sort of fondness; after the incident with her father in Vermont, every early memory was tinged with a discoloration, like photographs left out in the sun for too long. But now, she tried not to let the ugliness color the good parts of her past. The parts spent with her mom and Noah–even the contented moments tucked next to her father watching action movies–all of it was real, to her. Even though it all felt like another lifetime ago.

Adam had offered to give her a ride here, but like healing, this was something she had to do on her own. If she even decided to do it that was. She still hadn't fully made up her mind yet. She smiled thinking about Adam and Chelsea...Bryce, Erin, Andrea. This little found family felt like a gift. Even Spence had joined them in the compound. It was awkward between them at first. Yes, Fiona was grateful for Spence's help with what they all now called "The Derby Line Scenario," but she couldn't help harboring a lingering bit of resentment for his complicity in the hand she was dealt. He apologized profusely at first, but ultimately he shifted to a wait-and-see pattern. Gradually, Fiona came around. Gradually the anger and hurt packed their bags and left... without Fiona even realizing it completely. One day, they were there...the next, they were just gone. Like smoke.

Standing in the warm, early morning air, Fiona thought about all the people they helped this past year. The causes they impacted. Even though they left a small imprint, she felt as though they made a difference, that *she* made a difference. And maybe that small sense of pride and accomplishment was what finally pushed her to consider going back to her own roots–to make this pilgrimage back to Levittown–and what led her to be standing outside on her childhood street at five o'clock in the morning on a Sunday in early August.

Fiona would be lying if she said this was the first time she made this journey back home. Even though Chelsea was so sure she could just waltz back into her mother and brother's lives, Fiona didn't feel the same sense of confidence. She didn't even know if it was the right thing to do. They had mourned her already. Could they possibly open up their hearts to her again? After all this time? After all that happened? Would they even recognize her anymore? How would she even explain what had become of her? Perhaps she didn't need to. Perhaps family meant not having to explain.

Three other times, Fiona attempted to arrive in the place where she currently stood...at the corner of Surrey and Cotton Lane. The first time she only made it to the train station before she turned right around and went back to the compound where her friends waited for her. They embraced her with hugs when she returned and assured her that she didn't have to do anything that she didn't want to do. But the thing was, she *did* want to. She *desperately* wanted to. She just didn't know how.

On the second attempt, she made it into an Uber after the Long Island Railroad spit her out at the closest station, but didn't allow the driver to stop at this intersection–the closest intersec-tion to her childhood home. But now, the Uber waited at the curb, and the door was closed. She had gotten out of the car this time. And maybe that meant something. Or maybe today wasn't the right time either and she would try again next week or next month or next year. But one thing was for sure. One day she would do it. She would walk down the street where she used to ride her tricycle as a child and muster up the courage to knock on the door to number seven. Maybe she would see confusion in her mother's eyes...or maybe she would see simply love. She desperately wished for the latter.

She swallowed the heat within her down into her belly; it had been a long time since her flame arrived unexpectedly like that, but it was there just the same. And it didn't feel scary or threatening. It felt good...and right. It felt like a gift. Like an ability. So with her cheeks ablaze with emotion, Fiona took a step in what she hoped was the right direction. Perhaps fate would handle the rest.

The End

"Out of the hottest fire comes the strongest steel."
- Chinese Proverb

$\mathcal{Acknowledgments}$

Some words are easier than others...the words in this book didn't readily flow out of me, not at first at least. Until I truly uncovered Fiona's story, the words came awkwardly, stutteringly, painstakingly. This one was hard (well, they're all hard)–but it made the completion that much more satisfying.

I am so incredibly fortunate to have amazing and unfailingly supportive family and friends in my life that helped me help Fiona gain her footing. Brian is the fiercest advocate of my work and also the proudest husband. His belief in me helps me believe in myself–even when I am in the grip of self-doubt or in the clutches of Imposter Syndrome. Brian, and my boys–Jack and Max–push me to put myself out there, even though sometimes the intimacy of sharing my work with the world is downright terrifying.

This book would never have seen the light of day had it not been for my dear, lifelong, English teacher colleague friends Dave Goldman and Sean Breves. They have taken on Fiona's story as their own and have selflessly expended energy, time, passion, expertise, opinions, editing skills–and quite a bit of unlicensed therapy sessions–to help me make this book what it has become. I could never repay them for their efforts...and one day, when their books are also published, I will look proudly on; they are both incredibly talented authors in their own rights and I cannot wait to hold their books in my hands, as they have held mine in theirs.

I also want to express my deepest gratitude to my Red Penguin publisher, Stephanie Larkin. She took a chance on a new author and I am forever thankful. Joining hands with her has allowed me to fulfill a lifelong dream. I can't wait for what's in store for both of us!

And to my dear readers. Thank you for picking up my story and for spending time with Fiona. I hope you enjoyed the journey. Nothing makes me happier than hearing from you, so please feel free to share your feedback. An Amazon and/or Goodreads review is beyond appreciated. It is my hope that you saw a bit of yourself between the covers and that maybe Fiona helped to kindle that inner flame that burns within us all.

Sincerely,
Melanie Murphy

Melanie Murphy is a writer and high school English teacher from Long Island. She loves to include the diverse settings of New York in her fiction, as she explores nature's capacity for magic and the inherent strength hidden within us all. She lives in Massapequa Park with her husband, two sons, and her Labradoodle, Winnie.

www.ingramcontent.com/pod-product-compliance
Lightning Source LLC
Chambersburg PA
CBHW051529100726
47898CB00005B/1624